TERRAPIN

T. M. DORAN

TERRAPIN

A Mystery

IGNATIUS PRESS   SAN FRANCISCO

Cover art: iStockPhoto.com

Cover design by John Herreid

© 2012 by Ignatius Press, San Francisco
All rights reserved
ISBN 978-1-58617-721-8
Library of Congress catalogue number 20012936916
Printed in the United States of America ∞

The whole earth is our hospital
Endowed by the ruined millionaire
Wherein, if we do well, we shall
Die of the absolute paternal care
That will not leave us, but prevents us everywhere.

T. S. Eliot, *East Coker*

I

Day One

When the day that Dennis Cole had eagerly anticipated finally arrived, how could he have guessed that it would end so horribly?

Dennis was at the wheel of a Mercedes luxury sedan (he had his literary creation, Cole Porter Palmer, to thank for that) and was driving east on the interstate from Ann Arbor, Michigan, toward Comerica Park. Dennis and his friends Greg, Tony, and Ben had premium seats for the Tigers game against the Yankees. Afterward they would return to the Ann Arbor Hilton, where they would spend the rest of their weekend reunion.

"Do they have Glenlivet at the hotel bar?" Greg asked.

"You bet", Dennis replied.

"I didn't have time to unpack or get a drink", Greg added.

"You could have changed your shoes, at least", chided Tony. "Who wears Armanis and a sports coat to a ball game?"

"I do. You never know who you'll meet. I like to be prepared. That's the difference between us."

"That's one of the differences", Tony muttered.

"Got your cards, Tony?" Ben asked.

"Tony always has cards," Greg said, "but he doesn't know what to do with them."

So accustomed to this banter between his friends, Dennis listened without really hearing. Though they sounded caustic to strangers, the jabs were as comfortable to him as his morning coffee. He expected nothing but relaxation and enjoyment for the next three days, the separation from the world that always occurred when they got together.

Unfortunately, things had gotten off to an anxious start when a colleague at the university arrived in Dennis' office just as he was leaving for the hotel to pick up Ben, Greg, and Tony. Thirty minutes later, after listening to a tedious account of the professor's research on ultra-high-pressure water, Dennis was behind schedule and fighting Ann Arbor traffic. Still, they were on their way to the game. Dennis took the freeway exit for the ballpark; everything was back on track.

As red taillights massed up ahead, Greg said, "Wonder what the problem is."

Tony cursed and said, "I don't like to miss the first pitch."

"It's not bad", Dennis observed. "Cars are moving. I think I see an ambulance."

As they drew closer, they saw the ambulance and two police cars on the right shoulder.

"I don't see any wrecked cars", Ben said.

"There's a man on a stretcher", noted Dennis. "Must have been a pedestrian." His stomach lurched uncomfortably.

"Keep moving", Greg said, barely audible. He picked up the *Detroit Free Press* and began scanning the sports section. The inside of the car had grown quiet when Tony opened a bag of peanuts. The others could hear the nuts crunch between his teeth.

As they passed the site of the accident, only Dennis turned his head to look at the man being loaded into the ambulance. "I got a call from Jonas last week", he said, breaking the silence.

"Jonas Ratigan?" Tony asked.

Dennis glanced at Tony, and then at the ambulance behind him, in the rearview mirror. "Yeah, Ratigan; he asked me to help him find a job."

"He called me too", Tony said.

"He's a two-time loser, isn't he?" Greg scoffed.

"I told him I'd keep my eyes open", Dennis continued, realizing that he hadn't gone out of his way, as his father, TA, would have done.

"Don't bother; he made his own bed", Greg added scornfully.

"Haven't we all?" asked Ben.

"Isn't the witch dead?" Greg asked, ignoring Ben.

"I saw her obituary", Dennis replied.

"Did it say anything about Jimmy and Billy?" Ben wanted to know. "Wonder what happened to them."

"I sure could use a drink", Greg said over Ben.

According to the obituary, Dennis explained, Jimmy had survived both his mother and his brother, Billy. "I understand Jimmy is still living in the house", he added.

"Yeah, he's there all right", Greg said. "My mom sees Little Morgus once in a while. She told me he's gone gray. Cerberus finally kicked the bucket. Good riddance."

Dennis hadn't heard Greg's moniker for Jimmy Macklin—Little Morgus—in years, nor had he heard the name Cerberus, which is what TA had called the Macklins' dog. The nicknames stirred memories of their boyhood pranks and prompted mixed emotions. "There's more to that family than we knew", he said.

"Don't get maudlin on us, pal", Greg replied.

"We're supposed to be having fun," Tony reminded them, "and there was nothing fun about the Macklins."

"Speaking of having fun, my mom said they took the shackles off Jenny Holm", Greg said. "She's back in her house."

"Maybe they cured her", Ben offered. "It happens."

"She's a nutcase; always has been", Greg countered. "The asylum must be short of beds." Folding the paper and dropping it on the floor, he added, "I'll take the Yankees even up for twenty."

"Okay", Dennis said.

"Me too", Tony added.

"What's wrong, Ben? Not enough data?" Greg asked, looking over his shoulder.

"I don't care who wins, and I don't have twenty dollars to throw away."

"Then what are you doing with your fortune?"

"Smoking Cuban cigars and growing the best peaches in the world."

"They're illegal", Dennis remarked.

"The cigars or the peaches?" Ben joked. Then he leaned forward until his face was next to Greg's ear and said, "What's become of your uncle Adam?"

Tony laughed out loud and said, "Greg's twin uncle. See, he's starting to look like him."

Greg didn't flinch, even when Ben squeezed his shoulder. "Won't work, boys; not anymore. To the best of my knowledge, Uncle Adam is still haunting the bohemian alleys of Chicago. My mom gets a card now and then."

"He was an interesting character", Dennis mused. "A good magician too."

"Do you still have your rabbit's foot?" Tony asked Greg.

Greg smiled but didn't answer or produce the "rabbit's foot" Dennis knew to be a bone that Greg had encased in plastic and attached to a key chain. Greg claimed that the bone was from a human index finger; for a while after high school graduation, he would display the grotesque object at a bar or a party.

They pulled into a lot across the street from the stadium. The weather was ideal for an outdoor event, clear skies and comfortably warm, and the crowd was big and loud. The sign said that the parking fee was twenty-five dollars. Dennis took a fifty from his shirt pocket and handed it to the attendant. "Take care of the car", he said.

"Yes, sir, Dr. Cole."

"Yes, sir, Dr. Cole", Tony mimicked.

"Tony needs a woman", Greg said.

"Men who give other men advice about women are pathetic", muttered Ben.

"Is that a clinical diagnosis?" Greg rejoined. "Stick to things you know something about ... cigars and viruses. You notice I didn't include peaches."

"I'll remember that when they're ripe", said Ben. A virologist at the National Institute of Health, Ben had a small grove of peach trees on his property near Atlanta, where he experimented with synthetic hormones and viruses to make them more pest resistant. Once a year, a container of peaches would arrive at the homes of Greg, Tony, and Dennis. Even Ben's hobbies were connected to his passion for science, which had marked Ben's personality for as long as Dennis could remember.

The car doors slammed in unison, as if the four had attended a hundred games together, rather than one every five years. As Dennis followed his friends between the two huge tiger statues, he saw not just three men but also the boys and teenagers they had once been. In the course of that year, they would all turn fifty. Like brothers, many said—and had been saying since the days of their childhood on Lincoln Street. Not that they were much alike; in fact, they were different in temperament and interests, but what held them together transcended these differences.

The Yankees won three to two, and Greg made sure everyone within earshot knew that he was forty dollars to the good.

During the ride back to Ann Arbor, the night hid much of the decrepitude along the road, but it was doubtful the friends would have noticed, so intent were they on catching up. Only when they passed the site of the accident did their eyes drift and the conversation wane.

"When are you going to find another girl?" Greg asked Tony, who had never married. Dennis winced; only Greg would go there. After thirty-two years, the ghost of the lovely girl they all had loved, but no one more than Tony, still hovered over the group.

"I found her", Tony said, surprising them. "I should say, I found her, but she didn't want to be found."

Dennis said, "Out with it, brother."

Tony didn't answer right away. He looked out the window, with the familiar expression that meant he would speak when he was good and ready. Rushing Tony had never worked. He could be convinced, but not pressured into anything.

"Her name's Maddie. We met in Portland." Tony frowned. "I thought it was the real thing. I even asked her to marry me. I should have known better. It's been over three years since she broke off our engagement— ancient history."

"And you kept a little thing like a proposal from your best friends?" Greg asked.

"It all happened quickly. When she said no, I didn't feel like talking to anyone. At that point, what was there to say?"

Dennis sensed Tony's distress, and so did Greg, who changed the subject. "How about that Delta Tau girl? She lit your fire."

"You're an idiot", Tony replied. "And Jim Morrison's been dead a long time."

"Come on, baby, light my fire", Greg started singing.

"He needs a Scotch, or we do", Ben commented.

"You're a genius, Ben", Greg said. "Haven't I always said that boy's a genius?"

"You're all geniuses", Tony said. "That's the problem."

"Eva reserved the suite and left some goodies", Dennis remarked. "We're almost there."

"Then step on the gas", Tony said. "We're parched, and I can't take any more of Uncle Adam Junior's imprecations."

"How long have you been practicing that word?" Greg needled Tony.

Tony turned toward the window again and left Greg's question unanswered. Looking in the mirror, Dennis saw that Tony was smiling, so Greg had been successful in taking Tony's mind off that broken relationship.

When they arrived at the hotel suite, they found cheese, fruit, and nuts; two bottles of a nice Bordeaux; and two bottles of Glenlivet single-malt Scotch. Greg opened one, and four glasses touched with a loud clink.

They weren't in the room long. Tony checked his blood sugar with unconscious efficiency, like a bicyclist checking his tire pressure. The others were so used to the procedure that it scarcely registered. As they walked out, Dennis gave Greg a playful jab in the ribs. He felt something; it wasn't a wallet. For an instant, he wondered if Greg was carrying a gun. He dismissed the idea, telling himself that Smithsonian archaeologists working at desks didn't need guns.

The hotel bar was dimly lit. They found a table in a quiet corner that suited them. Greg produced the Glenlivet that he had hidden beneath his sport coat, and Ben muttered something about associating with jerks.

Dennis looked at each of them in turn. They hadn't been together for more than five years, except for that whirlwind funeral for Ben's wife in Atlanta. "It's good to see you boys", he said, taking off his suede jacket and hanging it on the back of the chair. "First time we've been together since——"

"Diane", Ben said inscrutably.

"Are you okay, Ben?" Greg asked. He had poured himself another glass of Scotch and hid the bottle under the table.

The big man grunted. "As well as can be expected. And make sure no one sees that bottle." That was as close to an admission of vulnerability as one was likely to get from Ben.

Ignoring the command, Greg continued, "The kids taking good care of you?"

"They're trying too hard. They have lives of their own. I'm okay", he repeated, as if saying it would make it so.

Greg put his arm around Ben. "Let me know if you need anything, brother."

"Can you make sure I don't screw up Thanksgiving dinner?" Ben asked with a sardonic smile. "Can you cook Cornish hen like Diane used to?"

Dennis remembered the dauntless Ben he had grown up with and said, "You're young enough to meet someone else."

"Thanks, but no thanks. And in case you haven't noticed, I look more like Frankenstein than Frank Sinatra."

"Frank Sinatra's dead", chimed in Tony. "You look better than that."

"Barely", Greg said.

"Are the girls well?" Dennis asked.

"Sure. Beth's finishing at Tech. Vera's teaching there now. Lori's engaged."

"That's news", Greg said. "Do you like the guy?"

Ben mentioned noncommittally that he had met him a few times. "Vera calls every day", he added. "I like talking to her, but I wonder how I tied my shoes before the girls came along."

"You never lacked for brains," teased Greg, "but in the shoe-tying department you were always an oaf. I recall an incident with shoelaces and a bicycle that ended badly."

"Now I'm an oaf; that's nice", Ben said without rancor. "I can manage well enough. I wear loafers, by the way."

"How about David?" Dennis asked Greg. He hadn't seen Greg's son in years.

"Doing fine."

"Still policing the border?"

"Still whacking the banditos", Greg said, adding some Scotch to his glass.

"See much of him?" asked Ben.

"Sometimes", Greg answered, with a tone of disappointment. "How about the nieces and nephews, Tony?"

"I see a lot of Jan's kids, especially Harry, who works with me in the business. I'm going to California next month to see Wim. Maybe I'll get to see his children, Paul and Jill; I hope so."

Everyone knew that Dennis and Marta had been unable to have children and that neither had living brothers or sisters. It would have been dishonest of Dennis to say that being childless didn't matter. Still, he enjoyed catching up with his friends and hearing about their families.

"Here's a penny for your oaf loafers", Greg said to Ben.

Ben pushed it away. "Keep it. You may need it, as profligate as you are with Scotch and money. As for the bike wreck, I landed on the grass and wasn't even scratched."

"*That* time you did. Don't make me go through the list of your crashes. We'd be up all night."

The sound of breaking glass interrupted their talk. Dennis hadn't noticed before, but a man was sitting two tables away. Beside him on the floor, a pool of red wine surrounded the remnants of a glass. The dark-haired man had a pronounced nose and chin, and concave cheeks. He was wearing a long-sleeved blue and white checked shirt that looked to be two sizes too large for his bony, wiry frame. The oddest wheelchair Dennis had ever seen was parked at the table. It featured a fifth wheel in the back, much smaller than the other four wheels, on a 360-degree pivot. The chair also had three miniature motors and a gold skirt around the entire perimeter of the seat, extending about eight inches toward the floor.

On the table in front of the man were a half-bottle of wine and a loaf of bread. He didn't seem to be particularly distressed at breaking the glass, but he looked up at the four men now staring at him. Greg nodded at him, and in response the man smiled and returned to his bread, tearing it into little pieces before eating it. For a moment, Dennis worried that Greg was going to say something sarcastic.

The waiter, approaching from the other side of the room, picked up the broken glass and mopped up the spilled wine before he came to their table. He wasn't young; he reminded Dennis of the mature waiters he had met in Mexico. He had a high forehead with wavy black hair, and he walked with a pronounced limp. "May I serve you something?" he asked.

"Cabernet, chilled, if you can manage it", Dennis said.

"A draft beer for me", said Tony. "Heineken."

"Make that two", added Ben.

All eyes were on Greg as he ordered, "A glass of water, no ice."

The waiter looked suspiciously at Greg before he left for the bar. Greg chuckled, and Dennis thought he winked at the man with the wheelchair; that would be like Greg.

"You shouldn't have brought that contraband Scotch", chastised Ben.

"Why not, Prince Charming?"

"It's the principle", Ben explained. "You can afford a glass of Scotch. We all can. We don't need to sneak it in."

"Listen boys", Greg said. "I have very rarely acted on principle; and when I have, it ended badly."

"It hasn't ended so well when you've acted on impulse either", Dennis added. "How's the job, Ben?"

"Fine", was Ben's laconic reply. "Same old stuff."

"What same old stuff?" Greg asked. "We're your best friends. We'd like to know what you're up to."

"If I could talk about it, I would."

"If you told us," Greg joked, "you'd have to put bubonic plague in our drinks, right?"

"If I told you, I'd bore you to death and be the target of every nerd, geek, and brainiac story you can retrieve from that fertile imagination of yours", Ben said.

"No need for me to pile on", Greg added. "You have damned thyself with thine own lips and thine own nerdness. Can you talk about those peach trees, or are they off limits too?"

"Since when are you interested in trees?"

"Since you got mysterious. Maybe you'll slip up and tell us one of your deep, dark secrets."

"If you must know, I'm working on next generation microbials, eradicating superbugs. Is that sufficient?" Ben said.

"If we must know? Of course we must know, Benedict", Greg said.

"Lysostaphin", Ben whispered. "That's all you're getting."

"Spell it", Greg said.

"S-c-r-e-w y-o-u."

"I second that", Dennis said. "We're all entitled to some trade secrets."

"Once upon a time, we didn't have any secrets from each other", Greg said jovially.

"Look where that got us", Tony said.

"Now it's your turn to reveal something", Dennis said to Greg, though he doubted whether Greg or even he was prepared to say anything of real substance about himself. The bizarre letter Dennis had received about his mother came to mind. He had locked it in his library drawer; he hadn't shared it with his wife, Marta. Could he bring himself to tell his best friends about that secret?

"Go ahead—ask me anything", was Greg's reply, but his demeanor had changed. Few would have discerned it, but Dennis had. What question did Greg fear? Dennis wondered.

Tony had brought out two packs of Bicycle playing cards and a handful of dominos. The cards were old; not battered, but well worn. He was building a structure with them on the table, using the dominos to prop up walls.

"Never seen you without those cards", Greg said. He could be counted on to say these same words every time they met. Greg picked up one of the dominos and flipped it from hand to hand. "The dominos are an innovation. You didn't learn that from Davey. That brother of mine was a purist. Mind if I huff and puff and blow that mess down?"

Tony ignored him and kept building.

"Tony, is that how you attract women?" Ben teased him.

Greg answered for him, "Yeah, babes go nuts over card houses."

Tony handled the cards as deftly as a magician, and the man with the wheelchair seemed to be fascinated by Tony's growing edifice. A new glass of wine and a slab of cheese now complemented the man's bread, and his eyes—greedily, it seemed to Dennis—darted back and forth between the house of cards and his food.

"And how is the author-professor?" Greg asked Dennis.

"As you see me."

"That's cryptic enough. And how about you and Marta?"

"Marta and I are okay."

"Just okay?"

"Just okay."

"Have you published any new pot-boilers lately?" Ben asked. Before Dennis could answer, Ben added, "If you must know, your stories are too episodic for my tastes."

"When did you start reading the *New Yorker*?" asked Greg. "It sounds as if you've been coached."

Ben smiled.

"He's been trolling for the opportunity to use that phrase," Greg said to Dennis, "and he's been coached; count on it."

"Professor Cole", a voice said.

Dennis looked up to see Joseph, the boyfriend of his assistant, Eva. The young man with large, dark eyes; black, curly hair; and a prominent but not disagreeable nose was always friendly and courteous to Dennis, so why did Joseph make him nervous? He didn't like to think it was the man's heritage. Did his unease have something to do with Dennis' protectiveness toward Eva? She was extremely competent—and pretty. Dennis admitted that she was the best assistant he had ever had, and he wasn't convinced that Joseph was good enough for her.

Dennis introduced Joseph to the others and asked, "What brings you here?"

"Eva's new car is outside. She wants you to see it", the man said.

"Is Eva here?"

"She could not come, but she is eager for you to see the car. Bright yellow . . . but you will see. Come."

Dennis found that he was annoyed at the idea of Joseph driving Eva's new car, then he bristled at himself for caring. The beer and wine arrived, and Dennis was glad for it. He was tired of watching Greg drink alone.

They all went outside with Joseph. Tony had eyed the card house apprehensively—it was five stories tall—but he came along. The yellow Mustang gleamed beneath the lights that illuminated the hotel entrance.

"Sit", Joseph directed them. The Mustang was nice, but Dennis told himself it hardly compared with his Mercedes. Still, Eva had been talking about buying it for months. The least he could do was make a fuss over it, though he wished Eva were there to hear his praises.

Ben was working hard to extract his big frame from the front seat. The others took turns and made suitably gracious remarks.

"Tell Eva we're impressed", Dennis said, after Joseph had completed their tour of the car. "And thank her for the refreshments."

Joseph got in the front seat and waved as he drove off. Dennis chafed at the man's nonchalance with Eva's new car. He wondered if he should talk to Eva about Joseph. Then again, her personal life wasn't his business, and taking such a liberty might cost him an excellent assistant.

When they returned to the table, their drinks awaited them, and the card house was still intact.

"When do we get to meet Eva?" Greg asked Dennis.

"Tomorrow, maybe. She has a busy weekend. She did her job, didn't she—nice suite, well stocked?"

"That's why I want to meet her. You've been bragging about her for years."

"Yes, she's good. What can I say?"

Greg raised his glass to Tony. "This might be your big opportunity, brother. You're a better catch than that Arab." Greg winked at Dennis. Most everything Greg said was meant to provoke Tony. It always had been.

Tony merely shook his head and took a sip of beer. "This is the worst Heineken I've ever had," he remarked, "or else the bartender gave me the cheap stuff instead."

"I'm surprised someone hasn't removed your head from your shoulders", Ben said to Greg. "You must be a riot at the tomb-raiders convention with remarks like that."

"I keep 'em honest, pardner." Greg's eyes were getting glassy. "Now, if you gentlemen will excuse me", he added, eyeing the pretty bartender across the room.

"Incoming, but an old warhead", Tony said.

"Probably a dud", Dennis added.

Greg cursed at Dennis and said, "I might need another room tonight, Professor."

Tony remonstrated, "Remember, Susan is like a sister to me." He pushed his chair back and was inspecting the card house. So were others in the room, including the man with the wheelchair.

Greg made his way to the bar and found a seat.

"He's getting too old for that nonsense", Ben said.

"More Gregory Pace bravura", Dennis observed. Seeing that Greg had left his rental-car keys on the chair, he put them in his jacket pocket so that they wouldn't get lost.

"Another round?" Tony asked. They all raised their glasses, Dennis reluctantly. He didn't want to get in the way of the celebration, but the day had taken its toll on him and he was exhausted.

Looking in Greg's direction, Ben muttered, "That idiot will spend the forty dollars he won trying to impress that girl."

"It's his forty dollars", Dennis said with a shrug. "He doesn't seem to be missing any meals."

"Maybe, but will he ever grow up?"

Several minutes later, Greg returned with a smile on his face and another glass of Scotch. "Her name is Christine", he said, enthusiastically.

Ben responded, "She's young enough to be—"

"Stop right there, pal. I already have a mother, and I don't need a pastor. I just came back to see how Tony's Tower of Babel is progressing. I've got a soft spot for those skyscrapers Tony and Davey used to build."

"You have a soft spot?" Ben questioned skeptically. "Where have you been hiding it?"

"Are you gracing us with your presence tonight, or are you flying solo?" Dennis asked Greg.

"We'll see", Greg said, walking back to the bar.

"Susan's an old friend", Tony said, rapping the table with his fist, and three stories came tumbling down.

"Don't worry," Ben said to Tony, "he's full of it. He'll be snoring in bed in an hour."

As Dennis listened to his friends, he realized that it was the same and not the same. Every time they got together, they wanted it to be the same, but it never was. Greg was becoming more and more a caricature of his younger self. Why didn't he talk about his work or his wife, Susan? What was he carrying beneath his jacket?

Ben was more cynical, and gaunter, than Dennis had remembered. Diane's death had hit his friend harder than any of them had guessed. Ben was right to suggest that he probably would be alone for the rest of his life.

Tony used to brag about being single, but Dennis wasn't sure that Tony believed in the superiority of bachelorhood anymore. His hair was grayer and his cheeks were puffier than they had been the last time they met. Dennis wasn't as self-confident as he used to be either. At best, he felt resigned to things as they were between him and Marta.

Dennis noticed the sudden movement of the man with the wheelchair. With just hands and arms, the man lifted himself, revealing that he had no legs. He wasn't wearing cut-off pants or regular slacks that were pinned back, but billowy brown silk pantaloons that had been sewn closed and which now hung vertically as they would from a hanger. He moved swiftly from the chair to the wheelchair, like a monkey; then he settled in the seat, activated the drive, and exited the room with amazing alacrity.

"I wouldn't want to arm wrestle that character", Tony said, when the man had gone. "Another round?"

"Not me", Dennis said.

Ben shook his head. "I'm going to bed. I can hardly keep my eyes open."

Tony removed one domino at the base of his card house, and the structure collapsed. "Should we wait for Greg?" he asked.

"He can take care of himself", Ben replied.

"That's debatable," Dennis countered, "but I'm turning in too. Greg has a key."

The three friends wound their way slowly through the hotel to their suite, bringing to Dennis' mind those swift and agile can kickers who once inhabited, and sometimes terrorized, Lincoln Street. So different and so much the same, he mused again.

As they were getting ready for bed, the conversation meandered. Tony described a house his construction company had built for a friend of his brother in Portland. He had even assembled a windmill on the property. Ben was expecting his peaches to be his best crop ever. Dennis was too tired to say much. After they had turned out the lights, they kept on talking until Ben and Tony fell silent. Dennis heard the door open and close as he was drifting off to sleep, never imagining that he would not see Greg alive again.

2

August 1969

Terrapin Township was one of a gaggle of communities that surrounded Detroit. It was bisected by Telegraph Road, whose claim to fame is that it goes from Michigan to California. Otherwise, there was little to recommend Terrapin Township to any but its residents, and even they were hard-pressed to identify its charms. The terrain was as flat as a washboard, and the only watercourse was the county ditch, an often stagnant effluence that featured gray water, weedy banks, questionable sediment, oily scum, and small but hardy crayfish.

There were certainly no landmarks of note; a handful of grade schools, half as many middle schools, and one high school. The Democratic Club boasted enthusiastic members, including mainstream Democrats, union members, fraternally minded men who enjoyed drinking beer away from their homes, a few ardent socialists, and one Bolshevik who owned a machine-repair shop and half a dozen rental properties in Detroit. The building that housed them was always on the verge of being an eyesore.

As for history, Terrapin Township was nothing but a farming community that had been overrun by post– World War II sprawl, which had petered out to shoebox houses by the time it reached the edge of town. Most of the farmers either sold out or were pushed out by the inexorable creep of the new suburban grids.

If there were any terrapins in Terrapin Township, they were well concealed. Some long-time residents swore that there were plenty of terrapins in the days of their youth and that the reptiles had been pushed south and west by the developers. In the heyday of the debate, a herpetologist at Michigan State University was approached to settle the argument, but he saw no need to enter a no-win fray. The intelligentsia in the township, if the politicians and educators could be so designated, pointed to the acknowledged founder of the township, Jeremiah Tarpin, as the inspiration for the name. It was an unresolved argument because few wanted it resolved. Why settle the only mystery in town?

Not that the township's history was entirely absent of color. Not too many years earlier, one Peter Macklin had been killed in his own front yard by a hail of bullets from what was said to be a gang of hit men from Detroit's Zerilli family. It was further speculated that Macklin had been an operative in that family's "business" and had gotten crosswise with the wrong people. A few said that money he had stolen from the mob was hidden somewhere on his property. That theory was buttressed by the eccentric and belligerent family Macklin left behind, along with the vicious canine that roamed the property.

At one point Macklin's widow sold off some of the land, and the almost identical houses on Lincoln Street were built. As TA Cole said, "The only thing this street has in common with Lincoln is its seven-letter name."

The residents of Lincoln Street were unabashedly working-class. Side by side were the Pompay, Cole, Carlson, Pace, and Linus houses. The Hulses lived directly across the street from the Carlsons. Each family had one sycamore tree near the curb. There were no other trees in any of the small yards except for the Carlson's backyard peach tree; otherwise, just a monotony of green lawn sprinkled in the summer with yellow dandelions.

The Cole house was even humbler than those of its neighbors in consequence of exclusively male residents and TA Cole's United States Marine Corps training. TA wasn't characteristically Marine-like in the sense of emotional rigidness, but he had wholeheartedly adopted the corps' minimalistic lifestyle. As Dennis had never known anything different, the Spartan living conditions seemed perfectly natural to him. He found it amusing that more than one neighbor, after visiting the Cole home, questioned whether the house wasn't larger than the others in the neighborhood. It wasn't. The feeling of more space was just an illusion created by a minimum of furniture and a lack of clutter in the house.

TA's room was especially barren, with just a small bed and a dresser. The closet looked oversize, so inconsiderable was TA's wardrobe.

The house was comfortable enough, but no one would call it appealing. Few items graced the walls. In the narrow hallway in the back of the house, far from ideal for viewing, hung a family photograph taken when Dennis was five and his brother was three. Dennis never tired of looking at it, even though it took an emotional toll to do so. The woman in the picture, Patricia Cole, was both familiar and strange. The familiarity was visceral rather than conscious; the strangeness came from Dennis' recognition that he had never, and would never, know what motivated and animated his mother. There was an inexpensive but nicely framed print of Rembrandt's

27

late-in-life *Return of the Prodigal Son* in the front room. Dennis never questioned why TA was attracted to this picture, and TA had never offered an explanation. It was like that with a lot of things. Also in the front room was a small, and obviously amateur, photograph of TA and Patricia on their wedding day. There wasn't a stitch of carpeting in the house, just an incongruous collection of threadbare rugs that covered areas of the wood flooring. Dennis sometimes wondered how much of this haphazard décor his mother had conceded to in her lifetime and how much of it TA had adopted after the accident; another unasked question.

Extended family was in short supply too. All of Dennis' grandparents had died before he was five; he had no memory of any of them. TA's older brother, Thomas Aurelius Cole, never married and lived in Manhattan. TA once told Dennis that his uncle was a financier. Thomas Cole had attended the University of Chicago and made a fortune out east, while TA had joined the Marines and fought in the Korean War. After that experience, he had studied philosophy for two years at the University of Detroit.

They rarely heard from Thomas, though he sent elaborate gifts on Dennis' birthday and at Christmas. Dennis had seen his uncle on only two occasions. Thomas had made a whirlwind visit to Terrapin Township several years earlier, opting to lodge at the Dearborn Inn rather than at the Cole home, and during that time it seemed as if Thomas and TA had to work at being agreeable with each other. Later, Dennis spent a weekend with his uncle in New York City, where he was constantly on the move and where Thomas had chaperoned him on visits to more museums than Dennis knew existed. Even though Thomas had been cheerful and accommodating, Dennis sensed that his uncle was uneasy with children. He lived in an old brick building next to a big park. A butler kept things tidy, and a cook prepared the meals. Though neither of them said anything unpleasant to Dennis, it was clear to the boy that neither the manservant nor the cook— Thomas referred to him as the *chef de maison*—had much use for him.

Patricia Cole's sister, Mary, lived in Harbor Springs, where she operated a bed and breakfast with her husband, Bert. They had moved there before Dennis was born and had adopted a native boy from Peru, a cousin whom Dennis had never met. As a matter of fact, he had no memory of meeting Mary and Bert.

On that August morning, Dennis stood facing the front-room window, but in his mind he was paying more attention to the man in the corner chair than to anything that was going on outside. The rain that had begun the night before had stopped; the clouds were breaking up; and Dennis was considering a run to the frog pond. TA was sipping black coffee from his favorite cup, chipped and stained, and was reading the paper.

From TA's youth to the time he joined the Marines, he had been called Timothy. Peter Kristov, his closest friend, began calling him TA when they served together in Korea, and the name had stuck. Now everyone except his brother called him TA, including Dennis. Dennis couldn't remember ever calling him Dad.

TA was a quiet man, even contemplative, though he could be gregarious when the spirit moved him. This aspect of TA's personality emerged most often, or perhaps it was extracted, when Peter Kristov visited. While a great advocate of personal freedom, TA applied strict limits to his own liberties, and Dennis sensed that his father expected the same of him. TA had few hobbies. Reading could be said to be his chief interest, and he favored mostly philosophical works and mystery novels. He also tended the aquarium in the basement; caring for the sea horses, Dennis believed, was as much avocation as hobby.

TA was an ordinary-looking man—just under six feet tall, trim but not especially athletic. He might have been more handsome without his distinctive nose, which Dennis had inherited. He was older than the other fathers in the neighborhood. By the time TA met Dennis' mother, he was almost thirty. No gray streaked TA's dark hair yet. He was still good for a game of catch but not much more when it came to physical activity. He liked to walk. Many mornings, weekend or workday, rain or shine, winter or summer, Dennis would wake to find TA at the kitchen table with his coffee, just returned from a walk around the neighborhood. Whether it was these walks or a telepathy that Dennis didn't understand, TA knew more about the people in this corner of Terrapin Township than could be explained by his insular lifestyle.

"Does Gordie ever bother you?" Dennis once asked him. He had never mentioned the Macklin's fierce mongrel to TA before.

"Cerberus never bothers me", TA had answered, a stoic expression on his face. "I've been up against worse than that dog", was his laconic summa on that subject.

In those early years, Dennis didn't think of TA as someone special, just someone reliable—someone who was there when he was needed. He provided the roof over their heads and took care of the big projects around the house that needed doing; and he made sure there was always plenty to eat. Dennis was responsible for his own breakfast and lunch and for keeping the house reasonably ordered.

After a quick bowl of cereal, Dennis looked at the clock on the kitchen wall and exited the house. The sky was clearing nicely, and even the wet grass would be practically dry before noon. Tony came out his front door at almost the same moment as Dennis, who heard Magdalena Hulse's commanding voice, "Anton, you take your insulin?"

The Hulses were packed into an eleven-hundred-square-foot house. It was the same size as the Cole house but appeared to be half as large, due to the number of people always coming and going. Originally from Holland, Mr. and Mrs. Hulse had three other children besides Tony: Caterina, who was already married and lived two blocks away; Jan, who worked for his father's construction company; and Wim, their eldest son, who was studying architecture at the University of Michigan.

If Dennis' home was silent most of the time, the Hulse residence was exactly the opposite—ringing with rampant conversation, argument, and laughter. The strongest personality in the family belonged to Tony's mother, Magdalena, who displayed that female solicitude which is scolding one minute but warm and offering food or an unabashed embrace the next. Her strong opinions and blunt delivery frightened Dennis sometimes, but she always made him feel welcome.

The boys met on the sidewalk in front of Tony's house and loped down the street without a word. Everything that needed to be said on that summer day could be communicated without words. They knew the street, and every house on it, as well as they knew the inside of their own houses. Dennis glanced at the Big Tree on his left, majestic and lush, as they came to the first corner. Fifteen houses down, the street turned north. Dennis and Tony crossed the street, hopped a chain-link fence into a backyard, and then vaulted another fence.

Tony looked like an enormous frog in his mint-green shirt. He had been wearing that same shirt for a couple of years, and it showed—the hem an inch short of reaching his beltless jeans, the material stretched at the chest and shoulders, and the sleeves extended only midway to his elbows. The shirt had been washed so many times that it was diaphanous and practically colorless near the seams. In Tony's absence, Lori Linus, who cared more about how Tony looked than he did, had started referring to the shirt disdainfully as "that green thing he wears".

The undeveloped property on the other side of the fence comprised no more than five acres and contained an old house and barn on a hill, a county drain that ran parallel to the fence line, two seasonal ponds that were never more than two feet deep, and a grassy field everywhere else. It was encompassed by the subdivision to the east, various businesses that fronted Telegraph Road to the west, the same subdivision to the north, and a dirt road with older homes and larger plots of land to the south, the same road that fronted the Macklin property. An odor of sewage often emanated from the county drain; the ponds—especially the one at the rear of the gas station—sometimes displayed an oil sheen; the hill served as a sled run in winter.

Never in living memory could any of the water in that field, moving or still, be said to be blue, much less clear. Depending on the weather and the time of year, the water was gray or, at best, a muddy green. Nonetheless, the field was a magical place for the boys, especially Tony and Dennis. Many a spring or summer morning they hunted for frogs in the ponds, for crayfish in the drain, for mice and rabbits on what remained of the old farm, and for snakes in the tall grass and under fallen branches. The monotonous sameness of the species—garter snakes, leopard frogs, common toads, and field mice—occasionally nettled the boys. A snapping turtle or a bullfrog would have been greeted like the appearance of a unicorn; even a garden-variety salamander would have been welcome, but the experience had always been more about camaraderie and the shared hunt and less about the quarry.

As they looked at the pond in front of them, Tony said to Dennis, "Are the sea horses scared of you?" Tony had seen a program on television about sea horses and had been peppering Dennis with questions about the little creatures in the Cole aquarium ever since they jumped the fence.

"They're not afraid of TA", Dennis said. "He moves slowly. Anyway, there's nowhere for them to hide."

"How does he get them out?"

"With a net and a cup. He uses the net to get them into the cup. He says if he takes them out with the net they might get damaged."

"Your dad is weird."

Dennis hadn't ever considered the possibility. Keeping sea horses in the basement seemed the most natural thing in the world.

"My dad says TA should have been a teacher", Tony observed.

"He fought in the war instead."

"He didn't get killed," Tony argued, "so he could have gone to school after the war."

Now Dennis was getting annoyed. What business was it of Tony's, or his father's, to criticize TA? Dennis would have expected something like this from Greg, but not from Tony.

"TA says life distracted him", Dennis said, realizing that he was at a loss for words because he suspected that Tony's dad was right. TA did seem out of place on Lincoln Street, and out of place at the machine shop, and out of place behind a lawn mower.

"How many sea horses does he have?" Tony asked.

"They belong to me too", Dennis answered. "If something happened to TA, I'd take care of them."

"They wouldn't let you stay in the house. You'd have to live with someone else."

Never before had Dennis considered the tenuous link between the well-being of one man and his life on Lincoln Street.

"We have eleven hippocampi", Dennis said, hoping that the Latin would intimidate Tony.

Tony was unperturbed by the big word. He said, "They're a lot like frogs, I guess."

"Not so much", Dennis said. "They don't hop, or croak, or eat bugs."

"They live in the water. They can stay still for a long time. They have big eyes", Tony countered.

"They aren't even amphibians", Dennis said.

"What if you let one loose in the pond?" As Tony said this, he had one eye out for frogs in the water.

"It would perish", Dennis said, using a favorite word of TA's. "The water chemistry is different in the pond. It would poison the hippocampi."

"Lori says it's going to poison us too", Tony said.

"She doesn't know what she's talking about. She's never even caught a frog."

Tony didn't impugn that observation. For Dennis' part, there were days when he wasn't particularly comfortable with the water flowing in the drain, but he wouldn't admit that to Tony, and certainly not to Lori.

"Do they have names?" Tony asked.

"Does who have names?"

"The sea horses."

"Hell no. We call them giraffe, zebra, dwarf, and long-nose; those are their names."

Tony said, "Do you think I could keep one alive?"

Dennis shook his head vigorously. He was peering in the direction of an especially loud croak. "I doubt it. It takes a lot of experience."

"I bet I could."

"Go ahead and try." Dennis was growing weary of Tony's questions and insinuations, and he was eager to pursue that insistent frog.

"Would you help me?" Tony asked him.

Dennis wasn't willing to admit that his collaboration with TA extended no further than handing him concoctions and devices. Despite his bravado, he wasn't at all convinced *he* could keep the creatures alive. "Sure", he said, hoping that Tony's interest wouldn't amount to anything.

There was a moment of silence before Tony said, "We have truck-ill-id-eye in our backyard." He pronounced each syllable as if the word had been carefully practiced.

Dennis wondered how long Tony had been preparing to say the word, and who had coached him; probably his brother Wim. Dennis boldly returned his friend's stare.

He had no idea what the word meant, only that it was Latin—he had heard enough Latin around the house to recognize it, if not understand it—and that it referred to a living creature. He judged that it couldn't be a commonplace animal, such as a toad, or even a butterfly, or why would Tony have taken such pains to learn the word? His mind was spinning, as it often did when confronted by a mystery. Surrounded by other houses and Lincoln Street, the creature would most likely have flown into Tony's yard.

"Does it like the flowers?" Dennis ventured. Magdalena Hulse reserved one quadrant of the yard, the rear right corner, for her flowering plants and bushes. Tony's eyes widened, confirming that Dennis had regained the advantage. His expression revealed doubt that he had baffled Dennis.

Dennis pressed harder. "They like only certain flowers", he said, having no idea which flowers and having no image of the bird, if bird it really was.

Tony didn't contradict him, which emboldened Dennis: "I've seen them in my yard too."

"You don't have any flowers, except clover and dandelions", Tony challenged.

Dennis tried to recover with, "I think they were after Delia's flowers", though the Pompays' yard was scarcely more inviting than TA's.

Tony still looked skeptical, but more crestfallen than anything else, as if a treasured balloon had been pricked. Dennis almost regretted having taken the offensive. Still, he told himself, Tony had set him up by giving him a mystery to solve.

Tony shrugged, turned back toward the field pond, and took two steps toward the margin that separated water from dry grass. "It rained", he said. Those two words contained a cornucopia of information, as well as an action plan for the better part of the morning. It pushed all thoughts of truck-ill-id-eye and hippocampi from Dennis' mind. Tony had already removed his shoes and socks and was rolling up his jeans. Dennis followed suit.

The grass and green plants were redolent of high summer, a fresh scent that defied precise description.

"We might need a bucket", Dennis said.

They were at the edge of the larger pond, actually a vale in the field that collected rainwater. They could hear the croakers, and a frog leaped from the grassy fringe into the water. An observer might have wondered how even the tardiest frog could be caught without a net and the skill to use it. But if the frogs had been conditioned to be wary, and if they possessed the supple athleticism to launch themselves into watery safety, so too had these boys honed their frog-catching skills since they had learned to walk.

They could move along the fringe of the pond like phantoms, their individual actions in perfect concert with one another, like two foxes stalking a rabbit. They could stand as still as trees, and then move as quickly as lightning when they had a mind to. They caught, in their bare hands, every third or fourth frog they stalked.

Their favorite tactic was to scare a frog into the shallows, mentally mark where the frog had descended into the foggy grass, wait until the water cleared, circle the place with mature caution, thrust a hand into the place where the creature had settled, and close it on the slick frog skin. It was a delicate matter to apply enough pressure to keep the creature from squirming away—these creatures were aquatic greased pigs—while not applying so much pressure as to damage, or even kill, the frog.

"It's a bullfrog", Tony whispered, freezing Dennis in his tracks.

"Do you see it?"

Tony nodded.

"You're sure?"

Tony nodded. He was always sure, even when he was wrong.

There was no need to say more. Tony stood in place while Dennis backed away and made a wide half-circle through the field until he was on the opposite side of the frog. Tony nodded and rolled his pant legs several inches higher while Dennis kept his eyes fixed on the spot Tony had indicated. Normally, they could expect the amphibian to lodge itself in the weedy bottom some six inches or so from the place where it had entered the water. Thus, an eye and then a darting hand would have to fix on this presumed location, for the animal could rarely be seen, even when the water cleared. No second chances; choose poorly or let the frog wiggle free, and it would propel itself through the stirred up, muddy water deeper into the pond, and to safety.

This one was a big frog for sure. A bullfrog in this pond would open up new sporting vistas. Dennis' right index finger pointed to the spot where the animal ought to be. That finger, and not words, guided Tony, whose right hand was poised above a clump of weeds that was more visible as the sediment stirred up by the frog's immersion settled.

Tony turned an eye toward Dennis, who nodded vigorously. Tony's hand shot into the water with barely a sound, like an expert diver penetrating a pool. The matter was instantaneously settled; either Tony had the frog or it had escaped.

"Got it", he shouted in that inimitable way that always reminded Dennis of Tarzan's jungle call. Then Tony's other hand went into the water to secure the prize. When the hands emerged, Dennis could see the creature's long legs dangling from his friend's clasped hands.

"Is it a bullfrog?" Dennis asked.

Tony might have been gazing into a crystal ball. He gave Dennis a queer look, then Dennis saw the blur of something eject itself from the boy's hands and escape into the water.

"It was a bullfrog", Tony insisted. "It was."

It might have been, Dennis admitted to himself, but hadn't he seen leopard-frog spots the moment the creature was between Tony's hands and its watery refuge? He looked quizzically at Tony, who now pleaded, "It was."

3

September 1969

Dennis squatted behind the parked car, a small gray shadow. Greg's brother, Davey, had already captured Ben, Greg, and Tony. Dennis was the only one still free.

Not only was Davey older and faster than the others, even faster than Greg, who was lightning quick, but he possessed an eerie sense that seemed to direct him to the hiding places of the younger boys. Now he was peering intently at the car that concealed Dennis.

Dennis wasn't slow, but he didn't like his chances in a footrace with Davey. Ben, Greg, and Tony were counting on him. There wasn't time for another game; it was a school night. Either the can would be kicked, or Davey would be bragging for another week.

A gusty breeze was blowing early fallen leaves down the street. Dennis knew he had to creep closer to the can before making a dash for it. He also knew that Davey wouldn't range far unless he knew, or strongly suspected, where Dennis was hiding; so it was a stalemate, a familiar stalemate, until one of them took a risk.

Almost any gambit was fair game, except for hiding inside houses. They often hid on house or garage roofs, lying so flat against the shingles that they later had to remove grit from their faces. Moving cars were sometimes used to shield a dash from one hiding place to another. Trees could be climbed, and often were. The Macklin property was a particularly inviting place to hide, if the canine sentry could be avoided.

The car that shielded Dennis from Davey was the Buick TA had purchased to replace the one that was demolished in Iowa. It was old now, with rusty patches, and not terribly dependable, especially in winter. A car had never been anything more than transportation to TA, but Dennis sometimes wished they owned a vehicle he could be proud of.

Dennis knew he'd make the first move, and he knew that Davey knew it too. He needed to reach the back fence before Davey caught him. If he could accomplish this, he might be able to follow the fence line, vault over the Pace fence, and kick the can before Davey intercepted him. While the Macklin property, with its vines and clutter, wasn't made for fast running, it would neutralize Davey's speed and might even give an edge to the smaller, nimbler boy.

He crept from behind the car, until Davey's surveying gaze fixed on him. The tremolo of a late-season cicada intruded on the silence. Dennis knew that Davey had spotted him because the older boy affected unawareness by turning away, and he could tell by Davey's posture that he was preparing for fast action. So was Dennis.

At the same instant, Dennis raced for his own backyard and Davey made a beeline at him. Was his gate closed or open? It couldn't be safely vaulted, and he didn't have time to open it and then beat Davey to the back fence. He heard Greg's encouraging shout from the can prison. A bee or a fly ricocheted off his cheek as he passed through the open gate. He heard the pounding of Davey's feet on the drive, the slamming of the gate as it closed behind him. That bought him another second, a fortunate second.

He heard a tinny voice say, "He's coming", and without looking—there was no time for that—he knew that the voice belonged to Ben's little sister, Carly, who was in the peach tree in their backyard. Not allowed to participate, Carly often ascended to that treetop perch and waited for backyard action, seeing herself as an elevated spy for Dennis and Ben.

He was up the hill and over the fence so quickly that he was already anticipating the accolades of his friends. He turned right, darted past the apple tree, nearly tripped on a root, and made for the vines. He was on the witch's land now but felt lucky that night; besides, he'd soon be back over the fence and on familiar ground.

Where was Davey? He hadn't heard the tinkling of the fence that accompanied a vault. Furthermore, he had no sense that he was being chased, and that was the game's essential instinct. He wondered if Davey had fallen or had been turned back by Gordie. Not Davey—he was indestructible. Dennis emerged from the chute made by the vine trellises. Now all that was necessary was a quick right turn, a vaulting of the Pace fence, a dash to the can, and glory.

He heard the dog before he saw its ominous form; the growling sounded like rocks being rubbed together. Gordie stood before Dennis, his heavy legs planted like tree stumps in the ground; his yellow-red eyes aimed at about the level of Dennis' waist. He had never felt such sudden terror before, not when the car was struck in Iowa, not even when he fell from the Big Tree. He was walled in by the trellises, and the dog would be on him before he could turn and run in the opposite direction.

The growl persisted, even as Gordie inched closer. Dennis was anchored to the ground by his fear. His mind was racing: Did he have a stone, anything in his pocket he could hurl at the beast, not to discourage him—that was a vain hope—but only to distract the dog long enough for Dennis to gain the fence?

As his hand fumbled in his pocket, Gordie leapt forward. Dennis groaned, and a voice, or so he imagined—he was never certain about this voice—enunciated a single word: "Stay."

The dog turned its head, sat on its haunches, and recommenced growling. Dennis didn't delay. He raced past the animal, vaulted the fence, and made for the street. That "stay" he thought he had heard stuck in his head. It so preoccupied him that he never saw Davey at the corner of the house, and he was stunned to find himself pinned to the grass on the Paces' front lawn.

"Game over", Davey shouted, as the three boys walked away from the can prison. By then, Dennis had wiggled free of Davey's now disinterested restraint and stood up. He knew his performance had been feeble.

"What was that noise I heard from the witch's yard?" Greg asked Dennis.

"Don't know", Dennis said. He had no interest in telling the story of his encounter with Gordie. He didn't even want to think about it.

"Let's go", Greg said, walking toward the garage. Ben, Tony, and Dennis followed him. Davey went into the house; the difference in age was beginning to separate him from the other four. Dennis wondered how long it would be before Davey declined to play kick-the-can with them. Even tonight, Davey seemed more distracted than usual, as if he worried that someone he knew, someone his own age, might see him with the younger boys.

Greg opened the garage door and turned on the light and the radio. The Pace car was hardly ever kept in the garage. Most of the time, Greg's mom made room for the boys in the garage by parking their Chevy in the driveway.

The garage was uncluttered and familiar. There was a regular door and an uncurtained window on the wall that faced the backyard. Beneath the window was a work-bench Bob Pace had built a few years before his sudden death. Most of the time, tools were scattered on the bench top; some were hanging on the Peg-Board to the right of the window. There was a card table near the back wall with a plug-in transistor radio on it. The west wall featured two baseball mitts hanging on nails, a cheaply framed photograph of Al Kaline that had been cut from a newspaper, and a pen-and-ink portrait of Bob Pace that Lori Linus had drawn for Greg after his father died. It was more than just a lifeless image. Something of the spirit of that complicated man seemed to reside in the picture.

"Are you sure you didn't hear anything in the witch's yard?" Greg pressed Dennis.

"I'm sure", Dennis said.

"See anything?"

"No."

Greg shook his head, lifted a hammer, and drove a nail into a section of two-by-four.

That command "stay", or whatever Dennis had heard or imagined, still reverberated in his mind, along with the frightening image of a menacing Gordie. Goose bumps coursed up both of his arms.

Lori arrived as she always did, suddenly and with sublime vigor, the light emanating from the open garage door having announced that the game was over. Lori's energy might cause one to think that she was loud or overbearing. In fact, Lori was the opposite of all that. Very little angered her. Stories about Jonas Ratigan's cruelty to small animals and the boys' disparaging references to the Macklins evoked her stern reprimand, but Lori tolerated the boys' teasing and laughed at their jokes. Her loud and husky laugh reverberated like big bells being struck.

Below the girl's high forehead were big expectant eyes set wide apart; her brown hair, thick and wavy, spilled over her shoulders. Lori was almost as tall as Greg and taller than Dennis. She and Tony were as close to being the same height as could be discerned. If anything, she was a fraction of an inch taller, though Tony denied it. Lori humored him, as she humored all the boys in their harmless affectations. The sturdily built girl wasn't a prodigious tree climber or a swift runner like Ben's sister, Carly, but she wasn't timid either. In her plodding way, she would go as high in the Big Tree as Dennis, that is, until she turned twelve and everything changed. She liked to ride bikes as much as any of them.

Lori's father, Larry, an emotionally remote man, was a surveyor for the state Department of Transportation and was often absent for days at a time. Her younger brother, Eddie, was afflicted with cerebral palsy, such a severe case that he couldn't walk normally. Lori's mother, Linda, seemed to be overwhelmed most of the time. Dennis had heard rumors that she was a chronic drinker.

While the boys' friendships were solidly built on their own merits, Lori was a kind of glue that strengthened them, or a kind of oil that lubricated the moving parts. Her private conversations with one or the other helped to keep frustrations from boiling over. Lori had earned their grudging admiration; no mean feat for a girl.

Dennis liked Lori a lot. He liked talking to her. Her perplexing questions made him think. Occasionally, he harbored a tinge of resentment for her special relationship with Tony, not because he aspired to that relationship with Lori himself, but because he had an apprehension about what it might portend.

"Who won?" she asked.

"Who do you think?" Ben said. A recent growth spurt had left Ben ungainly and as tall as Davey. He had the least to say of the group, unless aroused. Dennis had the sense that Ben was always watching and listening, always collecting information. He was a good student at school too, and not ashamed of it, as some boys were.

"You don't collaborate enough", Lori said.

"Where did you learn that word?" Greg teased.

Lori ignored him and walked toward the radio.

"What do you mean?" Dennis asked her.

"Davey's faster than any one of you, but he isn't faster than all of you together", she explained. "If you collaborated you could beat him. It's obvious."

"It ain't obvious to me", Greg said.

Dennis knew that Greg liked to pretend he was simple, even dense, until it came to something he wanted; then he displayed a keen intellect. Greg was lean and good-looking, with bright eyes, a mischievous smile, and long white-blond hair. He desired to be in charge, and he might have been a leader if he didn't try so hard.

"I bet you've never noticed how Davey pits you against each other before the game starts", Lori continued. "That's why he does it; to keep you from collaborating."

"Better shut up", Greg said. "He's coming. If he hears us, there'll be some clobberating."

Lori shook her head in frustration.

Davey was no taller than Ben, but he seemed to dwarf everyone in the room; only Lori didn't shrink at his entrance. The older boy exuded vitality. He had an athlete's build and an actor's features. His sandy, wavy hair, though tousled, couldn't have been improved by a comb. His eyes were remarkably dark for one so fair. His voice was easy on the ears. Only when Davey was genuinely angry, and that wasn't often, did he seem more terrible than companionable.

"Hi, girls", Davey said. He drained the Coke he was holding, crushed the can in his hand, and tossed it into the garbage can on the driveway as if he couldn't miss. "Meet up with Gordie tonight, Dennis?"

"Nope", Dennis said, hoping that Davey hadn't witnessed his distress in the Macklin yard.

"Gordie isn't the worst thing over there", Davey said, shuffling through some magazines on the corner of the workbench. They had belonged to the late Mr. Pace and had never been removed.

"What does that mean?" Ben asked Davey.

"That's for me to know and for you to find out", Davey said.

"You're full of it", Tony said, the first words he'd spoken since they entered the garage. When Davey glared at him, Tony's eyes fell to the concrete floor. Dennis suspected that Tony had spoken to impress Lori. As level-headed as Lori was, she wasn't immune to Davey's charms.

"We'll see who's full of it", Davey said, changing the radio station mid-song. "One night, I snuck up to the Macklin house from the road and saw something I'll never

47

forget." He waited until he had everyone's attention; even Lori was interested. "The old man has been dead for years—everyone says so—but I looked in the window and here's what I saw."

After another dramatic pause, he continued, "There's a chair in the front room with its back to the window. Someone was sitting in the chair. I could see a hat and part of a neck. It wasn't Jimmy or Billy. They were arguing in the hallway. Anyway, the witch was talking to the thing in the chair."

"Maybe it was a visitor", Ben suggested.

"No car in the driveway", Davey rejoined.

"Who do you think it was?" asked Dennis.

An odd smile creased Davey's face, making Dennis realize this was the question he wanted them to ask. "I'll tell you *what* it was", he said. "Those freaks keep the old man's body in the house. When no else is around, they put it in the chair and put the old man's hat on its head."

Tony laughed, but no one else joined him.

"Still think I'm full of it?" Davey asked Tony.

Though he could be the most obstinate of the four boys, Tony knew better than to press the point.

"Wouldn't there be an odor?" Ben asked.

"Not after all these years", Davey said. "He'd be a mummy by now. Anyway, who'd notice an odor around that place? It always stinks."

"That's the chickens", Dennis exclaimed, before he could check himself.

"Okay, Colonel Sanders", Davey said. "I told you what I saw and what I think. You believe whatever you want." With that dénouement, he left the garage and disappeared into the darkness.

"A witch, and now a mummy", Greg said.

And Cerberus too, Dennis wanted to say, but didn't.

As if the image of the mummified Peter Macklin had taken hold of his imagination, Tony said, "What happens when someone dies?"

There was a long silence; then Lori said, "My father says that when someone dies, he becomes nothing, but I don't believe it. It seems wrong to me."

Ben said, "Just because something seems wrong doesn't make it so. Whatever happens when someone dies, he's gone. We never hear from him again."

"TA says that sometimes saints speak to people, and they're dead", Dennis said.

Everyone except Lori looked at him as if he were crazy. "TA said it, not me", he added nervously.

"How can someone speak after he's dead?" Ben plied Dennis. "He doesn't even have a mouth."

"I don't know", Dennis responded. "I'm just telling you what TA says."

"People who hear dead people are nuts", Ben concluded.

"TA isn't nuts", Lori protested. "I believe him."

"I do too", Greg said, surprising them all.

Feeling a certain moral momentum, Dennis continued, "It has to do with God, not just the dead person. TA says it's God who does it."

"How can he be sure?" Tony asked earnestly.

"He can't be sure", Ben answered.

"What's a saint?" Greg asked.

"Like Saint Peter", Tony said, unwrapping a stick of gum and scrolling it into his mouth.

"A good person who dies and goes to heaven", Dennis said.

"Like my dad?" Greg asked tentatively.

No one answered right away. Dennis had heard Bob Pace curse often enough. When Greg's dad had been in one of his bad moods, Davey and Greg had given him a wide berth.

"Your dad was a good man", Lori reassured Greg. "Every time he saw me outside with Eddie, he came over and played with him. Remember how he used to pull Eddie around the block in the wagon? He used to take us both to the park too."

Greg smiled and nodded. "Yeah, my dad had a soft spot for little kids."

Dennis recalled overhearing Mr. Pace tell his sons that he felt sorry for Lori because she was expected to be a mother to her little brother, but he didn't mention this.

Ben returned to the previous subject. "Well, you can't see someone who's dead; that's for sure."

"Davey saw the mummy", Greg said.

"I'm not talking about that. I'm talking about after somebody's buried."

Lori looked at Dennis, as if hoping he had a rebuttal. In truth, Dennis was uncomfortable defending TA's position, a position he wasn't sure he believed himself. But finding it hard to resist Lori's silent entreaty, he said, "People see saints sometimes too."

Tony laughed. Ben just shook his head.

"TA says that people have seen saints, like the Virgin Mary."

"Like a ghost?" Greg said.

"Not exactly", Dennis said. "Ghosts are bad, or miserable. Saints are happy."

"What do they have to be happy about if they're dead?" Ben asked.

"How am I supposed to know?" Dennis replied. "Ask TA."

"They're happy because they live in heaven," Lori suggested, "and they don't have to be sad or worry anymore."

Dennis was surprised at the vigor of Lori's answer.

"I'm not buying it", Ben said. "People see a lot of things that aren't real. That's why they have asylums."

"And shock treatment", Greg added eagerly.

"The people TA is talking about aren't crazy", Dennis said.

"How do *you* know?" Ben countered.

"I don't know, but *you* don't know either."

"I'm going to be a scientist", Ben said, as if it proved his position and settled the matter.

"Go ahead", Dennis said, before realizing how feeble the response was.

"I'd like to talk to a dead person", Greg said.

"You'd pee your pants, or even worse", said Ben. "Anyway, that will never happen."

As Dennis was defending a problematical viewpoint, TA's viewpoint, he found it hard to summon the energy to refute Ben, who was a formidable intellectual adversary when aroused. He didn't like the idea of losing an argument, but he felt he had acquitted himself reasonably well. So long as Ben didn't insult TA, Dennis was happy to let the matter rest unresolved. Hearing angry barking, Dennis reflected that there were worse things than ghosts, and not far off.

4

October 1969

The days had grown shorter, and kick-the-can had given way to school and oppressive homework, but there was one autumn night that invigorated Dennis: Halloween. How many houses could he and his friends visit? How efficient a route could be planned to minimize backtracking and less profitable streets? How early could they embark and how late could they extend their trick-or-treating?

A hard rain and a stiff breeze the previous weekend had brought most of the leaves to the ground. These formed a wet carpet wherever one walked, and not a few found their way into houses. Except for the chrysanthemums and pansies, all the flowers on Lincoln Street had withered or been cut.

That afternoon, Dennis walked the field and the perimeter of a pond retaining only a small residue of water. Red berries, brown stalks, and silvery fronds had replaced most of the green plants. As Dennis stood beneath some late-defoliating pear trees, the wind gusted and bombarded him with multicolored leaves. As the sun peeked through the clouds, more leaves swirled above the treetops like bejeweled halos.

Dennis and his friends had decided to dress as superheroes. All of the costumes were homemade or patched together from closet articles, with a minimum of store-bought accessories. Dennis was the Green Lantern; Tony was Batman; Ben was Aquaman; Greg was—insisted on being—the Flash; Davey was—who else?—Superman; and Lori was Wonder Woman. She had started on her costume in August, long before the boys had given a thought to Halloween.

The six friends pawed around Dennis' front yard like race horses getting ready for the starting gate. It was twilight and darkening by the minute. Greg was especially eager to get going, and he let the others know it.

"Keep your pants on", Davey said to his brother.

Dennis sensed that Greg wanted to respond but didn't want to risk having his costume defaced by an irate Davey, who might push him down or even tackle him. Davey had displayed an annoying paternal demeanor toward Greg since the boys' father had died, and Greg resented it. Sometimes he could control his reaction to his brother, and sometimes he couldn't; but Dennis knew that Greg disliked Davey's patronizing attitude.

Four years had passed since the death of Bob Pace, and Greg hardly ever talked about it. Making ends meet hadn't been easy for the boys' mother, Wanda, but she was an independent and determined woman. She operated a machine at the Terrapin Tool and Die, where TA worked. Wanda's brother, Adam, who lived in Chicago, visited regularly and tried to lend a hand. He could have been a father figure to the boys if he hadn't been so flamboyant.

After sulking for a moment, Greg walked over to Dennis and whispered, so that Davey couldn't hear, "He's a shithead."

"Forget it", Dennis said, not wanting anything to ruin this special night.

"Easy for you to say. You don't have to live with him."

The side door of the Pompay house opened, and Alvin, the Cole's burly next-door neighbor, came down the steps, waded through a pile of leaves at the top of the driveway, and asked Dennis, "Is your dad home yet?"

"He has to work late this week", Dennis answered. There would be no one to distribute candy in the Cole house that night; to leave a house empty on Halloween made Dennis feel both guilty and apprehensive.

"Can you boys," Alvin looked nervously at Lori and smiled, "spare me a minute?"

"We have to get going", Davey said, looking up and down the street, where another summer had vanished.

"I won't hold you up for long. Just one photo. Delia told me that Dennis' dad would appreciate it. Here, squeeze together. Davey, you and Ben in the back. Closer. That's good. Smile everyone."

The flash went off. As soon as Alvin had lowered the camera, Davey ran across the street, followed by the rest.

Dennis felt the familiar thrill. The hunt was on.

5

Day Two

Dennis was dreaming he was a prisoner, that two men were dragging him somewhere—to trial, to execution? He couldn't remember what he had done to deserve it. More vivid than the experience was the sense of desperation, that there was nothing he could say or do to prevent these depredations.

"Get up", the voice said, repeatedly.

He didn't want to get up. He was exhausted.

"Get up."

He opened an eye. Ben was pulling on his arm so hard that his shoulder hurt. Tony had hold of the other arm.

"We have a problem", Ben said, and Dennis could tell it was serious.

He stumbled out of bed. The room was bathed in light. A glance at the clock revealed it was after nine. He wondered why he was so tired; then he remembered the long day at the university, the game, and the subsequent drinks with his friends.

Ben backed up to the bed near the window, where Tony joined him. Neither looked fresh or composed. Ben was running a hand through his sparse hair, and Tony's breathing was labored. At least, Dennis told himself, he wasn't the last one out of bed. No surprise there; Greg had been characteristically exuberant last night. Now the guys were going to make him pay for it.

Or were they? Something was wrong. The expected banter was absent; and, upon closer inspection, Tony didn't look well. In his muddled state, Dennis realized that there was more going on here than hazing.

He made his way to Greg's bed and, at first, thought he was dreaming one of those especially intense dreams that seem real. Greg, wearing his pajamas, was lying face-up on the bed, with a transparent bag over his head. The covers were pulled down to his knees, and his hands were visible at his sides. Dennis could see that an elastic band affixed the open end of the bag to Greg's neck. He could see Greg's face as one sees things underwater. If Greg had been strangled, there were no signs of it, no contusions that were visible on his neck, no blood anywhere, not even on Greg's hands or fingers, as would have been likely if he had fought to repel his attacker.

The scene was bizarre. Dennis, thinking it had been staged by the other three, began to laugh, but as his eyes moved from Ben to Tony, he could see no amusement in their expressions.

"He's dead", Tony said.

Dennis stood there, looking down on what used to be his friend.

Ben asked curtly, "Did either of you hear anything last night?"

Dennis began to shake. Something he couldn't control had been stirred.

Tony said, "I didn't hear a thing. I was so tired, I slept like a log."

"I thought I heard him come in. Then I was out like a light until you guys woke me up", Dennis explained.

Ben added nothing but stood there shaking his head.

Dennis reached down, took hold of the elastic with both hands, and pulled the bag over Greg's head.

"You shouldn't have done that", Ben remonstrated. "We need to call the police." Why hadn't Dennis, the mystery writer, thought of that? He felt foolish, but he wasn't about to put the bag back on his friend's head, so he dropped it on the floor.

The elastic left an imprint on Greg's neck, but there were no open wounds or angry welts. His face was bluish and chalky; and, thankfully, his eyes were closed. Greg looked as though he might have been sleeping, but for his eerie stillness and lack of normal color. Dennis prodded Greg tentatively, but there was no response.

How was it possible that Greg was dead? Something told Dennis that a professional killer must have been responsible. He remembered the hard object under Greg's jacket. Had it been a gun or a knife? He knew he ought to search for it, but what difference would that make now? Greg would still be dead.

Dennis felt the bile rising. He had to make two trips to the bathroom to get rid of it. As he was heaving, he wondered how the world could go to hell so quickly. He had never known a world that didn't include Greg. Some of his earliest memories involved Greg; for that matter, Ben and Tony too.

When the three were again assembled in the room, away from the body, Tony said, "I need some coffee."

"We need to call the police", Ben said again.

"Not yet", Dennis said resolutely.

"We have to do it", Ben said.

"Coffee first", Tony said. "My head is pounding, and I can't face that thing on the bed or the police right now. And we need to talk before we call."

They dressed, after a fashion. On their way out of the room, Ben put the "Privacy Please" sign on the door. Dennis was so distracted that he turned the wrong way and collided with a large dirty linen hamper. The maid, who was bending over on the other side of the hamper, cried out and then mumbled an apology. Dennis did not even reply but rejoined the other two, thanking Ben for his presence of mind in putting the privacy notice on their door. If the maid had gone into the room, the decision about the police would have been made for them.

The three men who entered the hotel restaurant looked awful—unshaven, disheveled, and wearing whatever had been handy. Dennis had thrown on jeans and a golf shirt, but Tony still wore his pajama top, partially concealed by a sport coat; Ben was wearing his slippers. Fortunately, they weren't many people in the room, and they pretended not to notice the three.

"That's better", Tony said after his first sip of coffee. Already, the cards were out, and Tony's hands were moving with what seemed to be a separate consciousness. In that terrible turmoil, he had remembered to put the deck in his pocket. Dennis remembered that his friend had also brought cards to the reception after Lori's funeral. Perhaps Tony needed to feel the cards in his hands, to know the sense of normality they gave him, as much as he needed the time and the coffee. He was doing card tricks, not building anything, the same tricks Greg's uncle Adam had taught him as a boy.

"We're in serious trouble", Dennis began.

"We didn't kill Greg", Ben protested.

58

"How do we convince the police of that? He was in the room with us. The door was locked. My fingerprints are now on that damn bag. There will be questions."

The others remained quiet, and Dennis couldn't help remembering the corpse on the bed. He didn't dare drink anything, not even water. "Are we sure he's dead? What if he's still alive?"

"I'm not a medical examiner. He looked dead, didn't he?" Ben answered.

"He wasn't breathing", Tony said. Tears welled in his eyes.

Trying hard to stay composed, Dennis added, "Are you sure?"

"You saw him", Tony said brusquely.

Ben rose with obvious difficulty and walked toward a window. For a minute, Dennis was alone with his thoughts. Greg couldn't be dead. This couldn't be happening to them. Dennis had a splitting headache. Was it the trauma of Greg's death, something as mundane as a lack of caffeine, or the result of vomiting? Ben and Tony didn't look any better. So this was the kind of trauma TA had experienced in the war, the kind of thing that TA had so rarely talked about. When Ben returned to the table, Dennis said, "I think Greg was carrying a gun."

They looked at him with a combination of fear and disbelief. He told them what he had felt under Greg's jacket the previous night.

"What does an archaeologist on vacation need with a gun?" Tony said. "This isn't a hunting trip."

"Who knows what he was up to", Ben said, shaking his head.

"Greg always had a screw loose", Tony offered.

"We have to call the police", Ben said. "The longer we wait, the worse it will be. Finish your coffee, and let's go back to the room. And this time, don't anyone mess with anything."

Preoccupied, Dennis hadn't noticed the legless man. The man with the wheelchair was sipping from a cup and watching them from the other side of the room. In the light of day, he looked more vigorous than he had the previous night, more intimidating, if such a word could be used about an invalid. With the same efficiency he'd previously displayed, he moved into his chair and wheeled to their table. He was wearing a powder-blue silk shirt and tan pantaloons similar to the ones he had worn the previous evening. Dennis noted that while the man may have been handicapped, he didn't lack for money.

Dennis watched the man approach with a mixture of annoyance and apprehension. While part of him welcomed any excuse to delay their return to the room, he wondered if this stranger had a reason for trying to inveigle himself into their company. But what could that reason possibly be?

"Did your friend have too much Scotch?" the man asked in a melodious baritone. Without waiting for them to answer, he added, "Scotch can have that effect. How well I know it." The man had a British accent, but it wasn't pronounced. At close quarters, his eyes seemed to bore into Dennis.

Ben said, "He'll turn up."

"No doubt. An interesting man, it seemed to me."

"We're just friends together for a weekend", Dennis explained.

The man's eyes moved from one to the other as he said, "Friendship is a beautiful thing."

"What's your business here, may I ask?" Ben inquired. Dennis was grateful that Ben had changed the subject, as he himself was too befuddled to take any initiative.

The legless man said, "Business is one way to put it, but I like to think of my work as a vocation. I've come to Ann Arbor for a seminar on high-canopy tree frogs. My condition, I'm sure you noticed," and something like a chuckle erupted, "has made me a devotee of those remarkable amphibians. They have such strong and supple legs, and my own legs—if you can call them that—are neither strong nor supple."

Dennis' and Tony's eyes met. For an instant, in spite of their anxiety, an imaginative conduit connected their memories. Just as quickly, the connection was broken, and the present moment, with its oppressiveness, returned.

An educated man, an entertaining man, an arrogant man, Dennis thought. His lively dark eyes and smooth olive skin signified good health, in spite of his affliction.

"But I'm curious", the man said. "Yesterday, there was laughter and card castles, not to mention your friend and the lovely bartender. Today, you look so morose and joyless."

Tony said what Dennis and Ben were thinking but wouldn't say. "What business is it of yours?"

"None of my business, but I am a curious man." He seemed neither chastened nor annoyed.

"Our friend overindulged last night, and we had a little more than was good for us too", Dennis said, wondering why he felt he owed this man an explanation. Why not let Tony continue to run interference, he asked himself. Tony wouldn't be badgered into anything by this man.

"That frequently occurs when friends assemble," the legless man said, "and it's the obvious answer."

Tony said, "It's the only answer you're going to get."

Dennis saw the two men lock eyes, as if arm wrestling. He felt uneasy. The legless man smiled at Tony and said, "I hope your friend's equilibrium is soon restored. I meant no disrespect to him, to any of you." Then he wheeled away slowly, never looking back at them.

"What do you make of that?" Ben asked.

"If you're suggesting that character had something to do with Greg's death," Dennis responded, "a person would have to be a fool to kill and then draw attention to himself like that. Whatever that man is, he isn't a fool. And how could someone in his condition get into our room and overpower Greg?"

"He may not be a fool," Ben said, "but he might be a madman. Lunatics have been known to kill and then brag about it."

"He gives me the creeps", Tony said. "Why was he so interested in Greg?"

"Maybe he's exactly who he said he is", Dennis said. "Whoever killed Greg got into a locked room. That character's nimble for an invalid, but he can't go through locked doors or scale walls."

Tony made them wait while he had another cup of coffee. Dennis found it hard to look at his friends. For that matter, he found it hard to concentrate on anything. Finally, Ben stood up, and the others followed his lead. The walk back to the room was the hardest thing Dennis had ever done. Ben led the way with his awkward loping stride. Tony brought up the rear, though he lagged so far behind that Dennis wasn't sure Tony had followed until they arrived at the suite. Ben couldn't find his key. He said, "I thought I put it in these pants. I must have lost it."

"No wonder", Tony said, and he unlocked the door with his own card key.

"I'm not ready for this", Dennis said, shivering. "I'm wide awake now. Maybe we should call the police and wait in the hallway."

Tony pushed the door open.

Dennis' eyes were immediately drawn to the bed where Greg had lain. When he didn't see him there, he looked at the other two beds; they were empty too. There was no sign of his clothes or his bag—nothing. The plastic bag that Dennis had removed from Greg's head and dropped on the floor had vanished too. They walked around the bedroom, the sitting room, the bathroom and found no trace of their friend, no evidence that he had ever been there.

Dennis was trembling; his skin was crawling; he sat on the floor as a hedge against the dizziness he was experiencing. Tony's face was ashen. He opened a bottle of Scotch, poured himself a glass, and drank it down like it was water. To Dennis, Ben seemed the most composed of the three. He made another search of the room, opening all the drawers and looking under the beds.

"Are you sure he was dead?" Ben asked them.

"Yes," Tony answered quickly, then added, "I thought so anyway. He didn't move at all. If he was breathing, it was too shallow to notice. You saw the color of his face." Tony dropped the empty glass on the carpet.

Dennis struggled to his feet. "He looked dead." It sounded ridiculous as soon as he said it.

"Then where is he?" Ben demanded.

"Does this mean we don't have to call the police?" Dark humor, but Tony didn't have his heart in it. He started to pick up the glass but sat in the chair instead and hung his head.

"I'd swear he was dead", Dennis said. He distinctly recalled gazing at that spectral face.

"Tony said he had a screw loose", Ben replied. "Maybe it's just Greg being Greg."

"Let's think", Dennis insisted. "We were sure he was dead when we left the room. Now he's gone; not just Greg, but all his possessions too. He has to be alive. I noticed that there were no signs of violence on Greg's neck, or his hands. Don't you think he would have fought someone who was trying to strangle or suffocate him? Why would someone kill Greg and then later risk coming back to the room to remove his body? And how did someone get into this locked room last night and kill Greg without waking us? It has to be a gag."

"A sick gag, if that's what happened", Ben said. "As long as we're thinking, how do we know that the person who killed Greg—if he was killed—is the person who moved the body?"

Tony, his eyes still directed at the floor, said, "So two different people broke into the room; one's a murderer and one's a comedian."

"An illusionist", Dennis corrected him. "What about the police?"

"No body, no crime", Tony replied. "We don't need the cops."

"We saw the body", Ben said.

"We saw what we thought was a dead body", Dennis objected. "Greg might be in the bar splitting a gut."

"If he is, I'll murder him myself", Tony said solemnly. Then he stumbled to the bed and sat down. He looked paler still and his eyes were lusterless. "Get me a syringe."

They knew what he needed. Ben opened Tony's bag and searched. He handed the syringe to Tony, who gave himself an injection.

"Are you okay?" Dennis asked.

Tony didn't answer. He dropped back on the bed and closed his eyes.

"When Tony feels better, let's go downstairs", Dennis suggested. "If Greg is alive, he'll turn up soon. He won't be able to resist a grand entrance."

"I'm back to thinking he was dead", Ben said. "It would have taken an award-winning performance to create that effect."

"We didn't check his pulse or take his temperature", said Tony.

"We were preoccupied with being terrified and sick", Dennis said. "We were in shock. Maybe he was counting on that."

Tony rolled to his feet. "Let's go. I'm not hungry, but I have to eat something or I'll get sick. If it turns out Greg is behind this, he's going to pay. There's a limit, and he's gone beyond it, if this is his doing."

They changed their clothes and washed up. Dennis saw Tony put a day-old strawberry in his mouth. He thought Tony looked better, and he felt better too, contemplating the possibility that Greg might still be alive.

Ben pulled out his phone. "I'm going to call Greg's mobile number."

Tony and Dennis waited. After a minute, Ben said, "This is—"

Tony grabbed the phone and terminated the call.

"What the hell was that all about?" Ben demanded.

Tony returned the phone to Ben, saying, "I'm not buying the gag explanation; not yet. And if it isn't a gag, it may be the cops listening to the message."

"I knew we kept you around for a reason", said Ben. "I should have thought of that."

"Even geniuses need help now and then", Tony muttered.

Ben placed the call again, waited, and said, "I need to speak with you right away. It's Saturday morning, and one of your colleagues has been trying to contact you. Call me."

"I'm not holding my breath waiting for Greg to call back", Tony said.

"Can't Greg's mobile phone be located?" Dennis said.

"Not by me it can't", Ben replied. "Even geniuses have their limitations."

"Whose half-dollar is that on the table?" Dennis asked. It sat in center of the table, separate from the refreshments.

No one claimed it. "Maybe it's Greg's", Tony suggested. Dennis picked it up and put it in his pocket. Ben grabbed his computer. The others didn't ask him why, but Ben rarely did anything without a reason.

The dining room was nearly full. When the waitress came to their table, Dennis and Ben ordered coffee. Dennis was hoping that more coffee would cure his headache. Tony asked for scrambled eggs and a beer. He set two packs of cards on the table but didn't open them. Ben powered up his computer.

Dennis and Tony left Ben to his work, figuring he'd let them in on what he was doing when he was ready. Tony ate his eggs with little enthusiasm. He hadn't even bothered to salt and pepper them. He handed Dennis a piece of toast, and Dennis forced himself to eat it.

Ben said, "Here's the personnel phone number for the Smithsonian. Call it."

Dennis complied. "It's a message system. Now what?"

"Of course; it's Saturday. Figure out how to find Gregory Pace."

Dennis waited, hit some keys, and waited again.

"Are you getting an extension?"

Dennis shook his head. He had an inkling of what Ben was up to.

Dennis said, "There appears to be no extension for Gregory Pace. What does that mean?"

Ben went back to work on his computer. "I think I have the email convention." Shortly, he looked up and said, "I tried three different variations using Greg's name and the convention. All the emails bounced; he must not work there. I have his home phone and email, not his work information. How about you?"

Dennis and Tony checked their mobile phones and shook their heads.

Ben said, "Here's a person we've known all our lives. He might have been murdered in our room. He claimed he worked for the Smithsonian, but that's doubtful. He was probably carrying a gun. Something weird is going on."

"The Smithsonian is a big organization", Dennis said. "Maybe—"

"Face it, Dennis," said Tony, "no phone and no email. Ben's right. What was Greg up to?"

"Here's my logic", Ben said, as if he hadn't heard them. "If Greg is dead, he was murdered. We can't guess why, but he seems to have been living a double life, since he told his closest friends that he worked somewhere he didn't. If he's not dead, it has to be a prank; that doesn't explain why he pretended to work for the Smithsonian. If he's dead—I think he is—the police will get involved sooner or later. If we wait, it will be *big*"—he paused—"*big* trouble for us."

"We can say we don't know anything about it", Tony said, spinning a pack of cards with one hand.

"We can say it and get thrown in jail", Ben countered. "Just because *we* can't find any evidence of violence in the room doesn't mean the police won't. If Greg was killed, they'll find something."

"I say we wait a little longer before calling the police", Dennis cautioned. The idea of involving the police conjured up strong emotions. In the absence of a corpse—he forced himself to remain hopeful that Greg was still alive—he had convinced himself there was nothing to be gained by contacting the police.

Ben shrugged. "It's a big risk."

"It's a bigger risk to involve them", Dennis retorted.

"What would Cole Porter Palmer do?" Tony asked Dennis, without any levity. Ben rolled his eyes and went back to work on his computer.

Dennis didn't have that answer. It had been easy to sit in the solitude of his library and compose cerebral mysteries. This was different. He was ashamed that Ben had been the one to take the lead in analyzing the situation. Sitting in this room, drinking coffee and talking about murder, or whatever had transpired in that suite, was the last thing he expected to be doing on this second day of their reunion.

"Are we in danger too?" Ben asked, without looking up.

"I don't have any secrets", Dennis said warily, though he couldn't help thinking about the oblique letter in his library drawer that might be fact and might be a vile fiction.

"You don't?" Tony countered, then wiped his lips with a napkin. His features were inscrutable, but Dennis knew what he meant.

"If Greg was murdered," Ben surmised, "the killer could have killed all of us too. That suggests Greg was the only target."

"Unless something happened and the killer got scared, and had to get out of the room", Tony said.

"That's a pleasant thought," Dennis said, "that we're here because something distracted the killer. I don't believe it. There's nothing that connects the four of us that warrants murder. Don't shake your head, Tony." He waited until both Tony and Ben met his eyes before saying, "If Greg was killed—I'm not convinced he was—we were safe then, and we're safe now. If Greg was killed, it was something that had to do with Greg, and Greg alone." Even as he was speaking, Dennis wondered how he could talk about one of his best friends so clinically.

"I'm not feeling well", Tony said. "I can barely keep my eyes open. We can talk more later, but I need to lie down."

"Go ahead, Tony. I'm exhausted too", Dennis admitted.

"I'll come with you", Ben said.

"I'll be okay", Tony replied. "If you find me on the hallway floor, just drag me back to the room." He stood up, using the table for support.

After Tony left, Ben and Dennis stared at each other across the table. Dennis thought he knew Ben as well as anyone. They had shared so many experiences. Still, at that moment, he might have been sharing a table with a stranger, so guarded did Ben seem to be.

"I'll take care of the bill", Ben offered. "Get some rest. I have things to do." He patted the computer.

"What are you thinking about?" Dennis asked.

"I don't know. All I have are questions."

"Tony looks bad."

"We'll keep an eye on him. He'll be okay. He let his sugar go."

"Maybe Greg will be roaring with laughter when I open the door to the room", Dennis said, but skeptically.

"If he is, slug him for me. Then I'll do the honors myself when I see him."

"Don't do anything foolish until we talk about it."

"Like calling the police, you mean."

"That's right", Dennis said, as he left the table.

Tony was already asleep when Dennis entered the suite. He felt drained, but his mind was racing. Was Greg really dead? If so, who killed him and why? Was that really a gun beneath Greg's jacket? If Greg wasn't associated with the Smithsonian, why had he pretended to be and what was he really doing?

Despite these questions, Dennis slept, and slept hard. Though the world seemed to be unraveling, he was not up to stitching it back together.

6

January 1970

So much snow, Dennis reflected, and wasted on a Saturday, when there was no school to be canceled. TA called it winter's harsh charm. He stared out the front-room window at well over a foot of snow on the ground and three-foot drifts. TA's car in the driveway was almost invisible beneath this white blanket. The sky was gray and low, and though it wasn't snowing hard, there were still snowflakes falling and blowing about.

A week earlier, they had taken down their Christmas tree, a scrawny specimen TA had picked up on Christmas Eve on his way home from work. They had decorated the tree together with ornaments that Dennis was certain his mother had acquired. The ornaments did for the tree what a nice suit and tie did for an ordinarily seedy man; they improved the tree's appearance, but couldn't make a paragon of it.

One morning after Christmas, Dennis had awakened to find TA kneeling before their manger. TA hadn't seen him, and Dennis—uncomfortable—had retreated to his bedroom until he heard TA in the kitchen.

That snowy morning, there was no one outside. Dennis could hear Judy Garland's voice coming from TA's room. Soon, the percolator would be tapping away and the scent of freshly brewed coffee would permeate the house. He wondered if they'd be able to clear the snow by Monday. Probably, he surmised, as long as they didn't get much more.

"Clang, clang, clang, went the trolley." The sound was so vivacious, it was hard to believe it was just a record. He imagined for a moment that Judy Garland had spent the night with TA, was serenading him. Maybe they'd share a cup of coffee at the kitchen table. He thought that Judy Garland was dead, but wasn't sure. She was Dorothy; that was the only thing he knew about her, and that she was a good singer.

TA emerged from his room in pajamas and slippers.

"Friendship, friendship, just the perfect blend-ship", Garland crooned. Dennis had heard that song often enough. TA had an extensive collection of Cole Porter songs. He especially liked renditions by Judy Garland, Ella Fitzgerald, and Frank Sinatra.

"Lots of snow?" TA asked.

"Lots."

TA went to the window, then walked to the kitchen to make the coffee. TA's day never started without this ritual. He came back to the front room, sat in his chair in the corner opposite the big window, and said, "I don't suppose we'll get a paper today; and if we do, I don't suppose we'll find it until next spring. Want to help me with the hippocampi?" TA never called them sea horses. He always used the Latin family name, and occasionally *hippos*.

"Sure."

"When you get a chance, you can clean off the car", TA said.

"Are you going somewhere?" Dennis said.

"Not today, tomorrow. I don't want it to ice up." TA went to Mass every Sunday and holy day, and to confession monthly. He encouraged Dennis to accompany him, but he didn't demand it.

Now both the record and the percolator were silent. TA got up from his chair to pour himself a cup and make another selection. There was a book on the table next to TA's chair: *The Judas Window*, by Carter Dickson. Dennis shared TA's love for mystery stories; he was fortunate that TA's collection was rich. TA sometimes ordered hard-to-find editions from The Mysterious Bookstore in Manhattan. Alvin Pompay once remarked that Dennis was too young to be reading these books, but TA disagreed, saying, "Reading is a consolation to me; I hope it will be for him too." As for the majority of the books on the front-room shelf—philosophy and other idea-laden works—Dennis knew them only by the authors on their spines: Aristotle, Marcus Aurelius, Thomas Aquinas, Augustine, Pascal, Edmund Burke, Montesquieu, Goethe, Kant, Fulton Sheen.

TA's battered bookshelf was about six feet long and five feet high, with cracked and chipped varnish. As with everything else TA owned, function predominated over form. Paperbacks stood side by side with bulky hardcovers; the only concession to order was the grouping of the books. The two top shelves contained TA's mysteries. The bottom shelves held his idea books.

One rainy Sunday afternoon, Dennis had picked up *The Crooked Hinge*, by J. D. Carr, and had read it until well past midnight. TA once told him that mystery stories were applied philosophy and that the best were exercises in reason and ethics; in that sense, the top two shelves were not so different from the bottom two. Dennis knew only that the mental puzzles provided enjoyment. If he learned from them anything of a philosophical nature, he did so in spite of himself. TA neither encouraged nor discouraged Dennis' interest in his books. If he did steer him toward one title or another, he was so subtle that Dennis didn't notice.

TA was a late-night reader. On one occasion, Dennis woke in the middle of the night to find his father, still dressed in his work clothes, reading *The Greek Coffin Mystery*, by Ellery Queen. In what passed for garrulity in TA, he said, "I thought I'd read a few pages and turn in, but now I'm a third of the way through. This is Queen's best—pure mind, not much passion or modern psychology. Aren't you feeling well?"

Dennis had told TA he was fine, just restless.

"Pick up a book and sit", TA had said, even though it was a school night.

They sat together for another hour, producing in Dennis such a poignant memory of their silent camaraderie that he wondered why he had never sought to replicate the experience. Perhaps he had been moved by an unconscious desire to keep this night a singular event.

TA re-entered the room, holding his coffee cup. "I think your boots are in the closet", he said.

"They're in the basement", Dennis said. How lonely the house could be, he thought, especially in winter. Dennis didn't blame TA, who did what he could to make their home a congenial place. It just so happened that both TA and Dennis were inclined to go inside themselves for revitalization.

After TA had dressed, they went to check on the sea horses. Walking down the narrow wooden stairs, Dennis

74

wondered once again how TA had gotten the thousand-gallon aquarium into the basement. The tank was eight feet long, five feet wide, and four feet tall. Adjacent to the aquarium, on a low bench, were a sophisticated filtration unit, a recirculation flow heater to maintain temperature, and a salinity probe.

The almost empty concrete vault was kept dark. The only light glowed from fluorescent bulbs in the aquarium cover. Inside the tank at any one time were up to a half-dozen species of sea horses. These delicate creatures paddled about the luminous space or attached themselves to rocks or undulating saltwater plants.

Peter Kristov had once mentioned a curio shop in Saigon that sold sea horses and suggested this might have been the origin of TA's interest in these creatures. At a gathering one night after Dennis had gone to bed, he heard Peter's booming voice saying, "Leave it to TA to be more interested in fish than girls"—not taxonomically accurate, but to the point.

At great labor and some expense, TA had created an amazing world in that otherwise barren basement. Many a night, Dennis would find TA, though tired from a long day at work, testing the water, repairing equipment, or ministering to ailing creatures. This work seemed to vivify rather than weary TA, and the two of them, especially when Dennis was younger, spent many, mostly silent night-time hours gazing through the glass.

On this particular visit to the aquarium, TA said, "*We* might not be very active today, but *they* seem to be. Hand me the algaecide."

TA moved a few inches from Dennis and peered into the water. Here before the aquarium, Dennis could be close to TA without feeling uncomfortable. From out of the sea grass closest to where they were standing emerged a giraffe sea horse with a particularly large coronet. Its prehensile tail curled behind it, and its pectoral fins moved so fast that Dennis could see only a blur. Moving toward it was a longnose sea horse, and the two animals passed each other.

"Have you seen the dwarf?" TA asked Dennis.

Dennis shook his head.

"I'm a little worried about her", TA said.

Dennis made a circuit of the tank. "There she is", he said, pointing at the sea grass. The dwarf's small tail was secured to a stem.

"How does she look?"

Dennis squatted and leaned closer. "Hard to tell. Maybe the others are keeping her from the food."

"Maybe", TA said. "I'll drop the brine shrimp close to her." He lifted a portion of the aquarium cover, scooped a small cup into an adjacent, but much smaller, aquarium, and deposited the contents into the larger one.

Dennis asked, "What's a truck-ill-id-eye?"

"Can you spell it for me?"

"No."

"Where did you hear it?"

"Tony had them in his backyard last summer."

"Did you ask him what they were?"

"No."

"Why not?"

Dennis was sorry he had asked TA the question. "I guess I didn't want him to know I didn't understand the word."

"There's no shame in that. What do you think it is?"

"I thought it was a bird. Tony admitted it liked his mother's flowers."

"Do you know of any birds that like nectar?" TA asked him.

"No."

"Have you ever seen a hummingbird?"

"In a book, I think. They're small, aren't they?"

"Very small. They like the nectar in flowers. We're not likely to see one in our yard, but Tony's mother is a splendid gardener. Just one species of hummingbird resides in Michigan in the summer. The movement of its wings reminds me of the hippocampi's pectorals when they're in motion. Look it up—I ought to trim these plants too", TA said.

When the work was done, they went upstairs and noticed that a snowplow had made a pass down the street. The street wasn't clear, but it might be navigable.

Dennis was preparing to find a book to read when there was a knock on the door. It was Tony. His brown coat was too small for him, and the index finger on his gloved left hand was bare from fingertip to first knuckle. He was wearing jeans and tennis shoes. Tony's one serious concession to the cold and snow was a black ski mask, a point of pride to Tony, as his oldest brother, Wim, had bought it for him. A sled attached to one end of a length of clothesline reclined on the snow-covered walk below the steps, which now made a kind of snow-ramp to the porch.

Dennis said, "There's only one species of truck-ill-id-eye in Michigan."

"Get your sled", Tony said, ignoring the comment.

In a hurry, Dennis retrieved his boots and sled from the basement and found his coat, gloves, and woolen hat.

The boys manhandled their sleds through the deep snow to the street. While they were deciding what to do, two doors slammed, and Ben and Greg joined them in the street. Dennis was struck by the different quality of sound when the world was inundated by snow—crisper, like the crisp air itself. Ben was the most prudently dressed of the four. He wore boots—like Dennis—ear muffs, and mittens. Greg was wearing his tennis shoes and a coat little more substantial than a windbreaker. His gloves were sound, though, and he wore a Tigers cap as well as a bright yellow scarf.

"Where did you get that thing?" Dennis asked, pointing to the scarf.

Greg shrugged. Then he said to Ben, "You look like a fag."

Ben was used to ignoring Greg. "Want to go to the hill?"

"We can walk down the middle of the street. No one will be driving today", Tony suggested.

As if on cue, a car came around the corner and crept toward them. It was Jonas Ratigan's old Chevy. There was barely room for a single car in the swath that had been plowed, so the boys had to lift their sleds to make room for the vehicle.

Jonas hit the brakes, slid too close to Dennis for comfort, and got out of the car.

"What are you up to?" asked the young man a few years older than Davey Pace. He wasn't wearing a coat and was smoking a cigarette; his dark hair was greased back in a stiff wave.

Jonas had the disposition of a hornet being pestered with a stick. His angular face and mischievous eyes could turn malevolent in a heartbeat. His nose looked as if it had once been broken, and he was missing a bottom tooth. Most parents in the neighborhood were suspicious of Jonas, and Dennis thought he intentionally cultivated his bad reputation.

"We're going to the hill", Dennis answered for all of them. He was the only one of the four boys who didn't fear Jonas, because out of respect for TA, Jonas treated Dennis better than the other kids in the neighborhood. Even though Greg and Tony knew that they could call on their older brothers in a pinch, Jonas could do a lot of damage by then. Moreover, Jonas was known to act first and think later.

The young man threw the cigarette as far as he could in the direction of Ben's house. Dennis could see a tee shirt under his long-sleeved shirt, but he thought Jonas must have been cold. He knew his next-door neighbor well enough to realize it would take a lot to make Jonas reveal any weakness.

"Want a ride?" Jonas said in his husky voice. Dennis wondered whether the cigarettes were responsible for the raspiness, as Jonas had been smoking for as long as he could remember.

Thinking that Jonas was inviting them to get into the car, Greg said, "We're gonna sled."

"That's what I mean, stupid", Jonas said. "I'll pull you. Tie your sleds to the bumper."

Ben looked skeptical. Tony's expression was invisible beneath the ski mask. Greg was already dragging his sled to the back of the car.

Jonas said, "Two of you tie to the bumper, and the other two can tie to the backs of the sleds, like a train."

"Will it be safe?" Ben asked.

Jonas cursed; then he hopped into the driver's seat, but he didn't shut the door. "Tell me when you're ready", he shouted. In the meantime, he lit another cigarette.

Reluctantly, Dennis joined Greg and tied his sled to the rear bumper as securely as he could. Tony tied his sled to Greg's; Ben tied his to Dennis'. The snow had stopped, and pale blue gaps broke up the clouds; but now the wind was blowing harder so it felt colder. While Dennis was busy tying his sled, Lori joined the group. She was wearing a pink snowsuit with an attached hood, and she wore ankle-length black boots and black gloves. As usual, her ensemble put the boys to shame. She placed her sled next to Tony's so that she was in between Tony and Ben. She clutched the handle of Tony's sled with her right hand, and he grabbed hers with his left, interlocking their arms.

"Are you ready?" Jonas shouted back at them through the open driver's window.

"Yeah", Greg said.

They were lying face-down on their sleds. Dennis gripped the handle with determination. The car jerked forward, wheels spinning and throwing snow in their faces. Dennis had never desired a piece of clothing more than he did Tony's ski mask at that moment. His face burned. He closed his eyes, feeling himself moving with increasing speed. The sled hopped up and down as it encountered bumps in the snowpack. The stench from the tailpipe came and went.

The sleds weaved with every slight veering of the car, and when they went around the corner, Dennis saw that Greg's and Tony's sleds were plowing the corner of the snowbank. For a moment, he thought that Lori's sled would be released by the impact, but both Tony and Lori held tight to the other's handle.

Dennis couldn't feel his face anymore. The car continued to pick up speed. The sounds of the engine and wheels echoed in the little canyon created by the snow-banks. There was nothing to do but hold on. He heard Greg's laughter and was embarrassed by his own fear. He looked back and saw that Ben's eyes were closed. Tony had lifted his upper body, reminding Dennis of seals he had seen on TV. Lori's head was raised, but she was other-wise flat against the sled.

Jonas must have made a turn in the opposite direction, because this time it was Dennis and Ben who received an icy sandwich from the snowbank. Dennis heard Ben yelp, and his own left hand felt as if it was being rubbed raw, in spite of the glove.

The crash wasn't abrupt, but that didn't make it any less scary. First the car began to veer. Then Jonas must have jammed the brake pedal, because the sleds hurtled forward. Greg and Dennis had to extend their arms and push against the bumper to keep from sliding beneath the car. Dennis felt Ben's sled crash into his; the next thing he knew, the car had jumped the snowbank. A split second later, he heard a crash as the car struck a tree. The boys' sleds piled up against the snowbank and each other.

The lines from the sleds had pulled free from the rear bumper. Greg's sled was upside down; he was beneath it, upside down too, in the same position as prior to the accident. Tony had managed to push off from his sled and had rolled into the bank some five feet from the others. Lori was still stretched out on her sled in the middle of the street two houses back. Tony must have turned her loose when Jonas lost control of the car.

They heard Jonas' disembodied voice cursing from over the bank.

Dennis got to his feet. He had bumped his head against something, but otherwise he seemed to be okay. Tony was already standing. Ben was on his knees on top of his sled. Greg, who hadn't moved, said, "That was a wild ride."

Jonas trudged through the snow to where the boys had tumbled and looked down at them. "Get the hell out of here. If the cops ... and Alvin", he said, as an afterthought, "find out what we were doing ..." He added a word that got their attention.

"Move those turds along, Lori-loo", he shouted, gazing mournfully at the damaged car. He had used that nickname for Lori since she was a toddler.

Jonas was lucky they were all capable of moving, Dennis thought, but he knew better than to say anything, TA or no TA. They were only a dozen houses from home, but no one had come outside yet. Greg rolled his sled over, got up, and joined the others as they made their way down the street as a procession of disheveled, snow-encrusted kids.

For a fleeting moment Dennis considered Jonas' plight. What on earth would his parents say or do about the wrecked car? His mother, Cordelia, was a strong-willed woman, but Dennis could not imagine her being unduly harsh to her son. His stepfather, Alvin, on the other hand, was more difficult to predict. He had the humble and self-effacing manner of many men who did manual labor for a living, but because of Jonas' predilection for trouble, his relationship with his stepson was stormy. And Alvin and Delia had a young son of their own, Caleb, which made living together even more challenging for that family.

"Anybody want to sled down the hill?" Greg asked.

Dennis said no. Tony, Ben, and Lori must have been as rattled as he was, because they expressed no enthusiasm for the idea of getting back on their sleds.

"That was cool", Greg said, once they had put some distance between themselves and Jonas.

"It was memorable", Ben said, extracting a chunk of ice from behind his ear.

They heard a siren.

7

March 1970

Dennis tied his tennis shoes, bolted out the door, and ran down the street, the same street that had been covered with snow just a few weeks earlier. The weather had been abnormally warm for March, and he had heard peeping at night, which foretold frogs and toads. He hadn't bothered to see whether Tony, Greg, or Ben wanted to accompany him. Tony was the most likely candidate, but even he didn't like to go frogging this early in the season. Dennis was usually the first one to sight frogs jumping from the banks of the little ponds, and snakes slithering in the grass.

The little leaves on the oaks and maples were wrinkly and tinged with red. Patches of green dotted the field but mostly bordered the pond, which melted snow had swollen twenty feet beyond its normal margins. He walked the entire perimeter of the water and didn't scare up a single frog. He heard no croaking or peeping either. At least the air smelled like spring, giving him the hope that a few more weeks would result in amphibious activity.

Turning to go, he thought he saw suspicious ripples next to a large tree limb that had fallen the previous winter. Had something that had perched on the limb dived into the water, or was something moving beneath it?

Everyone—especially Lori—worried about snakes, but there weren't any water snakes in these parts, just boring garter snakes and the occasional rat snake. The latter resided under the barn on the sledding hill, while the garters were almost always to be found in the open field.

Dennis was too curious to pass by the ripples without investigation. The water wasn't deep, and the limb was close enough to dry land to be reached by a moderate leap, an action Dennis had executed dozens of times.

Maybe the long winter had put him out of practice. He landed on the limb in good form, but when it rolled, he lost his balance. One leg went into the water, right up to his knee, and he felt his foot sink into the thick, cold mud below. He quickly extracted the leg and regained his balance, but minus his left shoe.

He swore loudly. He couldn't go home without that shoe. Losing it would be bad enough, but taking the risk that Tony, Greg, or Ben might see him shoeless was worse.

He hated soakers, and muddy soakers were especially distasteful. He rolled his shirt sleeve up to his shoulder, reached into the water, and dislodged the shoe. Holding the muddy shoe in one hand, he leapt from the tree limb to the shore. He did his best to remove the mud from his sock and shoe before he put them back on, but wet and filthy they remained.

No frogs and a soaker; a wasted trip, he told himself as he walked down Lincoln Street. He was almost home when he felt the urge to make a detour to the Big Tree. It was still too early in the year to expect any buds on so old and gnarly an oak. Maybe, he told himself, a few minutes in the tree would dry his shoe and sock a bit and make the mishap less visible to his friends. He swung easily onto the lowest branch and climbed another ten feet before he heard a voice and saw two people approaching the tree—Billy and Jimmy Macklin.

"Get off our property!" Billy shouted.

Dennis and his friends had always considered this small parcel of land on the corner, and especially the Big Tree, to be community property. The notion that someone owned it, especially the Macklins, was unwelcome, to say the least.

Now the brothers were standing beneath the tree. Both had oval heads, close-cropped hair, and button noses. Billy, though the younger of the two, was a head taller and fifty pounds heavier than Jimmy. Dennis didn't know Billy's age, but the boy, unlike his older brother, possessed a shadow of a beard. He looked up at Dennis through narrow eyes. Jimmy's eyes were like dark marbles stuck in his doughy face. His mouth was smaller, and his chin more pronounced than his younger brother's. By turns, he could be timorous or belligerent, not unlike the brown squirrels that inhabited the Macklin property. He was not mute, but he did not often speak unless aroused or agitated.

Billy wore jeans and a white tee shirt, none too clean, even by Dennis' standards. Jimmy, on the other hand, was dressed in a collared shirt and brown corduroys. Both boys wore dark boots.

"Get off our property," repeated Billy, "or I'll call the dog."

The Macklins referred to Gordie as "the dog". Dennis looked nervously across the field to their backyard. He spotted Gordie by the chicken coops. He didn't like the idea of being trapped in the tree by that beast.

Dennis descended to the ground not two paces from the Macklins. He wasn't much smaller than Jimmy, but Billy was another matter; he towered over Dennis, who doubted that either was a fast runner, something in his favor.

"Since when is this your property?" Dennis ventured.

"Since before your house was built and before you were born", Billy answered. "Want me to call the police?" Bubbly spittle formed at the corner of Billy's mouth as he talked.

"No", Dennis said hesitantly.

"And tell that Pace boy to stop stealing our grapes", Billy said.

"That's none of my business", Dennis said, raising his voice defiantly. Greg swore that the Macklin grapes were the most delicious he had ever eaten. He justified stealing them by insisting that the grapes that could be obtained by vaulting the fence and quickly snatching—that is, those within five feet of the fence—were community property. Though a doubtful legal principle, this notion came to carry great moral weight with the boys. Thus, the vines nearest the fence were denuded by early fall. For the most part, the Macklins wrote off this proximate fruit as grudging tribute. They didn't like the theft, but there wasn't any incontrovertible evidence to prove who took the grapes, or a practical remedy to prevent him. Of course, when Gordie's rounds brought him to the fence line, all of these principles and understandings were moot. In Dennis' estimation, even the best of these grapes were indifferent, as likely to be sour as sweet. He wondered if it wasn't the taste of adventure that made Greg so effusive about them.

"Did you fall into a swamp?" Billy asked.

Dennis imagined how dirty he must look. "I just finished saving a kid from drowning. I'm on my way to get an award."

"Smart ass", Jimmy hissed.

Dennis almost erupted with, "Listen, Little Morgus", but thought better of it.

Billy laughed, but not pleasantly. "Your friend Ratigan is a thug", he said.

"Tell him yourself", Dennis said. "He might like it, and he might not."

"Your father's not much good either."

Dennis flushed. "At least he isn't a crook like yours."

Billy Macklin's nostrils flared, and his hands balled into fists. Dennis tensed, preparing himself for a fight, a fight that could have been avoided and wouldn't end well. He knew that he ought to have gone home without antagonizing these two.

Billy hesitated and glanced back at his house, where Dennis saw that the boys' mother, the "witch", was watching them from the yard. Then Billy wagged a finger at Dennis and, with the back of his other hand, wiped his eyes. Dennis thought it was the dysphasic Jimmy who said, "Leave them grapes alone."

Billy began lumbering toward the house, and Jimmy beetled along behind him. As soon as the brothers had taken a few steps through the tall grass, Dennis ran for the sidewalk. He wouldn't put it past Billy to call the police, and he wanted to be out of sight if they showed up. He bounded down Lincoln Street like a spooked rabbit, muddy and rattled. Jenny Holm, who lived next door to Tony's family, was sitting so still on her front porch that he almost missed her. She was seated on a yellow chair, and her canary sweater and brown slacks made her hard to distinguish from her surroundings. When he saw that she was watching him, he slowed to a walk. He felt guilty about something, but he wasn't sure what.

Dennis had always been fascinated by Jenny. He thought that she would have been beautiful if she didn't have a perpetually troubled expression. Her golden hair fell to her shoulders. She had large, cat-like eyes, high cheek-bones, and full lips. Her chin was narrow and her nose was rather small, as if it declined to compete with those spectacular eyes. She was large in front and narrow at the waist. Dennis had seen some female movie stars who didn't measure up to Jenny when it came to looks, but there was a shrewishness in her demeanor that tarnished the allure.

"Sit with me", she said, in a tone more commanding than inviting.

Dennis ascended the porch stairs and sat in an empty blue chair. He was conscious of the mud on his pants and arm; it didn't smell good either, but Jenny's company was an improvement on the Macklins'.

"What have you gotten into?" she asked, turning up her pretty little nose.

Dennis knocked dried mud off his pant leg, which didn't satisfy her as it was now on her porch. She seemed to exert an effort to convert her frown into a smile. "Will you be happy when school ends?" she asked.

"Sure", he said. He didn't know how to address her. The mothers of his friends he referred to as Mrs. Pace or Mrs. Hulse. Jenny was a grown woman, but Dennis wasn't sure that she had ever been married. He had heard that she had two children, though he had never seen any children at the house. Some said her children lived with their father, and some insisted they were with their aunt and uncle. Dennis had never heard Jenny mention them.

"Did you fall in the mud?" she asked. "Your shoe is filthy."

"TA will put it in the washer."

Jenny Holm's gaze made Dennis uncomfortable. Her big eyes looked even bigger now. She asked, "Does your father have friends?"

"Yes", Dennis said nervously. He was wondering where *his* friends were when he needed them.

They sat in silence for a while, so long that he thought it might be acceptable to get up and leave; then she said very suddenly, as if she had been bottling it up, "Girl friends?" Now, those big eyes were pointed straight ahead, across Lincoln Street.

"I don't think so", Dennis said.

She put her hand on his clean arm and said, "Do you want your father to be happy?"

When people referred to his father, they sounded as if they were talking about a stranger. He said yes, wondering what kind of a question that was, and feeling even more nervous. He imagined Greg watching all this from a window across the street and began to flush.

"A man needs a woman to be happy. Your mother's been dead a long time."

He didn't need to be reminded of that.

Now she squeezed his arm with unexpected vigor and said, "You should help him find a woman who can make him happy."

Despite her million-dollar face, Jenny was giving Dennis the creeps, and he moved to the edge of his chair.

"I want you to do me a favor, Dennis", she said.

"Sure", he said automatically; anything to get out of here, he told himself.

She handed him a folded sheet of paper and said, "This is my phone number. I want you to give it to your father and tell him to call me. I can make him happy. Do you understand?"

He understood perfectly. That was why he felt so creepy.

Dennis took the paper. She got up from her chair and kissed him on the lips.

"You'll make him call me?"

"Yes", he said, getting up and running from the porch, never remembering that he had said it. The only thing he could think of as he ran past Tony's house was that if any of the others had seen that encounter, he was doomed to a month of ridicule. He had turned to cross the street when he heard a loud voice say, "Stoppen!"

He stopped and looked at Tony's house. The door was open, and a woman was standing half in, half out. With one crooked finger she beckoned him to the porch. He wanted to get home, but he didn't dare ignore Magdalena Hulse. Head bent, Dennis walked slowly toward Tony's mother.

"Vhat dat voman vant?" she asked him.

Knowing Dennis lacked a mother, Mrs. Hulse assumed that role with him, at least whenever Dennis was within eyeshot or earshot. She especially made a point to keep track of Dennis when TA was at work.

"Nothing", Dennis answered.

"Don't tell me nuttink", she said. Magdalena Hulse was short and compact, and she went to Mass every day. If she was overly scrupulous in some matters, she wasn't obsessively so, and her natural inclination was to be generous. She had lively, dark eyes and prematurely gray hair—Tony's older brother Jan took credit for that. Her thick, dark brows beneath an expanse of forehead touched above the bridge of her aquiline nose, and her expressive face was quick to smile or frown, depending on the circumstances. She and her husband,

Johannes, had emigrated from Holland when Caterina and Wim were little. Her husband and her friends called her Maggie.

"You tell me", she said to Dennis emphatically.

Dennis recounted his conversation with Jenny as coherently as he could. He left out the kiss, hoping she hadn't seen it.

"Dat voman got a loose screw in her brain. Stay avay from her. Give me dat phone number." She extended a hand, and Dennis put the folded paper in it. Hand and paper disappeared into Magdalena Hulse's apron pocket. "Your fahter don't need such grief as dat", she said, quietly. "By Gott, dat voman is a leecher. I tell Vim and Yan to stay avay, by Gott."

Magdalena looked down at his pants and shoe. "Have you been vit pigs?" She didn't wait for him to answer. "Here, you vait. I have nice piece of cake for you and your fahter." She disappeared and reappeared before the door fully closed behind her.

"Take", she said pushing the pound cake into his hands. "Don't go near dat harpy. You hear me?"

He heard her and said he wouldn't. Then he ran across Lincoln Street and into the house. The first thing he did when he got inside was take off his tennis shoe and sock. TA watched him with scant interest; he'd seen this act before.

"Any frogs?" he asked.

Dennis shook his head.

"Got a soaker?"

Dennis nodded.

"What were you discussing with Jenny Holm?"

Dennis walked downstairs with the shoe and pitched it into the wooden crate that served as a laundry hamper.

He came upstairs with one bare foot, hoping that TA had left the kitchen.

He was still there, with the paper and a cup of coffee in front of him. TA said, "How about tamales for lunch?"

"Okay."

"Find some shoes."

Dennis found last year's tennis shoes, which almost fit, and followed TA to the car. The inside smelled of oily metal. They rode the short distance to Telegraph and Broadway in an apprehensive silence, or so it seemed to Dennis.

The restaurant was a small block and brick building with spaces for a half-dozen cars. TA had introduced Dennis to tamales so long ago that he had no memory of his first visit to Zapata's. To him, it was as natural as eating cereal or Betty Carlson's peaches.

They sat across from each other at a tiny table, each with a plate of tamales and beans.

"See any snakes?" TA asked, with a forkful of tamale midway between his plate and his mouth.

Dennis shook his head. TA knew it was too early in the season for snakes. Dennis directed every ounce of his attention to the tamale on his plate. He heard the door open and close and Mr. Zapata's greeting, always in Spanish, even though he spoke perfectly good English. The aroma in the room was pleasant.

Glancing at the man across the table, Dennis remembered that less than a year after his mother's death, TA began dating. Several times a month, he went out on Friday or Saturday night. Dennis remembered one woman—Caroline—who accompanied them to a movie and the zoo. She was older than TA, and she understood that Dennis wasn't interested in another mother. She was courteous to him, but she didn't overdo her solicitude. He would have liked her if there hadn't been the complication of her undefined relationship with TA. Dennis had even seen her kiss TA on one occasion; not passionately, nor in a sisterly manner either.

As Dennis recalled, this dating went on for about a year, after which TA gave it up or did it so discretely as to render it invisible. As the years progressed, TA wasn't gone at night frequently, and never overnight, but he'd occasionally let Dennis know that he was going out. Dennis never felt the need to question him about where he was going, and wasn't sure he even wanted to know.

On those occasions when Dennis happened to be awake when TA arrived home, he had never detected the scent of alcohol or perfume. For all Dennis knew, TA could have been to church; their parish had twenty-four-hour eucharistic adoration.

Dennis was all but certain that TA never had anything to do with Jenny Holm. That was enough for him. But there was one brief period, when Dennis first began reading Hercule Poirot mysteries, in which he set out to learn what TA was up to. As an exercise in detecting, Dennis went through TA's pants and jacket after he had been out, but to no avail. Unlike the stories Dennis had been reading, there were no clues—nothing other than keys, coins, and the hard candy TA enjoyed.

As matter-of-factly as he could, Dennis asked the man seated across from him, "Does a man need a woman to be happy?"

"Some men need a woman to be happy. Some are better off without a woman. Some devote their lives to God's work."

"Which one are you?" Dennis said, still not daring to look up from his plate.

TA laughed. "I'm the kind only a few women can tolerate."

"Like Mom?"

"That's right. Like Mom."

Dennis said, "Are you looking for a woman?"

"I can't say I am", TA said wistfully. "I'm getting set in my ways. It wouldn't be gracious to subject a woman to that."

Dennis said, "I don't think Jenny Holm would mind."

"What makes you say that?"

"She asked me to tell you to call her."

TA said, "Do you think Mrs. Holm is the right woman for me?"

Dennis didn't answer.

"Tell me what you think", TA insisted.

"I don't think so, but it's your decision."

TA seemed to be pleased by this response. He said, "It *is* my decision, but a person's choices affect other people. People can make choices, but they can't choose the consequences. They'd like to, but they can't. You may have noticed that Jenny Holm is a very attractive woman, but I don't dare touch her with a ten-foot pole."

"Mrs. Hulse says she has a screw loose."

"Maybe. She's troubled."

"Where are her children?" Dennis asked.

"With their aunt and uncle."

Dennis said, "Did you ever see them?"

"Only when they were little. Dick Holm was with them then."

"What happened to him?"

"He ran off, or she ran him off. They fought. One day he was there, and the next day he was gone. He never came back. The kids left soon after."

Dennis said, "She's pretty."

"I suppose so. Very pretty, in fact. Some women—and men—are dangerous. She's one of them; the kind who lured Odysseus to a lee shore."

Dennis didn't know Mr. O'Deesus, or Lee's Shore, but the way TA put the matter, it didn't sound good. Dennis said, "What's a leecher?"

"I'm not sure. Where did you hear it?"

"Mrs. Hulse. She was talking about Jenny Holm."

TA said, "Unless I'm mistaken, the word is *lecher*."

"What's a lecher?"

TA said, "Technically, it's a man whose sexual urge is uncontrolled."

"Can a woman be a lecher?"

"I can't say whether the definition is that broad. I don't think it's a common trait in women, but I suppose it's possible."

"Is Mrs. Hulse right?"

TA said, "On that point, I choose to remain silent."

Dennis had learned that this could mean many things.

TA said, "I suggest you give Jenny Holm a wide berth. How is your tamale?"

Dennis looked up and met TA's eyes. When they walked outside, TA put his arm around Dennis' shoulder. That didn't happen often.

"How about ice cream?" TA asked.

8

Day Two, Afternoon

When Dennis opened his eyes, Tony was tying his shoes and Ben was sitting at the desk with his computer.

"What time is it?" he asked.

"Three", Ben said.

Dennis rubbed his eyes. "I didn't mean to sleep so long", he said. "How do you feel, Tony?"

"Better."

"Let's get something to eat", Dennis said.

"Then we have to make a decision", Ben insisted. "There's no trace of Greg. And if he's in trouble, we'll need to help him."

Dennis said, "What do you mean?"

"I mean, if he's alive and up to something, we'll need a weasel to find a weasel."

That didn't convince Dennis. They made their way to the hotel restaurant. When they were seated, the same waiter who had served them the previous evening approached their table.

"I am happy to see you again", the man said. "But where is your friend?"

"Busy", Tony answered peremptorily.

They ordered. The waiter was preparing to leave when Dennis said to him, "Did our friend speak to you after we left?"

The man said, "Your friend was at the bar. Christine, the bartender, is a magnet for men."

"Did he talk to anyone else?" Ben asked.

"I don't think so." The man gave them an inquiring look. "Is something wrong?"

"No", Ben replied quickly. "We had a wager with him. We're just checking."

"Good lie", Tony said after the man had left. He seemed to have recovered from his earlier sickness.

"I'm not a weasel-hunting weasel, but I can lie when I need to", Ben explained. They looked at each other with stone faces, as if Ben had not needed to explain. "We've got to make a decision", he pressed again.

"Let's talk to the bartender first", Dennis suggested.

No one objected, but Ben said, "Then what? Do you expect her to have answers?"

"I don't know what to expect", Dennis said.

"How about calling Susan?" Ben offered.

Susan could no longer be avoided. Greg's wife was a woman they had known since high school, a friend.

"We have to call her", Ben insisted. "We might as well do it and get it over with. She might know something."

"She wasn't here", Dennis protested. He didn't want to compound the anguish he was already feeling. "What could she know?"

"She's his wife", Ben countered.

The waiter returned with their drinks, just water. After they had ordered food and before the man left the table, Ben said, "Is the bartender—the woman who worked last night—here today?"

The waiter nodded.

Tony said, "Will you send her over here?"

"She's not supposed to leave the bar."

"It has to do with our friend who spoke to her at the bar last night", Tony said. "Tell her it won't take long."

"I will see", the man said, his face registering suspicion.

"We have to talk to her", Dennis said as the man turned to leave, regretting the passion in his voice. He heard the chime that indicated he had received a text message. He retrieved his phone and read it: "Hope you're having a great time. How are the accommodations? Need anything? Eva."

Ben said, "What now?"

"Eva hopes we're having a great time and asked if we need anything."

"Can she send along your detective, Cole Porter Palmer, and a bloodhound?" Tony said querulously. "I need a real drink."

"Do you think Greg's lie about where he works has something to do with his disappearance?" Ben asked them, ignoring Tony's remark.

"We don't know that he lied", Tony insisted.

"Don't be so damned naïve, Tony", Ben said. "Greg was living a lie, or at least a deception."

"He's our friend. I'm not jumping to that conclusion until there's more proof", Tony said. "Where's that waiter?"

Instead of the waiter, they saw the attractive bartender walking toward them. Most women—and men for that matter—look better at a distance. This woman was an exception. She had bright blue eyes and a lovely complexion, like fine china, but she lacked the hauteur of many beautiful women; her smile was warm and inviting.

"How can I help you?" She sat un-self-consciously in the chair where Greg should have been sitting.

Dennis looked at the other two and saw that they were waiting for him to speak. The woman was waiting too.

"We made a wager with our friend last night", he began. Her smile dissolved, and anger flashed in her eyes. "Not that kind of wager", Dennis said reassuringly. And her composure had returned by the time he finished explaining that they had bet Greg on the outcome of a game and that he had left without paying what he owed them. "Did he mention that he was going anywhere last night?"

Now there was a hint of amusement on the bartender's face. "No", she answered. "Somehow—maybe it was the man in the wheelchair—we got talking about my brother, Jeff, who has cerebral palsy. He said he knew a doctor in D.C. who is doing work with young cerebral-palsy sufferers. When he got ready to leave, I wondered if he would use it to try to hustle me. He didn't. He gave me the name of the doctor, said he would leave the phone number at the front desk, that I was welcome to use him as a reference. I appreciated the chance to talk to someone about Jeff. He cared—I'm sure of it."

It had taken a stranger to remind Dennis that his friend had many dimensions, not all of them tedious or frustrating. Greg had always been there when any of them needed help. If he wanted them to believe that he worked for the Smithsonian, maybe there was a reason.

"I still have the card he gave me. I hope he's all right."

Dennis said, "I hope so too. If Greg thought that doctor can help your brother, he probably can."

Ben said, "Did he say anything about meeting someone later?"

"He said that he was in town with friends", she answered warily.

Dennis could see that Christine was no dummy. They couldn't go much further without rousing her suspicions. On the other hand, they were desperate for information.

Ben said, "Did Greg talk to anyone else in the bar?"

"Not to my knowledge", Christine answered. "When he left the bar, he moved off my radar. Even the good guys do; that's how it works. I have to go now." She was already out of the chair, and she passed the waiter on his way to the table with their food and drinks.

After they had been served, Dennis said, "Do you believe her?"

"I don't know what to believe", Tony said. "If Greg was murdered, why was he killed *here*?"

They ought to have been hungry, but Dennis was hard-pressed to eat his soup and the bread and cheese he had ordered. He watched Tony, who needed to eat, and was glad to see him consume a sandwich. When Ben finished his chef salad, he said, "I'm calling Susan." After a minute, he shook his head and said, "The Arlington number I have for Susan has been disconnected. When was the last time Susan answered the phone when you called Greg?"

Dennis said, "I don't know. Quite a while, I guess."

"Me too", Ben said. "Have either of you talked to Susan recently?"

Dennis was embarrassed to admit he hadn't. There had been only cards, or messages through Greg.

"What if they aren't married anymore?" Ben asked.

"He would have told us", Tony protested.

"He lied to us about the Smithsonian."

"We're his friends", Dennis remonstrated. "One lie, and maybe for a good reason—Do a search for Susan Pace."

"Or Decker", Tony added.

Tony got the waiter's attention and ordered a beer for himself and a glass of wine for Dennis and Ben.

Ben said, "No hits for Susan Pace and Arlington. I'll try some other combinations."

Tony and Dennis waited. Dennis didn't feel the urge to vomit anymore, but his head still hurt, and there was no way he could erase the image of Greg's ashen face from his memory.

Ben said, "Where was Susan from originally? It's a long shot, but we might as well try it."

Tony said, "A small town in Pennsylvania, not far from Pittsburgh." He shut his eyes, searching his memory, then said, "Imperial. Her dad worked there before they moved to Michigan."

"Eureka", Ben exclaimed. "Susan Decker, Imperial, Pennsylvania. Here's the phone number."

Tony said, "What's she doing in Pennsylvania?"

"Good question", Ben said. "I have my suspicions."

"If this is our Susan, what do we tell her?" Dennis said. "What do we ask her?"

Tony said, "I say we tell her he didn't show yesterday. We can ask her how we can get in touch with him."

"She'll give us his home phone and email; then what?" Dennis said.

"We'll have to tell her he was here yesterday . . . and missing this morning", Ben said. "And that we're convinced he hasn't gone off with someone."

"You expect Susan to believe that?" Dennis asked.

"It's the best we can do", Ben countered. "Are you ready?"

"I'm not, but you better call anyway", Dennis said.

When Dennis pictured Susan, he didn't see a fifty-year-old woman but the vivacious girl he had known in high school. He'd had a crush on Susan once, but had lacked the self-confidence to do anything about it. He saw Ben make the thumbs-up sign.

"Hello, Susan, this is Ben Carlson. . . . I'm okay; how are you and Greg doing? . . . Is that so? I didn't know; he didn't tell us. . . . Yes, that's Greg. Hey, thanks for the note you sent when Diane died. I wasn't thinking clearly, or I'd have noticed it didn't come from both of you. . . . Yes, it *has* been difficult, but I'm managing. . . . We located you using the Net. . . . Yeah, Decker and Imperial. . . . It's good to talk to you too, but I do have something on my mind. Greg met Tony, Dennis, and me yesterday in Ann Arbor. . . . Yes, they're here with me. . . . No, not Greg; that's why I called. . . . No, nothing's wrong."

Another lie, Dennis thought.

"He's gone missing. . . . Since last night. . . . We don't think so, Susan. . . . No, honest, we don't think so. It might be a prank—then we'll look like idiots—but do you know anything that might explain it? . . . Do you know where he's working now? . . . We just found that out. What the hell has he been up to? . . . He doesn't tell us much either. . . . Sorry to pester you, Susan. I feel bad about calling you out of the blue. . . . Yes, we're a little worried too. . . . How is David? . . . That's good to know. Well, take care of yourself, Susan. . . . I will. Goodbye."

Ben looked up at them. "They divorced four years ago. Greg hasn't worked for the Smithsonian for at least three years. She has no idea what he's up to or what might have happened. Oh, she said to say hello."

"That weasel", Dennis said.

"Now do we call the police?" Ben asked them.

"I say no", Dennis retorted. "If he's dead, he's dead, and if he isn't dead, he faked it. He hasn't made getting to the bottom of it any easier with these lies."

"He's not the only liar at this table", Tony said.

Ben gave Tony a sharp look and said, "If we don't call the police, we're at a standstill; and if we're at a standstill, we might as well go home. But if we go home without calling the police, and they confront us later on, we'll have hell to pay. I'm not going to jail because you guys are too stubborn to do what's necessary . . . what's required by law."

"Let's do a search for Greg as we did for Susan", Dennis said, ignoring Ben's remarks. "See what turns up, and we should check the room again."

The waiter returned with the wine and beer. They were silent until he left; then Dennis consumed his wine greedily.

Tony said, staring into his beer glass, "I removed the privacy sign." Ben gave him a nasty look. "The maid's probably been through the room. There was nothing there, Ben. We searched the room from top to bottom."

"We're in big trouble if the police find out we let them clean the room after what happened", Ben said.

Dennis said, "That's why they're not going to find out."

"Here's something interesting", Ben interrupted them. "A paper presented two years ago by Dr. Gregory Pace entitled 'Weapons of the Early Indo-European Migration'."

Tony said, "We already know he's interested in that subject."

"His affiliation is listed as the U.S. Army War College in Carlisle, Pennsylvania", Ben said.

Dennis said. "Do you think he's a spook?"

"It's as good a guess as any", Ben answered. "It might explain everything."

"Then it may not be a matter for the police after all", Dennis said.

"Whether it's spy business or police business doesn't matter", Tony said. "It's our business. Greg is our friend. We owe him our best." He lifted his empty glass. "From one weasel to another!"

9

July 1970

It was a rare morning, even for a Michigan summer. The aquamarine sky was empty except for a three-quarter moon that shone almost as brightly as it did at night. The cool, almost cold, air created pockets of mist like little clouds above depressions in the field. The brilliant early light produced long, crisp shadows and dozens of shades of green and brown. Even the dead elm trees seemed to possess a spark of vitality, as if the vigor of that day might resurrect life from dead limbs.

Dennis had gone to the field as soon as he awoke, not waiting for Tony or any of the others, as if he'd been beckoned by someone, or something. The frogs had not been roused yet; the only sounds came from the cars and trucks on Telegraph Road. As he made a circuit of the larger pond, which was receding by the day, he saw a dragonfly skimming the water. By the time he returned to where he had started, the mist had dissolved.

When Dennis arrived home, he noticed that the grass needed cutting and made a mental note to mow it some-time during the day. This was the first summer that TA trusted him with the lawn mower. When TA did yard work, modest as it was, he always wore his blue work cap and occasionally his jacket; most of the time he was in a tee shirt. TA wasn't one for weeding, so he mowed down both grass and weeds with ecumenical impartiality. Apart from the sycamore by the street, there was little in the Cole yard to get in his way. The incline by the back fence was more nuisance than obstruction.

The mower resided next to a rusting barbeque grill, which produced remarkably good hamburgers and hot dogs. Propped against the back of the house, both devices were shrouded with a tarpaulin when not in use. The otherwise empty yard might have bordered a Marine barracks rather than a home. On one occasion, Cordelia Pompay had stolen into the yard while TA was at work and planted a stand of petunias. For some weeks, the flowers stood out like an island of color in an otherwise pale-green and brown sea. Whether an autumn frost took them, or raccoons, or TA's mower, Dennis never knew, but the flowers never appeared again. Even Delia was no match for TA's relentless austerity.

Later that morning, Dennis and his friends found themselves gathered on the sidewalk with little to do. Dennis tried to convince them to accompany him to the Little Store, but to no avail. Ben was going to the comic-book store, and Tony and Greg intended to play Monopoly, a game Dennis despised. Without a word being said, they all understood that they would reassemble for kick-the-can in the evening.

Dennis decided to walk to the store by himself, but when he reached the corner of Lincoln and Mary streets, he heard Lori's husky voice behind him. He turned and unwrapped a caramel candy while waiting for her.

"Want one?" he asked Lori.

She shook her head. "Tony said you're going to the Little Store. Can I come?"

"Sure." He started walking past the Big Tree. Though it didn't display any visible signs of distress, its leafy plumage was already ripening to yellows and browns. No one said anything until they reached the next corner. Then Lori broke the silence and asked, "What do you want to do when you grow up?"

Dennis hadn't thought about it—that seemed a long way off—but he wasn't surprised that Lori had. He pondered the question for a minute and said, "I'd like to clean up the county drain so more things could live there."

"Don't frogs live there?" she asked.

"They don't live in the drain; it's too dirty. They live in the ponds. What do *you* want to do?"

Lori's face was wreathed with a big smile. "Promise you won't laugh."

He said, "Why would I laugh? You didn't laugh at me."

They had turned the corner and were walking down an unpaved street lined with homes that predated the development where Dennis and Lori lived. Not far ahead, on their right, Dennis could see the back of the field and the frog pond. The county drain, enclosed for several hundred feet, passed beneath the street a half-block ahead.

She said, "Do you know that block in downtown Edison with the brick buildings on both sides?"

"The old brick buildings with the stone animal heads on top?"

"I want to have an art gallery and a studio there; not very big but with lots of windows. The gallery will be on the first floor, and the studio will be above it. I want to make portraits that show what the person is seeing, make you feel what he's feeling."

Dennis thought of Lori's portrait of Bob Pace, how it captured the look of determined resolution that somehow defined Greg's father. He sensed the joy in her words; he had never heard her speak with such excitement.

Lori said, "When I was little, we took a trip to Charlevoix. I've never forgotten it. I want to have a studio in Charlevoix too and spend the summers there. Tony could do the building and carpentry and make the picture frames. He's very good with his hands."

"Have you told him yet?" Dennis said.

She looked at him warily and said, "Not yet. Please don't say anything. Promise?"

Dennis nodded.

"We'll have a big telescope on the roof. At night, we'll look up at the stars or down at the streets."

Dennis rarely thought about the future, while Lori seemed to have everything planned. He said, "Are you drawing anything now?"

Lori hesitated, then said, "I'm working on a portrait of Jonas. I'd never tell him; that makes it difficult, having to draw without being able to look at the subject. I don't even have a good photograph of him."

"Why Jonas?" Dennis asked. Jonas Ratigan seemed an unlikely candidate for Lori's art. He knew she didn't like Jonas, so why would she bother to draw him?

"I don't pretend to understand him," she said, "and what I do know about him I don't like very much. It's silly, but I see him as a sort of werewolf. Not with long hair and big teeth, but like a man who's watching the moon emerge at night and knowing what that means, what's going to happen next with that sense of both fear and exhilaration. That's how Jonas strikes me—always on the verge of something dangerous."

Dennis looked at Lori as if he were seeing her for the first time. He didn't know what to say, but her description of Jonas made strange sense. He was a sort of werewolf.

She bent over and picked up a stick, snapped it, and threw the larger end into the ditch by the road. Then she used the other end as an imaginary pen, drawing something against the canvas of the sky. She said, "Do you think we'll actually do these things someday? My mom and dad aren't very happy. Maybe there are things they wanted to do but never did do, or could do."

He saw that she wanted an answer, but he could offer little reassurance. A lot of the adults Dennis knew seemed more resigned to, than motivated by, their lives. "We can," he said, "but who knows? I haven't thought about it much."

"Maybe people don't want it badly enough," she offered. "Maybe they get discouraged and give up too soon." She looked down at the walk and said, "I love my brother, but I get sick of it all sometimes. It's not just Eddie ..."

Dennis thought that she wanted to say more; her expression became stormy.

"I *do* love him. I know life isn't easy; but I have dreams, and I won't give them up."

"Maybe he'll get better."

She looked at him in the way his teacher looked at him when he wasn't paying attention. Then she beamed a smile at him and said, "Maybe he will—Is your dad happy?"

For a moment, he wondered who she was talking about. Then he said, "I don't know." He didn't know for sure because TA never told him.

"What do you think he'd do if he could?" she asked.

It was an odd question, one Dennis had never considered. When he pictured TA, he visualized him in his blue jacket and hat, or reading in the chair, or standing over the aquarium with a bottle or a net in his hand. That he might be interested in doing something else never occurred to Dennis.

She didn't wait for him to answer, saying, "I wonder if that will happen to us, what happened to our parents, or to people like Jenny."

Dennis said, "What happened to her?"

"She's not happy."

"How do you know?"

"I don't know how I know, but I'm sure of it. Can't you see it in her eyes? I made a portrait. I started over five times. My dad won't let me show it to anyone. It isn't very flattering, but it's how I see her. I think it's how she sees herself. Have you ever heard of Circe?"

He shook his head.

Lori said, "I read about her. She was a goddess, a witch, an enchantress. In my portrait, Jenny is practically naked, with her chin pointing to the sky, her eyes wide open, her arms outstretched."

No wonder your dad won't let anyone see it, Dennis was tempted to say, but he had a desire to see it himself. He said, "What gave you that crazy idea?"

"That's what I see when I look at her", Lori said. "I can't help it. I don't know how to explain it, but I had to draw that picture."

Dennis said, "You're going to have quite a gallery with pictures like that. I'm not sure Edison is ready for it."

"It's my dream."

After hearing Lori describe her dream, it wasn't hard for Dennis to see it too. It made a vivid image.

They sat on the curb outside the Little Store and ate strawberry twists and shared a can of Coke. Lori became quiet. On the way home, Dennis wondered if she regretted sharing her dream with him. When she went into her house and closed the door, he felt sad.

Greg's garage door was open, and Dennis walked up the drive into the Pace yard. He was still thinking about his conversation with Lori. When he turned the corner into the backyard, he saw Greg lying on his stomach on the incline in front of the fence, so the Monopoly game must have been suspended. Greg had one end of a pea-shooter in his mouth; the other end rested on one of the fence links. Dennis knew from experience that Greg was waiting for one of the Macklin chickens—better yet, Gordie—to come into range. It was a tricky proposition, as the grapevines and rubbish supplied copious protection from the pea-shooter. Greg had been known to lie in that spot for an hour or more awaiting his prey.

The previous year, Dennis and Greg had entered the backyard one morning to discover that a dozen bean plants, at least six inches tall, had been transplanted along the fence line on the Macklin side. They never discovered who had done it. Even though Wanda told Greg to leave them alone, he had taken this transplantation as a personal affront, had uprooted them, and had stomped them into the ground.

Now Greg might have been a statue, so still was he. There was no sign of any movement on the Macklin property, just bees darting around the vines.

Dennis fought back the urge to call out and left the Pace yard. He removed the last half of the twist from his shirt pocket and put it in his mouth. Striding back to his house, he saw Delia Pompay and Betty Carlson sitting on the Pompay porch. Delia called out to him, "Here's a pie for you and your father. Come and get it."

Carly Carlson was sitting on the Pompay lawn with an open book in front of her. She looked up and stared at Dennis as he walked toward her mother and Delia.

Betty Carlson said, "These are last year's peaches, but they're still good." She handed him a box. It was warm and emitted a sweet aroma that made his mouth water.

Dennis thanked her. He was reasonably comfortable with Ben's mother; as a neighbor, she was courteous and generous, but as an elementary-school teacher, he thought, she would be intimidating. He sensed a hardness in the woman's character. She was tall—what was called willowy—and had a small nose and straw-colored hair. Dennis had never seen her when she wasn't attractively dressed and made-up, even when she was working in her yard.

"Make sure you save a piece for your father", Delia admonished him. She was wearing a bright red and gold bathrobe instead of street clothes.

Dennis noticed an odd rigidity in her face, as if her mouth had lost its mobility. It seemed to him unnatural in so animated a person.

"I don't look so good, do I?" she said.

"You look okay to me", Dennis answered cautiously.

"Liar. Didn't TA teach you any better than that? I look terrible. I'm sick; that's why."

Betty looked nervous but kept quiet. Betty Carlson and Delia Pompay were not known to be close friends, even though they lived only two houses away from each other. So Delia's illness explained why Betty was here,

Dennis thought. He looked down and saw another boxed pie on the concrete porch. He glanced at Betty, whose eyes were boring into him. Ben had inherited his mother's intelligence, but Dennis saw little of Ben in those penetrating eyes.

Delia said to him, "Would you ask your father to visit me tonight? I'd like to talk to him. I have to go to the hospital tomorrow."

"I will", Dennis said. He couldn't help noticing how different these two women were. Delia was partial to bright colors. She would be stout if she weren't careful. She wasn't unattractive; her facial features and her flamboyance reminded Dennis of Lucille Ball. Delia could be morose, but she was energetic when she had a mind to be. Dennis once heard TA mention to Peter that Delia had lived in Greenwich Village, and that Jonas' father still lived there. While few would think of Delia Pompay as motherly, she doted on her son Caleb, a boy so young that Dennis had consigned him to the same category as the neighborhood dogs and cats.

"Don't forget", Delia said.

"When will you come home from the hospital?" Dennis asked.

"That's a good question. Maybe a week, maybe longer. We'll see."

"What's wrong?" he said, before he realized what he was asking.

Betty Carlson looked down at her lap, but Delia was unperturbed, at least outwardly. She said, "I have to have my breasts removed. There's cancer in them."

Betty took her hand. If a dog took a cat's paw, it wouldn't have surprised him more. Delia closed her eyes. Dennis thought she was going to cry, but she bit her lip, and all he heard was a single sob. He noticed that Carly had stopped reading and was watching them.

"Don't worry", she said to him. "Just don't forget to tell your father."

He didn't forget to tell TA, but he wasn't able to talk to him before he left the house for kick-the-can because TA was working late again. He made himself a plate of macaroni and cheese for supper and left a plate for TA before he went outside. He was so preoccupied with his conversations with Lori and Delia that he was the first one captured, and he spent the rest of the game confined to the can prison. He didn't mind. It gave him a good vantage point when TA's car came down the street.

But it didn't come, and when the game was over, the boys assembled in Greg's garage. Dennis, Greg, Ben, and Tony hadn't been inside the garage for long—just long enough to initiate their idiosyncratic routine, to turn on the light and the radio, and to get themselves a can of pop—when Davey strode in and said, "What's this about you girls digging tunnels?" He was eating an apple. Dennis noticed that Davey's blond hair was getting longer. The boy had pushed it straight back and it fell over his collar. He was much taller than Dennis now; for that matter, Greg was quite a bit taller than Dennis too.

No one answered Davey. Greg, with a guilty expression, looked down at his shoes. The boys had indeed been talking about finding, or building, a passageway from house to house, but it was supposed to be a secret.

"Anyway," Davey continued, taking another bite, "you don't need tunnels. There are already tunnels underneath these yards and streets." Then he waited for the inevitable amazement to appear on their faces.

Davey said, "Uncle Id"—that was his name for his Uncle Adam, because Adam was fond of saying *id est* whenever he launched into one of his innumerable stories—"told me about the time he went into a huge sewer below Detroit. That was when Id was young, before he moved to Chicago. He was in a boat. He said it reminded him of the *Phantom of the Opera*."

"How could they see down there?" Ben asked skeptically.

"They brought flashlights, big ones. They could go anywhere down there. No one could see them."

"What were they doing down there?" Ben persisted.

Dennis could tell that Ben's questions were annoying Davey, who had set up the boys to be so dumbfounded they'd be speechless.

"They were inspecting the sewer because a new sky-scraper was being built on top of it." Davey answered matter-of-factly.

"What was it like inside the sewer?" Tony asked, with an appropriate sense of awe.

Davey had a talent for suspense, and timing. He waited until they were all growing impatient, then answered, "Id said there were millions of giant cockroaches all over the walls. And they had to be alert, because if there was a storm, the sewer would be flooded and they'd be trapped."

"What happened to the cockroaches when there was a storm?" Tony asked.

"How the hell should I know?" Davey said peevishly.

"Where did they go in the boat?" Dennis asked.

Davey said, "They went all over the city, and no one above the wiser. Id said they might have gone all the way to the river, but they were afraid of getting lost."

"It sounds fishy to me", Ben said.

"Are you calling my Uncle Adam a liar?" Davey demanded. He flipped the apple core at Ben. It bounced off his chest and landed on the workbench.

Ben knew better than to press the point. He walked toward the radio. Dennis tried to imagine how it would feel to get lost in a place with millions of cockroaches, especially if the flashlight batteries went dead.

"The point is," Davey continued, "there are sewers underneath our yards too. All you have to do is tunnel from the sewer to the basements."

Ben turned around and said, in a disparaging tone, "Is that all?"

"It's a hell of a lot easier than digging tunnels from house to house", Davey said.

Greg said to his brother, "Why did Dad call Uncle Adam 'Uncle Eve'?"

Davey grinned and said, "You're too young to know. Someday you'll figure it out." He delivered this statement as if he were thirty rather than thirteen. "See you girls later", Davey said, leaving the garage.

"I have to get going", Dennis said, realizing that Davey's story had distracted him from watching for TA's car. He ran down the driveway and crossed the Pace and Carlson lawns to his side door. TA's car was indeed in the driveway, and there was a light on in the kitchen.

When Dennis entered the house, he met TA coming upstairs from the basement. The man was still wearing his blue jacket but had removed his cap.

TA said, "Thanks for the mac and cheese."

"Delia wants you to visit her", Dennis said breathlessly. "She's going to the hospital tomorrow."

"I know."

"Is she going to die?"

"We're all going to die", TA said. "If you mean, is she going to die soon, I hope not."

"She said she has cancer."

"She does. It's daunting, but Delia's strong, and she's fortunate to have Alvin supporting her. My father, your grandfather, died of cancer."

"Are you going to see her?" Dennis said.

"Of course. I'm going now."

"Davey said there are sewers underneath the neighborhood that are big enough for boats", Dennis said, eager to change the subject. "His Uncle Adam was in one."

TA said, "A lot of tall tales contain a kernel of truth. There are very large sewers, and there are sewers beneath this neighborhood; but our sewers aren't that big."

"How big are they?"

"I'm not sure … twelve inches, maybe twenty-four. It would be hard to squeeze into one, and if you did, you wouldn't smell very pleasant when you came out. Now, I'd better be going. I'm late."

"There's pie in the refrigerator", Dennis said. "Mrs. Carlson made it."

"That's very kind of her. Eat as much as you want."

TA went out the side door and Dennis went to the refrigerator. Next time he saw Davey, it would be Dennis who did the dazzling.

10

July 1971

The bright summer day would be hot by noon, and no one needed a weather forecast, or even a cloud, to know that rain was likely.

Dennis and Greg were up and outside earlier than the rest of their friends. They were leaning on the fence in the Pace backyard and looking at the vast expanse of the Macklin property.

The other side of that chain-link fence might as well have been another world. There were no concrete driveways or sidewalks, no manicured lawns or flower-beds, no garages or streetlamps, or gutters where the water collected when it rained. A dozen old trees almost as tall as the Big Tree made the yard a shadowy place for much of the summer and fall. Maybe it was the chickens, or the kitchen garden, or the tall grass, but, in spite of Gordie's territorial hegemony, wild animals were far more prevalent there than on the Lincoln Street side of the fence. Dennis had seen many squirrels on the property, along with stray cats, raccoons, skunks, and even pheasants. He never saw a snake, perhaps because Gordie was a kind of Macklin-property Saint Patrick. Small brown bats emerged at night; from where, Dennis did not know. Oddly enough, they never seemed to cross the vertical plane of the fence line, as if they were constrained by a magic spell.

Not far from the fence was the dilapidated frame that supported the grapevines. They did not produce much fruit because the nearby trees had grown so tall that sunlight could barely penetrate their canopies. Still, grapes developed in the late summer, and Dennis was always amazed that such seemingly lifeless vines could produce anything at all. Someone—it might have been Delia Pompay—had told him that Mrs. Macklin, the witch, made a potent wine from the grapes. Mrs. Pace had told the boys that the Macklins once kept a pigpen in the yard and that one of the pigs had gotten loose and disappeared when the Lincoln Street neighborhood was being constructed.

"What happened to it?" Ben had asked.

Wanda had evasively replied, "Construction bacon, I suppose." She went on to explain that the township made the Macklins give up all of their pigs, as the property had been rezoned for residential, not agricultural, use.

When Dennis had asked TA about the fairness of this decree, the man had replied, "In this world, it doesn't pay to be a pig"—another unsatisfying answer.

The township must have issued a variance to the Macklins, because they were allowed to keep their chickens. Not a particularly discriminating guard dog, Gordie both terrorized and protected the chickens. Davey, who knew more—or pretended to know more—than the younger boys, claimed that the dog had been named after the Detroit Red Wings star Gordie Howe. That was consistent with the only adornment on the property: a flagpole bearing the United States flag and a Red Wings banner.

Propped against the nearer chicken coops was a miscellany of screens and framed glass, and off to one side was a series of plots where Mrs. Macklin grew peppers, beans, and carrots—this according to Wanda Pace. In those days, Dennis had seen nary a pepper, bean, or carrot, as Gordie's presence discouraged even the notion of closer examination.

Sometimes, Dennis thought he heard emanating from the rather run-down wooden house melodies as haunting as the place itself. When he mentioned it to TA, he was wryly informed that even the Macklins had electricity and may have discovered record players. It was times like this when Dennis suspected TA knew more about the boys' obsession with the Macklins than he let on.

Was it the heat or the plummeting barometric pressure on that sultry day that prompted Greg to suggest that he and Dennis open the Macklin chicken coops?

Greg now stood half a head taller than Dennis, and the summer sun had bleached his hair almost white. He resembled his older brother but lacked Davey's commanding presence. Greg had always been impulsive, and growing up without the steadying influence of his father, he could be reckless.

"What about Gordie?" Dennis asked.

"We'll bring hockey sticks with us", Greg said, laughing. All too often, that engaging laugh, having the effect of a snake charmer's pipe, would militate against ample evidence that his schemes were foolish, or worse.

This time, Dennis remained skeptical. He weighed a hockey stick against that beast and didn't like the odds.

Greg said, "Maybe I'll bring a chicken back. We can keep it in the garage and have an egg whenever we want one."

Dennis said, "I don't think it works like that. Anyway, a chicken isn't a candy bar. I can take or leave an egg."

"We can sell the eggs for money."

"To who, the Macklins?"

"Are *you* chicken?" Greg said, with a big grin.

"No."

"Then let's go", Greg said, putting his foot in the fence links and propelling himself up and over.

Dennis wondered what had happened to the hockey sticks, but he vaulted the fence anyway. Greg's schemes were all but irresistible, even when the desired outcome was highly improbable. As they crept through a gap in the grapevines, Dennis wondered whether Greg had sat up all night planning this escapade, as his friend was smarter and craftier than he ever let on. They had to cross a corner of the vegetable garden to get to the coops. Greg tramped through it with little regard for the small plants and shoots, crushing more than a few. Dennis heard violin music—a familiar tune, though he couldn't name it. They scared a rabbit that had been eating its breakfast; it made a dash for a clump of overgrown bushes and disappeared. Dennis thought about making a smart remark about Farmer McGregor but was too frightened to formulate a coherent sentence.

"Come on", Greg exhorted, now several steps ahead.

They circled the junk heap and heard a cacophony of clucking and squawking that signified the chicken coops.

"Just one", Dennis whispered as loudly as he dared.

"You keep a lookout for Spartacus"—that was Greg's version of Cerberus—"and the witch." Greg knelt next to a small door, not a door proper but a tangle of wooden slats and wire that looked like a transplanted window frame. He flicked the latch and pulled open the door. Immediately, several chickens rushed out into the open.

"Let's go", Dennis insisted. His heart was pounding. Looking at his friend, he was amazed to see that Greg's face was suffused with joy.

Three more chickens were loose when Dennis saw a low, bulky form protrude from around the corner of the coops. Before he actually saw it, he'd heard a human voice. That single word—"Gordie"—left no doubt that it was a command to act, and act quickly.

Greg was around the corner of the junk heap before Dennis found his wits. He followed as quickly as he could, but Greg was the faster runner and was through the vine gap well ahead of him. By the time Dennis squirmed through the vines, the snarling was so loud that he expected to be brought down any instant.

He stumbled two paces from the fence and, from the ground, saw Gordie dart through the vines like a hot knife through butter. Dennis heard himself shriek, and he crawled to the fence. He was halfway over when he felt the teeth in his right calf. The grip was so powerful that he felt himself being dragged back to the Macklin side of the fence. He heard a crack, and his leg was free again. When he fell over the fence and looked up from the ground, he saw Greg waving a hockey stick at a snarling but chastened Gordie.

"Let's go", Greg said urgently. "I don't think the witch saw us, but she'll be here in a minute."

They ran down the drive, crossed Lincoln Street, and made for Tony's backyard. Dennis hoped no one had seen them. They huddled under Tony's bedroom window; actually, Tony shared the room with Jan.

Both Dennis and Greg were panting and sweating; their pants, especially Dennis', were filthy.

Greg laughed. "Did you see those chickens scatter when Spartacus showed up?"

Once he was aware of Gordie, Dennis hadn't seen anything except for Greg's back. "Do you think she saw us?" he asked.

"The witch?"

"Who else?"

Greg seemed to be considering the matter. Then he said, "I don't think so."

Dennis realized that his leg hurt. There was blood on his pant leg. He rolled the material up and saw two puncture marks in his calf, still leaking blood.

"Better hope Spartacus doesn't have rabies", Greg said, chilling Dennis. Then Greg rapped on the window.

Jan came to the window first, shook his head, vanished, and was replaced by Tony, who pushed open the sash.

"What's wrong with the front door?" he said.

"Spartacus bit Dennis", Greg said vehemently, as if the dog had flown over the fence and attacked them while they were minding their own business. "Go get Lori."

It seemed longer, but it was less than ten minutes later when Tony and Lori came around the side of the house and joined Greg and Dennis.

"Let me see", Lori said. She was carrying a paper grocery bag.

Dennis showed her the pant leg, then rolled it up to reveal the wound. Lori opened the bag and took out a bottle of iodine. Then she said to Tony, "Go get a pair of your jeans."

"What?" Tony said.

Lori said, "Just go." She cleaned the bite with a wet napkin—also obtained from the bag—and liberally applied iodine to it. It took three Band-Aids to dress the wound, but when she had finished, Dennis felt better, at least emotionally. He hadn't been able to take his eyes off Lori while she worked. She had taken charge, directing the boys. More surprisingly, they had obeyed her. Tony grimly handed Lori the jeans. Seeing his consternation, she said to Tony, "He's only going to wear them for a few hours. I'll mend these holes, and then you can have your precious pants back."

"They're almost new", Tony said.

Lori snorted derisively. "Change", she commanded Dennis and turned her back on him.

Was he supposed to strip to his underpants in broad daylight? Apparently so. Greg and Tony were snickering.

"Hurry up", Lori said. "I don't have all day. I have a brother. I've seen more than I care to see."

Dennis changed as quickly as he could, almost falling down when his leg got hung up on the fabric and he lost his balance. This capable girl was far different from the Lori who had shared her dreams with him. He felt even more respect for her. He handed her the damaged pants and put on Tony's.

Lori draped the jeans over one arm and picked up the paper bag. As she marched out of the yard, they heard her say, "It wouldn't kill you to say thanks."

"What happened?" Tony said when Lori was gone.

Greg provided a blow-by-blow account.

"Did it hurt?" Tony asked Dennis.

"What do you think?" Dennis said.

"I wacked Spartacus good", Greg said proudly.

"Want to go to the frog pond?" Dennis asked them.

"Not with my new jeans you're not."

"Let's go to my house then", Dennis said. "We better stay away from Gordie for a while."

Greg clucked and flapped his arms.

The three boys had just crossed the street when a police car pulled up next to them. First Gordie, now the cops, Dennis told himself, as he anxiously waited for the car door to open. Instead, the passenger-side window came down.

"Where do you boys live?" asked one of the two officers.

Receiving no answer, the officer said more sternly, "Where do you live?"

"I live here", Dennis said, pointing to the house, exceedingly grateful that TA had left for work. Greg and Tony told the policeman where they lived too.

"What have you been doing this morning?" the officer said, opening the door and getting out of the patrol car. He wasn't tall, but he had a big face and a nose to match. If he had shaved that morning, he'd need to do it again before supper. He moved slowly and kept looking from one boy to another.

Greg said, "Nothing . . . sir."

"You sure of that?"

"We're sure", Greg said.

"What do you two have to say?" the officer asked Dennis and Tony.

"I was in the house until a few minutes ago", Tony said promptly.

Dennis said, "Nothing." He was so scared that he had almost told the truth.

The officer's eyes bored into Dennis. "The woman behind you reported trespassers and vandalism of her property."

"Did she see who did it?" Greg asked.

The man ignored his question and said, "So none of you were on that woman's property this morning."

They all said no. A terrifying thought came to Dennis. What if the policeman told him to roll up his pant leg? How lucky that Lori had talked Tony into giving up his jeans.

"I imagine you know there's a nasty animal on the other side of the fence."

They said they did.

"If it gets hold of you, it will be ugly." The policeman got back in the car but didn't roll up the window. "If this happens again, there'll be big trouble. Stay out of that yard and quit tormenting those people."

Greg said, "We weren't . . ."

"Shut up. You heard me." The car drove away.

Greg smirked after the car had turned the corner. He said, "Think he suspects us?"

"Is the pope Catholic?" Tony said. "It's bad enough to get in trouble for things you do. I don't like getting in trouble for something I didn't do."

"That makes up for all the times you did something and didn't get caught", Greg said philosophically. "Anyway, that cop was fishing. He doesn't know anything."

Dennis' leg was itching. They split up and headed for their own houses; even Greg had been flustered by their encounter with the police, though he tried hard to hide it. Dennis couldn't remember the last time he had spent an entire summer afternoon indoors, but he was worried about the bite, worried about the police, and especially worried that TA would find out. He read most of one of TA's Nero Wolfe mysteries, but it was hard to keep his mind off that awful minute in the Macklin's yard.

Midafternoon, Lori knocked on the door and they traded jeans. The tears in the fabric were almost invisible, so expertly had she mended them. This time, he managed to express a timid thanks as she walked away.

Not long before Dennis expected TA home from work, he went into the backyard. His eyes hurt from reading. The sky above was clear, and the air hot and humid, but he could see dark clouds to the west. He often climbed to the top of the hill and looked over the fence, but not today. He wondered if the Macklins had corralled the chickens. He mostly wondered how he had let Greg talk him into another one of his stupid schemes.

Dennis' thoughts were interrupted by Jonas Ratigan, who was ambling toward the fence that separated their properties.

"Come here", Jonas said, with his arms dangling over the fence, his long and dour face supported by the crossbeam.

As Dennis approached the fence, Jonas, who was no stranger to the police, asked, "What did the cops want?"

"They wanted to know if we were on the witch's property."

"Were you?"

Dennis couldn't lie to Jonas. His and Greg's insurgency was still fresh in his memory. He nodded.

"I saw her chasing a chicken. Did you do that?"

"It was Greg's idea."

"That little creep. He's got potential after all. Hop over."

Dennis vaulted the fence. Notwithstanding Jonas' quasi-friendship, Dennis was not especially comfortable in his presence. Jonas was unpredictable and, at times, explosive.

As if sensing Dennis' apprehension, Jonas said, "I want to show you something."

Delia and Alvin's yard was bare except for a picnic table and side-by-side lilac bushes against the back of the house. As it was July, the lilacs were green; there was no evidence of the sweet aroma that pervaded the property in May and early June. There was a niche where the plants abutted and Jonas led him there. Both crawled into this space between the bushes until they reached the back wall of the house. It felt close there, like the inside of a burrow, and cooler than it was in the sunshine. Dennis' leg smarted, but what he saw made him forget his discomfort.

Jonas had constructed a cross out of two Popsicle sticks, and to this cross he had pinned a large leopard frog, forelegs and backlegs, to the vertical and horizontal members, as if it were a crucified man. He had also jammed a small firecracker into its mouth. The creature was still alive, but Dennis could see that it was desiccating in the heat. Every now and then, it twitched.

Dennis had never experienced before what he felt then. It wasn't anger; certainly not like the anger he felt when he thought of the driver who had caused the accident that killed his mother and little brother. Rather, this was a kind of interior chill. He and Tony caught frogs and snakes for sport, but they always released them; and they took good care of the creatures while they held them in captivity.

Jonas backed up, signaling that the demonstration was at an end. When they were both back on their feet, Jonas took hold of a silver chain around his neck and pulled something from beneath his shirt. Dennis examined it as it lay cupped in Jonas' dirty hand—a swastika surmounted by an eagle.

"Know what this is?" Jonas asked. He didn't wait for Dennis to answer. "SS insignia. Don't tell anyone."

Dennis said he wouldn't.

A car pulled up in the Pompay driveway, and the driver honked the horn. Jonas returned the object beneath his shirt and made for the driveway.

Dennis must have stood in the Pompay yard for five minutes, but he lacked the courage to do what he thought he should. Wouldn't Jonas know if he did what he was considering? What would Jonas do to him when he discovered that the creature was gone? Muddling the matter even further was Dennis' vague awareness that he was showing more solicitude for this frog than he had shown for the Macklins' chickens or, for that matter, the Macklins themselves. He shivered and noticed that a cool wind was blowing, the sky darkening.

He climbed the fence deliberately, lacking the energy to vault it. TA was cooking supper when he went inside, but Dennis had no appetite. A sudden downpour began drumming on the roof; it got so dark in the kitchen that TA had to turn on a light. Dennis expected TA to say that he had heard from the police, or the witch, or Magdalena Hulse—who might have seen the police car—but the inquisition never materialized. He ought to have felt relief, but he didn't.

Dennis woke up after midnight, troubled by the image of the crucified frog. The rain had stopped, as suddenly as it had begun, before he had gone to bed. His bedroom window was wide open, admitting a cool breeze and a fresh fragrance. He heard a night bird and another sound—doleful—that might have been a cat. On the third impulse, he rolled out of bed and went outside. Feeling the cold, wet grass, he realized that he was still in his bare feet, but he scaled the fence and darted toward the lilac bushes. The niche was directly beneath Jonas' bedroom window, but he had come too far, physically and emotionally, to go back.

The lilacs were laden with water from the storm, and Dennis got wet crawling between them. The frog was still there; he could feel it, even if he couldn't see it. Without the benefit of sight—it was as dark as a cave—he removed the pins and then the firecracker from the frog's mouth. Squatting there between the bushes, he enclosed the little animal in both hands and waited. His knees and back began to ache, and still nothing happened. Why couldn't he admit to himself that the creature was dead? Still he held it, dead or barely alive—it didn't matter anymore—warming it with his hands.

Did he feel a tremor, or was it his imagination? The next time, he was sure there was movement. Still, he held it tight. More minutes passed; the frog was now twitching with regularity. As quietly as he could, Dennis carried the creature to the back fence and released it in the Macklins' yard—Gordie or no Gordie: there were worse things than a ferocious dog.

This frog was the last one Dennis ever held. He could never again summon the joy he'd once felt for the hunt. TA, sitting at the kitchen table, was waiting for him when he came in by the side door.

"Need anything?" TA asked.

"No", Dennis said.

"Hungry?"

"A little."

"How about some pancakes?"

TA had already gotten up from the table when Dennis said, "Okay." He knew TA had to be at work at seven while he, Dennis, could sleep as late as he desired.

"Want me to add some blueberries?"

"Okay."

TA joined him at the table and ate a pancake himself, though Dennis suspected it was just to be comradely. In his pajamas, with his hair uncombed and the stubble of a beard, TA looked old to his son. Dennis wasn't in a mood to talk, and TA didn't press him. When Dennis finally went back to bed, he stared at the coal-gray ceiling, stared at it for so long that he lost a sense of time, stared at it until he heard the Macklins' rooster crow. Only then did he turn over and go to sleep.

11

July 1972

They hadn't gotten to the end of the street when Ben looked behind them and growled. He locked his brakes and put his feet on the sidewalk.

"Where are you going?" Ben asked his sister, Carly, who stopped her bike next to his.

The gangly girl with a mop of red hair and freckled face said, "I want to come."

"You can't", Ben said. "Go home."

"Why not?"

"It's too far for you."

"I can keep up. Please?"

Carly Carlson, at eight years old, was almost as tall as Dennis. Because she was still so young and growing so quickly, it was hard to say what she'd look like when she was older. To Dennis, she was just Ben's little sister.

"I said go home", Ben repeated firmly.

"I can ride as far as you can", she argued.

Dennis didn't doubt that. Carly's athleticism rivaled that of the Lincoln Street boys.

"Please let me come, Dennis", she pleaded, with tears in her eyes.

"Listen, Carly," Dennis said, "we're going a long way. Next time you can come."

She glared at Ben and reluctantly turned her bike around. Ben shook his head as she rode away, then asked, "Didn't I say the same thing you did?"

Dennis shrugged.

"She likes you. She'll do anything you tell her."

Dennis suspected as much, but winning an eight-year-old girl's affection wasn't a badge of honor on Lincoln Street. "Let's go", he said.

Ben had recruited Dennis to accompany him to the Sears store twelve miles away. No one knew about the trip except the two of them, and only Ben knew the reason for it.

Ben wobbled precariously for a dozen feet before getting his bike under control, and Dennis gave him plenty of space. Ben was the least graceful of the four boys on a bike. Truth was, he was a less accomplished biker than Lori, and certainly less athletic than Carly. The fact that he didn't see well and needed thick glasses didn't help. For one reason or another, every so often, his foot slipped off the pedal. When he stopped quickly, it was anyone's guess what would happen. The previous summer, Ben had sported an egg-size bump on his forehead after he had crashed his bike into a parked car and had been propelled onto the roof.

"When are you going to tell me why we're biking to Sears?" Dennis asked.

Ben stopped his bike again and lurched forward, regaining his balance before the bike toppled over. "Here", he said, handing Dennis a folded paper from his back pocket, an advertisement for a chemistry set.

"I'm going to buy it", Ben said. "It's on sale."

Dennis handed the ad back to Ben and asked, "Why didn't you ask your dad to take you?"

Ben's shoulders sagged, and he inadvertently crumpled the paper when he put it back in his pocket. Then he said belligerently, "He told me I couldn't buy it."

"He wouldn't pay for it?"

"I didn't ask him to pay for it. I'm spending my own money. I saved it. Let's go." Ben re-mounted the bike and pushed off with the grace of a walrus lumbering off an ice floe.

Ben's father, Jack, was a draftsman for a Detroit engineering company. Neither Ben nor Jack had ever said a word about it in his hearing, but Dennis suspected that Jack was disappointed at Ben's disinterest in sports. Ben wasn't contrary by nature, but he wasn't disposed to do things just to meet someone else's expectations either, including his father's.

They were riding through the neighborhood just east of their own, amid houses almost identical to their own, on streets just like Lincoln Street. They passed the church that TA and Dennis attended. Dennis had never seen it on a weekday morning, barren of cars and people.

Dennis was finding it hard to keep up with Ben. That rankled him, as normally it was Ben bringing up the rear. This morning, Ben gave Dennis the impression that he was on an important mission. He didn't look back; he just kept pedaling. Dennis stood up and pedaled faster until he reached Ben's side.

"If we're riding twenty-four miles, you better slow down", Dennis said.

Ben eased off a little—not much—and Dennis sat down again.

"Why doesn't your dad want you to have it?"

"Because he's an idiot", Ben said loudly. "He wants me to play football and basketball."

"Why don't you?" Dennis said, knowing the answer, and knowing that the question was unnecessarily provocative.

Ben gave Dennis a savage look and said, "I don't want to; that's why."

"If that's what you told your dad, no wonder he's mad."

"I didn't say it like that, but he knows how I feel."

"How do you plan to hide a chemistry set?"

"I'll think of something. He doesn't pay any attention to me. I could bring a bazooka home, and he wouldn't notice."

"Slow down", Dennis insisted. He was sweating, and it was still early in the morning.

Ben was gripping the handlebars so tightly that his knuckles where white. Looking straight ahead, he said, "I heard him say that Carly's the only boy in the family."

"When did he say that?" Dennis asked.

"A few days ago."

"Who cares?"

"I care. When he told me I couldn't buy the chemistry set, I'd had enough."

Dennis said, "So you're going to torture me and you to get back at him?"

"I'm going to buy the chemistry set. If you think it's torture, you can go home."

"Maybe I will", Dennis said angrily, but he kept pedaling.

They'd reached Limerick High School, a Terrapin Township rival. Dennis might have been driven past the school, but he had never had the opportunity to examine it leisurely. It was a newer school, like Terrapin Township High, and architecturally similar.

"Let's stop", Dennis said, locking his brakes and hearing the tires squeal. He took a half-smashed candy bar from his pocket, tore off the wrapper and threw it on the ground, broke the bar in two, and gave half to Ben, who had reluctantly halted. Then he set his bike on the grass and sat down.

Ben, still standing and holding his handlebars, took a bite and said, "Were you sitting on this thing?"

"It was in my front pocket."

"How long?"

"I'm not forcing you to eat it", Dennis replied.

As if Dennis' dilapidated candy bar had prompted thoughts about sanitation, Ben said, "I'd stay out of the county drain if I was you."

"What's wrong with it?" Dennis demanded defiantly.

"Do you know where that water comes from? It's full of germs."

"So what", Dennis said. He admitted to himself that the water in the open drain never looked or smelled good, but he wasn't about to share those observations with Ben.

"Do you want to get sick?"

Dennis, licking the candy off his fingers, said, "I feel fine."

"Don't say I didn't warn you when you catch bubonic plague."

"What's that?"

"It killed everyone in Europe in the Middle Ages", Ben said.

"That was a long time ago. They didn't have medicine and doctors then." Dennis had had enough lecturing by Ben. "Incidentally," he added, using the word introduced by his uncle Thomas when he had visited in the spring, "you'd better be careful with that chemistry set or you'll blow your head off."

Ben snorted. "Do you think they'd sell a stick of dynamite to a kid?"

"You don't need dynamite. I heard TA say you can blow stuff up with fertilizer and bleach."

"That's stupid", Ben said. "And when I get my microscope, I'll show you what's in that drain water."

"When you've read as many books as TA has, you can call him stupid. Until then, keep your mouth shut." Dennis was regretting coming along with Ben.

"I didn't call him stupid", Ben protested. "I said it was a stupid idea."

"Same thing. Just because your dad's a jerk doesn't mean TA is too."

"I guess not", Ben conceded, and Dennis could tell his friend was eager to change the subject.

They'd crossed a larger road, not so large as Telegraph but a demarcation between the cities of Limerick and Edison, and took a detour through an abandoned train tunnel. Along the track, and spaced every hundred feet or so, were concrete arches that still contained the metal connectors with which the trains had once been electrified. The inside of the tunnel was strewn with trash, and the concrete walls were peppered with graffiti, some of it produced by a deft, if not inspired, hand. They had to dodge broken glass. Coming out on the opposite side, they welcomed the light, warmth, and fresh air.

"Let's stop at the drugstore on Edison", suggested Dennis, who was tired and thirsty. Ben gave his grudging approval to this side trip. Dennis had expected a little more enthusiasm for his suggestion, as there were beads of sweat all over Ben's face and arms; even his hair was wet with perspiration.

When they reached the drugstore, they leaned their bikes against the brick wall, an old wall of an old building, probably built when Edison was a two-lane macadam road. They had to wait fifteen minutes for the store to open, a delay Ben didn't relish, but he acquiesced without protest. He stood by his bike and used the time for a meticulous cleaning of his glasses while Dennis peered through the none-too-transparent store window.

When they walked through the door, Dennis realized how warm it was outside, even though it was still early in the day. Ben displayed impatience as Dennis examined the comic books, even though Ben had a substantial comic-book collection himself. For the most part, Dennis ignored him. He selected four new comic books and a bottle of Coke, but when he got to the register, he realized he was a dollar short.

"Can I have a dollar?" Dennis asked Ben.

Ben said, "Didn't you save any money for lunch?"

Dennis shook his head.

Ben reached in his pocket and said, "I brought three extra dollars. Here." He handed Dennis a crumpled bill.

Dennis finished the Coke before he got back on his bike, giving Ben the last swallow. Even though Ben hadn't wanted to stop, he looked better for having done so.

Riding together, just the two of them, and far from home, Dennis had the urge to ask Ben a question he didn't dare ask TA—a question he had been pondering for some time. He had been working up to it for several miles, trying to decide how to say it, and wondering if Ben would take him seriously. At last he said, "Ben, I want to find out who killed my mother and brother, but I don't know where to start."

Ben gave Dennis a quizzical look, then said, "If the police couldn't find out, what makes you think you can?"

"I want to try."

Ben said, "What does your father say?"

"I'm not going to ask him."

"Why not?"

"Because he'll tell me to forget it."

Ben was silent for so long that Dennis thought he had forgotten about it. When they stopped for a red light, Ben said, "There must be a police report. I read once that some accident information is available to interested parties. You could write them and request it."

"What if they tell TA?" Dennis said.

Ben said, "You can't make an omelet without . . . spilling milk. Anyways, the cops are too busy to contact your father."

Dennis admitted the police report was a place to start, surely better than what he had today, next to nothing.

"You better type the letter. I've seen your handwriting", Ben said.

They were back on their bikes again. The breeze created by the motion along the road was pleasantly cooling.

"TA doesn't understand why it's important for me to know", Dennis explained.

"At least you can talk to your father. At least you can trust him", Ben said.

Dennis wondered what Ben meant. Before he could ask, Ben added, his voice cracking and his eyes directed at the road, "I found a bra on the floor in the backseat of the car."

Dennis said, "When?"

"A week ago. He comes home really late one night a week. Mom says he has to work late. I went to the car the next morning to get my magazine, and I found it." Ben was sweating again, and his face was beet red. To Dennis, his friend looked more angry than tired or embarrassed.

"Do you know who it is?"

"No, but I'll find out. You can bet on that."

Dennis would never bet against Ben when it came to a mental challenge. "There might be another explanation", he said.

"Like what?" Ben retorted.

"I don't know. TA says don't jump to conclusions."

"I have evidence. That's different from jumping to a conclusion."

Dennis pondered what Ben had told him and said, "Next time your dad comes home late, go to the car and see if you smell perfume. If he was in the car with a woman, you'll be able to smell something, but it will probably be gone by the next morning."

Dennis took Ben's lack of a rebuttal as confirmation that his idea was sound. He'd always thought that affairs were something that strangers and people on TV were guilty of, not people you knew and saw every day.

"What did you do with the bra?"

"I put it in the garbage so my mom and Carly wouldn't find it."

"What color was it?"

"Who gives a damn?" Ben snapped.

"Did your dad say anything?"

"No, and I didn't ask."

"Do you think your mom knows?"

"I don't know. She never said anything."

"What would she do if she found out?"

Ben said, "She wouldn't like it, but I don't think she'd leave him."

"Don't they talk to each other?"

"They talk, but they don't say anything ... that matters."

Ben's color had abated a little, but he was still sweating; Dennis realized that he had picked up the pace again during the conversation about his father. In the distance, Dennis could see the large spherical water tower that marked their destination. He was hoping they had a water fountain in the store, as he had no money for another Coke. He was getting hungry too; all he had had for breakfast was a bowl of cereal.

The Edison businesses abutting the road made Dennis think about his conversation with Lori, her dream of a studio. Looking down side streets, he saw older wood-frame houses and not a few vacant lots. If Terrapin Township consisted of newer blue-collar homes, then Edison's blue-collar homes were of a much earlier vintage.

The last few miles were tedious, with the boys exhibiting none of the enthusiasm they had at the onset of the journey. When they finally locked their bikes on the metal stand and entered the cool building, both were exhausted and looked it.

TA had taken Dennis to this Sears on several occasions. It had two floors connected by escalators, hard-to-find elevators, and just about anything one might be looking for, including a lunch counter that had been made irrelevant by Dennis' expenditures in the drugstore. For his part, Ben was on a quest, and Dennis dutifully followed. Ben snatched the last chemistry set on the shelf, with the closest thing to a smile that Dennis had seen all day. The boys marched to the checkout counter, and Ben put his money on the Formica surface. The attendant counted it slowly, then said, "There isn't enough money here."

Ben's brow creased. "Nineteen, ninety-five, with tax", he said plaintively.

"This item isn't on sale anymore", she said. "It went off sale at midnight."

"How much is it now?" Ben said.

"Twenty-two, ninety-five, with tax."

Ben reached into his pocket again, this time with the expression of a tentative magician doubting he could produce a rabbit. He had told Dennis he'd brought three extra dollars, but he had given one to Dennis.

"This makes only twenty-two", she said. "I can't give you the sale price. Get another dollar from your parents and come back. I'll hold it for you. We're open till seven."

Ben slowly collected his money and put it back in his pocket. Dennis was sure that his friend's grim expression meant he was going to scream at him, and he felt guilty.

"Let's go", Ben said under his breath. He didn't say a word about the dollar or the fact that Dennis had spent all of his own money. Ben led the way to the lunch counter, took a seat, and gestured for Dennis to join him.

"Two burgers and fries," Ben said to the waiter, "and plenty of water."

12

August 1972

"Let's go again", Tony said, as he and his friends disembarked from a roller coaster that needed a fresh coat of paint and smelled of oil. Dennis was willing; for weeks he had been looking forward to this excursion to Bob-Lo Island Amusement Park.

"Twice is enough for me", Lori said.

"One more time", Tony countered, watching boys and girls fill the seats.

"Give it up, Tony", said Greg. "Twice is enough for this kid stuff. I have a better idea."

Lori retreated half a step; everyone else moved closer to Greg.

"I'm staying on the island tonight", Greg said in a hushed tone.

Ben turned his head toward the embarking roller coaster. Tony shifted from one foot to the other, not paying any attention to the ride or the exuberant children. Dennis, strangely troubled and looking down at the dirt path, crushed a beetle making its way to the cover of the lawn.

No one spoke until Greg said, "See that metal building?"

Their eyes followed the line of his finger past several rides and a concession stand to a pale green structure about a hundred yards distant.

"I checked it out while you guys were on the Mad Mouse. The door was unlocked. It's a perfect place to spend the night."

"What if they lock it at night?" Dennis asked.

Greg gave Dennis a look that combined pique and condescension. "If they don't lock it during the day, with a million kids around, why would they lock it at night, when no one's on the island?"

"It's a stupid idea", Lori said.

"I'm staying, and you're not talking me out of it, Lori, so don't try."

"I've never talked you out of anything, but it's still stupid."

Greg turned to Tony. "I need you to call my mom when you get home. Tell her I'm staying with you tonight. If she wants to talk to me, tell her I'm out with Dennis. She won't be a problem. She's always tired when she gets home from work."

"How about Davey?" Lori said.

"He won't even notice I'm gone", Greg said.

"What if you get caught?" Lori asked.

"I won't get caught."

She smiled sadly at him.

"So that's why you brought the backpack", Ben deduced.

"That's right, Sherlock. I've got everything I need: food, a flashlight, comic books, and plenty of Coke."

Lori asked, "How long have you been planning this?"

Greg gave her an appreciative look. "Since the beginning of summer."

Ben said, "You won't be able to take the boat back until tomorrow afternoon. Tony won't be able to fool your mom that long."

Greg said, "I have faith in Tony."

"Well," Lori added, "don't be too sure you've thought of everything. Please don't do it, Greg."

Ignoring her, Greg asked the others, "What do the rest of you say?"

"It doesn't matter to me", Ben said. "I won't be spending the night in a shed."

"I'll call your mom and tell her you're with me", Tony said.

"Sure you will", Lori said, hotly. "You're all stupid."

"Don't you like adventures, Lori?" Greg asked.

"An adventure that matters, sure. Not this nonsense."

"Let's not let this spoil the rest of the day", Dennis interjected, watching the kids run from ride to ride.

They found a consensus there, at least. Ben led the way to the next ride, and soon they were acting as if Greg's announcement had never been made. As the afternoon waned, the five friends turned toward the boat dock. No one had mentioned Greg's scheme for hours, and Dennis half-expected Greg to board the boat with them. Greg walked with them as far as a stand of tall poplars and said nonchalantly, "Don't forget to call my mom, Tony, and make it sound convincing."

Tony said he would.

"Still worried, Lori?"

She didn't answer. Dennis thought Lori looked even more troubled than she did earlier.

The uneasiness that Dennis had felt when Greg described his plan had crystallized into a resolution, a feeling rather than something reasoned. "I'm staying with Greg", he stated. He expected a disparaging remark from Lori, but received a solicitous look instead.

"I don't need a chaperone", Greg said. Dennis suspected Greg's comment had more to do with Lori's relieved expression than disdain for his offer.

"I'm staying", Dennis said again.

"Suit yourself", Greg said. "There's plenty of room in the shed. Just remember whose idea it was."

"You can keep the idea", Dennis said. "Tony, would you call TA too?"

Tony hesitated, then said, "TA won't be as easy to fool as . . ."

"Go ahead and say it," Greg said, "as my mom. Maybe Ben better do it."

Neither Tony nor Ben looked pleased by that suggestion.

"I'll do it", Tony said. "I don't need any help."

Lori squeezed Dennis' hand discreetly as they parted company. After Lori, Ben, and Tony had vanished into the crowd, Greg pulled on Dennis' arm and led him into the stand of poplars. There wasn't much cover, but it was better than being out in the open. Dennis was amazed at how quickly the park emptied and grew silent. Soon only a few of the attendants were cleaning up their game stalls. If they noticed Greg and Dennis, they didn't show it by saying anything to the boys.

Greg said, "We have to get into that building without being seen. After that, it will be easy."

Whatever the night would bring, Dennis was sure it wouldn't be easy.

After they had entered the building, Greg closed the man door behind them. There was a large roll door on the opposite wall that was already closed. The floor was constructed of paving bricks that looked to Dennis as if they had been there for a long time, perhaps before the structure was built over them. Greg led Dennis to the far corner of the building, where crates were stacked two or three high, creating a wall taller than a man. On their way, they passed spare parts, power tools, and a raised area where a carousel leopard and horse were awaiting repairs. Greg going first, they squeezed between the crates and the wall into a small open space in the corner.

"This hiding place is better than I expected", Greg said, taking off the pack and sitting down on the brick floor. Even though it was still light outside, it was gloomy inside the building. What was left of the golden daylight seeped through cracks in the siding; a few bare bulbs suspended from the ceiling also provided some illumination.

Dennis said, "Is this where you went this morning?"

Greg nodded and began unpacking his bag. There emerged six cans of Coke, two handfuls of candy, a flashlight, four bun-less hot dogs in a plastic bag, a transistor radio, a few comic books, and a paperback copy of *Murder in Mesopotamia*. Greg spread these things out on the floor and handed Dennis a Milky Way bar.

Dennis was reminded that Greg could be a fox as well as a mule. His friend didn't have the least interest in mystery stories, but he knew that Dennis loved them. Therefore, Dennis concluded, Greg had planned on Dennis' spending the night with him. Why else did Greg bring the mystery novel? But how had Greg known that his friend would stay, Dennis wondered, when Dennis himself hadn't decided until the last minute?

Greg aimed the flashlight at the corner of the ceiling directly above them, where a huge hornet nest hung.

"Hope it doesn't fall on us while we're sleeping", Greg said, sardonically. "Better keep your shoes on."

Sleeping, with or without shoes, seemed out of the question to Dennis. The air inside the shed was uncomfortably hot and humid, and Dennis was sure he had seen some cockroaches scuttle beneath the crates.

"Do roaches bite?" Greg asked, with something like clairvoyance.

"I don't think so."

"They're hard as hell to kill."

Dennis, who had never managed to catch, much less kill, a roach, said without conviction, "They won't bother us if we don't leave food out."

"Did you see the horse?" Greg asked.

It took a while for Dennis to realize that Greg was referring to the carousel animal.

"I'd like to bring it home and wire it to the back fence", Greg added. "Let's see what Spartacus makes of that."

"He won't make anything of it. No scent."

"Spartacus has no sense either. Want to read?" He tossed Dennis the Agatha Christie novel.

"What time is it?"

Greg looked at his watch. "Six."

Dennis had finished the candy bar. Now he opened a Coke. He hadn't realized how thirsty he was.

They ate, drank, and read for what seemed like a long time, until no more light seeped into the building, until only the ceiling bulbs and Greg's flashlight wedged between two crates illuminated their reading material.

Some mosquitoes found their way through cracks in the walls and located Dennis and Greg, provoking occasional slaps. Greg said, "That one got me. Look at the blood." Dennis had been right about the roaches. He saw several more and concluded that the shed must be teeming with them. They uncomfortably reminded him of Davey's story about his uncle Adam and the sewer.

More than once, Dennis asked himself why he had volunteered to stay with Greg. He couldn't help thinking about TA and his own bed. It was almost ten when Greg said, "Lori was right. I didn't think of everything. I need to go to the bathroom."

Dennis had been thinking about the same thing. He said, "We shouldn't go outside. We can go somewhere inside the building."

"What I have to do I can't do in the building", Greg said, with as close to chagrin as he was capable of displaying. "I'm going to the bathroom. You coming? Yes or no?"

"No side trips."

"Who ... me?"

Dennis got up and led the way from their hiding place into what now seemed a shadowy cavern. They exited the building through the man door. Greg would have let it slam shut—the wind had picked up considerably—but Dennis caught it with his foot and closed it silently. The sky was purplish-black, with shreds of dark clouds in the western sky illuminated from below by a now-invisible sun. In the same direction, a stand of tall beech trees were seething in the strengthening breeze.

Dennis looked back at the building. He was apprehensive about this foray into the park. Not Greg; he strode ahead with palpable bravado, kicking stones and leaping over a short fence.

Bats were out; lots of them. Dennis was used to bats, but in this place they seemed more menacing. Moths were swarming around the flood lamps. He saw a bat dart in and take one.

"Do you know where you're going?" Dennis asked in a loud whisper.

If Greg heard him, he chose not to answer. He was a dozen strides ahead of Dennis now, and lengthening his lead. Dennis trotted to catch up. Greg made a right-hand turn on a gravel path that went east into deeper darkness and more beech trees. The leaves and branches were twisting and turning as the wind gusted.

They passed beneath a flood lamp and found themselves among a battery of rides. Dennis remembered riding them, but they looked eerie in that motionless, riderless state.

Greg looked at Dennis and said impetuously, "Want to turn one on?"

Though they had seen no one, Dennis doubted that all the park employees had left the island. "Do you know where you're going?" Dennis said, not liking the plaintive sound of his voice.

Greg circled the carousel. They were at the door of the restroom.

"Better use it while you can", Greg said, pushing open the door and disappearing inside.

On their way back to the shed, Greg did not retrace their steps. Instead, he turned toward a concession area, as if he were in no hurry to return to their hiding place. Dennis felt uneasy following his friend. Greg looked as though he were strolling down Lincoln Street, without a care in the world, but Dennis could not shake the feeling that there was something terribly wrong with their being in the closed amusement park, and deceiving Wanda and TA.

"Wonder where they put all the good stuff?" Greg said, pointing at the food stands.

"Who cares?" Dennis said.

Greg looked at Dennis as if he were crazy.

In between two of the stalls was a dumpster. In the shadows produced by a flood lamp on the other side of the path, Dennis saw a scurrying rat with something in its jaws. About ten feet in front of them was a hopping object—a fat toad, and an old one. Dennis wasn't sure what signified an old toad, but this one looked especially warty. For a moment, he thought that Greg was going to attack it, but just as his friend took a step in its direction, they heard a loud voice; rather, a shout.

"Hey!"

Like brother rabbits surprised in the act of sharing lettuce in someone's garden, Greg and Dennis bolted as one. Dennis had seen that the man was fat and wore overalls. As they ran, he could hear the man's bellowing voice; whether directed at them or calling for reinforcements, he couldn't tell. He saw the back of Greg's red-checked shirt in the gloom, a moving chessboard several steps ahead. Next, Dennis heard a loud voice to their left. Greg turned in that direction, as if he knew where he was going. Even though this action would bring them closer to the second voice, Dennis followed. Sure enough, Dennis saw a tall, balding man standing on the side of the footpath—saw him before he saw them, as the man's back was turned. Greg and Dennis darted off the path and crept into a birch copse, where they squatted down and waited. They both knew better than to speak.

Five minutes might have passed before Greg trotted out of the copse, saying, "I think we ditched them. Come on."

Dennis was far from convinced, but he followed Greg anyway, knowing that their only hope was to get back to the building.

Greg had, or pretended to have, an intuitive sense of the location of the shed, even in the dark. They crossed the path, or different paths, twice before they came in sight of it. Though they had left by the side of the building with the man door, they had returned on the roll-door side.

"Crap", Dennis said, seeing that the roll door was open.

Greg looked at him, grinned, and said, "We're going in anyway. When they come out, you go in. I'll meet you." Greg ran off before Dennis, crouched in the shadows some thirty feet from the roll door, knew what was happening.

Not long after Greg ran away, Dennis heard a cry from the far side of the building. At first, he thought Greg had been caught, but he knew Greg well enough to recognize it as his dramatic, rather than distressed, cry.

Soon the fat man and the bald man came out of the roll door and turned the corner of the building. Dennis was on his feet and had already taken a step when it dawned on him that there might be others inside. He stopped for a brief moment; then he ran as fast as he could into the building and to the hidden alcove.

Sitting in that secluded corner of the building, he didn't feel nearly as safe as he had before they had made their excursion to the restroom. More troubling, he realized that he was trapped in that space if someone should find it. That thought had barely come to him when someone did burst in—Greg, smiling and sweating profusely.

"Cretins", was all Greg said, sitting down and unwrapping a candy bar.

Dennis put a finger to his lips. They could hear voices.

"See anyone?" Dennis thought that he recognized the fat man's voice.

"No."

"Let's look around."

Dennis' finger remained pressed against his lips. He could hear the men moving about the building. One of them sneezed twice in succession. As quietly as he could, Greg put everything back into his bag.

"Damn rats. All over the place", the second voice said.

Dennis could see flashlight beams reflecting from the metal walls of the building. Now, even Greg seemed apprehensive. The boys sat statue-still. They felt as if they waited an hour for the men to complete their search, though it was actually less than fifteen minutes. Once, someone climbed on the crates that made up one wall of their shelter. Instinctively, both of them pressed their backs against the crates and crouched as low as possible. Any second, Dennis expected one of the men to drop into their hiding place. The scuffling continued, and Dennis was terrified to see that Greg's bag could be observed by someone standing on the crate nearest to the wall. Greg saw it too. Dennis thought that he was going to make a dash to retrieve it, but Greg just shrugged and sat back resignedly.

First, the flashlights went off. Then they heard voices, though they couldn't make out the words. Finally, the roll door closed.

Now it was Greg with a finger to his lips, and Dennis knew what was meant by that gesture. Suppose the men had pretended to leave the building but were actually waiting for the boys to emerge.

They waited. Occasional scuffling interrupted the silence, which Dennis took to be the activity of mice or rats. It was Greg who finally stood up and said in a conversational voice, "Jonas said I couldn't do it."

Dennis, pretty sure he knew the answer but wanting to hear it for himself, said, "Couldn't do what?"

"Couldn't stay on the island without getting caught."

"Since when did you start listening to Jonas?"

"He said I couldn't do it. I proved him wrong."

"We're not home yet."

Greg shrugged, as if getting off the island was just a detail. He removed a switchblade from his pocket and wedged it between two of the bricks.

"Did you tell Davey?"

Greg shook his head and said, "He would have squealed."

"Davey would have?"

"Yep."

"I wish I had a big brother."

"I wish I didn't have one. Do you think Tony called my mom and TA?"

Dennis said, "We can count on Tony."

"I'm glad you stayed", Greg said, his eyes directed at the brick he was trying to dislodge.

"I didn't do anything", Dennis said, recalling his fears.

"You made Lori happy by staying. She's gotten strange. She's different now."

"What do you mean?"

"Different. I'm different too."

"What are you talking about?" Dennis said.

"Different. If you don't know, I can't explain it."

Dennis said, "What are you doing?"

The brick began to come up. It was slow work.

"What's it like living with TA?"

"It's okay."

"Do you miss your mom?"

"I don't know. I guess so." Dennis was surprised to hear Greg ask that question, and not a little cautious about answering.

"I wish TA was my dad."

"You have a mom anyway."

"It's not the same. I like talking to TA."

"Do you remember your dad?"

"Sure. He paid more attention to Davey than to me." Greg wedged his finger between the raised and the adjacent undisturbed brick, and slowly lifted the one he had been working on. Then he reached into his bag, removed the flashlight, and turned it on, vastly increasing the light in the alcove.

They both stared at the bare ground where the brick had lain and saw something that looked very much like a bone.

"How did you know it was there?"

"I didn't."

Greg picked up the bone and rubbed off some of the dirt. Then he held it up for examination, as someone would hold a french fry.

Dennis moaned in spite of himself.

"Maybe that fat guy is killing kids", Greg said.

Of all the thoughts that had passed through Dennis' brain that night, this was the most chilling, even if it was preposterous, and he said. "How do you know it's a human bone? It could be from an animal." Then he remembered TA saying that Indians had once used the island as a burial ground and that artifacts were discovered here occasionally.

"It's part of an index finger", Greg said, pointing with it and reminding Dennis of a painting with a man and God nearly touching fingertips. He had seen a photograph of the painting in one of TA's books. "I wonder where the rest of the skeleton is", Greg added, looking at the adjacent bricks as if he were an archaeologist at a dig.

"Leave them alone", Dennis said.

"Aren't you curious?"

"No."

"I am. We might find more."

"More what?"

"We'll see what Lori says about this."

"I don't think a bone will change her mind."

"A skull might change her mind. Do you ever think about your brother?"

Dennis wondered how Greg's mind could be so at ease as to dance from subject to subject. "Sometimes", Dennis lied. Hardly a day went by when he didn't think about Andrew. "What time is it?"

"One-thirty."

"Let's go to sleep."

"Sure. Why not?"

Greg switched off the flashlight, cradled his head on his pack, and closed his eyes. It took a long time for Dennis to fall asleep; and, when he did, his mind was fecund with dreams. He woke up so suddenly that he had no idea where he was or how he had gotten here. It was still dark in the building, but there were rosy hints of dawn seeping through the cracks in the walls. He remembered everything as he sat up, stiff and sore, dirty and hot.

"Shhh", Greg said. He was sitting with his back against a crate. Then he whispered, "They opened the big door. Someone's in the building."

Looking down at the empty soda cans and candy wrappers, at his filthy hands, Dennis realized that he could never return to this island with the sense of wonder he had once experienced. The magic had been spoiled. He resented Greg for it, and he suspected that Lori had seen this outcome, instinctively if not consciously.

"When can we get out of here?" Dennis whispered. He had slept, but he was still exhausted. He noticed that the brick Greg had pried up had been replaced. Greg must have done it while he was sleeping.

"Not until the boat docks, and the kids get here. I'm not going to get caught when we're so close."

"To what?" Dennis said bitterly.

"To doing what I set out to do."

"Are you satisfied?"

"I will be when we get on the boat. All the rides are free today, since we're already on the island."

Dennis said, "Free? We slept with roaches and rats, and a skeleton underneath us."

"That was a bonus."

"Lori was right. You *are* an idiot."

Greg picked up a comic book and started reading.

They heard the kids when the boat docked. That raucous roar couldn't be silenced by those flimsy walls. Greg put the comic books, the flashlight, the radio, and *Murder in Mesopotamia* back in the bag. All the food and soda had been consumed. As they were leaving the hiding place, Greg surreptitiously put something in his pocket. Dennis couldn't see it clearly, but he would have bet it was the bone.

The boys left the building through the man door and joined the crowd that was joyously making its way to the attractions. They entered the flow, but Dennis didn't feel part of it, not as he had just twenty-four hours earlier.

"There's that fat slob that tried to catch us", Greg said, pointing at a young man in gray overalls. In the light of day, the man didn't look particularly threatening to Dennis.

"Want a hot dog?" Greg said, with a big smile and a gleam in his eye. "I'm starving."

13

Day Three

The following morning brought more evil news.

When Dennis emerged from the bathroom, he saw someone moving in the dark; it was Ben. The three friends had shared a somber supper in the hotel, revisiting what they had learned and didn't know, and reluctantly decided to get another night's sleep before taking any action. Dennis turned the dead bolt before retiring, and he didn't hear a thing all night, though he hardly slept soundly. His chaotic dreams woke him a couple of times, but he could not remember them.

"Is Tony still asleep?" he whispered to Ben.

He saw Ben nod his head and could see a form in Tony's bed.

After both men had finished dressing, they decided to wake Tony; but as hard as they tried, he wouldn't stir. With each shake and prompting word, they became more anxious.

"Roll him over on his back", Ben suggested.

When they did, they discovered that Tony was barely breathing.

"Call 911", said Ben.

Dennis dialed the number and told the dispatcher to send an ambulance. His heart was pounding so hard he thought it would tear his chest open.

"Where's his medicine bag?" Ben asked. "We'll need it for EMS."

"In the bathroom", Dennis said. "Did you hear anything last night?"

"Nothing", Ben replied.

Dennis said, "I turned the dead bolt. No one could have gotten in."

Ben said, "Someone got in the night before."

"Maybe through the window."

"There's no sill, and we're on the third floor", Ben said. "This isn't a comic-book crime."

The paramedics worked on Tony for ten minutes before putting him on a stretcher and wheeling him out. Ben and Dennis could tell by the technicians' intensity that Tony's condition was serious. While the paramedics peppered Ben and Dennis with questions, both resisted making any mention of Greg.

As Dennis watched Tony go, he looked at his friend's ominously flaccid features and felt utterly hopeless. At that moment, he didn't see a stricken man but his long-ago frog-catching partner. He resisted the urge to run from the room and drive home, and he tried to remember everything that had happened the previous day. He admitted to himself that Tony had eaten too little and drunk too much; he had likely neglected his meds too.

"We should have paid more attention to Tony yesterday", Dennis said. "We knew he was sick, and we know he's careless."

Ben said, "Do you think that explains it?"

"Tony has diabetes." Dennis hesitated before adding, "This doesn't have to be connected to Greg."

Ben said, "You mean Greg's murder."

"I'm not sure what I mean."

There was a knock on the door. The two men looked at each other.

"Who's there?" Dennis said without moving.

"Eva."

Dennis took a deep breath before he went to the door and pulled it open.

"Surprise", she said, smiling.

Eva Bright was a tall woman, at least an inch taller than Dennis, with short dark hair. Her dark eyes and brows were the most outstanding of her features, enough to warrant a second look. Eva was sultry rather than beautiful. Her fingers were long and thin, and her nails were painted violet. Her graceful movements suggested dance training in her past. Though it was the weekend, she wore a violet pantsuit and heels.

"We've had a bad morning, Eva", Dennis said. "Tony's in a diabetic coma, we think. They just took him away."

"I'm so sorry. Can I do anything?" Eva said. She had a warm voice. Her smile was replaced by a pronounced frown.

Dennis introduced Eva to Ben, and they shook hands tentatively.

"Can I have breakfast sent up?" Eva asked.

"We'll go down", Dennis replied. "I need to get out of this room."

"Where is your other friend?" she asked.

Dennis said, "He's been called away ... business." He thought he sounded unconvincing, but it was the best he could do.

"Is he coming back?"

"We don't think so", Dennis said.

"This weekend is an awful bust, isn't it?" she said.

"You can say that again", Ben replied, glancing at Dennis.

"Your new car looks great though", Dennis said, but distractedly.

"I love it. Joseph likes it too."

Dennis said he had noticed that and tried to keep the disapprobation out of his voice. With all he was experiencing, this wasn't the time to indulge his ambivalence toward Joseph.

"I told him to show you everything", Eva continued. "Did he?"

Dennis assured her that Joseph had done a thorough job. Normally, conversation with Eva was a calming and reassuring experience, but now he couldn't wait for her to leave.

"I wish I could help", she said earnestly. "Are you sure there's nothing I can do?"

"I'll call if I think of anything."

"Promise? Day or night."

Dennis nodded. Ben had turned his back on them and was unpacking his laptop. He said, "Let's get something to eat. We might get a call from the hospital. I don't want to make that trip on an empty stomach."

"I better go", Eva said. "You promised to call. Don't forget." She gave Dennis a hug, an out-of-character gesture, and left the room.

After giving Eva a head start, Dennis led Ben out of the room.

"Could we trust Eva to do some research on Greg?" Ben said.

"Wouldn't that be suspicious?"

"I suppose so. I'm not thinking clearly. It's time for us to throw in the towel. I've given up on a happy ending."

They ate cheerlessly and, for the most part, silently. Every few minutes, Ben would return to his computer, while Dennis made notes on the paper placemat.

"I don't think this has anything to do with Greg", Dennis said, trying to convince himself as well as Ben.

"Even if it doesn't, it does", Ben said. "I doubt if Tony would have been so careless without the drama."

"Do you think this will bring the police down on us?"

"Like flies", Ben said.

"People get sick all the time."

"Let's make sure we don't get sick too", Ben said.

"What does that mean?"

"You know damn well what it means. The Lincoln Street herd is thinning. Time will tell if it's coincidental or intentional. I'm not a big fan of coincidences. We need to keep a close eye on what's going on around us."

Ben was making sense, frightening sense.

"We better call Jan", Dennis said.

"It's only seven out west", Ben said.

"So what? Wouldn't you want to know if it was your brother?"

Ben shrugged and sipped his coffee. "We don't *know* anything yet."

Dennis said, "We know Tony's in the hospital, and we know it's serious." Without waiting for a reply, Dennis called Jan's number. "No answer." He called again, then again. This time he nodded at Ben.

"Hi, Jan, this is Dennis. I'm sorry to call so early, but Tony's in the hospital. . . . Yes, his sugar. . . . Well, it might be serious; we don't know yet. He was not well this morning, and we called 911. . . . The University Medical Center, I think. . . . Yesterday he had too much beer and didn't eat well. . . . I know we're getting too old for that, but you know Tony; he has a mind of his own.... We'll let you know anything we find out. Will you let Wim and Cate know? ... Ben and Greg are fine; me too.... You know we will. So long.

"That wasn't fun", Dennis said.

Ben said, "The conversation, or the lie about Greg? We're partly to blame."

"We're to blame for a lot of things, but not this", Dennis protested. "Tony's always done what he pleased, and he got worse after Lori died. How often does he take your advice? He hardly ever takes mine."

"Did it ever occur to you he doesn't need our advice?" Ben said. "What do we do about Greg?"

That mastodon was in the room again. Dennis said, "We still don't know anything for certain."

"We know he's been absent for over a day. We know he's either dead or pretending to be dead. We know that someone got into the room with—or after—Greg." Dennis started to object, but Ben raised a hand and said, "Hear me out. Either someone got in and killed him or an accomplice got in and helped Greg create the illusion. We know he doesn't work for the Smithsonian. We know he's been divorced for years. We know he's affiliated with the War College. We know that if he cooperated with whatever happened that night, he kept it from his best friends. We know he came back to the room after we were in bed. We know he talked to the bartender, and maybe others, before he came up to the room. We know that all his personal effects were removed from the room."

"And here's what we don't know", Dennis said determinedly. "We don't know if he's really dead. We don't know where he's been working for the past three years. We don't know if he was carrying a gun and, if he was, why. We don't know why he was killed, if he was. We don't know why this happened in Ann Arbor. We don't know if anyone else was in the room with Greg; he might have concocted and executed everything himself."

It annoyed Dennis that there were so many unanswered questions. For all they knew and for all their questions, where was the means (the how), the motive (the why), and the opportunity (the who)? Dennis shoved his hands in his pockets and felt the half-dollar. He took it out, set it on the table, and said, "What do you think happened?"

"I think someone came into the room and killed Greg. It probably was connected with what Greg was doing for the government. The room was being watched. After we left, all the evidence was removed."

Twirling the coin with his finger, Dennis said, "Why kill him in a room with three other people? Why not in the stairwell, or in the elevator? Better yet, if Greg lived alone, why not kill him at home? How could the killer know we wouldn't call the police? Ninety-nine out of a hundred people would have."

Ben said, "I don't know. I thought of that too."

Dennis said, "Maybe Greg works for the government, and this is a way for him to drop out of sight. He must have had help putting it together, and it must be something serious. What's more believable than his best friends reporting they'd seen his dead body, even if no one can find it? If that's the truth, whatever he's up to must be important. If this was an ordinary murder, it defies logic that the killer would have come back in broad daylight to clean up."

Ben said, "I don't buy it. Greg would have known we'd be suspects. Regardless of the peril he might have been in, why would he do that to us? And could Greg—knowing what he knows—count on us to contact the police? And what if we'd examined the body more carefully? No performance, by Greg or anyone else, could have withstood that test. Sorry, your solution is pulp fiction."

Cole Porter Palmer had never been popular with Ben Carlson, and Dennis thought he knew why, as Palmer's close colleague bore more than a passing resemblance to Ben. He said, "Greg would have known we wouldn't examine the body."

"Would anyone else?" Ben said.

"Of course not. We ought to go to the hospital. Then we'll take a drive. We haven't been out in two days."

They returned to the suite, and Dennis said, "This room is a chamber of horrors."

Ben grunted and began cleaning up.

Means, motive, opportunity—they could be devised for a story, Dennis told himself, but in real life they seemed so confused. Marta was unaware of everything and was unlikely to call him this weekend, knowing how he valued these gatherings. He had a yearning to see her and talk tō her, more than he had in years.

There was a knock on the door, and it startled Dennis. He froze.

"I'll get it", Ben said.

The familiar waiter stepped into the room, far enough to view the sitting area of the suite. His hands were at his sides, like a soldier, or a prisoner. He said, "I saw them remove your friend this morning. I'm sorry."

"So are we", Ben said.

"I remembered something", the man said.

"What?" Ben said, with suppressed eagerness. Dennis unfroze and drew closer.

"Your other friend, the one you asked about yesterday ... I remembered something. It must have been after he spoke to Christine. I passed him; he was in a dark alcove outside the bar."

Ben said, "Was he alone?"

"Yes ... I think so. He was speaking on a cell phone ... with passion."

Dennis said, "Could you hear anything?"

"No, nothing. But there is a small table in the alcove and there was something on it I have never seen before."

"What?" they both asked.

"I cannot say for certain. It looked like a small computer but smaller than any I have ever seen. Folded up, it might have fit in a shirt pocket. There was something like a thread attached to this object and to the phone your friend was holding. When he finished, he put his head down on the table as if he were going to sleep, but then he roused himself and stumbled away."

"Why didn't you mention this before?" Ben said.

"You were interested in whom he met, and he was all alone in the alcove. I hope this information is helpful, gentlemen. And I hope your sick friend is well soon."

"What's your name?" Ben said.

"Jorge Estrada", the man said. He left the room and pulled the door closed.

Ben said, "Do you think that was the object you felt under Greg's jacket?"

"It might have been. Maybe I convinced myself it was a gun, and my mind did the rest."

Dennis' phone rang. He turned away from Ben. "Hello? ... Speaking. ... Why do you need to know that? What's happened? ... Is that all you can tell me? ... His name is Jan—Johannes—Hulse.... Listen, I'm Tony's friend; can't you tell me anything? ... Can't you make an exception? I'm in town and his family is far away.... I see. Goodbye."

Dennis looked up. "The hospital needs to talk to Tony's next of kin. I think he's dead."

14

August 1973

Though the days when Dennis and Tony stalked frogs and snakes on that nondescript but magical patch of land had come to an end, Dennis found himself sitting alone on a high spot overlooking the field. The pond had dried up in the summer heat, and noisy grasshoppers bounded through the tall, golden grass. They landed on Dennis as if he were a bush or a stone, and he didn't bother to discourage them.

Now thirteen, Dennis increasingly sought solitude. He was experiencing thoughts and sensations he had never experienced before, and he remembered Greg's words on the island: "Different. If you don't know, I can't explain it." Ben, Greg, Tony, Lori, and Dennis too—they were all different. Their friendships remained strong; but at the same time, they were under siege in a way Dennis couldn't describe. So many of the things they used to do together, took for granted they would always do together, had been left behind. No more kick-the-can or climbing the Big Tree. Dennis noticed his sled was missing, and he didn't know whether TA had stored it in the basement or put it in the trash. No matter; the hill was hardly worth the effort anymore. He didn't miss the things he and his friends used to do together as much as the camaraderie and the spontaneity that now seemed so hard to recapture.

He got up, shook himself free of grasshoppers, and walked home. On the way, his eyes were drawn to the Big Tree. He had no urge to climb it or even stand below it. The ancient oak had given up its meager production of leaves by August, and it occurred to him that the tree was struggling to survive. School was starting again next week, a new school for all of them, a prospect that made him more melancholy than usual for late August. TA was at work. The house would be empty, as he liked it when he felt this way.

As Dennis walked past Greg's house at a brisk gait, he saw the yellow Gremlin parked in the driveway. There had never been a spot of rust on that car, and the chrome always gleamed with a dazzling brilliance. It belonged to Greg's flashy Uncle Adam, also known as Uncle Id, from whom Greg had received his middle name. Greg wasn't proud of this inheritance. Dennis recalled one occasion when Greg had told someone his middle name was Allan, rather than Adam.

Wanda Pace liked to say that Adam was "funny", and Dennis suspected that if he had been anyone else's brother, Wanda would have used more colorful words to describe him. Dennis understood that Uncle Adam worked in the Chicago theater world, though he wasn't sure what he did. For years, Greg's uncle had been delighting the boys and Lori with magic tricks. His costumes were hardly more outré than his normal ensemble, which included bright scarves and equally bright jackets. Dennis had a strong suspicion that Greg's uncle used makeup, and he also guessed that this was one of the things that made him "funny". TA had nothing to add to Wanda's description of her brother. TA's friend Peter Kristov called him a sissy.

Even though Adam was rarely without a big smile, Dennis didn't think the man was particularly happy. One night, after drinks at a Pace driveway gathering of neighbors, Adam's laughter suddenly changed to unabashed weeping. Wanda took him inside the house, and the next morning, car and uncle had vanished.

Dennis walked around the side of his house to the backyard. He had thoughts of resting on the cool lawn and looking up at the sky, as he used to do. Because it was a weekday, he expected the other backyards to be empty, but as he came around the corner of the house, he heard angry voices. A rubicund Alvin Pompay had a hold of Jonas' collar, and Jonas was trying to pull away. Dennis stepped back behind the house and watched them with one eye.

"Let go, old man", Jonas said, in an anguished tone Dennis had never heard from him before.

That enraged the normally docile Alvin. He began punching Jonas in the stomach and slapping his face. Jonas fought back, but he was no match for the bull-like Alvin. After a few seconds, Jonas fell to his knees in a defensive posture, but he still kept screaming at his stepfather.

"You fat nigger."

Alvin then pummeled Jonas. Dennis saw blood on the older man's fists; whether it was Jonas' or Alvin's, he couldn't tell. Dennis wondered if he should do something—call out or run for help. He even wondered if Alvin was going to kill Jonas.

The close-cropped lawn with its absence of trees and the fence on three sides gave the yard the appearance of an oversize boxing ring. The fight ended suddenly. Alvin dragged Jonas to his feet. He held the young man's collar and shook him like a rag doll. Jonas' face was red, and his nose was bleeding. He put one hand in front of his face as if to ward off Alvin's next blow.

Alvin drew back his big hand, then lowered it again and said, "Don't talk to me that way ... ever ... never." Then he released Jonas, who staggered backward.

The two men stood there glaring at each other until Alvin turned and marched into the house through the side door. Dennis could hear Jonas cursing, but not so loud that someone in the house or front yard could hear. He heard a snapping sound from the Macklin yard and peered in that direction. The witch, barely visible through the trees and bushes, was shaking a rug from the back door of her house. There was no one else in sight.

Dennis made for his own house. Notwithstanding Jonas' benignity toward him, he knew better than to approach his mercurial neighbor now. It would never do for Jonas to know that Dennis had witnessed him being un-manned. The air was close inside the house. The place seemed even emptier than usual that afternoon. Dennis didn't even remove his shoes when he lay face-down on his bed. He didn't expect to sleep, but he did. He dreamed that he was being chased by Gordie, a common nightmare. This time, the dog bit him repeatedly, and when he tried to run away, it seemed as if he were running in mud. He woke up tired and frustrated.

TA would be home before long, so Dennis made tacos for dinner. The man came in, grimy and tired, with a smile and a one-word greeting. After TA had removed his jacket and hat and took the first bite, he complimented Dennis, then said, "Anything happen today?"

Dennis wanted to say something, to ask questions, but he said, "No." He couldn't get out of his mind the image of Alvin beating Jonas, but he couldn't talk about it either, not with TA, not with anyone. The rage he had seen was so incompatible with the Alvin he thought he knew that he could not make himself articulate it. Had Jonas finally provoked Alvin past his ability to restrain himself? If so, did that mean that anyone, even TA, even he, could be driven to brutality?

TA was watching him in that knowing way of his. He said, "Feeling all right?"

Dennis nodded. "Just a bad dream."

TA squeezed Dennis' shoulder as he went to the sink with his dish. After a few minutes, Dennis heard the shower and knew that TA had embarked on an evening ritual that would involve a book, music, and several cups of coffee.

The boys and Lori had planned to get together in Greg's garage that night. After the melee in the Pompay yard, Dennis was ambivalent about leaving the house again, but when the time came, he decided to join his friends. He was the last to arrive. The radio was on, and Elton John was singing "Rocket Man". The shadows cast by the lightbulb bizarrely elongated his friends' arms and legs, making them momentarily unrecognizable. Greg was sitting at the workbench, with his back to the others, and Lori was sitting next to him. She was wearing jeans, a pink long-sleeved tee shirt, and white tennis shoes. In contrast, the boys looked as if they had put on the first things they saw in their closets, and then slept in them. Tony was examining Lori's pen-and-ink sketch of Bob Pace. Ben was tuning the radio.

There was little enthusiasm that night. The coming school year, while not dreaded, wasn't exactly welcome either. "The witch gave me the evil eye today", Greg said, turning around.

"Where was she?" Dennis said, recalling their harrowing escape several years earlier. He still had a thin yellow scar where Gordie had bitten him. Greg's remark about the witch also brought Dennis back to that afternoon, to the snapping rug, and, especially, to the fight between Alvin and Jonas. He didn't want to think about it.

"She was standing by the fence and looking at the house", Greg said.

"Your house?"

Greg nodded.

This reminded Dennis that one of their eighth-grade teachers had an affection for the word *cerebral*, so Greg had dropped the name Spartacus and replaced it with something that sounded like "cerebral-less", a name closer, at least phonetically, to TA's appellation for the dog. When Dennis complained, TA had laughed out loud and said he couldn't do better than Greg if he pondered the matter for a month of Sundays.

"See if the Tigers are on", Greg said.

There was a crackling sound, followed by Ernie Harwell's sonorous voice saying, "That ball was corralled by a nimble gentleman from Terrapin Township. And speaking of Terrapin Township, warm birthday greetings to long-time Tigers fan Eroica Macklin."

"Did you hear what I just heard?" Dennis said.

"What's so strange about her having a birthday?" Lori said.

"She must be a hundred", Tony said.

174

"She's not even seventy", Ben observed. "She just looks older."

"If she's a witch, she might be a hundred", Greg said.

"Don't be stupid", Lori said. "You're not in kindergarten."

"Didn't you have a meeting with one of the teachers?" Greg said to Ben, ignoring Lori.

"So what", Ben said noncommittally.

Lori said, "Ben and Dennis are in advanced placement. They get to start earlier than us plebeians." She had read a book about ancient Rome last year, and a few words had taken root in her vocabulary.

"What's the school like?" Greg asked Ben.

"Big."

"Who was the teacher?"

"Janet Winter. She teaches English."

"Do you like her?" Lori asked.

Ben said, "She's a harridan."

"What's a harrigan?" Greg asked.

"Harridan", Ben corrected him.

Dennis couldn't be sure, but he often suspected that Greg was playing a private joke on them, as intelligence and creativity were required to affect such vacuity.

"What did she do to you?" Greg asked Ben.

"She didn't do anything. I told her I got a collection of O. Henry stories from the library for my first assignment. She wasn't amused."

"Was she supposed to be?" Tony said, turning away from the portrait.

"O. Henry isn't on her list of approved writers", Ben said. "I told her I was almost finished with the book. She wanted to know why I thought O. Henry was suitable for advanced-placement English. I told her I liked the stories."

175

"That was a mistake. You're not supposed to like it", Dennis interjected.

"Adam said literature is supposed to be enjoyed", Ben said sullenly.

"So what happened?" Greg said, flinching at the mention of his uncle.

"She told me to find another book on the list and read it quickly."

Lori was trying hard not to laugh.

"I'm glad I'm a plebian", Greg said.

15

September 1973

That night, Dennis exited the Hulse home through Tony's window. The boys reserved that mode of egress for the nighttime hours when they wished not to be observed coming and going. Dennis glanced at Magdalena Hulse's garden in the corner of the yard, now practically fallow. Standing in the Hulse yard, dark and silent, he had an urge to vault one fence after another, to go all the way to the corner of Lincoln and Lee streets without being detected. The chain-link fences were no problem, but he didn't want to be mistaken for a prowler. He didn't relish the idea of the police being summoned or of being chased by one of the men through the neighborhood.

As he hesitated, he could almost hear Greg whisper, "Chicken."

Dennis made for the Holm fence and vaulted it with one hand. He knew that the worst he'd encounter in Jenny Holm's yard were cats. There was a half-moon, shrouded in an orange haze, and the air was still summer-warm. He could smell autumn, but there wasn't that fallen-leaves aroma yet.

He stopped to consider whether he'd have enough time to vault all the way to Lee Street. It was a school night, and though TA wasn't fastidious about Dennis' comings and goings, he made a pretense of it for the first few days of school.

Jenny had converted one of the rear bedrooms to a sitting room and had replaced the small window with a picture window. The light coming from the window caught Dennis' attention, even as his hand was clutching Jenny's fence in anticipation of a vault into the next yard.

He released his grip and turned to face the window. The sheers were closed but not the curtains. Standing in the center of the room, holding a cocktail glass, and staring out the window was Jenny. She was wearing a thin, pale-red negligee, and nothing else. He could see her body almost as well as if she were naked. The negligee might have added mystery to the image, but it didn't conceal a thing.

Dennis was as transfixed as if he had been paralyzed by a strong drug. His eyes traced the woman from her toes to her face. A sensation that he had never experienced before overwhelmed him, excited him, troubled and confused him. It was as if an invigorating nectar had been injected into his bloodstream. His heart pounded, even as his breathing came in fits and starts.

He wondered if she could see him. His mind turned peripatetically to occasions when he had looked out of a lighted room into darkness. Whether anything in the yard was visible to Jenny or not, how could she be oblivious to the possibility of an observer outside her window? How could she not realize that a man outside could see everything and might be stirred to do something foolish, or even desperate?

For a moment, Dennis' world constricted to Jenny, and only Jenny; nothing else existed. All he knew was that he wanted to touch her, hold her. Finally, he forced himself—it wasn't easy—to remember that this was Jenny Holm. Hadn't TA suggested she was mentally ill? Wasn't Jenny more to be pitied than desired?

She hadn't moved except to sip her drink. He told himself that even if she didn't know who was outside her window, she must suspect that someone was watching. A short-haired cat rubbed against her calf. Unperturbed, she continued to stare out the window, looking at him or past him, inviting him or teasing him like some merciless siren.

He felt compelled to get out of Jenny's yard, but was so mesmerized, he could barely stir. He knew that TA would be looking for him, and he feared being discovered here. Every time he tried to turn away, his eyes were drawn back to Jenny. He had the mad urge to tap on the window; could something so beautiful be bad?

He took two steps toward the window and lifted a hand. Remembering Magdalena's words years ago, he couldn't help looking guiltily toward Tony's house. His hand came down and he ran, not toward the next fence but in the direction of Jenny's driveway. When next he was conscious of his actions, he was walking down Jenny Holm's drive toward Greg's house.

The Pace house and garage were dark. He had turned toward his own house when he saw a figure approaching from his right. Though he couldn't make out her features, he knew Lori's gait and form too well to mistake her for anyone else. Her braids bounced against her shoulders and her neatly cuffed jeans topped her white tennis shoes.

"Hi", Lori said to him. She was close now, and she joined him as he walked past Greg's and Ben's houses.

He stopped directly below a street lamp. Now he could see her more clearly, her ordinary features and plump cheeks. But she could see him more clearly too. He wondered if she could read the excitement, and the shame, on his features.

"What are you doing out so late?" he said.

She looked down at the pavement. "I've been with Eddie ever since I came home from school. Dad's out of town, and Mom isn't . . . well. I needed to get out of the house."

Lori would never dissimulate, even when the truth was uncomfortable. That bothered him sometimes, because he knew he lacked her courage to admit vulnerability.

"Where were you?" she asked.

"Tony's."

"You came from that yard", she said, pointing toward Jenny's house.

"So?"

She noticed his defensiveness and said, "It wasn't an accusation. I was just surprised to see you come from her yard."

They were in front of his house now. One more step up the driveway was all that was needed to bottle the memory of this night. To anyone other than Lori, he wouldn't have said a thing. The mutual bravado of the boys would have made the experience a caricature of what it had actually been. And TA, though he might have understood, would pose provocative questions that Dennis wasn't ready to answer. He felt compelled to tell someone, even if he didn't know why—to purge himself of guilt, to affirm his incipient manhood, to articulate something he hadn't understood. Before he knew it, he had told Lori the entire story.

She stood impassively as he related what had happened. Her face might have colored, but he couldn't be sure under the hazy light of the street lamp. When he had finished, he unclenched his tightly balled fists and took a deep breath.

Lori said, "She knew exactly what she was doing. That's what I drew without ever having seen what you saw."

"How could she know I'd be there?" Dennis protested.

"You or someone else, sooner or later. She might be there every night."

Every night. That was something Dennis hadn't considered. One part of him wished that he would never experience those sensations again; another part was eagerly anticipating the next occasion. He also admitted to himself that he resented Lori's suggestion that Jenny hadn't intended the experience for him alone.

Lori added, "You said the lights were on. Tony, or his brothers, could see enough to make them curious if they were outside."

It was Tony she was worried about. That stood to reason.

"Stay away, Dennis", she said. "That witch is up to something."

Two witches in one neighborhood were more than Dennis could handle. He felt exhausted, and now he felt ashamed that he had confided in Lori.

Lori plucked something from his hair, a burr or something like it. He had a visceral memory of his mother, and it warmed him in a way different from the way Jenny had.

"Promise you'll stay away", Lori said forlornly.

"Okay."

"Do you mean it?"

Dennis thought he meant it but wasn't sure. He said, "I mean it."

She smiled at him and turned to go home. It struck him that in Lori's search for respite from her care for Eddie, she had stumbled upon someone else who needed help.

There was a light in the front room when the door closed behind Dennis. He went the other way to his room and sat on the bed in the dark. The experience in Jenny's yard and his conversation with Lori prompted a flood of strong emotions. Though he was exhausted, he doubted he could sleep. His eyes, now accustomed to the dark room, moved toward the dresser. He had been determined to avoid TA, but whatever had been stirred in him that night, whatever had caused him to confide in Lori, had made him bold, even reckless. Now the knowledge of what was in the dresser compelled him to get up from his bed. He removed the envelope from his drawer—it was hidden beneath his socks—and opened the door.

TA had moved from the front room to the kitchen table. Even as Dennis took those few steps down the hall-way, he questioned what he intended to do. He knew it was foolish; worse than foolish, it would be fruitless, but he couldn't resist. TA was sitting beneath the light, not reading or eating. A coffee cup sat in front of him. Ella Fitzgerald was singing "You're the Top", but the volume was so low it was hard to hear the words. Dennis sat in the chair opposite TA and set the envelope on the table between them.

TA opened it and read without asking questions or remarking. Dennis could tell that TA was suppressing strong emotions as he read, though the man did his best to conceal them. TA examined each page as if it were a legal document in which every word was critical. When he had finished, he put the pages back in the envelope and pushed it toward Dennis.

Dennis waited for him to say something. Finally, Dennis said, "What should we do next?"

"It couldn't have been easy to get this information", TA said.

Dennis thought it was a compliment, but he wasn't sure. TA was smiling, but it seemed less than genuine to Dennis, and he wasn't used to that from TA. He asked a second time, "What should we do next?"

TA looked at Dennis in a way that made him uncomfortable and said, "You may be too young for this, but I'll ask it anyway: What is freedom?"

Dennis shrugged, wondering what freedom had to do with the information in the envelope. TA's question reminded him of the books on the bottom shelf of TA's library, the books Dennis scrupulously avoided. He had asked TA about the police report in that envelope and what they should do next to identify the man or woman who had killed their wife and mother, their son and brother. He was tempted to answer that he didn't care what freedom meant unless it got them closer to the truth.

TA said, "Freedom, interior freedom, the only freedom that matters, is an inner peace that comes from consenting to what is."

"I don't care about that", Dennis said. He hadn't expected cooperation, but he resented TA's dismissive attitude toward his question.

TA ignored Dennis' passion and said, "Consenting means accepting that something happened, that it's necessary to go on in spite of it. It doesn't mean we don't try to put things right, or make them better when we can, or that we shouldn't learn from what happened, or that we shouldn't be contrite for what we did. It means we shouldn't carry the burden with us like emotional handcuffs. It also means that, with our consent, some-thing good might come from what happened."

Dennis didn't comprehend all of what TA was saying, but he understood enough. TA was advising him to abandon the investigation. Dennis said, "Shouldn't the person who did it be punished?"

"Maybe he should. We don't know."

Dennis said, "I want to know."

"Why?"

"To make him pay; that's why."

TA made Dennis meet his eyes. "I don't want you to have to be the one who pays, any more than you already have."

"Those detectives", Dennis said, pointing toward the bookshelf in the other room, "are after the truth. So am I."

"Those are stories. You're my son."

The relationship between TA and Dennis rarely admitted father-son intimacy. In that sense, it was a strange relationship, though it didn't lack camaraderie or warmth.

TA's hands engulfed the cup. He leaned forward and said, "You brought up the subject, so hear me out. There was a Jewish woman who lived in Holland, not a particularly religious woman for most of her life. The Nazis confined her to a ghetto in Amsterdam. She kept a diary of that experience; it was before they shipped her to Auschwitz and killed her. In her diary, she insisted that even though the Nazis took away her freedom of movement, they didn't have the power to take away her interior freedom; that is, her freedom to consent to what was happening to her, and her belief that something good could be made of it, even if that good was utterly invisible to her.

"There was a soldier on the other side of the world who fought in a war. The brutality was unbelievable. This soldier learned what hell looked like; he'd seen it for himself. One day, the soldier did something he will never forget, something he never should have done, something he never believed he could do. I suppose there were reasons, or excuses, for what he did. It's enough to say he did it, and he won't ever forget it. For years it haunted him. It nearly destroyed him. Then, he met a priest who told him about consent and interior freedom. The act itself can't be undone, and the soldier can't forget it, but he won't let it control his life, and he believes that something good may yet come from it."

Dennis said, "You think we should let him go free."

TA said, "First of all, you don't have the power to free him from what he did. No one does. What I told you has nothing to do with that person's freedom. It's about your freedom. You have a choice."

Dennis opened the envelope and reread the brief report. How many times had he done this, looking for a pearl of a clue to the person's identity? He had hoped that TA's response would be satisfaction, even pride, though he had suspected that TA's reaction would be more complicated than that. Why wouldn't TA want to see this person punished? And what did he mean when he said it was about Dennis' freedom? He hadn't done anything wrong. The image of a virtually naked Jenny Holm flashed into his mind, making him wonder if TA had somehow learned what had happened that night. Then there was TA himself; what had he done wrong, for surely he was the soldier in the story. He even wondered if there was a son out there who was determined to bring this soldier to justice.

The perpetrator's truck must have been badly damaged, because TA's car had been demolished. Much of the information in the police report had come from TA's recollections of the moments before the truck crossed the yellow line and barreled into their Buick. The blue paint on the wreck of their car confirmed the color of the truck. It might have been an older model Ford, according to TA. He had no memory of the driver, who could have been anyone: young or old, man or woman. The person hadn't stopped to assist; had limped off—mechanically speaking—leaving a trail of oil for several miles before it was lost on a dirt side road. The truck was never found. Now, eight years later, Dennis was furious that the police hadn't pursued the matter more assiduously.

Dennis was surprised that TA hadn't warmed his coffee. He wasn't particular about the brand of his coffee, but he liked it blisteringly hot. He just sat there looking at Dennis. After some time had passed, TA took a deep breath, sat back in his chair, and said, "What do you hope to accomplish by pursuing this? Can you hope to find the driver, if the police haven't, after all these years?"

Dennis said, "The police didn't try to find him."

"Or her", TA said. "You don't know how hard they tried."

"They didn't try", Dennis insisted. It took effort not to raise his voice.

TA said, "Emotion won't get you any further with this." TA waited for Dennis to say something, but he was too conflicted to think clearly.

"What do we know about the driver and the vehicle?"

"We don't know anything", Dennis said curtly. "That's the problem. The police didn't care if he got away."

"As for not knowing anything," TA said, "that's not accurate. As for the police, that's speculation. We know that the vehicle was a blue truck, even if I wasn't sure about the make and model. We know that the vehicle was badly damaged. What does that suggest?"

These questions surprised Dennis. Until now, hadn't TA been discouraging pursuit of the perpetrator? "I don't know", he said.

"Think."

It was hard to think. He was tired. He could still hear Ella Fitzgerald, and every now and then the image of Jenny behind the glass and beneath that transparent gown intruded on his thoughts. Dennis turned this information over in his brain. "If the truck was badly damaged, it couldn't have gone far."

"Good. Let's say it couldn't have traveled too many miles. That limits it to the county. Do you think it likely that a damaged vehicle, driven by a stranger; that is, someone from outside the county, would risk having the truck repaired so close to the accident, especially as it's a crime to flee the scene of an accident? People might have died."

"People did die", Dennis said bitterly.

TA said, "I'm looking at it from the driver's perspective. He couldn't have known that someone was killed, but he, or she, knew it was a bad crash and knew it was a serious crime to drive off. The truck wasn't abandoned. That means there's a high probability that it was repaired inside the county. What do we know about the area where the crash occurred?"

What was TA up to? Dennis wondered. Was this a real-life mystery story, a lesson in logic, or something altogether different?

Dennis said, "We don't know anything about Iowa. I don't."

"Think."

"There are a lot of farms in Iowa."

"Iowa is more than farms," TA countered, "but the area where the accident occurred is rural, sparsely populated. There's just one small village in the county. We already surmised he wasn't an outsider, so where could the driver have gone to get the vehicle fixed?"

Dennis said, "To the village, I guess ... if they have a repair shop."

"They do have a small repair shop. Are there any other possibilities?"

For the first time, Dennis suspected that these were more than extemporaneous questions. TA had already considered them. Dennis said, "Maybe he could fix it himself."

"Now you're thinking. How many blue trucks do you think there were in the county in July of 1965?"

"I don't know", Dennis said.

"Think", TA said patiently.

"How can anyone know that?"

TA said, "Someone can know, but I'm asking for your opinion."

"A dozen?" Dennis said.

"Good. Actually, there were seven."

Dennis' heart felt exactly as it did when he was chasing a fly ball, knowing that the fence was looming but loath to take his eyes of that spinning white orb. How much did TA actually know?

TA said, "I was in Korea with a guy who joined the Iowa State Police. He agreed to check for me, though I didn't tell him why.

"There were seven blue trucks registered in the county on the date of the accident: two Fords that were state conservation vehicles with lettering on the sides; a Chevy that belonged to a minister's widow; a Chrysler that was owned by a farmer on the western edge of the county— over twenty miles from the accident site; and a two-toned Chrysler owned by a postman who lived in the village. That leaves two more."

"What were they?" Dennis asked eagerly.

"One was a Ford, owned by a young farmer with a wife and three small children. He lived five miles from the accident. The other one was also a Ford that belonged to a single man who lived about nine miles from the crash site. He trapped mink and weasel along the Squaw River."

TA took a sip of coffee. Dennis glanced at the stove clock and saw it was after eleven. The record had stopped and the house was silent. "Why are you telling me this now?" Dennis said.

"You suggested that the other driver could have been anyone. I wanted you to think about it differently."

"Do you know who was driving the truck that hit us, and killed Mom and Andrew?"

"No. I didn't pursue it any further."

"Why not?"

"I decided it was too dangerous", TA said.

"Dangerous to who?"

"To me. It would have been dangerous to me. That's all I can say about it."

"So a killer was allowed to go free", Dennis said contemptuously.

"If we're going to reason this out, then let's be precise about it. That person in the blue truck may have been distracted, or careless, or grossly negligent, but I'm almost certain he didn't set out to kill anyone; that's manslaughter, not murder. You've read enough Christie and Carr to know that. You said he's free. Is he?"

"He isn't in jail, where he belongs."

TA said, "That's one way of looking at it. I can't criticize that viewpoint. I came to a different conclusion."

Dennis knew that he couldn't convince TA to see things his way, nor would Dennis adopt TA's viewpoint. He gathered up the papers, recalling the conversation with Ben a year earlier that had prompted his research. How could Ben, someone who hadn't suffered the terrible loss the Coles had, understand the necessity for pursuing this person, and not TA?

Dennis was overstimulated. There was the recent Alvin/Jonas fight, strictly speaking, more of a beating than a fight. There was Jenny Holm and the charms she so uninhibitedly revealed to him. And now this.

"Think about it", TA said.

Dennis started back to his room. He could imagine TA as a soldier—barely—but a killer? Then he asked himself: Wasn't that what soldiers did, at least those who saw combat? When Dennis considered TA's Marine Corps service, he had never entertained the idea that TA might have killed or that what TA experienced in the war still affected him so profoundly.

He closed the door of his room and replaced the envelope in the drawer; then he stretched out on top of the bedspread. TA didn't like air conditioning, so windows were open most summer and autumn days and nights. As Dennis' room faced the back of the house and the Macklin property, little light—unless there was a bright moon—penetrated the window. He heard a horn and the sound of a car on the gravel street, but this was background noise that scarcely registered in a mind that was pregnant with emotions and ideas.

The most vivid of these were two recurring images. He saw Andrew hurtling from the backseat, striking the windshield with a sickening shattering sound, exiting the car, bouncing on the hood, and skidding down the street. In the other image, he looked into the backseat of the car and saw Patricia Cole twisted like a pretzel on the floor behind the passenger seat. No matter how hard he tried, there was no eradicating these images.

TA had rushed to Andrew first, instinctively kicked open the door and ran to the boy. It was no use. And no use with the lifeless form in the backseat either. Dennis had never before, or since, seen such a mixture of grief and fortitude as was demonstrated by TA that day; no doubt it had formed Dennis, and was still forming him, though that notion could not have been articulated by the boy.

The idea that the person in the blue truck was living a normal life infuriated him, and nothing TA could say or do would change that. Dennis had the police report, and now he had TA's reluctant help in reasoning from that information.

He had to know. He could petition the police to reopen the investigation, but on what grounds, or based on what new information? If the police hadn't been able to make an arrest eight years ago, they would be even less inclined to act now. He could go to Iowa, but then what? He'd have no transportation, he'd be in unfamiliar surroundings, and he'd have little time to act before TA, or the police, found him and sent him back to Michigan. He thought about corresponding with someone his own age in the county where the accident occurred. He might be able to identify a pen pal through his school, but turning a correspondent, if one could be identified, into a collaborator was easier said than done.

If he was determined, even obstinate, he wasn't impulsive. As sleep descended, he resolved to consider everything, to ask advice—discreetly—if necessary, and then to act. But when he slept, it was not the person in the blue truck who inhabited his dreams, nor Jenny, but Lori, who kept asking him questions he couldn't hear, and who wept when he didn't respond. He woke in the middle of the dream and the middle of the night, troubled about many things, and he was late for school the next day.

16

Day Three, Afternoon

Lunch left Dennis and Ben unsatisfied. Dennis had had to force himself to eat ever since the morning they discovered Greg. He managed to talk Ben into a ride in the car as a way to relieve the oppression they were both experiencing. They walked to Dennis' car and took a drive to nowhere in particular. Dennis wound through Ann Arbor until he reached North Territorial Road and then went west through mostly undeveloped country. Not infrequently, tree limbs from both sides of the road intertwined above the sedan. The area was rich in wildlife, a habitat for deer, coyote, and pheasant. The ponds were home to snapping turtles and bullfrogs. The two men said nothing to each other, and after half an hour, Dennis found a pull-off area, turned around, and began the return trip to Ann Arbor. Glancing at Ben, Dennis reflected that though this excursion wasn't as satisfying as those long-ago bike trips had been, there was still a sympathetic rapport between them, even in silence.

Ben's phone rang, breaking the silence and startling Dennis. He answered apprehensively and hesitated before speaking. "Hello, Susan. . . . No, nothing yet. . . . We don't think he's coming back either. . . . No, we haven't talked to anyone about Greg. . . . I don't think you should do that, Susan." Ben looked at Dennis and with his hand over the speaker framed with his lips the word *police*. "Maybe his disappearance has something to do with his job. We don't know what Greg is doing, but we learned that he published an article at the War College.... CIA? No, we didn't know about that.... Greg not truthful? You must be pulling my leg. Listen, we've had another jolt. Tony had to be taken to the hospital.... We think diabetic coma.... Yes, it's very serious, but the hospital won't tell us anything.... Yes, I promise to let you know when we find out more.... You can say that again. Thanks, Susan. Bye."

When Ben put his phone back into his pocket, he bent his head and groaned.

"Your back hurting again?" Dennis said.

Ben nodded and said, "Driving aggravates it, and I haven't been able to do my exercises. Getting older hasn't helped."

"Can't it be fixed?" Dennis asked.

"The pain, or the memory of waiting in that ditch until the police arrived, wondering how bad I was hurt, wondering if I would ever walk again? The doctor says surgery may, or may not, repair it. I guess I'll live with it.

"Listen, Dennis, Susan is no fan of Greg's, but she still cares about him. He applied to the CIA toward the end of their marriage but told her they rejected him. It wouldn't surprise me to learn he's in the espionage business. Instead of stealing grapes and tormenting chickens, he may be stealing state secrets and tormenting terrorists."

"It's a free country. We have our own limits on candor", Dennis said. "Greg isn't here to defend himself."

Ben smiled. "Remember the time in Fort Lauderdale? Greg got wasted and the bar owner wanted to bounce him. I've never seen you so protective of anyone. By the time you finished, even I believed Greg was a victim of circumstance, and I knew him. I don't suppose he ever realized how good a friend he had."

"You and Tony were right beside me."

Ben said, "That's because you were driving. We didn't want you and Greg to leave without us."

"I was driving? I guess I was. Was that the trip I let the lizard loose in the car and you went berserk?"

Ben said, "I still have nightmares about that."

"It wasn't a big lizard."

"It was big enough."

"How are your mom and Carly?"

"Mom's OK. When my father died, I suspect she felt a kind of grief, but some relief too. She knew about his extracurricular activities. She might have known it all along but kept quiet for our sakes, Carly's and mine. My parents were never close, so by the time he died she'd been alone a long time. Carly's a corporate warrior. She's another one who thinks I need taking care of, collaborates with my girls to make me happy. Her heart's in the right place, but it gets annoying."

"You're lucky", Dennis said.

Ben looked at him and said, "So are you."

Dennis knew Ben was referring to Marta.

"I'd like to see Carly again", Dennis said.

"She still lives in town. She had a crush on you. I'm sure she'd like to see you too. Don't try to push her around like we used to. She's pretty good at pushing back these days." Ben shook his head and said, "I'm glad you dragged me out of that mortuary."

"Can't you stay a few more days?"

Ben said, "This isn't my place anymore; hasn't been for a long time. The girls are in Georgia. Did you ever wonder how I ended up living sixty miles from that freeway ditch? I drove past once. It's as ordinary as can be, but it still looked like hell to me."

Dennis had wondered, but he had never dared to ask Ben how he could stand living so near the site of where his car was run off the road. It stung a little to hear Ben say that Michigan wasn't his home, even though Dennis knew that was true. Ben had been living in Georgia a long time; longer than he had lived in Terrapin Township.

"Diane shouldn't have died; Tony should be married to Lori; Greg and Susan shouldn't have split up; and you and Marta ought to have lots of kids", Ben said with emotion. "Sometimes, when I'm home alone at night in that quiet house, I think about things like that. What do you think TA would have made of all this?"

Dennis recalled TA talking with Delia in their front room, after her cancer had returned. Hope amid misery had been TA's message, but Dennis was poorly suited to articulate it. "I don't know", he answered.

Ben took Dennis' equivocation in stride. "I'll be back here in a month or two to see my mom. I'll call you."

Dennis doubted it. Things had irrevocably changed. Ben would always be his friend, but the special thread that connected them had been severed, or at least frayed. All too soon, Dennis parked the car at the Hilton, and they went back inside. Just the sight of the hotel rekindled feelings of desperation and sadness.

When they opened the door to the suite, the maid was cleaning inside. They were supposed to be checking out—Dennis had forgotten.

"Can we stay a while longer?" he said. "I'll call the front desk. Our friend was taken to the hospital this morning."

She smiled at them nervously and walked toward the door.

"Just a minute", Ben said to the maid. "Did you clean the room yesterday?"

"Yes", she replied.

"When you cleaned the room yesterday, did you find anything?"

"No", she said firmly, as if Ben's question might be an accusation.

Dennis said, "Did you notice anything different, anything at all?

"No, sir", she said.

"Sorry to trouble you", Dennis said, "I'll call the front desk and let them know we'll be late."

The maid put a hand on the doorknob, then turned and said, "Someone moved the food and beverages and put a coin in the middle of the table where they had been. I knew about the food because I was cleaning the room when it was delivered."

"And you replaced the food and left the coin on the table", Dennis said. He knew that he had not moved the food, and he couldn't remember his friends doing so either.

"Yes, sir."

Ben asked, "Where did you find the food and drinks?"

"On the counter near the sink."

After she had left the room, Dennis said, "We didn't move that food. And we were too stunned to pay attention to food and spare change when we first discovered Greg, and then when he went missing."

Ben didn't dispute Dennis' recollection. He said, "Why would Greg's killer go to the trouble of moving food around after removing the body and everything associated with Greg? And why leave that coin behind?"

"We don't know that the killer, or Greg, did it", Dennis answered.

"None of us put that coin there."

Dennis said, "No one remembers putting the coin there, or has admitted it. Listen, all I'm suggesting is that we don't have proof that Greg or, if he was killed, his killer did it. The maid might be mistaken, and what could a half-dollar have to do with this business?"

When Dennis told the management about Tony, they were intent on making him as comfortable as possible; he was told that they could stay as late as necessary. When Dennis informed Ben, his friend said, "I intend to be on that flight to Atlanta today. We both know Tony is dead. Why else would the hospital ask for his family, and why else would they keep us in the dark? There's no point in staying. I'll deal with Greg and Tony in my own way; and if it turns out that Greg is alive, there will be a reckoning that Mr. Pace will never forget."

"I don't blame you", Dennis said.

Ben's phone rang. He frowned and said, "Hello? . . . Who is this? . . . Who? . . . That's not good enough; I need a name. . . . We haven't seen him since yesterday. . . . Nothing happened, and nothing went wrong. Who are you? . . ." Ben wrote a phone number on the hotel stationery. "How did you get my name and number? . . . It *is* my business. If that's your attitude, don't expect anything from me. . . . Okay, that's a start. Did the two of you work together at the War College? . . . Do you think Greg's work has anything to do with his being missing? . . . We've established that you're concerned about Greg; so are we. But you know who we are, and we don't know who you are. . . . So you can't tell me anything, but you want me to tell you everything. . . . How the

hell did you learn that? . . . I heard you the first time. . . .
I'll think about it."

Ben terminated the call. Dennis had crowded so close
to the phone he could hear the murmur of the other
person's voice.

Ben said, "That was a so-called colleague of Greg's.
He admitted they were connected to the War College,
but he wouldn't tell me his name, what the two of them
did, or how he knew that Greg was gone. He knows
who we are. Oh yeah, he told me Tony's dead."

"Another spook," Dennis said, "or maybe the person
responsible for Greg's disappearance."

"Or both, but if he's responsible, why does he need us?"

Dennis sat on the bed. The stranger's assertion that
Tony was dead made him feel lightheaded. He tossed his
things haphazardly into his bag. He couldn't wait to get
out of there. Ben was the lucky one; he would never
have to see this hotel or this town again.

When Dennis had finished with his own bag, he collected Tony's things. Inexplicably, he took time to fold
Tony's clothes, as if this mundane act was a valedictory
to his friend. When he came to the cards, he put them
in his own bag instead of Tony's, as they were the only
tangible remnant of Tony and their friendship. In his mind's
eye, he could see those card houses: on tables and floors;
in apartments and airports and restaurants; majestically
tall; low and sprawling; fortress-like or fragile like a Jap-
anese pagoda. Even when Tony was resting, he was building. He needed to build as Dennis needed to write. These
cards had been Tony's pen and paper. Perhaps they were
a talisman against a relentless darkness.

"Have you changed your mind about what happened?" Dennis asked. "Do you still think that someone

entered the room and killed Greg, then came back and removed everything?"

"That call proves Greg was mixed up with something. The waiter seeing him in the alcove with that device is suspicious too. If Greg wanted to drop out of sight, he'd do it differently, not by torturing his best friends. He wasn't an angel, but he wasn't that insensitive. What about the Scotch and the cigars?"

"I'll take the Glenlivet, and you keep the cigars", Dennis said. "You're probably right. If Greg were alive, he would never have left the Scotch behind."

Ben made a sound that passed for a laugh.

"I wonder where that half-dollar came from?" Dennis said.

Ben said, "I don't think Greg's disappearance hinges on that coin, if that's what you mean. We were in a hurry; as you suggested, it could have been one of us that left it here; Greg most likely, or the maid could have found it on the floor and put it there without thinking."

Dennis removed it from his pocket. It was an ordinary half-dollar, not a high-tech camera or listening device or whatever else spies are wont to carry; not ancient but not new either, minted in 1981. He tossed it to Ben, who turned it over and flipped it back to Dennis.

"This is the end of the road", Ben said. "We can't button this up like one of your mystery stories. We're out of our element, even out of our league. It's taken down two of us." He shook Dennis' hand perfunctorily, zipped his bag and wheeled it to the door. "I'll be late if I don't get going."

Dennis said, "How can you go back to Atlanta as if nothing happened?"

Ben looked at Dennis from the door, and said, "The last trip we took with the kids, before it stopped being cool to be with their parents and before Diane got sick, we were at the beach. I got up early one morning, went down to the beach, and started walking. I hadn't gone far when I found a big terrapin. It might have been a turtle or a tortoise; I don't know. It made me remember the old stories when we were growing up. Who knows what happened, but it was upside down. At first, I thought it was dead, maybe cleaned out by sand crabs. When I picked it up, I saw movement inside the shell. I put it back on the sand right side up and waited. After a while it began to extend its feet but it must have been paralyzed by fear because it retracted them again. Whatever happened to that creature left a mark on its psyche."

"Turtles don't have psyches", Dennis said.

"The hell they don't. You weren't there. It wasn't normal. I'm telling you it was big and strong, but it wasn't normal. I waited for over an hour before I went back to the cabin, and it never moved. When I came back the next day, it was dead. I'm not going to become that animal just because something bad happened to me—us—that we can't undo. I'm going back to Atlanta, and I'm going to work tomorrow; I'm going on, as I did after Diane died. If they make me come back to Ann Arbor, so be it. Whatever happened to Greg and Tony—to all of us a long time ago—can't be undone. I'm a scientist. That gets in my way sometimes—Diane was right about that—but sometimes it comes in handy too, and this is one of those times. I'm going to let the police, if this is police business, do their job. I'm not going to die on this beach. I'm swimming out to sea."

Dennis' phone rang. He wondered if he would ever hear a phone ring again without experiencing that feeling in his stomach. Ben was halfway out the door.

"It's Jan", Dennis said to Ben. "I'm sorry, Jan. . . . No, they wouldn't tell us anything. . . . Diabetic reaction? We thought so. . . . He wasn't feeling well yesterday, but we never guessed it was serious. When we found him this morning, he was unresponsive. . . . No, I don't think he suffered. . . . Greg? He had to leave early, but I'll let him know. . . . Jan, Tony was a great friend. We all have great memories. Please let me know about the services." There was a long pause, during which Ben nervously gripped and un-gripped the handle of his bag. "Yes, I will, Jan. You too."

"Tony *is* dead", Dennis said after he hung up. "The family is making arrangements. Jan will let us know."

Dennis and Ben stared uncomfortably at each other. Then Dennis extended his hand, and Ben took it again. They stood there, hands clasped, as if one or both would say something, but they didn't. The door closed, and Dennis was alone in the room.

He felt it was time to call Marta and confide everything; well, almost everything. He needed her desperately, but he wondered where he'd find the energy to tell half-stories and half-truths. Where he'd always found it, he told himself. He put the half-dollar back in his pocket and finished packing.

17

May 1975

With four boys sleeping side by side on the floor, the sound of snoring could hardly be ignored, but Dennis seemed to be the only one awakened by it. He was sure that Greg, Ben, and Tony were asleep in their bags on Greg's wooden bedroom floor.

Greg's clock told twelve-thirty. Dennis admitted to himself that what had been special earlier in the evening— spending the night with his best friends—had now become tedious. The floor was hard; the room was warm and stuffy, and Ben's snoring was maddening. It wasn't soft and regular enough to produce a lullaby effect. On the contrary, minutes of silence were punctuated by sudden blasts.

These four were still good friends; but, truth was, they had gone in different directions in high school. Ben and Dennis had been elected to the National Honor Society— Dennis because of natural talent, and Ben because of talent *and* effort. Ben was also active in the Science Club. Greg made the football team as a wide receiver and defensive back; disinterest in academics kept his grade point average just below the NHS requirements. Tony was engaged in his father's business. He often helped Johannes Hulse with construction projects after school and on weekends. Lori was in the Drama Club and was editor of the school paper. Days went by without their talking to each another.

Dennis supposed that Tony was the least changed of his friends, not that Tony hadn't matured; in fact, he had more responsibility than the others. Tony had never been flashy or showy, but his compass had always been true. In contrast, Greg had become more audacious with the years, as if he felt the need to compete with Davey for notoriety and attention, a frustrating and, ultimately, losing battle. Greg's precocity could be endearing, but it could just as easily cross the line to belligerence. Ben was more independent, less confiding. As for Dennis, he would have found it difficult to describe what had happened to him. In truth, he had been ungrounded by the changes that were going on inside him, and by a world that influenced him more than TA liked.

Davey was sleeping in the next room. He was graduating in June. David Pace was the person every boy wanted to be. It was hard for Dennis to imagine that Davey used to play kick-the-can with them, so lofty did he now seem. Greg's brother was tall, good-looking, athletic, and popular, but for one so young, he took these qualities in stride with nonchalant grace. He'd recently purchased a motorcycle. That very night, just as Dennis was preparing to leave the house, he heard a loud roar, and a familiar one. Down Lincoln Street came the motorcycle, going too fast for a residential street. As the bike passed below a streetlight, Dennis could see Davey's long blond hair cascading over the collar of his leather jacket. Whether Davey saw him, Dennis couldn't say, but Greg's brother raised one hand as he passed the Cole house and then turned into his own drive.

If Dennis were honest with himself, he would admit that his inability to sleep on Greg's floor had another cause besides Ben's snoring. That morning, he found on the kitchen table an unfamiliar black scrapbook. It had no labels or markings on the cover, and Dennis at first ignored it; then curiosity got the better of him. When Dennis opened the book, he was startled to see articles that Patricia Cole had written for the *Detroit Free Press*. Dennis knew that his mother had been a freelance journalist—TA had always been proud of that—but he had never suspected that something like this collection existed, though he now realized it was the most natural thing in the world for his mother, or TA, to keep copies of her published work.

Dennis was sure that TA had meant for him to see the scrapbook. He read every article; a few more than once. Reading his mother's words was almost like listening to her voice, an experience Dennis had never dreamed possible.

The articles concerned the cultural and historical heritage of Detroit and its surroundings. Patricia Cole hadn't written with a broad brush about big things. Rather, she had selected some detail—a stone and flower garden at Greenfield Village, an opulent eighteenth-century home on a formerly grand boulevard, a piece of art that had once belonged to an early French settler and now graced an auto baron's parlor—and explored its origin, its contribution to the community, and its charm. Even though Dennis was not particularly interested in the subjects she had chosen, he found himself drawn to her graceful, accessible writing style and learned that his mother had been enchanted by art, music, architecture, and the natural world.

Dennis found troubling the lack of resemblance between the author of the articles and the mother his imagination had invented. This woman was bolder and more cosmopolitan than his imagined Patricia Cole. She had interests that went beyond being his mother and TA's wife, and she intruded on his iconic image, forcing him to re-imagine her.

One of the articles included a small photograph of Patricia Cole that Dennis had never seen before—a picture of a serious, unsmiling woman who was both familiar and strange.

TA had given Dennis the opportunity to examine the scrapbook alone, and the articles remained on his mind throughout the day; they were on his mind now as he lay awake on Greg's floor. He wondered why TA had chosen this particular time to share the articles with him, and whether TA had done so gratuitously or with an intended effect.

With care, Dennis emerged from his sleeping bag, located his tennis shoes, and crept between Greg and Ben to the window. With long-practiced skill, with barely a sound, he slid the screen to one side, pitched his shoes into the yard, lifted himself with both arms, and tumbled headfirst over the sill, tucking and rolling on the grass. After closing the screen, he put on his shoes, not bothering to tie them, trotted to the fence, and vaulted into Ben's yard.

As soon as his feet touched the ground, the scent of peach blossoms wafted over him. As he passed beneath the tree, the air was noticeably cooler. Something bounced off the back of his neck, causing him to flinch and slap, but whatever it was didn't linger. He vaulted the fence into his own yard, noticing that a low mist clung to the bottom of the incline at the rear of the property, from Greg's yard all the way to the Pompays'. That drew his eyes to the Macklin yard; and, when he looked up, he saw a bat dart left and then right.

The full moon was high in the cloudless sky. It was so bright that it produced nighttime shadows and, like the sun it reflected, prevented Dennis from keeping his eyes fixed on it for any length of time. To Dennis, the moon seemed filled with some inner energy, even life, of its own, though he knew that it was nothing but inorganic rock. Lifeless matter, yet radiant with an intense, crystalline beauty—Dennis could almost believe that someone had hung the moon in the sky intentionally, for no other reason than for it to be admired on just such a night.

Dennis entered his bedroom in the same way he had exited Greg's—through the window. He removed his shoes and climbed on his bed without bothering to get under the covers.

After his heart rate and breathing had slowed, Dennis heard a woman's voice in the house. Her words were unintelligible, so he crept to his bedroom door and placed his ear against it. He wondered if TA had taken advantage of his absence to invite a woman—a girlfriend—to spend the night. He still could not hear well enough, so he slowly opened the door. The voices were audible now, and recognizable. One of them belonged to Delia Pompay; the other was TA's. Dennis crouched low in the hallway, like a baseball catcher, with his back against the wall, ready to dash into his room at the sound of footsteps. He glanced at the family photograph on the opposite wall. Yes, he could see the serious-looking woman from the scrapbook in this familiar image of his smiling mother; perhaps they weren't incompatible after all.

"I haven't been well", he heard Delia say. "I'm afraid the cancer is coming back."

TA said, "You don't know that. It doesn't pay to worry about what you don't know."

"I'm afraid I do know."

"Have you been tested?"

"Not yet."

"Don't wait, Delia. You know that better than me. Does Alvin know about this?"

"I haven't told him. You know he's been working in Bay City since the ground thawed. I don't want to worry him. It's hard enough for him, being so far from home. He's living with a bunch of men in a flea-trap hotel; Alvin never complains, but I know he hates it."

TA said, "He has a right to know. Alvin can handle it."

"I'm not sure any of us can handle it, when it comes right down to it."

Dennis heard TA clear his throat, as he often did when he was excited about something. The man said, "Not on our own we can't. I learned that a long time ago."

There was a period of silence before Delia spoke again, and when she did, Dennis could hear the emotion in her voice, even from the hallway.

"When I was a girl, I had big plans. I left home as soon as I could and moved to New York. I was an actress and a dancer then, and I got some work—nothing big, but enough to pay the bills. It wasn't as glamorous as I'd hoped, but it was exciting. My mother was worried, but I didn't care. Now I know all about a mother's worry."

"We've all had to learn a parent's worry from experience", TA said reassuringly.

"Did I ever tell you that I was in the Broadway production of *The King and I*? I was a substitute for a girl who hurt her ankle. It lasted for only a few weeks, but it was marvelous—the clothes, the audience, the set. Yul Brynner had the lead. He greeted me one night when we passed in the wings; the memory's as fresh as if it was yesterday."

She paused, but TA did not say anything.

"Stars are people just like the rest of us," Delia said, "and some are not as good as the rest of us; but I can't help feeling like I do, like I'd been plucked from the ordinary world and set down in a magical land. It was over too soon. Raymond was helping the carpenters; that's how we met. Funny, isn't it, how something so good can turn out bad?"

"And a bad experience can produce something good", TA condoled. "Don't forget that."

"Do you think so? Raymond swept me off my feet. I wasn't a fool, so why did I believe everything he told me? I've heard it said that eggs shouldn't dance with stones, but some stones look like eggs; they look like eggs until one has gotten too close. Then, it's too late for the egg."

As Delia spoke, Dennis had a difficult time connecting the woman in the front room with the woman who had lived next door his whole life. It was as if an entirely different person had commandeered Delia's voice.

"Well, I moved in with him," she continued "and we lived together almost a year before we married. I kept acting and dancing; but I was too distracted to make anything out of it, and the jobs got harder to find. In the beginning, I was reliable, if not gifted; but after Raymond, I was no different from a thousand irresponsible girls who wanted their names in lights without working for it. Sometimes, I wish I could start all over again, but I'd never give up Caleb, or even Jonas. Is that hard to believe—that I wouldn't give up having Jonas?"

"Not at all", TA said.

"After we got married and especially after Jonas came, things went from bad to worse; I had to leave Raymond. Of course, by then, it was too late for a career. I came back to Michigan, to Detroit. Thank God I met Alvin. My mother thought I was crazy, but I'd seen enough bad to recognize good when I saw it."

"Alvin's a good man", TA said.

"And Alvin has tried hard with Jonas; it hasn't been easy. Our peculiar marriage doesn't help either. I knew it wouldn't be easy, but I never imagined all-out war between Jonas and Alvin."

"Family life is challenging", said TA. "Stepfamilies even more so."

"I've learned to take life as it comes rather than as planned. It was a hard lesson. When they took my breasts, there were days, at the beginning, when I didn't care if I died."

TA said, "This was given to you, or permitted, for an important reason."

"Do you really believe that?"

"I do believe it. I believe that good, great good, can come of it."

"How? What should I do?"

"It's not for me to tell you what to do. You know you're not in control of this thing."

TA said something Dennis couldn't hear, and Delia started crying. Dennis felt ashamed for hiding in the hall and eavesdropping on this poor woman's problems, but he wouldn't leave either.

Delia's sobs gradually subsided. Dennis heard her say, "Thank you, TA. Who will take care of Caleb?"

TA said, "If it comes to it, Alvin will. He's a good father, but you already know that. That's not something you need to think about tonight."

"How can I avoid thinking about it? I'm worried about Caleb ... and Jonas."

TA said, "Everyone worries about their children, if they're good parents."

"Dennis is a good boy," she said, "and he'll be a man in a few years."

There was a pause, during which Dennis inched toward the lighted room.

TA said, "I'm proud of him, but a darkness, an obsession, got hold of him after his mother and Andrew died. We've talked about it, but he's determined to exact justice, whatever that means."

"He'll get over it", Delia said.

Dennis resented TA's talking to Delia about so private a matter.

"I want to see Caleb grow up, graduate," Delia said, "but I don't expect to."

"Embrace every day you have with him. All parents should. Illness, and loss, sensitize us to that truth, that priority."

"You're right", she said.

TA said, "I've known people who died in their twenties and thirties who lived more fully than many in their seventies and eighties."

"Like Patricia?" she said.

"Like Patricia."

"You miss her."

"I will always miss her."

"She was a beautiful person."

"I still have a hard time talking about her, even with Dennis. The pain has never gone away."

"You are good at concealing it."

"I have to be. I have work to do. I have a son to raise."

"I'll try to remember what you said about making every day with Caleb count. It won't be easy."

"It never is. Sometimes, it feels like firing a popgun at a tornado, but I'm convinced the popgun is more powerful than we could ever imagine."

She said, "If something happens, will you watch out for Jonas? He doesn't like Alvin, and after so many years of Jonas' insults, Alvin has washed his hands of him. I don't blame him. Alvin was always good to him, but Jonas treats him like a fool. No man can tolerate that, especially from his wife's son."

TA said, "I'll do my best. I see something of myself in Jonas."

Dennis was amazed to hear this. What on earth, he wondered, could Jonas and TA have in common?

Delia voiced the same sentiment. "You're not at all alike."

"Not now, perhaps. At one time, I was a rebel. That's not all bad if you're rebelling against something that ought to be opposed. I wasn't. The Marines cured me of that. Unfortunately, that experience left its own scars. Sometimes, I wonder if the cure was worth it."

Delia said, "If it made you the man you are today, it was worth it. Jonas is sly and secretive, and of all the interests he could have—that Nazi nonsense. That goes in the face of everything I've ever believed. He's out all night; you know about his trouble with the police.

Between the cancer and Jonas, the sense of despair can be overwhelming. I miss Alvin, but I'd never say anything. That would only make it harder for him, and it wouldn't change anything."

Dennis' legs were so cramped his muscles were burning. For a minute, he thought they had finished. He was on the verge of returning to his room when he heard TA say, "I happen to believe in the possibility of human restoration, of becoming the person we were meant to be, the person that will make us happy, but it's all tied up with freedom. A person has to choose this restoration for himself. Others can help with advice, and especially example, but no one can make the choice for another person."

"You're an amazing man", Delia said.

TA said, "I'm someone who's learned to take life seriously. I'm convinced that life has purpose and meaning, and it can be discovered."

"Thank you, TA", Delia said. "It's after two. I'm sorry I stayed so late."

"I'm glad you came, Delia."

With the sound of rustling, Dennis darted into his room, but just as he was preparing to lie down, he knew that he had to return to Greg's house. If TA checked his room, Dennis didn't want to be found there. Also, Dennis regretted abandoning Tony, Ben, and Greg on what might be the last night they would spend together as they had done as boys. It was two-twenty when he slid open the window and exited the room.

As he traversed the yards, he had the strangest feeling. Everything in his house and in these yards was the same as ever, but alien too, as if familiar things had been turned sideways. Maybe it was the moonlight, or the unexpected

conversation between Delia and TA, or something altogether different; he was too tired to ponder it.

When he passed through Greg's window he was greeted
by an explosive snore, which provoked a dreamy word
from one of the sleepers. Dennis was back in his bag and
no one the wiser. His last conscious thought was about
Delia's conversation with TA. Her desperation, her fear,
her pitiable plea for Jonas were memorable, but in the
darkness, on the floor of Greg's room, it struck Dennis
that he had learned as many new, and even unexpected,
things about TA as he had about Delia.

18

October 1976

Dennis walked into the front room expecting to see TA ensconced in his reading chair and absorbed with a book. TA was where he ought to be, but he wasn't reading and he wasn't alone.

In the too-small chair by the window sat a bear of a man, well over six feet tall and as sturdy as a lumberjack. The man was unconventionally handsome, having a prominent chin and nose, and big gray eyes. He was clean-shaven this time. Sometimes he sported a beard, sometimes a moustache, sometimes both. There were flecks of gray in his hair.

"He goes and he comes", TA once said of Peter, whom he had met in Marine boot camp. Between that experience and serving together in the Korean War, the two men forged a special friendship, in spite of drastically different personalities and interests. Peter never married. "That doesn't mean he's a saint, or a monk", TA had said more than once. At some point, Peter settled near Tucson, from where he often called TA. For a while, he had a Native American girlfriend. "It's a miracle an Apache and a Cossack haven't killed each other", TA said after one such call.

Dennis supposed that he was the closest thing Peter had to a son. He certainly treated Dennis like a son—hugged him every time they met with that vice of an embrace, kissed him without a hint of bashfulness, and even disciplined him when he thought it was necessary. TA didn't mind; he trusted Peter as he trusted no one else.

Peter Kristov could make TA laugh; not grin or chuckle—laugh. And that was no mean feat. Peter's hilarious stories, most of them containing an element of truth, were legendary. More surprising was that Peter could tease TA. No one else Dennis knew would ever presume to do such a thing.

"You're a foot taller", Peter said, as he rose, rather ascended, from his chair to greet Dennis. "You won't be a runt like your dad. But he runs fast. Remember, TA, the time that girl's brother chased you all the way to the base?"

TA only laughed and shook his head.

Peter could exaggerate, but Dennis knew the man to be honest and dependable, meaning fiercely loyal to his friends. When it came to taking care of himself, on the other hand, TA's friend was less conscientious. On his last visit, Peter had arrived at the house the morning after a festive evening minus his shoes and socks. The fact that there was a dusting of snow on the ground mattered less to Peter than the fate of his Italian-made shoes.

After the usual bear hug and "How the hell are you?" Peter turned back to TA. "Have you heard from any of the boys?"

"I had a card from Paul Paniak", TA answered. "He's living in Las Vegas now."

Peter laughed and said, "That's a good place for him."

TA laughed too. "Remember when he came after you in boot camp and said you could have the first punch?"

"Yeah. He wasn't the smartest guy I ever met. Best offer I ever had."

"He went down hard."

"Like I said, Las Vegas is a good place for him." Glancing at Dennis, Peter said, "This young man is growing up."

"He wants to go to the University of Michigan in a few years", TA said, smiling at Dennis.

"Do you remember me telling you I always had an itch to go north and pan for gold?"

"I remember", TA said.

To Dennis, this had all the hallmarks of another Peter Kristov tall tale, but he knew that playing along was part of the fun.

"I'm thinking of going to Alaska", Peter continued. "They say that's where the best panning can be found. Would you two like to come?"

"It's tempting", TA said, winking at Dennis.

"You bring your toothbrushes, and I'll take care of all the rest." Now Peter reached into his pocket and attached an artificial moustache to his upper lip.

"You're not wearing that thing with me tonight", TA said.

"You carry around a sea horse in a jar. What's the difference?"

TA said, "Just one time, and it was you who put me up to it."

Peter removed the moustache. "I have four of these. I left two at home."

"I wish you'd left them all at home."

Peter beamed a grin at Dennis and said, "Behaving yourself?" Then he put a cupped hand over the side of his mouth that faced TA but said loudly enough for TA to hear, "I hope not."

The big man brought an indefinable élan to the house. He amused Dennis and invigorated TA. Dennis told himself that this particular visit was especially fortuitous. As it was a Friday night, Peter and TA would surely go out and not come home until late.

"Mind if I steal the old man tonight?" Peter said, intruding eerily on Dennis' thoughts.

TA did not wait for Dennis to answer, but asked "Want me to get some food from Zapata's?"

"No thanks. I'll make something here. I'm going to Greg's."

"That boy bears watching", Peter said. "He impresses me as a fast learner."

TA said, "It's been tough on Greg and his brother since Bob Pace died."

"Everything in this life is temporary, TA. You know that. Fortunately, the bad things are temporary too. Sure we can't bring you some tamales, Dennis? Your dad can afford it."

"I'll be fine", Dennis said.

"We'll all go to breakfast," Peter said, then added, "but not too early."

As soon as it started to get dark, Dennis slipped out the side door and made his way to the Pace garage through the backyards. Greg, Tony, and Ben were already there.

"Ready?" Greg said. He put on a black ski mask through which only his eyes were visible.

Ben and Tony were holding their masks, and Dennis had his concealed beneath his shirt.

"Ready?" Greg asked again, and Dennis could sense his friend's impatience.

"Did Cerberus take the food?" Ben whispered, as he stretched his mask nervously.

"Every bit of it", Greg said, not in a whisper. "He likes McDonald's burgers."

The sedative that was added to the burger had been one of the thorniest problems. Ben had worked on it. They wanted to render the animal insensible, but they didn't want to kill it. The Carlsons knew a veterinarian, and Ben managed to find out the right dose without raising undue suspicions. Of the four, only Ben could have managed that part of the mission.

"How long will that mongrel be knocked out?" Tony asked.

Ben said, "I told you he got an overnight dose."

"If he ate the whole burger", Dennis added.

"That's not a problem", Greg said loudly. "I watched."

"Keep it down, Greg", Tony said in a hushed tone.

Greg grinned. "Scared?"

Ben said, "If we get caught, we'll have plenty to be scared about."

Dennis pondered how the mask had transformed Greg into something menacing. In a certain sense, so long as he and the others resisted putting on their own masks, they were not fully committed.

Greg turned to Tony and said, "Did you take your shot?"

Dennis couldn't remember Greg ever talking about Tony's diabetes.

Tony said, defensively, "Mind your own business."

Greg said, "Tonight, it *is* my business; did you?"

"Yeah."

They stood in the dark, as if they were waiting for someone to make the decision to embark. The garage light started flickering; then it went out. They heard a drawer being pulled open. Then, as their eyes were getting accustomed to the dark, they saw Greg's shadowy form replacing the bulb. The new light seemed garishly bright.

"Let's get going", Greg said, as if they had planned no more than a walk around the block.

Dennis put on his mask, then Tony. Taking a deep breath, Ben put his on last. They opened the side door. A large, yellow harvest moon ruled the clear sky. Not ideal for this mission, Dennis observed silently, while knowing that Greg would not let anything interfere with the plan.

"Who thinks it will be in that chair?" Greg whispered as they approached the back fence.

The others were too preoccupied to answer. The walked up the incline side by side. As one, they grabbed the fence cross member and vaulted in an easy motion. That action conveyed them to an older, more ominous, world. Despite the knowledge that Gordie had been incapacitated, each retained a visceral apprehension of meeting that creature in the dark. They followed the line of the grapevines, rounded it, and found the rubbish pile. The turf was lumpy and matted, different from the lawns north of the fence. As they passed the coops, Dennis could hear the chickens; smell them too, reminding him of his and Greg's previous invasion of the Macklin property. Dennis had the irrational fear that Greg would succumb to the urge to break a pane of glass in one of the discarded windows, but his friend ignored them.

The moon was so bright that Dennis could see every step the others took. In every other respect, he told himself, this was a good night for the mission. TA and Peter would be busy. Davey was out with friends; he had reached an age where he might have caused trouble had he learned of their plans. Greg's mom was working late. The Red Wings had a home game. Several hours earlier, Tony had confirmed that he had seen the Macklin car leaving the driveway. Gordie had been neutralized.

"Nothing to it", Greg said, as if reading Dennis' thoughts.

Tony knocked on a tree. Dennis wasn't particularly superstitious, but he didn't like Greg's bravado so early in the mission.

Dennis saw a light in the back of the house, but it didn't worry him. There was no sign of Cerberus. Like a cloud of black smoke, they crept around the side of the house and halted at the corner of the front porch.

A critical moment had come. They all knew it wouldn't do to fumble around at the front door. Not only was there a bright full moon; a porch light also illuminated the front yard. Dennis had the crazy thought that anyone who saw him could see through the mask, could even see through the mask of his face, deeper still.

"Do you have the key?" Tony asked Dennis.

"I'm not an idiot", Dennis said, annoyed that he was asked that question. Still, when he reached into his pocket he felt anxious until his hand closed on that cold metal object. His nervousness was partially vitiated by a keen anticipation.

Would it work? he wondered. Like the business of drugging the dog, the key couldn't be tested beforehand. This was *his* measure, and he had done all he could to be up to it.

Dennis had learned about the skeleton key quite innocently. Ajax, the school janitor had showed him the key one day after Dennis had tutored the man in math. He forgot how he had learned that Ajax wanted to achieve a modest competency in math, but Dennis had volunteered to help him in exchange for free candy and soda from the cafeteria. Ajax was proud of the key. "Opens

every door in the building, even the principal's office",
the man had said intemperately. Ajax trusted and liked
Dennis and was grateful that the boy was helping him to
rectify a longstanding source of shame.

It had been an easy matter for Dennis to palm the key
before he left school on Friday. There was no risk, he
told himself. Though Ajax esteemed the key, he rarely, if
ever, used it. Moreover, Dennis would return the key to
its little box in the back of the drawer before first class
on Monday.

But would it work? He had asked himself this question
over and over, and he had been thinking about it all day.
This wasn't a school door. Since he had purloined the
key, Dennis had tried it, with success, on every lock he
could find. That didn't mean he was brimming with confidence. What if the Macklin lock was too old to admit
the key? He would look like a fool after all their planning.

"Ready?" Greg said.

Greg took their silence for an affirmation. He leaped
the low porch railing and ran to the front door. Dennis
came next. He didn't wait for Tony and Ben. He felt
boxed inside his own world, a world with a keyhole staring at him, a world where a lone night bird piped, where
wood creaked, and where his hands shook.

He used both hands to insert the key into the lock. His
heart thumped when his attempt to turn the key met with
resistance. He remembered Ajax saying that less than full
insertion was necessary with some locks. He retracted the
key an almost imperceptible distance and turned it. He
heard a click and the handle rotated in his hand.

"It's open", he said, with a sense of triumph.

He felt hands slap his back. This is good, he told himself, or why else would he feel so good?

Greg pushed past him and entered the room. He had heard Davey's story about the corpse in the chair so many times that this house had taken on mythological proportions. The light that penetrated the window and the light from the back of the house didn't illuminate the room, but it wasn't dark either. Gordie was sleeping at the rear of the room, from which the hall extended to the rest of this architecturally haphazard structure. The animal didn't stir. Their eyes were immediately drawn to the chair that backed up to the front window.

It was empty.

Dennis took in the rest of the room: a threadbare rug featuring what might once have been yellow roses; an old chair partially covered with a chintz drape; a framed photograph of a young man and woman and two little boys on the rear wall; a barely recognizable nylon dog bone in the middle of the rug; and a hat stand in the hall corner opposite Gordie, with a man's hat placed on the top prong.

"Do you think they moved him?" Greg said.

"Are you joking?" Ben said. "Let's go."

Greg said, "We came to see a body, not an empty room. Maybe they have him stored somewhere."

"I've seen enough", Ben said. "I'm getting out of here."

They heard a sound from the rear of the house.

"Shut up", Dennis said.

Ben said again, more insistently, "Let's go."

"Not yet", Greg retorted.

The next thing they knew, Jimmy Macklin was standing at the end of the hall. It was hard to say who was more surprised. They stared at each other across the room.

Jimmy was wearing red and black striped pajamas, top and bottom. His small feet were bare. A button nose

223

protruded from his nondescript face. It looked as if he hadn't shaved that day, and his hair was uncombed.

"Gord!" Jimmy shouted. The dog might have been the handiwork of a taxidermist, so still did it remain. Apparently, Ben hadn't underestimated the dose.

Dennis felt naked. He had a fear that the masks were useless, that Jimmy recognized them through the fabric.

It happened so quickly that Dennis never remembered who made the first move. Did Tony move toward the door, or did Jimmy run at them? Later, Dennis concluded that Jimmy somehow comprehended that they had done something to Gordie. What other explanation was there for this man, this puny man, to charge the four of them?

Jimmy was within a few feet of Tony when Dennis extended a leg and sent the young man sprawling. Jimmy's head struck the uncovered wooden floor with a loud thump. He didn't move after that. Jimmy looked like a scarecrow that had been blown over by a strong wind. Ben bent over the still form. Greg stood in a crouch with his fists balled, as if ready for a fight.

Then he grabbed Ben's shoulder and said, "C'mon."

They piled out the door, not even bothering to pull it closed, as if an army of Gordies were snapping at their heels. It took less than a minute to reach the fence and only a few seconds longer to get inside the garage.

Ben handed his mask to Greg and said, "Get rid of these things."

Dennis pulled off his mask as if it were teaming with lice. His face was itching and bathed in sweat. Greg stuffed all the masks into a concealed niche behind the workbench as the others moved toward the door.

The wail of a siren stopped them dead in their tracks.

Ben cursed and said, "The cops are here already."

Dennis said, "We can't go outside. They'll stop us for sure if they see us."

"We can cross the backyards", Ben countered.

Dennis said, "Not Tony. He has to cross the street."

"Then Tony can go to your house. We're screwed if they find us here together."

"Why should the cops come here?" Tony said. "They have to be looking for thieves, not kids. We have every right to be here."

Ben shook his head. "What if they find the masks?"

"They won't find them", Greg said. "Nobody ever found anything Davey and I put there; not even Dad."

"He may not have known where to look, but the cops will", Dennis said. "Jimmy saw what we were wearing."

"You're a bunch of queers", Greg said. "I'll bring clothes from the house, and we can all change. Tony and Dennis can wear my stuff, and Ben can wear Davey's." Before anyone could speak, Greg dashed out of the garage. As Dennis, Ben, and Tony stood close to each other, they could still hear intermittent sirens.

Dennis' thoughts were a jumble. He told himself that he would never listen to Greg again; how many times did he have to learn that lesson? He felt a strong urge to open the door and run as fast as he could to his own house. He wondered if he had killed Jimmy.

Greg returned more quickly than Dennis had expected, with clothes draped over both arms. "Put these on", he said. "I'll take your clothes and stash them in the house."

"Is your mom home yet?" Dennis asked.

Greg nodded.

"Did she say anything?" Dennis said.

"She was too tired to notice. She's watching TV."

After they had changed, they all sat on the floor. Greg turned on the radio as if it were an ordinary night.

"How long should we stay here?" Tony asked.

"Hour or two", Greg answered.

Dennis said, "Davey could have seen someone in the chair. Maybe it wasn't Macklin, or maybe the body has been moved since then."

"I don't think so", Ben said. "Do you remember the man's hat on top of the stand by the hallway? Looking into the window from outside the house, the stand and the hat would line up with the chair where Davey saw the body. Actually, Davey said he saw the top of a head, a hat. It's possible that as he looked through that grimy window, the hat on top of the stand appeared to be on the head of someone in the chair. So Davey was telling the truth about what he thought he saw. The part about seeing the corpse's neck was just his imagination adding a detail, or it could have been the fabric."

Dennis shook his head at their stupidity. They'd experienced all the terrors of that night, not to mention the subterfuge, the lies, and the possibility that Jimmy was badly injured, for nothing but an optical illusion.

They all jumped at a knock on the side door.

Tony said, "Don't answer."

"That would be suspicious", Ben said. "They can probably hear the radio." He glanced at Greg disdainfully.

Dennis got up and opened the door. Lori walked past him and said, "I don't like the looks of this. What are you up to?"

"No good", Tony said, laughing nervously. The other three boys were now standing.

Lori started laughing too, then stopped as she looked from face to face. "You're not kidding, are you?" Lori's

226

auburn hair hung below her shoulders. She was wearing some makeup; not a lot, but enough for those who knew her well to notice. Her fingernails were polished a pale, almost opaque pink.

"I'm just kidding", Tony said, in response to a jab from Greg.

Lori said, "You're not kidding. You're not even wearing your own clothes. I'm not going to make you tell me what you're up to, but I know you're lying."

"Believe whatever you want", Dennis said curtly.

Lori flushed, and Tony flashed Dennis a nasty look.

"I can see I'm not welcome", Lori said.

"Yes, you are", Tony said, glaring at the others.

"Of course, you are", Greg said, but not convincingly.

Dennis told himself that what had begun so auspiciously was ending disastrously. A fruitless breaking and entering; Jimmy injured or possibly killed; police on the prowl; the unanticipated anxiety over the masks and clothing; and now this conflict with Lori, which was escalating into a conflict between the four boys.

"There's an ambulance at the Macklins' place", Lori said. She was watching them like a hawk.

Tony's eyes fell. Dennis noticed that Ben was staring past her. Greg's eyes never wavered from Lori's, and there was an ironic, if not forced, smile on his face.

Dennis noticed that Greg's hand was in his pocket, and he was almost certain that Greg was clutching the bone he had found on the island, which had become for him a kind of talisman. Greg had the bone encased in plastic and hung it from a keychain, displaying it when he wanted to amaze or intimidate someone. He had gotten the idea that carrying it was good luck. He was right about one thing, Dennis reflected: they were in desperate need of good fortune tonight.

"You hurt someone, didn't you?" Lori said.

"We didn't mean to", Tony replied.

"But you did something stupid and hurt someone."

Greg turned his back on Lori and walked to the workbench. Dennis followed him.

"I don't want to know any more", Lori said. "I'm leaving."

"No", Tony pleaded.

Dennis wondered if anything could be done to repair the rift. They all stood still, as if waiting for someone to make the first move. Dennis noticed that no one had turned on the light, not even when Lori arrived, but enough of the moonlight pierced the window to make people and objects faintly visible.

Lori said, "Do you want me to do something for you?"

The boys looked at each other. It seemed an honest enough question. "Are the police outside?" Ben said.

She walked toward the door, looked back at them, wistfully it seemed to Dennis, and exited.

Dennis said, "If the coast is clear, we can get out of here."

It didn't take long for Lori to return. The expression on her face, a gray face in the pale light, gave them the answer before she gasped, "The police are parked in the drive."

"Did you see them?" Tony said.

"No ... just the car."

"Let's get out of here", Dennis said. "If they find us together ..." He glanced at Lori and didn't finish. He darted to the door and put his hand on the knob. Simultaneously, there was a knock on the other side.

They were as motionless as five stone pillars, lacking even the appearance of vigor that some statues exude.

Dennis remembered the time when he and Greg had contemplated cutting an opening in the rear of the garage and concealing it, in case they had to make a hasty exit. They weren't even ten at the time and couldn't have imagined something as dire as this.

Another knock, and then the distressed voice of Wanda Pace: "Greg, open this door. I have to talk to you."

Greg pushed past Dennis and opened the door. Wanda's face was red and puffy, her eyes wet with tears. A police officer followed her when she stepped inside the garage.

Dennis wanted to say, "We didn't mean it", but he literally bit his tongue to prevent the words from coming. Wanda seemed oblivious to everyone but Greg, and the officer's eyes were fixed on him too. Dennis heard Wanda's broken voice: "Davey ..." But she couldn't finish. Her misery was so intense that the officer had to grab her arm to steady her.

Dennis took a step toward Greg. Lori's hand found Tony's. Ben was hunched over, shrunken, it seemed to Dennis. A world that had turned upside down with Jimmy Macklin's injury was on the verge of coming completely undone.

"Son," the officer said to Greg in a loud, jarring voice, "your brother's dead."

The mixture of shock and pain on Greg's face made him look like one of those men in a war movie who has just been shot and doesn't yet know he has been fatally wounded. Wanda Pace collapsed sobbing into her son's arms, and the policeman said to the others, "I suggest that the rest of you go on home."

When Dennis entered the kitchen, he found TA at the table with a cup of coffee, looking as though he had been waiting up for him. As if anticipating his son's question, he said, "Peter got a phone call and has to go home tomorrow, so he decided to turn in early."

"Davey's dead", Dennis nearly shouted, despite his effort to stay calm in front of TA.

"What happened?" TA's voice cracked.

"Motorcycle wreck. He was speeding and lost control, went off the road and crashed."

"I have to see Wanda", TA said, abruptly rising from his chair.

He opened the closet door and put on his blue jacket, saying, "I expect I'll be late. Don't worry if you wake up and I'm not here." The man went to the side door and halted. Dennis still refused to look at him.

"Alvin said Jimmy Macklin was injured tonight. Apparently, a gang broke in, and he confronted them."

Did TA want Dennis to object to that characterization of the night's events, to say that no one intended to hurt Jimmy, that they never intended to hurt anyone? He wouldn't say it. He wouldn't betray the others. Dennis meekly asked, "Is he okay?"

"He is not. They hope he'll be able to come home from the hospital tomorrow. Billy and Eroica were at the hockey game, but Jimmy wasn't feeling well enough to go. Strange that the dog didn't make a fuss; a lot of coincidences.

"Anything you want to tell me?" TA asked.

"I'm glad Jimmy is okay", Dennis mumbled.

"I didn't say he was okay. I said he was in the hospital."

Still Dennis did not look up. He wished the man would leave and stay gone a long time.

"Dennis," TA said, with more gravity than usual, "don't be the dog that keeps returning to its own vomit. It makes a miserable sight, and it's bad for the dog."

Dennis heard the door open and close.

19

Day Four

Dennis was driving along the winding road that connected his neighborhood to Ann Arbor when he had to stand on the brake pedal to avoid a darting rabbit, scattering unsecured objects in the backseat. He cursed loudly and pulled over onto a narrow shoulder to compose himself.

His nerves were shot, and not being able to sleep the night before hadn't helped. He had told Marta what was necessary—that Tony had died—and had dissimulated about Greg. Though sensing he was being less than honest, she had not pressed him, knowing well his moods and seeing his grief. Later that evening, she had watched him as he sat with the paper and a glass of wine; he had feared that she was going to ask more questions, but when their eyes met, she had merely smiled and left the room. Dennis yearned for his wife's friendship and counsel, but not enough to overcome his nearly pathological need for secrecy.

Downtown Main Street was late rising and late to bed. A small army of street people shared the territory with university professors, students, bankers, and artisans. Dennis was especially fond of the corners of town that were less visited: the Alexander G. Ruthven Museum, small courtyards and restaurants in Kerrytown, the quiet neighborhoods around St. Thomas Church, and the antiquarian book-stores on Washington Street. But Dennis took no delight in passing through Ann Arbor this morning, and he wondered if he would ever be capable of uninhibited joy again.

The south side of town, the area in the vicinity of Interstate 94, had none of Ann Arbor's highbrow charm. The large indoor shopping mall anchored this side of town and defined its urban-sprawl character and construction, which consisted of modern, nondescript office buildings and national chain stores looming behind huge parking lots.

Dennis parked the Mercedes in front of the hotel and turned off the ignition, but getting out of the car was another matter. Though he had told himself that returning to the scene of their misery was a worthwhile mission, he wasn't exactly sure what to do now that he had come.

The radio was still playing. He turned it off. His chest felt tight; each breath was labored, though he had done nothing strenuous that morning. He was having a hard time believing that, just three days ago, he, Greg, Tony, and Ben had been together in this parking lot and had been anticipating a joyous three days together.

He forced himself to open the car door. Next he had to force himself to get out of his seat. Every act required more will, more conscious effort than when the events of the last few days were unfolding. Then, a kind of combat mentality had taken charge and, with it, the consequent rushes of adrenaline. Also, the more analytical Ben had assumed a leadership role. Without his support and utterly drained by shock and grief, a mist of sadness and lethargy had descended on Dennis.

He walked through the hotel entrance and went directly to the empty lounge. In his mind, Dennis vividly recalled the legless man and his skirted wheelchair. He saw Tony's card house on the now-empty table; he recalled Joseph's visit to their table and Greg's abandoned rental-car keys on the chair.

He wondered if this visit was just self-inflicted punishment for still being alive, while Greg and Tony were dead. He didn't know for sure that Greg was dead, but he felt that he was. He insisted to himself that involving the police wouldn't bring Greg back; and, if Greg had been murdered, he didn't have the energy—not yet—to pursue his friend's killer.

He took the elevator to the third floor and walked down the hallway to the suite. The door looked like every other door in the hallway. Did he really expect to find or learn something here? These halls were cleaned every day; the suites and public spaces too. If something had been left behind, it surely was gone by now.

Left behind, like Greg's car keys. Dennis had picked them up, but where had he put them? Not in his pants pocket with his own keys. He wracked his brain to recall what he had been wearing that night—the fawn suede jacket that Marta had bought him for his birthday. It was still hanging in the back of the Mercedes.

So what, he told himself. Why would Greg leave anything important in a rental car? But he knew he had to see for himself. As he made his way to the parking lot, he made an exterior circuit of the hotel, paying particular attention to the side of the building where their suite was located. As he was staring up at the third-story window, his phone rang. He didn't recognize the number—it was a Detroit exchange—and was tempted to ignore it, but he finally decided to answer.

"Dennis?" the woman's voice said.

"Who's this?" he asked cautiously.

"It's Carly Carlson. Can you meet me? It's important."

Dennis' heart began to pound again. He said, "Is Ben all right?"

"I ought to be asking you that question", she said. "When I spoke to Ben last night, he was distraught about something. When I asked him what was wrong, I couldn't get a straight answer out of him. I'd rather not go into it on the phone. Can you meet me ... please?"

Dennis said, "I'll meet you, Carly, but I doubt if there's anything I can tell you." Defensive walls and deflecting shields were already being constructed in Dennis' imagination.

"So you say", she retorted. "I'm coming from Dearborn. Can we meet at Kellogg Park in downtown Plymouth at noon?"

"All right", Dennis said. That would give him some time to formulate a strategy.

"Thanks. See you then", Carly said and hung up.

He stood there with the phone in his hand, wondering what Ben might have told his sister. He knew that Carly was intelligent, with wits equal to Ben's and more practical cleverness. Dennis made a mental note to call Ben before the meeting with Carly. He was determined to be as prepared as possible.

Looking up at the suite window, he concluded that it would be next to impossible for someone to enter the room from the outside. That wall was in partial view of the entrance and in full view of a side lot illuminated by half a dozen lampposts. Even an acrobat would be taking irrational risks in trying to enter the room by that window. And how would he open the locked window if he reached it?

Dennis had almost forgotten about the rental keys by the time he got back to the Mercedes. They were in his coat pocket, as he had remembered. How long, he wondered, would it take the rental company to start searching for the vehicle? Tomorrow at the latest, he told himself.

Dennis scanned the lot; then he pushed the alarm button on the fob. Loud noise came from a black Cadillac, all by itself in a corner of the lot. As he approached the car, he saw that the plate matched the keys. He looked this way and that, telling himself it was foolhardy to do what he was doing, unlocked the car, and got in. The interior was empty, except for a black portfolio on the floor below the front passenger seat, almost invisible against the black interior.

He picked it up and unzipped it, and a clutch of photographs fell out. There was a professional portrait of Susan that must have been taken a decade or so ago. There were two photographs of Greg's son, David—one as a young boy on a white beach; the other, more recent, with his arm around his father. There was a faded and familiar photograph of four boys and a girl in superhero costumes. And there was a black-and-white photograph of Davey standing next to his motorcycle.

He opened the portfolio. There was a scrap of paper with the word *Jonas* written on it, along with a phone number. He found a receipt from a Hilton in Lagos, Nigeria. The only other item was a catalogue for a fine-wine auction.

Meager content, Dennis told himself. Still, the photographs said something. Greg had kept them close, even on what was supposed to be a three-day trip. And what had Greg been doing in Nigeria? Did that secret life that Dennis suspected Greg was living have something to do with the bizarre events at the Ann Arbor Hilton?

Dennis replaced everything in the portfolio, zipped it up, and exited the car with it. He opened the trunk—empty.

His mind had already returned to the coming encounter with Ben's sister. He had always liked and respected Carly, but he dreaded meeting her when he was in such a fragile mental state. He told himself that he should have pleaded ignorance and resorted to an excuse. Now that he had committed himself, he had to learn what Ben had told her before their meeting in the park.

Dennis didn't think Ben would reveal what had happened, not even to his sister, but he wasn't sure about anything anymore. Before Ben left for Atlanta, he had been emotionally wobbly, something Dennis had rarely witnessed in his friend. If Ben had spoken to the police and to Carly, where did that leave Dennis? He was sure that, at the very least, Ben would alert him, and Dennis hadn't heard a word from Ben.

Dennis walked to the Mercedes, opened the rear door, and tossed Greg's portfolio on the backseat. Once inside, he called Ben. When there was no answer, he hung up and tried again. No answer this time either. He left a message for Ben to call him as soon as he could. He wasn't looking forward to being interviewed by Carly without first hearing from Ben.

Dennis eschewed the freeways and took secondary roads, the route that travelers from Ann Arbor to Plymouth might have followed eighty years earlier. It gave him time to settle, if not compose, himself, and to reflect on what he knew about Carly.

It wasn't uncommon to see articles about Carly Carlson in the Detroit press, or to hear her voice on the radio. Once or twice, he had even seen her on television. She was a marketing executive for Ford. As such, she was also active in philanthropic and society circles. He recalled that he had seen her interviewed after the marathon in downtown Detroit. How impressed he had been by her grace and aplomb, not to mention her athletic ability.

As a girl, Carly had been a prodigious climber, swinging from limb to limb like a young gibbon. Now she was climbing the corporate tree with comparable agility. Dennis hadn't seen Carly for almost a decade, since Jack Carlson's funeral. The photographs and images he had seen more recently depicted a stunning, self-confident woman with short red hair and a splash of freckles that enhanced, rather than disfigured, her appearance. Dennis tried to remember if she was married; he didn't think so, but he seemed to recall that she had a long-standing partner. With her busy schedule and responsibilities, if she was taking time to meet him, it must be an important matter. Ben had told him that Carly was taking a keen interest in his welfare; that would explain her call if she had gotten the sense that Ben was in distress.

When he got out of the car at Kellogg Park, Dennis wished he had taken the trouble to change his now wrinkled and sweaty shirt. He didn't like the idea of making a bad impression on Carly, who was sure to be impeccably dressed. Then he reminded himself that she wasn't coming for a personal or professional visit.

Carly was already standing by the fountain in the park, even though Dennis was a few minutes early. It was impossible to miss her. The statuesque woman wore dark slacks and a green sleeveless silk blouse that dramatically contrasted with her red bob.

"Hello, Dennis", she said, sizing him up in a way that suggested her expertise in assessing a person's quality. "You look warm."

They shook hands.

"Do you want to sit inside? We could have a cold drink in one of the restaurants", she said.

"Suit yourself", he said. "You look great."

"Do you mean it?"

"Of course I do", he said inelegantly.

"That means a lot coming from you. I had a crush on you for the longest time."

Was the comment as ingenuous as it seemed, or was it a means to an end? He knew enough about Carly to be certain she shouldn't be underestimated. He wished he'd tried Ben one more time and told himself that if he got a call he would excuse himself and take it.

"Let's stay here", Carly said, seating herself on a park bench. "I spend so much time indoors that I welcome the opportunity to be outside."

"I don't suppose you want to race me up that tree", Dennis said, still standing and pointing at a large, leafy maple.

"Not today." Then she smiled at him, and he thought it was genuine and sat down beside her.

"How's your mom?" he asked.

"Well enough. She's in Northville. You know that, though. Mom has always had an independent streak; now she can indulge it. Sometimes, when I visit, we talk about the Lincoln Street band of boys—all of you; Davey and Lori too. Tell me something, Dennis. Did you know that my father was an adulterer?"

The question had come out of nowhere. He looked her in the eye and said no.

He thought he saw something like disappointment. She said, "Ben told me that he had confided in you. Your answer helps to calibrate my expectations."

She was telling him that she had established he was a liar. So that was how it was going to be, he said to himself, a contest of words and wits. "I'm willing to stipulate that I'm a liar", he said curtly. "What can I do for you, Carly?"

Dennis heard his own sarcasm and haughty dismissiveness, which had become automatic reflexes whenever he felt threatened. TA had often talked about choices, and Dennis was uncomfortable with the thought that this defensiveness might be a choice.

He and Carly were quite alone by the fountain. The breeze, conveying beads of moisture as it passed through the fountain spray, felt refreshing. Carly did not immediately answer his question, but cocked her head and regarded him as one might an obstinate child.

"You said you talked to Ben", Dennis prompted her.

"I don't want our first meeting in ages to be antagonistic," Carly said, "but I have to know what's going on. I said what I said to get your attention. Now please tell me why Ben was so shaken up when I spoke to him."

Dennis softened a little, but remained on guard. He was unable to separate the tomboy kid sister of his friend and the marathon-running champion of industry who was conducting this inquest. He said, "I saw Ben off to Atlanta yesterday. He must have told you that Tony died earlier in the day, at least that's when we were notified. It's no wonder Ben was upset."

"He was more than upset", she said. "He was evasive when I asked about Greg. Hell, he was evasive when I asked about you. I asked him if there had been some kind of trouble. When he didn't give me a straight answer, I asked him if the police were involved, and he flew off the handle, which isn't like Ben, and hung up. I am very worried, Dennis."

Dennis shook his head. "Why would the police be involved? You know that Tony was a diabetic. It was a hell of a shock. Why read any more into it than that? Ben has known Tony forever. That's enough of a reason for him to be upset."

"Why wouldn't he talk about Greg?"

"You know Greg. He can be vexing."

"Then tell me what Greg did this time", she said. "I'm a big girl. I can handle it. I already know Greg isn't perfect."

Dennis thought that she might have added, "And you aren't either." He said, "You want to know about Greg?"

"Yes."

He said, "Truth be told, he left early, before Tony died. Something came up."

She said, "Does he know about Tony?'

"Of course he does."

"Then you or Ben called him and told him. That means you have Greg's number. Mind giving it to me?"

He said, "Why do you want to talk to Greg?"

"That's exactly what Ben said. Humor me, Dennis."

He said, "I don't have my phone. Give me your email, and I'll forward it later."

The look on her face was a mixture of frustration and sadness. She said, "You had it this morning when I called. If I call your number now, will I hear a ring?"

He told himself he might as well see the bluff to its conclusion. "Go ahead."

She lowered her head and said, "I'm worried about my big brother. He's not as confident as he'd like you to think. Diane's death devastated him. The girls and I are trying to reintroduce him to a world outside of work. It would hurt me terribly to see him knocked down again."

He had an urge to take her by the hand, but under the circumstances, it seemed ludicrously hypocritical. He said, "I'd never do anything to hurt Ben."

"Not intentionally, you wouldn't. But I know your little band of brothers has small and big secrets, has for a long time. You're clams in a row when it comes to these secrets. One time, Ben slipped and let your literary alter ego out of the bag. Don't worry; I've kept it to myself. I'm practiced at keeping secrets too.

"So, is there anything else you can tell me? I'm asking as a friend, someone who has warm feelings toward you. I know I won't be able to pry it out of you if you're determined to hold it back. I guess I'm begging, Dennis."

He could believe it, by the expression on her face. If ever he would have emptied the tub of deceit and torment he harbored, it would have been at that moment. Was it fair to withhold what he knew from Carly, an old friend who had Ben's best interests in mind? He was very close, but he couldn't do it. He said, "We were looking forward to the weekend together"—truth. "When Greg left, we had no idea where he had gone"—lie. "Then, when Tony died, we were stunned"—half-truth. "That's all there is to tell"—lie .

She was watching him carefully as he spoke. When he had finished, she stood up, put her hand on his shoulder, and said, with resignation in her voice, "Fine. I wish you well, Dennis."

Before he could answer, she turned and walked toward the Penn Theater. He watched her get into a Lincoln and drive away.

Dennis' forehead was wet with sweat; his arms and back too. He walked in the opposite direction, found an outside table at the Box Bar and ordered a Stella Artois, but remembering Tony, he called the waitress back and made it a Heineken.

When it arrived, Dennis recalled Tony with a bottle of Heineken to his lips, and Greg saying, "I'm not old. And I'm as strong as an ox."

"And almost as intelligent", Ben had said, causing Tony to erupt with laughter.

But Dennis was all alone, and he didn't feel like laughing.

20

May 1978

Dennis never forgot waking the day of his high school graduation. Right up to the moment when he opened his eyes, he had been immersed in a dream that featured Tony, Ben, Greg, Lori, and Davey. They were playing kick-the-can on a stormy night. One instant, they were eight years old, and the next, they were seventeen, but their aging hadn't inhibited their zeal for the game. Jimmy Macklin had emerged from behind Jonas' old Chevy and kicked the can while Davey was busy pulling a sled down the snowless street. Then Davey approached Lori and held her hand. Dennis remembered searching the street for Tony, but he couldn't find him. A manhole cover rattled as if someone had just pulled it back into place as he entered the sewer. Greg tackled Jimmy and pinned him to the pavement. Dennis heard a siren and warned Greg to get off Jimmy and out of the street, but his friend didn't seem to hear him.

When Dennis woke up, he heard himself say, "Not that." Not what? he wondered as full consciousness returned. He was startled to remember that he was seventeen, not because he wasn't ready to graduate and get out of Terrapin Township but because he felt time had accelerated faster than he could keep up with it.

The day had all the outward appearances of being a typical spring Saturday. He had slept until almost noon, and TA had gone somewhere in the car. He consumed a bowl of cereal and a candy bar in silence and walked aimlessly into the front room. He wondered if his friends' families were already organizing or decorating for a party or family gathering; there would be no such celebration at the Cole house.

He hadn't been staring out the window for long when TA's Buick pulled up in front. The passenger door opened, and Jonas got out. He was wearing his black leather jacket and was smoking a cigarette. He looked as if he wanted to head straight to his side door, but TA must have said something, because Jonas put his head back inside the car and remained there for close to a minute. Dennis was surprised; he couldn't remember any other occasion when TA and Jonas had gone somewhere together.

When the conversation ended, Jonas walked briskly to his house and went inside. Dennis heard the screen door slam. TA continued to sit in the car for a minute or two and then walked to the front porch. Dennis let him open the door.

"Good afternoon", TA said, after examining his watch.

"Where did you and Jonas go?" Dennis said.

"Jonas and I didn't go anywhere", TA said. "I gave him a lift home from the shopping center."

"Didn't he have his own car?"

"He did."

Dennis followed TA into the kitchen, where the man poured himself a glass of iced tea. He recalled the Chevy that Jonas had crashed into the tree. Had the dream portended something real? "What happened to his car?" Dennis asked.

"It's still at the shopping center."

"Is it wrecked?"

"No", TA said. He put the container of tea back in the refrigerator.

Dennis was annoyed by TA's reticence. He said, "Then why did you drive Jonas home?"

"I'll tell you if you insist, but I'd rather not", TA said.

The choices TA gave Dennis could be maddening. This time, Dennis didn't demur. Maybe it was TA's nonchalant approach to Dennis' graduation, or maybe it was the idea of TA and Jonas doing something together; whatever it was, Dennis was determined to get to the bottom of it.

"I want to know", he said.

TA said, "I'll tell you if you promise to keep it between us."

Dennis made a barely perceptible nod and waited.

TA took a long sip of tea and said, "I happened to be in Woolworth's at the same time as Jonas was caught stealing a lighter. I talked the store out of pressing charges."

"How?"

"I told them I've known Jonas since he was a boy. I paid for the lighter. I agreed to take him home with me, and I suggested that I would tell his parents."

"Why did you do that?"

"I thought it might make a difference, to Jonas."

Dennis said, "He's been in trouble plenty of times before." He recalled Jonas' fight with Alvin, something he hadn't told anyone else.

"I know that", TA said.

"When are you going to tell the Pompays?"

"I suppose I should, but I don't think I will", TA said.

"You said you would", Dennis countered, delighted for once to have the moral advantage over TA.

TA said in reply, "I don't think it's the best thing to do. And, in a way, I'm keeping a promise—to Delia—by not telling."

"You're going to let him get away with it?" Dennis was sure TA wouldn't have let *him* get away with shoplifting.

TA didn't look ruffled by the question and gazed at his son. Dennis remembered the night of the Macklin break-in. TA hadn't pressed Dennis for information the way Dennis was pressing now.

TA said, "Jonas didn't exactly get away with it. He got caught. He was humiliated that I witnessed it. I know that Jonas has always looked up to me. And I have the lighter." He removed it from his pocket and with sleight of hand made it disappear, as he had made quarters disappear when Dennis was young. This time, though, the object didn't reappear behind Dennis' ear.

"What time should we leave for the ceremony?" TA asked. He was still watching Dennis.

"It starts at seven", Dennis answered.

"I had our suits cleaned. They're in my closet."

Dennis grudgingly admitted to himself that TA may have given some thought to his graduation, though laundering suits couldn't be compared to a party.

"Your mom would be proud of you."

Dennis didn't know that he wanted anyone to be proud of him. He wanted to graduate and move on with his life. He, Ben, and Lori had been accepted at the University of Michigan. He supposed that Tony would go to work for his father. As for Greg, what he'd do next was a mystery; maybe to him too.

Dennis went in search of TA when the time approached for them to leave for the auditorium. He found him in the basement, his shirt sleeves rolled up several inches, a net in one hand and a probe in the other. He looked at Dennis guiltily and said, "I'll just be a minute. The alkalinity has been spiking."

Dennis walked closer, thinking how odd the two of them looked in that basement in their white shirts and ties. To him, the sea horses looked active enough. The zebra darted from a frondy plant to the opposite side of the tank and anchored itself to another plant with its prehensile tail.

"How does it feel to be graduating?" TA asked.

"Good ... strange", Dennis replied.

TA said, "I remember when they discharged me from the Marines. I had a new suit and money in my pocket. I'll never forget that feeling. Enjoy it."

Staring into the tank, Dennis said, "What do you think will happen to Jonas?"

"I admit it doesn't look good, but there's still hope for him."

"How can you say that? He's always in trouble."

"A lot of people get in trouble. That doesn't mean they can't change, and it doesn't mean they can't learn to make good choices."

"Jonas won't ever change", Dennis remarked, now looking at TA, and recalling Jonas' torture of the frog. "Why did you say you used to be like Jonas?"

"When did you hear that?" TA was gazing at Dennis quizzically, if not suspiciously.

Dennis, feeling chagrined, hesitated before saying, "I don't remember."

"I recognize in Jonas some of my rebelliousness as a young man", TA explained. "I'm not proud of that part of my history, and Jonas isn't as proud of it as he pretends to be. I haven't lost hope for Jonas." He netted the longnose and inspected it up close before returning it to the tank.

Dennis said, "I'm not going to pretend that Jonas can be different. I know him too well."

TA's eyes narrowed, and he said, "There's a difference between hope and pretending, but you've put your finger on something important. Hold this probe for a minute."

TA poured a third of a beaker of milky liquid into the water; then he carefully rolled up his left sleeve and dipped his hand into the water, producing little disturbance. He plucked several blackening leaves from one of the larger plants. Dennis saw one of the sea horses—a pygmy—attach itself to TA's index finger. TA waited patiently until it disengaged before extracting his hand.

"The difference between hope and pretending is there's a reason for one and not for the other. I have hope that the adjustments I'm making in the water chemistry will benefit the hippocampi. I would be pretending if I thought I could make them live forever. Hope relies on facts, evidence, experience, but it goes further."

TA used the net to remove a clump of debris from the surface of the water. "Hand me that probe again please."

TA inserted the probe into the water and looked at the gauge on the wall.

Dennis said, "What's your evidence?"

"Jonas has confided things in me that he hasn't told anyone else. You know about his relationship with Alvin, and you know why it's more complicated than most stepfather and stepson relationships. That's my evidence, scanty as it is, and my reason for hope. Now, we have a graduation to attend. Ready?"

Dennis followed TA up the stairs. TA inspected Dennis' tie and proclaimed him fit. For his part, Dennis was pleasantly surprised at the figure TA made in his navy-blue suit, with a white display kerchief in his breast pocket and gold striped tie. TA's shoes shone like mirrors, and he had taken special care with his razor; he was lacking only a uniform to turn out for review or a parade.

Because they would be seated in alphabetical order, the five friends managed to meet before the ceremony, before they put on their caps and gowns. Lori startled the boys in her flattering dress and pumps. She seemed more comfortable there than the rest of them, though even she looked uneasy.

Dennis was almost sure that Tony was wearing the same graduation suit that Jan had worn several years earlier. Jan was taller than his brother, so Tony was constantly pushing the sleeves off the tops of his hands.

In his jacket and tie, Greg looked uncharacteristically uncomfortable. His girlfriend, Susan Decker, had joined the five friends, and Greg spent a lot of time whispering to her. In his senior year, Greg had done remarkably well academically, not because he was going to college that fall—he wasn't—but because Susan's father had suggested that he was lazy.

Ben was valedictorian of their class, and he conveyed his usual equanimity. Few of his classmates knew that he had purchased a green and white Metropolitan, and that he planned to tour the country in it before going to college in the fall.

After they were seated, Ben was introduced by the principal and gave his speech. It was short but eloquent. While Ben had always been a superior student, he had never been a comfortable public speaker, but he delivered his speech so well that Dennis was convinced that his friend could do anything he set his mind to do. Dennis was the

249

first to stand up and clap when he had finished, and he was sure that Ben noticed.

The principal's speech was neither brief nor inspiring as far as Dennis was concerned. After five minutes or so, the man's words began to run together and Dennis lost touch. When he had finished, the principal introduced a United States senator from Michigan, Ulysses Bridgeman. It was well known that the principal, the senator's cousin, had been working for most of the school year to get the legislator here.

The senator spoke with easy grace and a self-effacing style, contrary to his reputation as a political brawler. "I'm especially pleased", Senator Bridgeman said, "to have my son, Michael, and my daughter, Madeline, here with me tonight. Though they aren't classmates of yours, I invited them to accompany me. You may find this hard to believe, but many senators are fathers too. As you know, I'm often away from home, so this evening was an opportunity to spend time with them too, as I spend time, important time, with all of you."

Senator Bridgeman had the gift, or maybe it was a practiced talent, for making each person in the auditorium feel as if the senator were talking directly to him. Dennis was impressed by the man's style but not so much by his ideas, which seemed to him rather pedestrian and stale. His standards for rhetoric, he supposed, were a fruit of the training he had received from TA, who had bombarded him with challenging ideas since he was old enough to reason. Dennis soon lost interest in the speech, which was the usual graduation pep talk about making a positive difference in the world, until it peaked in intensity at the conclusion with "a life both productive and fulfilling".

When Dennis next looked up, he saw that the senator had been joined on stage by his son and daughter. The man put an arm around each of them with palpable pride. That seemed to Dennis to be the most authentic thing the man had said or done that night.

What would it be like, he wondered, to be Michael Bridgeman, the son of a senator, rather than the son of a factory worker? What couldn't be achieved with such an advantage? The boy next to the senator didn't look special. Pimpled and scrawny, he could be anyone, though his clothes were slick. He hardly noticed the girl, who was some years younger than her brother.

Dennis was so distracted by his own thoughts that the girl in the next chair had to nudge him when it was time for his row to rise and process to the front. Receiving his diploma and shaking hands with the principal didn't deliver the sense of accomplishment and joy Dennis had expected. Many of his classmates were beaming, but he found it hard to summon any emotion except relief.

The auditorium was clearing out, and the Bridgemans had left the stage; but no, not exactly. The senator's daughter, who might have been ten, was still there. With dark eyes and dark shoulder-length hair, the girl was unremarkable except for the intensity with which she scrutinized the audience. Dennis wondered how she could have been left behind and then figured the senator was politicking somewhere.

"Come on", Greg said, interrupting his thoughts, and Dennis followed him and his other friends to remove their caps and gowns and find their parents, who were huddled together outside.

Nervously, Lori explained her mother's absence by saying that she was ill. TA and Betty Carlson looked to be at ease. Magdalena Hulse wore a cheerful smile and a flowery hat that Dennis suspected had accompanied her from the old country. But the rest of the Lincoln Street parents looked as uncomfortable as their children. Tough-on-the-outside Wanda was teary-eyed. Jack Carlson was fidgeting with his keychain. Jan Hulse's hands were folded stiffly at his waist, and his lips were pressed together. Dennis thought he looked as if he might have been at a funeral, so discomfited was his demeanor. After some desultory conversation, the families went their separate ways, except for the Linuses and Hulses, who had planned—probably Lori had planned—to have dinner together.

It had been a day to remember, Dennis told himself, not because it was especially gratifying or joyful, but because he was relieved to put high school behind him. He expected TA to drive directly to the house, but instead, they went north on Telegraph Road and parked behind Zapata's.

"How about a tamale?" TA said.

In their suits and ties, Dennis and TA looked out of place in the almost-empty diner. How different the day would have been if his mother were here, Dennis reflected. What would this day have been like if she had planned it?

Dennis had loosened his tie, but not TA. His tie was intact and centered, and the silk kerchief was still in place. Mr. Zapata set a cup of coffee on the table, along with fresh tortilla chips, salsa, and guacamole.

TA said to Dennis, "You'll be moving to Ann Arbor before long. We'll go to the store for some things. When is Ben leaving on his adventure?"

"Next week."

"Jack and Betty are worried."

"Ben can take care of himself", Dennis said, defensively, but not convincingly. Ben had proven capable of delivering his valedictorian address, but his bicycle mishaps were still fresh in Dennis' memory.

"Johannes was proud of Tony."

"How do you know? He didn't say anything."

"Johannes isn't a talker. He talks with his hands, his tools. He was trying to honor Tony in his own way. Lori looked good, didn't she?"

Dennis said he thought so too. That night, Lori had looked like a woman rather than a girl. Moreover, she had behaved like a woman.

"She's quite a young woman", TA said, stealing Dennis' thought. "Little Wendy has grown up."

"Why wasn't Linda there?" Dennis asked.

"I think you already know the answer."

"It was her daughter's graduation."

"That probably made it harder, not easier. I'm not excusing it, just offering an explanation."

"I think it's disgusting", Dennis said.

"It's an important day.... I wish your mother and brother could be here."

TA had finally said what Dennis was thinking. Seldom in the years since his mother and brother died had the void their loss created seemed so large. Dennis looked around the modest dining room and thought about the many times he and TA had come here over the years. He remembered one occasion when his mother had joined them. He couldn't recall what they had talked about, only that Patricia Cole had seemed out of place here.

Mr. Zapata set the plates of tamales and rice in front of them and refilled TA's coffee. "Salsa good?" he said.

"Sure is, Luis", TA said.

Dennis said, "I miss them too. We let them down. We should have been relentless."

"Relentless?" TA said, cupping his coffee mug in both hands.

Dennis said, "I'm talking about the person who killed them."

"That's old ground."

"It isn't settled ground", Dennis said.

TA said, "Debating you isn't as easy as it used to be. Maybe I've created a monster."

"Are you trying to change the subject?" Dennis said.

TA finished his tamale and said, "What do you intend to do about it?"

Dennis put his fork down on the table and said, "Nothing. You know I had a copy of the police report. In eighth grade, I seduced a girl in Pocahontas County into making inquiries for me."

"Seduced?"

"By mail. It wasn't worth it. I ran out of options, so I gave it up. Does that make you happy?"

"No. It doesn't make me unhappy either. Using people can get to be a habit."

"I learned my lesson", Dennis said.

"Because it occurred to you what you were doing, or because she wasn't useful?"

"Does it matter?"

"It matters", TA said.

"This isn't about that girl. It's about Mom and Andrew ... and justice."

"Justice can't be achieved by injustice."

Dennis said, "The justice I'm talking about involves life and death, and you're worried about a girl?"

"That's one way to look at it: that there are shades of justice, and only the most serious are worthy of concern." TA paused and then said, "There is a ruined millionaire at large on the earth. He promises a lot, but he can't deliver."

For a moment, Dennis thought TA was quoting from one of his books, but TA's impassioned expression dissuaded Dennis from that opinion. TA was admonishing Dennis in that indirect way of his, but Dennis wasn't having any of it tonight. He shook his head and said, "I'm tired. Let's go home."

"Sure", TA said, and he led Dennis to the car. The old car labored, but it finally started. TA looked tired too. It struck Dennis that the man next to him was part of his past. He turned on the radio as they drove down the road.

21

Day Four, Afternoon

Instead of having one beer at the Box Bar, Dennis had three. He managed to eat a burger too, but he had little doubt that he was over the legal limit for blood alcohol when he got behind the wheel. He couldn't make himself go home. Instead, he had an overwhelming urge to return to the place where it all started.

Dennis forced himself to be cautious on the road. When he pulled up in front of the Pace house, he was more relieved not to have been stopped by the police than happy to be there. Happy. Even before the weekend, he wasn't sure he could have said what that meant. Contentment, professional success, a comfortable marriage perhaps, but happiness was another matter. He pushed open the car door. The hot air was oppressive. In spite of the car's air conditioning, he was still sticky from his Kellogg Park meeting with Carly. He couldn't get her misery out of his mind, all the more because he knew what it cost that proud woman.

He knocked on the Pace door repeatedly but got no answer, so he walked around the house to the side gate, opened it, and stood in front of the closed garage door. He didn't bother to look into the garage window as he passed. He went straight up the hill, grabbed the top fence rail, and leaned over. He wouldn't have dared to attempt a vault, even if he wanted to get to the other side, which he didn't. He just needed to be here, in this place, at the locus of so much that had made him who he was.

The trees in the Macklin yard shaded him, and the breeze freshened. He could feel his mind emptying of some of what he had experienced in recent days. Then, as if the vacuum needed to be filled, old memories rushed in. He saw the witch as he had seen her years ago. He saw Jimmy and Billy in the kitchen garden, weeding and hoeing. He saw Gordie patrolling the vast expanse of yard. He saw TA leaning over their back fence, cigarette in hand, before he'd given up smoking after the accident in Iowa.

In reality, there was next to no activity in the Macklin yard; just a few chickens pecking at the ground next to the coops. He neither saw nor heard any evidence of a dog. The vines were overrun with scrub and weeds. If there were grapes, they were too puny to be seen. Looking down the fence line, he saw no trace of the Big Tree, not even the stump he had seen on his last visit to the neighborhood. It dawned on him as he leaned against the fence that it was easy to be nostalgic about a tree, while a couple of hours ago there had scarcely been room in his heart for the woman who had once climbed that tree with him.

There was Betty Carlson's peach tree—though she no longer lived there—not looking especially vigorous. Even fifty feet away, he could see a cloud of wasps surrounding it, something Ben's mother would never have tolerated.

He came through the gate, made sure it was latched— Wanda Pace had always been adamant about that—and walked down the drive.

"Nice car for a Terrapin Township boy", a voice said.

He wouldn't have seen her if she hadn't spoken. The thin gray woman on the Linus porch was sitting in a fraying lawn chair with a glass of iced something on the concrete at her feet. A small black and white cat, not a kitten, was curled into a *U* on her lap.

"I'm not a stranger, Dennis", she said, forestalling his movement toward the car.

He walked to the corner of the porch and said, "Hello, Mrs. Linus."

"Call me Linda, and join me for a few minutes ... if you have time."

Joining Linda Linus was one of the last things he wanted to do. He was good with trees and ghosts; not so good with people, especially someone toward whom he had never been inclined, not because he disliked Linda Linus but because she had been an all-but-invisible neighbor, not to mention a burden on Lori. Without having seen or spoken to this woman for over twenty years, Dennis could see that she had a relentless enemy. Gravity had bent her, twisted her, tugged on her face, especially her cheeks and eyes, had given her the appearance of a birch tree after an ice storm. Age had surely accounted for some of this, but it seemed to him that gravity had singled her out for its conspicuous ravagements.

She got up with visible effort and unfolded another lawn chair. By the curve of her spine he suspected advanced scoliosis. The impression she conveyed to Dennis was that of decrepitude. She had an old bird-like face. Her eyes were the only part of her that seemed alive. Despite the heat, she was wearing an old beige sweater and dark brown slacks. He couldn't help looking from Linda Linus to the beverage at her feet.

"It's just tea", she said intuitively. "I quit drinking in 1992. I've never forgiven myself for missing Lori's graduation. They tell me she looked beautiful."

He didn't know what to say. Had his censorious glance been that obvious? As she stroked the cat, he noticed a hole in the right elbow of her sweater. Neither the admission of her alcoholism nor the hole seemed to affect her tranquility. She said, "Pardon my selfishness in calling you over here. Whenever I see one of Lori's best friends, I can't resist. I'm convinced that something of her resides in each one of you. The only one I ever see anymore is Greg. He visits his mother occasionally. Gregory Adam was a rascal. Not a scoundrel like Jonas, perhaps, but disposed to mischief. I could have watched that boy for entertainment all day long if I'd been sober. The Carlsons and Hulses are gone, and your father, of course. I especially miss him."

"So do I", Dennis said unguardedly. He hadn't admitted that to anyone else except Marta.

The cat purred, and Linda emitted something like a purr too.

"I didn't have many conversations with your father, but some of them were memorable. He stopped to talk to me and Larry when he was walking, especially after Lori died. He never avoided the subject that so many people wanted to dance around. I appreciated that. We both sat with Wanda that night Davey died. My God, that was an ordeal. It put me out of commission for a solid week. I don't know what I would have done without your father."

Dennis said, "He was a deep thinker."

Linda said, "He was more than that. I thought you'd have figured that out by now."

Dennis was sure that Linda's observation wasn't meant as a criticism.

"Can I get you an iced tea or a Pepsi? Sorry, no beer in the house anymore."

"Pepsi, if it's not too much trouble."

When she got up, he remembered her debilitation and almost called her back. The cat jumped from her lap an instant before she began to rise. It took a while but Linda Linus returned with a glass of ice and a can of soda. As soon as she sat down, the cat sprang back up and resettled itself.

It was pleasantly warm on the porch, with the shade the house provided and a little breeze. There was a dilapidated car in the driveway of Jenny Holm's house, a ramshackle structure on a street of now older, but still tidy, homes. He wondered if Jenny was inside and whether she would recognize him if she was.

As if reading his mind, Linda said, "Jenny brings me soup sometimes. It's from the can and I've never actually seen her, but I know. I leave the plastic bowl on the porch at night and it's gone in the morning. We've never said more than a few words at a time to each other. Maybe I'm the only one left, the only one left that unhappy woman doesn't despise."

Dennis saw Linda glance toward the Pace house.

"She's a lot like me really; terribly lonely, but afraid of close relationships."

Dennis said, "You don't impress me as someone who's afraid."

"Not anymore, but for a long time I was. It's a shame we don't get second chances."

Dennis didn't see a trace of life in Jenny's house. The lawn, weed infested, needed cutting. He wondered what

Tony's once-so-familiar house would look like if he happened to step inside it. Another box, with walls and appliances, he told himself; not the home, not the Maggie and Jan and the kids he had once known.

"I didn't think cats liked to be that close to people", Dennis said.

"He's an outlier. There are outliers in every tribe. The house gets lonely. He's a loyal companion."

Dennis said, "Is Mr. Linus still working?" He remembered that Larry Linus had always been a compulsive worker, seeking all the overtime he could get.

"Larry died in 2001. He had been retired for only a year. I'm not one for cautionary tales. Every story is unique. Work was Larry's way to cope with my addiction, Eddie's handicap, and then Lori's death."

Tony must have told him about Larry Linus' death, but Dennis hadn't cared enough to remember; the lapse embarrassed him. He wondered if he had ever met someone as frank as Linda Linus had become.

"Lori liked you", she said.

"Did she ever tell you about the time she doctored my leg?"

"No. Tell me."

He told her, leaving nothing out. Her honesty made him more honest. "It wasn't easy for Lori with the four of us."

"She never complained. Lord, that Gregory was a terror." Linda was looking down at the cat. Tears were coursing down her cheeks.

He said, "Linda, look at me."

She looked up, a premonitory terror on her features. He was sure it was a reflection of what she saw in his face.

"Tony died yesterday."

She shook her head and said, "I'm sorry I called you back. I should have let you drive away. I didn't need to know that. When Lori died, I succumbed to a melancholy madness. Even though I haven't seen him in years, Tony was a lifeline to her memory."

"I'm sorry."

"I am too. More of Lori is gone with Tony. I realize that's selfish and unfair to Tony, who was like a son in those days. It's how I feel. What happened?"

"Diabetic complications. Ben, Greg, and I were with him in Ann Arbor."

"Well ... it will be a long night", she said. "The demons will be out in force."

Dennis looked up and down Lincoln Street and said, "Does anyone play kick-the-can anymore?"

"No, never. How are Greg and Ben?"

"Fine ... they're fine."

"Sure?"

He said, "Tell me something I don't know about TA."

A bee was crawling on the rim of her glass, and two more were pestering them. She pitched the dregs of the tea and the ice cubes into the tiny flower garden that fronted the porch. "TA didn't get on a soapbox, but everyone saw how he behaved when the Pompays moved in—Don't look at me like that. That was 1958."

Dennis said, "I never thought of TA as anyone special."

Her eyes flashed, and she said, "Your father was respected. We knew his history, and we knew him. Alvin was a black man in an all-white neighborhood. I don't expect you to understand what things were like then. That's because of the way TA raised you. Because of the respect we had for TA, there was a lot less antagonism toward the Pompays than there might have been. Give him some credit."

Dennis remembered TA and Alvin going to fix flat tires when neither man's tire looked to be in need of air. It was common knowledge that they enjoyed each other's company, not to mention a beer or two. He remembered TA's respectful words whenever he spoke about Alvin, especially that late night when Dennis had overheard the conversation between TA and Delia.

Linda asked him, "Are you happy?"

"Sure", he said mechanically. He knew he was supposed to be happy, so that's what he told her.

"You don't look happy. I heard you're married. You're not separated, or divorced, are you?"

"No."

"There's no such thing as perfection when it comes to marriage. Sometimes, accommodation is better than the alternative."

He said, "Are you speaking from experience?"

"Yes", she said. "If Larry were here, he'd say the same thing. For a long time, I wasn't a barrel of fun. We persevered."

"Was it worth persevering?"

"I can speak only for myself. Yes, it was."

"That's good to know." He placed the empty glass on the windowsill.

"You're troubled about something", she said, looking at him with penetrating eyes.

"It's Tony", he said.

"You told me Tony died yesterday. If I'm not mistaken, this is an older trouble."

Dennis didn't contradict her.

Linda Linus said, "I want you to take something home with you, even though I'm loath to part with it." She struggled to her feet again. He could see something etched on her face: pain, but mostly resolve. This time, Dennis stood and helped her into the house, but he sensed that to accompany her any further wouldn't be welcome.

The inside of the house was dark; curtains were drawn, and no lights were on. As his eyes accustomed themselves to the gloom, he noticed the indigo brocade curtains, anomalous in an otherwise colorless room. It was cooler than he expected, though she had no air conditioning. There was the odor of an old person fending for herself. He returned to his chair on the porch and waited, looking across the street at Jenny's house. Linda returned sooner than he had expected. She handed a picture to him, sat back, and closed her eyes. Immediately, he knew that it had been drawn by Lori. It was a portrait of TA, little larger than a sheet of notebook paper, oil on canvas stretched and stapled to a wood frame. Someone had covered it with plastic wrap, not recently, but probably not as long ago as when Lori had painted it.

The likeness took his breath away. The image was not of the man Dennis remembered in later years. This was the virile man of Dennis' youth. TA was looking out of the picture, but not at the viewer. The face was paler than the living subject, and the eyes were almost black, instead of gray-green. The unbuttoned green sweater over a white shirt was the only concession to color in the picture. The painting was especially vivid around TA's eyes, and more abstract on the periphery. TA was looking past everyone and everything, at peace, but hardly at rest. His expression was neutral, neither happy nor sad. Dennis could hear Lori's voice across time: "Do you think your father is happy?"

The best of Lori's art was a window, not only to the merely visible, but also to the interior of the subject. Had TA sat for her? One might be inclined to think so, but Dennis knew that Lori produced her pictures from photographs and memory.

"It may be her best work", Linda said.

Dennis said, "Her best painting."

Linda smiled at him and said, "That's right. You always were precise with words."

He thought it was a compliment, but he wasn't sure. As generous as was this gift, he could see it had taken a lot out of her to give it up. He asked himself if he should refuse it, even though he knew it was impossible now that he had seen the picture.

"Thanks", he said. "How many more do you have?"

"Several", she said. "This is my favorite."

"Lori told me she drew Jenny, and that she was working on a portrait of Jonas."

The cat was back in Linda's lap, purring loudly as she stroked it.

She set the cat down on the porch and stood up, laboriously, walked the two steps to where he sat, and ran her fingers through his hair as if he were a small boy. Then she turned her back on him, faced Lincoln Street, and said, "I've learned something, Dennis. A person isn't irrevocably chained. Tormented, surely; but still free to act. The first step toward liberation is to recognize this truth. I'm far from perfect, but I'm living proof that it's possible to change. I may be dragging a chain behind me for the rest of my life, but I can go where I want to go now. I'm not a prisoner. Neither are you."

Linda's words were eerily familiar. He stood up and said, "I guess I'll be going."

"I didn't mean it when I said I regretted inviting you to join me. I enjoyed talking to you, Dennis. Lori liked you, and I always trusted her judgment."

"Me too, Linda", he said, as he took leave of Lori's mother.

22

August 1978

The radio was on, but no one was listening; not really listening; not like they used to; not like that summer night when all four boys and Lori sang "Mr. Tambourine Man" with such gusto.

"When do you move into the dorm?" Susan Decker asked Dennis.

Dennis had known Susan since his freshman year in high school, but not well until she and Greg connected in their senior year. Susan was a beauty, first runner-up for prom queen and with a mind to match. She was as tall as Greg. Her long auburn hair glowed. She had a hawk-like nose and solemn eyes that made her more, not less, attractive. Perhaps her warm smile contributed to her magnetism. Behind Greg's back, word was she could do better. Most knew not to voice that sentiment around Dennis, Tony, and Ben, who nevertheless were well aware of the prevailing view at school. Greg was too, but it didn't seem to bother him. He had never lacked confidence.

"Weekend before Labor Day", Ben answered for both him and Dennis. They were to be roommates.

There was a card table in the middle of the garage with five beer cans on top of it. Wanda didn't mind the boys drinking there unless they got noisy. Dennis figured that TA had guessed he and friends drank beer when they got together, though he hadn't said anything. Perhaps TA thought there were worse things they could be doing. Also on the table was a three-story card house. With another pack of cards, Tony was practicing a new trick, but without enthusiasm.

Dennis was looking out the window, but because of the darkness outside and the light inside, he saw little more than his own reflection.

"Does your dad have a lot of work?" Greg asked Tony.

Tony turned his head but not his body and said, "He's busy enough. I'm helping him remodel an apartment in Dearborn."

"Let me know if your dad needs help", Greg added.

"How's your back?" Susan asked Ben.

Ben walked gingerly to the table and sat at right angles to the card house. "About the same", he said.

Greg said to Ben, "I'd like to kill that idiot. I'd do it too."

Susan cringed, but neither Dennis nor Tony paid much attention. It was just Greg being Greg as far as they were concerned.

Ben said, "I saw Jimmy Macklin today."

Dennis leaned closer to the grimy windowpane for a better glimpse of the Macklin yard, but all he could see was the fence.

"Grapes are ripe", Greg said.

Dennis supposed that Greg had made the first of his annual forays over the fence to sample the grapes, though he hadn't invited Dennis to join him. Greg rarely came to the Cole house, now that he had Susan.

The card house collapsed, and Susan started. "Sorry, Tony", she said.

Greg said to Ben, "When will you have that clown car reassembled?"

Ben didn't waste a second in replying. "That clown car made it to Florida and back this summer. That's farther than your sorry ass is likely to go."

Greg marched toward Ben, and Susan quickly moved between the two. Greg said, "Are you saying I'm stupid?"

Dennis didn't see how Greg could infer that meaning from Ben's words. It seemed to Dennis that this was another case of his friend willfully misunderstanding, which Greg was inclined to do when it suited his purposes. Greg's frustration, always simmering beneath the surface these days, needed an outlet, and Ben was a convenient target.

"He didn't mean it", Susan said to Greg, grabbing his arm.

"Whose side are you on?" Greg snapped.

Now Tony turned around and said, "Lori's been dead for less than a month. She'd be proud of all this, wouldn't she?"

His voice snapped like the crack of a whip. Tony's eyes were turning red and watery, and his friends could tell he was fighting back tears. Lori's heart attack and sudden death had cut all of them to the quick, but it had devastated Tony. All trace of the guileless boy he'd once been had been obliterated. Even the things he used to enjoy doing—the card houses and tricks—he did mechanically, joylessly. In recent years, Tony had learned to be conscientious about his diabetes. Now, his mother had to watch after him and remind him to take his insulin, the way she did when he was ten.

Something had been amiss with Lori's heart from the time she was born, the doctors told her family; small comfort, that. In her grief, Lori's mother, Linda, had

269

become even more invisible. Her father, Larry, was spending more time at home. Devoted to Lori's memory, Tony had been helping out her parents. He'd even taken Eddie for walks around the block, the way Lori used to do.

TA had been somber enough. He had a special affection for Lori, and her death had visibly moved him. Some years back, he had taken to calling her Wendy, a sobriquet he only used in conversations with Dennis. It finally dawned on Dennis that TA saw him, Tony, Ben, and Greg as Lori's lost boys.

The mention of Lori's death altered the atmosphere in the garage; now it was crackling as if with static electricity. Greg snorted at Ben and walked to the workbench.

"Want to help me, Tony?" Susan said nervously, as she sat down in front of the cards. Wordlessly, Tony joined her.

"Have they found the creep who ran you off the road?" Susan asked Ben, who hadn't moved since the contretemps with Greg. It was a subject the boys avoided, or addressed tangentially. The wreck had strained Ben's back severely. He had been in plenty of pain ever since; Dennis knew that much.

Maybe it was because Susan had asked the question, but Ben said more about it than he had to anyone else.

"They haven't found him. It was a truck—dark blue or gray—and only one person was inside . . . I think. He had seen my Michigan plates, been on my bumper for miles. Maybe he was waiting for just the right time and place. He got alongside me and pushed me into the ditch. Next thing I knew, I was upside down in the bottom of a swale. I mean the car was upside down. I bounced around and ended up on the roof. I couldn't move. I knew my back was hurt. Finally, a state trooper showed up and called an ambulance. When they turned the Metropolitan over and towed it out of the ditch, it still ran. Except for the dents, broken windows and headlights, it was okay. Too bad I can't say the same about myself."

Dennis said, "You're alive. You can walk."

"I can walk", Ben said half-heartedly. "My father said it was stupid to go in the first place." Ben shook his head and said, "Maybe that idiot in the truck didn't like Yankees. Maybe his girlfriend ran away to Michigan. Who knows?"

Dennis could sense a wave of despondency descending over them. He watched Tony place the cards with a steady hand and practiced dexterity. Tony let Susan help, even though she was clumsy with cards. Dennis said to Tony, "Is Wim going to Oregon?"

"I guess so", Tony said, without looking away from the cards. "He told Dad that when he's established out west, we can do some building there too."

Ben walked toward the open garage door and nodded at Dennis as he departed. Tony and Susan were so intent on the card house that they didn't notice.

Dennis watched Ben's broad back as he limped down the drive. He had never seen it before, but now he noticed Ben's resemblance to Jack Carlson. A gust of wind—it had been still all night—blew into the garage and scattered the cards.

"Damn", Susan said. Tony reached down, picked up the cards that had blown off the table, and arranged them in a neat pile. He said, "I'm going home." Then, looking around, he said, "Where's Ben?"

Greg crushed a beer can on the floor.

"He could have said something", Tony said, but without rancor. "See you later." Susan kissed Tony on the cheek. When he stepped outside, Dennis saw him glance at the Linus house, at the window of what had been Lori's room.

"Want another beer?" Greg asked Dennis when Tony had gone.

Dennis thought about it and said no. Greg had taken the chair next to Susan that Tony had vacated. She was building another card house, but perfunctorily, and with no particular care.

Greg said to Dennis, "Davey taught Tony to build card houses. Remember?"

With Ben and Tony gone, Dennis was thinking about Greg and Susan. They were an odd couple, a far-from-likely pairing in Dennis' estimation. He himself had no objection to Susan, thought she was good for Greg, a stabilizing influence. Not too many years earlier he would have scorned the notion of someone *stabilizing* any of them. He wondered whether it was graduation, Lori's death, or something more complicated that had so radically changed his thinking.

Greg now possessed a rugged handsomeness, while still retaining a hint of the boyishness that appealed to some girls. He moved with easy grace, not unlike his brother had, but when it came to conversation, grace was not a word that would have been used to describe Greg. He could be loud and contentious, even obnoxious, though his friends made allowances for it. Susan tried to ignore it. For her part, she was smart, upbeat, and confident for so young a woman. Her father was the county sheriff, and her mother taught courses in finance at Wayne State University. Dennis had been attracted to Susan since their first day in French class, but he had been too timid to approach her as anything but a friend. Once Greg had marked her as his girlfriend-to-be, Dennis' friend had set out determinedly to win her, which he did.

Greg retrieved two cold beers from the refrigerator, sat down next to Susan, and put his arm around her.

Susan whispered something in Greg's ear. They both laughed conspiratorially.

Dennis said, "I better get going too."

Greg said, "Stick around", but Dennis knew Greg's tone of voice well enough to recognize that he didn't mean it. Dennis murmured a goodbye and walked into the darkness. The wind that had blown over the cards also carried a misty rain, a warm rain. Dennis could not remember being so confused and anxious. He knew this was connected to all the change he was experiencing, but how to dispel it was another matter.

As he passed the Linus house, he saw that Larry—he thought it was Larry—was sitting in the dark on the porch. The Linuses had no awning, which meant that Larry was getting wet. If Dennis hadn't seen the glowing end of his cigarette, he might have missed him.

"Dennis", the man said softly, in what might have been a greeting or a question. Dennis waved, walked to the bottom of the drive, and turned right on the sidewalk. Across the street, there was a light in the Holm kitchen window. As he walked toward his own house, Jenny stepped out onto the porch and shouted a malediction at him. He thought he heard TA's name too. He wanted to shout back at her, but he was too tired for a confrontation.

The Carlson house was dark. Jack and Betty had been deeply troubled by the attack on Ben and by his debilitation. TA had told him so, and Dennis could see it for himself in their faces. They weren't accustomed to mindless malice. TA was another matter. Dennis suspected he had seen plenty of malice in his day.

There were three cars in the Hulse driveway, and every window glowed with light. The front door was open, with just a screen separating it from the Lincoln Street night. He heard voices as he passed by.

Alvin's truck was in the Pompay driveway, and the side lightbulb, absent a fixture, was lit. As Dennis looked around the side of the house, he saw Alvin, Delia, and Caleb at the picnic table in the backyard. They were sitting beneath a table umbrella; there was a lantern on the table, and Delia held a fly swatter in her hand.

The light in the front room meant that TA was reading. Dennis opened the door and walked inside, feeling an oppressive fatigue. He waited for TA to look up from his book, before Dennis said, "It was a blue truck that ran Ben off the road."

If Dennis detected concern on TA's features, it was quickly gone. TA said, "How is Ben doing?"

"The same."

"I'm sorry to hear it. Sometimes injuries like that take a while to heal. Jimmy Macklin was dizzy for a long time after he was attacked."

Dennis knew that TA suspected his involvement in the Macklin home invasion, as TA sometimes put it. He wondered if TA was trying to humanize Ben's assailant, and even the man who had killed his mother, by this remark. It had the opposite effect. It made Dennis even more bitter, and it widened the gulf that had been growing between them.

"Resentment is a hard master", TA said. He didn't wait for Dennis to answer, nor did he seem to expect it.

Dennis wasn't in the mood for advice. He said, "Jenny Holm called you a bastard."

"When?"

"A few minutes ago, just after she finished calling me even worse."

TA said, "Why did she say that?"

Dennis said, "An old grudge, I guess. She blames me for not giving you her phone number."

"She's not fully responsible for what she says and does", TA said. "You're old enough to understand that now."

"I'm tired of hearing about people who aren't responsible for what they do", Dennis said angrily.

"I didn't say she wasn't responsible", TA rejoined. "I said she wasn't *fully* responsible. I don't suppose living with the choices she's made is easy."

Dennis didn't care that Jenny Holm was miserable. He went to his room and flopped on the bed, still dressed in his clothes. The glow in his window came from the Pompay's backyard. He could hear Delia's voice through the open window, regaling Alvin and Caleb with the story of how she had been an extra in *The King and I*.

"Getting to know you, getting to know all about you."

23

Day Five

Dennis took some comfort in being back in the familiar surroundings of his office. His teaching load was light; just one class and two graduate students. That was good, he reflected, as he felt like a man who had been pitched overboard in the ocean and was clinging to a plank. He had been torn between attending Tony's funeral in Oregon and waiting in Ann Arbor to hear from Greg, or about him. In the end, inertia prevailed and here he remained. Tony's family would be disappointed, but this ordeal had been too much, and going risked questions he wasn't prepared to answer.

Dennis' office featured a heritage bookshelf on the east wall and an enormous old desk. When seated, the entire lower half of his body was hidden by the rich wood fascia on three sides. On the south wall were a series of sashed windows. He wasn't supposed to open them, but he sometimes did. He enjoyed extending his head out of the third-floor office and looking down at the activity in the street.

He placed the picture Lori made of TA on top of the bookshelf, leaning it against the wall. Every time he looked at it, he recognized the *vita contempliva*, rather than *vita activa*. Dennis knew this about TA, but he wondered how Lori had discovered it.

"I have the research contracts, Dr. Cole", Eva Bright said, as she walked into the office. He hadn't spoken to Eva since she visited him and Ben in the hotel. Her business-like words belied the concern he could see on her face, a face he had come to know well, and liked. Eva could be protective of Dennis when she sensed that an administrator or colleague was being mendacious, but she never overdid it, and her professionalism never lapsed. She knew what made Dennis comfortable, and she conformed to that standard. He appreciated that quality and her talent in anticipating his needs.

"Are they ready to be signed?'

"Yes."

"You've looked them over?"

"They're good."

He signed them. "Is lunch with Dr. Foster still a go?"

"Yes, the Gandy Dancer at twelve fifteen. You have a table near the train window."

"Anything else, Eva?"

She hesitated. He could tell she had more to say. He could see it in her eyes. She said, "Have you heard from your friend?"

"Ben?"

"No, Greg."

He admitted he hadn't. He looked down at the work on his desk, hoping that she would take the hint and leave him alone.

"Maybe you should call the police", she said, after several moments of silence.

"Eva, I don't have any reason to believe he's in trouble. If I involve the police, it might embarrass him."

"Don't you think he would have called and told you he was okay?" she said.

Of course, Dennis thought, but he said, "Greg has always been unpredictable ... and impulsive."

Eva, used to a certain order, if not tidiness, in the office, glanced at and then walked toward TA's portrait, above eye level but not so far up as to be inconspicuous. Dennis had wondered how long it would take Eva to notice the painting.

"Who's this?" she said.

"TA", he said, adding, "My father."

"It's very good. Who drew it?"

"A friend." Even with someone he knew as well as Eva, he was reticent to talk about TA and Lori. He had too many regrets.

"Were you close to your father?"

That was a question Dennis had never been able to answer, not even to himself. He said, "We got along."

"I loved my father very much", Eva said. "He died quite a while ago, but I've never forgotten him. I'm sorry about your other friend, Tony."

He said, "I am too. It's hard to accept; hard to believe."

She said, "Sudden death, when you love someone, is a terrible thing."

He suspected that she was talking about her father and agreed, "It is terrible." Then, in a voice that told her he had work to do, he said, "Thank you, Eva."

She gathered the contracts and walked out of the office. He knew that Eva was just trying to help. Her advice had always been sound. He reminded himself that she was worried about him, about the emotional toll of Greg's disappearance and Tony's death. But talking about it would have been excruciating, like peeling off a fresh scab.

His phone rang. It was Susan's number. He had ignored two previous calls, but it was obvious she was going to persist until he answered. And if he didn't answer, she would surely call the police, if she hadn't already.

"This is Dennis Cole", he said.

"Hello, Dennis. You didn't avoid me in the old days."

Her strong voice evoked the image of that beguiling seventeen-year-old girl. "I wasn't avoiding you, Susan", he said.

"You can do better than that, Dennis."

"I haven't heard from Greg", he said, preempting her.

"And you haven't called the police, I bet."

Dennis said, "Not yet." He decided to go on the offensive. "I've been preoccupied with Tony's death."

"I didn't know. The last time we talked, Tony was in the hospital and Ben promised to let me know how he was doing. I guess I don't rate the courtesy of a call when a friend dies. The five of us haven't been that close of late, but there was a time—"

"I'm sorry, Susan", he interrupted her, back on the defensive.

"What happened to Tony?" she said.

"He went into a diabetic coma."

"Had he been sick?"

Dennis said, "If he was, he managed to keep it a secret. He wasn't well Saturday morning, but we thought it had to do with Greg's disappearance."

Susan said, "You didn't see Greg after you left the bar Friday night?"

"I heard him come into the suite; at least, I thought I did."

"But you didn't actually see him", she said.

"No."

"How I wish I could look you in the eye, Dennis. You were never a good liar where I was concerned. Did Ben agree with the decision not to call the police?"

Two women he liked and respected had called him a liar in the past twenty-four hours. "Ben and Tony agreed", he said. "The waiter remembered that he'd seen Greg later that night. Greg was alone, according to the waiter, using some electronic gadget. Then we learned about the Smithsonian and the War College. We concluded that Greg disappeared for a good reason." Dennis didn't dare mention the phone call from the man who refused to identify himself.

"Good reason or no good reason, here's the deal", she said. "You have twenty-four hours to call the police; then I'm going to do it."

"Susan—"

"That's the deal. I don't know what the hell's going on, but I'm going to get to the bottom of it. I may not be married to Greg anymore, but I owe him that much, and I owe our son that much too. If I don't hear from you by noon tomorrow, I'm going to call the police. I'm doing you a favor, for old time's sake. I'm giving you advance warning."

"Okay", he said, but she had already hung up. They—he—had been foolish to believe they could manage this thing themselves. He must talk to Ben, to make sure their stories matched. It struck him that one of the most common mystery-story devices, and one he had used himself often enough, is the failure of accomplices to align their stories. When separated and interrogated, the whole house of cards comes tumbling down. He also realized that this thing had gone on too long for him and Ben to escape censure—if not formal charges—when all the facts were known. They would have to steel themselves and see it through. Dennis was forced to admit to himself that he, Ben, Tony, and Greg had formed a club—no, that was too tame a word—a *cult* of deceit.

When his phone rang again, he expected it to be Susan. "Is this Dennis Cole?" It was a female voice, but not Susan.

"Who is this?" he asked abruptly.

"It's Veronica Carlson. I want to know what happened last weekend." Ben's oldest daughter sounded on the point of hysteria.

"Vera?" was all he could think to say.

"What happened last weekend?" It was an order, not a question.

Dennis said, "What's going on, Vera?"

"My father is dead." She said, sobbing.

"Dead? What are you talking about?"

"He left a note ... said he couldn't live without our mother anymore ... and shot himself!"

Ben commit suicide—impossible, Dennis told himself. He felt as if he were tottering on the edge of an abyss. He was at a loss for words, almost as if saying nothing would make time retreat to what had been before Vera called.

Vera said, "What happened last weekend? We need to know. You don't have the right to keep it from us."

He didn't have the right, but that didn't mean he would reveal more than he had to. If he hadn't recognized Vera's voice, Dennis would have thought it was a sick joke. He couldn't believe what he was hearing. He said, "Sunday, Tony went into a diabetic coma and died. It shook us up, but I never imagined it would affect Ben—your dad— like that. I don't believe it, Vera."

She started crying again. "What did my father say to you?"

What did Ben say? What did any of them say, he wondered, that he could reveal without prompting more questions? All Dennis could think of was Ben's story about the turtle; how could that be reconciled with suicide?

"When?" Dennis asked.

"Yesterday." Then all he could hear was her weeping.

"Is someone with you, Vera?"

"Yes, we're all here."

"Does Carly ... does your aunt know?"

"My sister called her."

How long would it be, Dennis wondered, before he heard from Carly? She might be on her way to Ann Arbor as they spoke.

"She's coming to Atlanta today", Veronica Carlson said.

"Is there anything I can do, Vera?"

"Nothing", she said. "No one can do anything." The phone went dead. Dennis could barely think. He didn't believe in coincidence, yet he refused to believe that the deaths of his friends were connected.

He called Eva Bright. "Cancel my lunch, and get Marta on the phone." He sounded curt; it took so much energy to speak. He couldn't wait to talk to Marta, but when he heard her voice, he didn't know what to say. She knew that Greg had vanished, and she knew about Tony. He had told her that much, but only Dennis knew that he, Tony, and Ben had seen Greg in the room with a plastic bag over his head.

"What's wrong, Dennis?" Marta said to him.

He said, "I just got a call from Vera Carlson. Ben killed himself."

"No ... when?"

"Yesterday."

"Dennis, what happened last weekend?"

"You know everything I know."

"I doubt it. I never have", she said.

"I called to tell you about Ben, not to be interrogated."

"I'm sorry about Ben and Tony", Marta said. "I'm just trying to make sense of everything. Are you going to Atlanta?"

"I haven't decided." He had decided. He wasn't going anywhere. All of a sudden, Dennis' sense of personal peril was overwhelming. If the evidence wasn't incontrovertible, it was compelling.

Marta said, "What could have made Ben do such a thing?"

"Vera said he left a note saying that he was depressed about Diane. I suppose Tony's death pushed him over the limit." Even as Dennis said this, it sounded like so much sophistry.

"You don't believe that", she said. "Ben isn't the type; he's anything but that type. Do you want to tell me anything else about Greg?"

"I haven't heard from him."

"Aren't you worried?"

"I'm worried, but what the hell can I do about it?"

"You can call the police", she said.

"I could", he said.

"Then let them call you. They will soon enough", Marta said impersonally. Then, her voice changed and she said, "I'm so sorry, Dennis."

"What's happening?" he said.

"Do you mean to say you don't have any ideas?"

"I'm too mixed up to have ideas."

"When are you coming home?"

"I don't know."

"Come home now."

"I can't. I have work to do."

"Work", she said scornfully. "You may not have ideas, but I've had an idea."

"What is it?"

"Goodbye, Dennis." She hung up.

What had he expected Marta to say? Naturally, she would want to know why a rational man like Ben would kill himself. Didn't he have the same question?

Moments later, Eva Bright paged him. "What should I tell Dr. Foster?"

Dennis said, "Tell him it's an emergency." He couldn't go into it again with Eva, not after the conversations with Vera and Marta.

He had to get out of the office. Never before had this room felt so claustrophobic. He left his jacket and waited at the campus bus stop, oblivious to everything around him, and too distraught to drive. His mind was reeling. He thought again about Ben's story about the reptile on the beach and his friend's determination not to perish like that animal. That was the Ben Carlson Dennis had known. But the notion that Ben may not have killed himself turned his blood cold, because murder was the only other explanation. This alternative was so unthinkable that Dennis had to consider the possibility of suicide. Hadn't Ben been home, in Atlanta? Hadn't he left a note? Hadn't he suffered many emotional hurricanes? Wasn't he in chronic pain? But the nagging question Dennis couldn't dispel was this: How could a man so bent on responding to setbacks with fortitude have shot himself a day later?

He disembarked from the bus at the transit center, with its gull-wing overhangs, in front of the Alexander G.

Ruthven Museum. The neo-Renaissance building housed the university's collection of paleontological, natural-science, and Native American displays. Two life-size recumbent pumas in black terrazzo flanked the entrance doors. He had never been able to walk through those doors without experiencing a sense of renewal. This time, he would settle for a brief respite from misery.

As he had expected, it was cool and silent in the two-story lobby, with its walls of polished marble and its gray and pink marble floors. It was TA who had introduced Dennis to the museum. He remembered how he had lost himself in the dioramas of prehistoric Earth, with TA's disembodied voice supplying a gentle commentary. Dennis took his time; no one bothered him—that was one of the things he liked about the place. Uncon-sciously, he had sought a place where respite—what passed for respite—could be found. He began to breathe deeper, and the shackles on his thinking were loosed. When his phone rang, he almost let it go to voicemail, but the unfamiliar number compelled him to answer.

"Is this Dennis Cole?" the voice said.

"It might be", was Dennis' cautious reply. He didn't recognize the voice.

"I spoke to your friend about Gregory Pace."

"So?" Dennis said defensively. He couldn't help won-dering if this man was a cold-blooded killer, an assassin. Had all of this mayhem proceeded from Greg's clandes-tine occupation?

"So Ben Carlson is dead now", the voice said.

Dennis' chest tightened. How did this person know about Ben if he hadn't been personally involved? "That's news to me", Dennis said, with all the resolve he could muster. "What do you want?"

"I want you to tell me the truth about Gregory Pace. That business might have something to do with the others."

Dennis said, "Ben told you everything we know. And if Ben is dead, as you claim, how do I know that you aren't responsible?"

"You are taking the news of your friend's death well. Why are you lying?" the man said.

"If I'm lying, I have a good reason. I don't know who you are or what you're up to."

"Greg and I were colleagues ... and friends."

Dennis couldn't ignore the man's reference to Greg in the past tense. "Greg and I have been friends for fifty years", Dennis said.

"I know that. Perhaps I can help you."

Dennis said, "What's your name?"

"Believe me, my name wouldn't mean anything to you. What if I told you that after Greg left the hotel, he—or his body—was moved to the street outside your office building, and was then moved to North Territorial Road west of Ann Arbor?"

"How do you know that?"

"I have it on good authority."

"Then tell me if it was Greg, or his body."

"What will you tell me in return?"

Dennis said, "You seem to know everything about Greg ... and about us, and I don't know anything about you. I'd say you have an unfair advantage."

"You're an engineer. You've heard of electronic implants, haven't you?"

"I have."

"And global positioning systems that can locate devices that emit signals?"

"Of course."

"Then put two and two together."

"You're saying Greg had an implant and that you tracked him after he left the hotel."

"That's right."

"Was the implant removable?"

"Only by someone who knows what he's doing."

"Could Greg have removed it?"

"Greg was someone who knew what he was doing", the man replied.

"Are you in Ann Arbor?" Dennis said.

"Yes."

"Were you at the hotel when Greg disappeared?"

"I was."

"But you don't know what happened."

"I have ideas."

"Care to share them?" Dennis said.

"Not yet."

"Whom do you work for?" Dennis said.

There was a delay; then the voice said, "The government."

"CIA?"

"No", the voice said. "This isn't getting us anywhere. You know more about Greg; tell me. We both want to learn the truth."

This was more than Dennis could stomach. What was truth anyway? He hung up, put the phone in his pocket, and wandered to the rear of the museum. He was all alone there with his heartbreaking memories of Greg, Tony, and Ben. In the shadow of the giant raptor, the shadow of a far-distant past and his own, he bent his head and wept.

24

May 1980

It was abnormally warm and sultry for Memorial Day. There were low gray clouds that threatened rain. Lawn chairs of differing colors and patterns made a circle on the Pace driveway, with a cooler in the center. On a separate card table were bags of potato chips, popcorn, and the remnants of several peach pies that Ben had brought in lieu of his mother and father. There were plates on the ground next to the chairs, with early flies helping themselves to the spoils. From somewhere on the Macklin property, Gordie was barking.

Wanda went in and out of the house to replenish the beer and snacks. She was a large-boned, muscular woman with big callused hands, almost as tall as TA. Her hair could be described as graying blond. She wore a tent-like gray and green checked blouse that draped over old blue jeans. When she sat, she took a chair next to TA, though they seldom conversed away from the shop.

Since starting college, Dennis had not seen much of Wanda, and it struck him, as it never had before, that Davey's death had diminished her. Exteriorly, she was still the strong, acerbic woman he had always known, but the inner spark that once powered her wit and words—the mischievous amusement that used to seep from her eyes and mobilize her mouth—was missing. Now that Greg had joined Dennis and Ben at the University of Michigan, Wanda was alone more than ever, and that too was taking its toll.

TA had arrived last and walked around the circle, shaking hands. Bareheaded that day, he looked young for fifty-one, in spite of his wartime experience and years of factory work. As TA aged, his sunken eyes and hawk-like nose had grown more prominent, but he had managed to stay trim and virile enough to do what he wanted to do.

Tony had brought along Eddie Linus, who was having difficulty getting a potato chip into his mouth. Tony reached over and guided the boy's hand. "Drink some soda", he said to Eddie, lifting the can with a straw from the pavement.

Wanda was watching her brother Adam and his friend Sebastian from Chicago. "Does your friend *do* anything?" she asked.

Adam winked at Greg and said, "He does well enough, sister."

"He's lovely", Wanda said cheerlessly.

"That means my sister approves", Adam said to Sebastian. Then he said to Wanda, "Sebastian is an actor."

"Of course he is", Wanda said, emptying the dregs of her beer can on the lawn.

Tony said to Adam, "Were you really in a boat inside a sewer?"

Sebastian looked at his friend and raised his eyebrows theatrically.

Adam had a friendly face and a ready smile with exceptionally bright white teeth. That day, he wore a pink silk shirt, gray pants with fine navy pinstripes, and burgundy loafers without socks. He had big rings on both his forefingers, one with a red stone and the other with a blue one. On his head was a gray beret. "I was very young," Adam said about his job as a sewer inspector, "and I needed the work. It was a horrifying experience, I assure you."

Tony said, "Cockroaches?"

"Everywhere. Thank God the little beasts were on the walls and not in the water. And the rats—you can hardly imagine."

"Unpleasant", Wanda said.

"It was dreadful, sister."

"How you stank", Wanda remembered. "How he stank, Sebastian."

Adam said, "That experience convinced me that I was meant for the theater."

"How big was the sewer?", TA asked.

"Thirteen feet in diameter, built entirely with bricks. Very old."

"How big were the cockroaches?" Tony asked him.

"As big as my ... my hand", Adam said, giggling at Sebastian.

Adam turned to TA, saying, "Wanda says you're a philosopher."

"Hardly. I have no formal training."

Adam pressed him. "You studied at college, didn't you?"

"For a while."

"Formal studies are overvalued. Give me talent and passion."

Sebastian said, "Hear, hear" and went for another beer. There were already three cans next to his chair.

Adam said to TA, "What is your philosophical lodestar? Are you a religious man, or are you an advocate of freedom?"

290

"Both", TA said.

"I didn't think that religion and freedom were compatible", Adam said. "Don't you agree that each man must decide for himself what will make him happy?"

TA took a sip of beer. He pursed his lips and seemed to be staring past Adam. Dennis knew that look. TA said, "People make choices, but there are consequences that can't be chosen. What may seem at first to produce happiness can bring misery. Making choices calls for discernment, and discipline. Sometimes, the right choices are counterintuitive, and inconvenient."

"It smacks of repression to me", Sebastian said petulantly. "Those pernicious inhibitions have bowed many a promising man."

TA looked Sebastian in the eye and said, "Repression is a poor caricature of virtue."

Sebastian smirked and said, "I hadn't taken you for a moonbeamer."

TA said, "If you're accusing me of caring about things that can't be seen or heard or touched, I plead guilty. If you are suggesting that my interests aren't grounded in reality, you are wrong. I've been splattered by reality more than once."

Adam looked as if he was following the debate between TA and Sebastian with delight. He said, "But what is reality? *Id est*, let's say you own a hunting dog that has no interest in hunting, and no aptitude for it. This dog is fascinated by birds, but seems to have no instinct for chasing them. Should the animal be made to hunt?"

TA grinned at Adam and said, "Maybe the dog should not be *made* to hunt, but it's still a dog, not a bird. It ought to be the best dog it's capable of being."

"Perhaps it should have been a bird", Sebastian said.

TA said, "Perhaps it was meant to be a dog, but different from other dogs, for a purpose."

"What might that purpose be?" Adam asked him.

TA said, "It depends on the dog"

"A Terrapin pedagogue; a most unlikely breed to be sure", Adam said. "Even if one is inclined to be virtuous, it's my experience that virtue is more attractive as an abstract exercise than a practical discipline. I can't quote chapter and verse, but it's that willing spirit and balky flesh thing. For myself, I am averse to the passionless life, despite the urgings of polite society, and sister."

"For God's sake, Adam, this is a picnic, not a theater", Wanda said.

Adam Zelinski looked at his sister, not unhumorously, and said, "This is not an act, sister. This is the real me."

"You can be annoying, Adam. Can't we talk about the weather?"

Sebastian said, "It looks like rain to me."

"Oh my," Adam said, "isn't that Jonas Ratigan bounding toward us?"

Dennis had been so intent on the conversation between TA, Adam, and Sebastian that he hadn't noticed Jonas and his brother, Caleb, coming down the sidewalk. Jonas opened a chair and placed it next to TA. He looked around the circle apprehensively. When his eyes rested on Adam, it seemed to Dennis that Jonas regarded Greg's uncle as a frog that needed to be pinned to something. Caleb sat on the Pace lawn outside the circle. Dennis was amazed at how he had grown. Caleb Pompay, at thirteen, was as tall as Dennis and thirty pounds heavier. He was square-headed like his father, but he had his mother's bright eyes.

TA shook Jonas' hand, and Wanda passed him a beer. "How's your mother?" she said.

Jonas took a long drink before he said, "That's what I came to tell you. Alvin took her to the hospital last night."

"When?" TA said.

"Late . . . early in the morning . . . maybe two o'clock; it was still dark when he came into my room and said they were going."

Wanda said, "Have they called you?"

Eddie Linus began to groan. His upraised hands were twitching. Tony reached over and clutched one of his hands, which quieted the boy.

"Not yet", Jonas said.

"Do you want me to go to the hospital?" TA said.

Jonas shrugged.

"Let me know as soon as you hear", TA said. "Are you still cabbing?"

Jonas nodded and went for a second beer. Once he had erupted with his news, it was as if he had nothing else to say. He was evidently uncomfortable in this gathering.

"Where are you driving?" Wanda asked Jonas.

"I have the Detroit-Airport run. Everyone's in a hurry."

"In a hurry chasing their tails", Adam volunteered.

"Or someone else's", Wanda added, *sotto voce*.

Greg didn't get his hand up quickly enough to prevent expelling beer from his nose and mouth.

Adam said to Sebastian, "I must write sister into my next farce. What wicked wit!"

"Let us know if we can help", TA said to Jonas.

"I think she's dying", Jonas said plaintively. No one contradicted him. Even TA was at a loss for words. Jonas got up and walked down the driveway with the beer can in his hand. Caleb followed him like a big puppy. For all the animosity between Jonas and Alvin, Dennis reflected, Jonas still accepted Alvin and Delia's son as his brother.

Tony put an arm around Eddie, who had begun to groan again. Eddie Linus had aged but was still small, and his cramped limbs made him look even smaller. His features were rigid, like a mask; in spite of this affliction, Dennis recognized Lori's eyes and nose. Eddie had long hair the color of roasted corn. He wore a stained white sport shirt and gray shorts, with sandals on his feet.

Dennis heard thunder. All eyes shifted from Eddie to the other side of the street when a front door opened and Jenny Holm emerged. She walked—unsteadily, it seemed to Dennis—across the road and sat down in the now-empty chair next to TA. Wanda Pace looked scandalized, Adam and Sebastian delighted.

She was wearing a mint green miniskirt and a black blouse that revealed the greater part of her breasts. Her eyes looked cloudy to Dennis. Makeup and carmine lipstick had been applied liberally, but hurriedly, or carelessly. She wore a string of costume-jewelry pearls around her neck. Dennis noticed several gaps where beads were missing. Only her luscious golden hair was a reminder of how beautiful Jenny had once been.

She whispered something in TA's ear that made him blush. Dennis knew from firsthand experience that Jenny was bold, but he hadn't expected public effrontery. Dennis saw that Ben was smirking at Jenny's comedic attempts to insinuate herself into TA's affections. TA's and Dennis' eyes met, and Dennis saw the caution in TA's expression.

"How are you, Jenny?" Adam said. "May I introduce my friend Sebastian?"

A sinister smile appeared on Jenny's lips, and she looked across the circle—triumphantly, it seemed to Dennis—at Wanda Pace. "Pleased to meet you", Jenny said to Sebastian. "I'm very well", she said to Adam. "Love your beanie."

"It happens to be a beret, but thanks for noticing", Adam said, giving the cap a pull.

This new development, Jenny's arrival, reminded Dennis of when Tony added one card too many to an unbalanced card house. Wanda's eyes burned, and her lips were clenched. "May I have a beer?" Jenny said. Even a simple question, coming from Jenny, carried a false note.

"Must you?" Wanda replied.

"Oh yes, I must. Give me one for TA too." Jenny looked at TA and said, "Or would you prefer to share mine?"

Seeing TA's cautioning expression, Dennis kept the caustic comment he was considering to himself. When she handed the can to TA, Jenny stroked his hand with her fingers.

Eddie raised himself on his canes and crept around the circle until he was standing between, and slightly behind, TA and Jenny. He gazed at the woman and then self-consciously turned his head and wiped the drool from the corner of his mouth on his sleeve. He said something to Jenny, but she ignored him.

"He said your hair is pretty", Tony translated.

Jenny ignored Tony too, sipping her beer, then whispering something to TA. Adam had the look of someone who yearned for pen and paper. Tony got up and walked toward Eddie, but Wanda said, "Let him be. He has a right to enjoy himself too. Everyone else is."

TA turned in his chair and asked the boy who was almost a man, "How's school, Eddie?"

Eddie's head jerked up and down, and he grunted before he said, "Good. I like school." But TA's tactic of changing the subject had not deterred Eddie, and he spoke again to Jenny. This time, the woman turned her head and said something in return. TA's disapproval was evident, and Adam must have heard too, because his supercilious smile dissolved.

Wanda said to Jenny, "Where's your boyfriend, the one who comes after dark? I invited him too."

Jenny glanced slyly at TA.

"Not TA", Wanda said. "He's allergic to spiders."

"I don't bite", Jenny said coyly. "Have you ever considered makeup, Wanda? It might help. Then again—"

Wanda stood up. Dennis worried that she was going to pounce on Jenny, but mostly he was distressed for Eddie. Wanda pounced all right; she said to Jenny, "How are your children? It's been ages since I've seen them. They aren't lost, I hope."

Jenny dropped the half-filled can of beer on the pavement. The golden liquid made a small rivulet as it meandered between Dennis' feet on its way to the street. Jenny's hand was shaking, and rage contorted her face. She stood up and said, "You stupid bitch."

Jenny Holm stormed through the center of the group, pushed between Dennis and Greg, and almost ran across the street, as her upset beer can and Dennis' rolled down the driveway in tandem. She entered her house and slammed the door.

"Atrocious manners", Sebastian said, winking at Adam. He wasn't looking at Wanda, but Dennis suspected that Adam's sister was included in Sebastian's verdict.

Adam, having regained his aplomb, said to TA, "A person would have to be endowed with an excess of *le force vitale* to keep up with that houri."

"*Le force macabre*, I should say", Sebastian piped.

Dennis glanced at Greg, who winked at him. Ben seemed fascinated by the spectacle. It was hard to say what Tony was thinking; he was watching Eddie with concern.

"I'm sorry", Wanda said, but it was abundantly clear that she was sorry for her guests' discomfort, and not for what she had said to Jenny.

Eddie Linus was the only one who appeared to be unaffected. He said something that sounded like "good riddance" and made his way back to his own chair. So Eddie understood what was going on around him, despite his debilitations, Dennis noted. Why did that surprise him; hadn't Lori suggested as much?

TA broke the silence. "Today's the day for remembering."

"Memories can be treacherous", Adam said. He looked at Wanda, whose owl-like features were expressionless.

"Will you let me buy you a new hat?" she said to her brother.

Adam said, "Perish the thought, but thank you, dear."

Dennis felt a raindrop, and TA must have too, because he looked up at the darkening sky and said, "That hat may come in handy soon. As for memories, good and bad, they are part of who we are."

"And what if memories wreck you?" Sebastian asked scornfully. "My father is an Air Force general. Try to imagine my memories."

Looking at that iconoclastic young man, now wearing a sad expression, Dennis tried to plumb such a relationship. "Destruction can be creative too, if it's properly understood", TA said.

"Bah", Adam exclaimed.

TA said, "I choose to remember—and to honor— Bob Pace, Lori and Davey, Patricia and Andrew," he gazed long at Dennis and continued, "fallen comrades, a certain Chinese soldier, and lots of others. They all contributed to who I am now."

"Did people you know die in Korea?" Greg asked, surprising everyone except TA, who just nodded.

The rain came. TA and Adam helped Wanda move the cooler and snacks into the house, and Greg and Ben folded the chairs. Dennis saw the pain still etched on Sebastian's features. He said to Dennis, "What a gig you've got."

Dennis got to the front door before TA. He looked up and down the street. He remembered.

25

October 1981

Dennis, Greg, Tony, and Ben were alone in the bar on Washington Street. Dennis and Ben were beginning their fourth year at the University of Michigan; Greg his third. Tony was working full-time with Johannes in the family business but spent a lot of his free time with his friends in Ann Arbor. The beer was cold, and it came by the pitcher; no food was served, not even chips or popcorn, which didn't bother them.

The place was equipped, if you could call it that, with mismatched wooden tables and chairs, a poorly constructed bar that separated the proprietor from the customers, and one serve-all restroom. There was hardly room on any of the walls for another line of graffiti. The wood floor was littered with the detritus of carry-in snacks. The ceiling panels, perhaps to hide the staining, were painted black. The bar was cold in winter, hot in summer, and damp when it rained. The only concession to décor was a University of Michigan flag nailed to one of the walls; even this had been a depository for graffiti.

It was the anniversary of Davey's death.

"Is Susan coming?" Dennis asked Greg.

"She hates this place, and she's mad at me."

"It's a tradition", Dennis said. "She ought to know that by now."

"She knows. It doesn't matter."

Ben stood up, stretched, and said, "My back hurts like hell."

Another pitcher of beer descended to the table. Greg immediately filled his glass, then the others.

They were all drowning in their individual miseries that night. For his part, Dennis fumed, as he often did, at the people who committed the heinous acts that irrevocably changed the lives of so many, and then went on with their own lives as if nothing had happened.

Tony, pouring himself another glass of beer, said, "Do you remember when Davey snuck up on us that night in the tree house?" He laughed but no one else joined him.

Dennis figured that it must have taken Davey an hour to paint his face that night.

"It was funny at the time", Tony said.

"It isn't funny now. It wasn't your brother that was killed", Greg said to Tony.

Tony said with passion, "Have you forgotten Lori?"

Dennis hadn't forgotten Lori, but he didn't have anyone to blame for her death, except God. His antipathy was directed at the man who had killed his mother and Andrew, and the man who had run Ben off the road. "What gets me is that there are people walking around, free as hell, that shouldn't be", he said.

"You're right about that, brother", Greg said. He drained his glass and refilled it.

"I wonder if we could find that bastard that ran you off the road", Dennis said to Ben.

"Then what?" Ben said, shaking his head.

"Then we make him pay", Greg said.

"It won't fix my back."

It struck Dennis that their association produced little joy anymore. Greg's bitterness about Davey's death hadn't diminished over the years; on the contrary, it had grown like a cancer. Ben had chronic pain; he was not so much aggrieved as weary. Ben, Dennis, and Greg managed to get good grades, in spite of drinking too much and smoking pot when they could get it. Tony was hard to read. He had always been quiet, but his silence had been companionable once; now he was just as likely to be uncomfortably sullen. He never dated, hardly showed any interest in Susan's efforts to pair him up with her friends. What these four now shared was a common animus toward the world, an emotional entropy.

"This place is a dump", Tony said. "Why do we keep coming here?"

"For the beer", Greg said slyly, "and the rustic charm. And no one bothers us."

"We could stand to be bothered once in a while", Tony said.

"I'll tell Susan you said that. Next time she finds you a girl, do something about it."

"Let's take a drive", Dennis said.

"One more pitcher", Greg countered.

"Okay, one more", Dennis acquiesced.

Greg said, "The beer will do Ben good. Look, no more pain."

Ben shook his head and said, "Promise?"

26

Day Five, Late Afternoon

Back in the office, Dennis was preparing to go home, knowing he would have to face more of Marta's probing questions. He opened his desk drawer and brought out the Glenlivet, poured himself a few fingers of the golden liquid and raised it high in a silent toast to Greg, Tony, Ben, and Lori. As an afterthought, he raised the glass to the picture of TA. Then he returned the bottle and the glass to the drawer and packed his briefcase. He had just stood up to leave when there was a knock on the door.

"Come in", he said wearily.

The man who opened the door was slight, but he had a big head. His eyes were watery, and his bulbous nose was pink at the end. His face was carelessly shaved, especially beneath the chin. He had a crop of thick gray hair that he had attempted to brush, but with uneven success.

"Yes", Dennis said, not discourteously, but not in a welcoming way either.

"I'm Lieutenant Jones. I'm with the Ann Arbor police."

Dennis wondered if alarm registered on his features. Something told him the man in the doorway would recognize it. With all that had happened, he had known it was just a matter of time before the police contacted him.

Still, a flesh-and-blood policeman at his door stirred strong emotions.

"I wonder if you'd answer some questions, Dr. Cole."

Dennis sat down and waved the man to the wooden chair on the other side of his desk. He didn't like long conversations, especially with loquacious academics, so he had selected a less-than-comfortable, slightly unbalanced chair from a second-hand store to promote short office conversations. The policeman sat down on it as if he was oblivious to any lack of comfort or to the tepid welcome. "Lieutenant Jones", he repeated. "You live in Barton Hills."

Dennis thought that a reply was expected and said, "I do."

"Nice houses there. My wife likes to drive through at Christmas. She likes the decorations."

Dennis wished he had had more of the Scotch.

"You know why I'm here." It was a statement rather than a question, and it confirmed Dennis' initial impression that this man wasn't someone to be trifled with.

"I think I do."

Jones said, "Your friend Gregory Pace is missing; isn't he?"

Dennis said, "I don't know that for a fact. I know that he left our hotel suddenly last weekend."

"Tell me what happened."

Dennis told him what they had told everyone else: that they thought Greg had returned to the room after they had gone to bed and that he was gone the next morning when they woke up.

The man listened, and he watched Dennis. "That's your story, Dr. Cole? Did he leave a note? Surely, he wouldn't go without leaving a note."

"No note."

"Did he call?"

Dennis hesitated before saying no.

"Perhaps he sent an email."

"No."

"When someone is murdered, it's dangerous to lie, even if you're innocent. I don't recommend it."

Dennis said, "Do you think I killed Greg? He's my friend. I told you he vanished from the hotel. We came to suspect that he was involved in covert government work."

"I didn't say you killed him. I said it's dangerous to lie in a murder investigation." Lieutenant Jones leaned toward Dennis and smiled. "I enjoy your books. Never would have guessed that Henry Drake is a Michigan professor."

Dennis wasn't about to let this man unnerve him. He wondered if this was a subtle hint that the police were investigating him.

Jones smiled slyly. "I've been told your friend had the libido of an alley cat."

"That's not true." Who could have told him this, Dennis wondered.

"He didn't like the ladies?"

"I didn't say that."

"What did you say?"

Even though Dennis was convinced that Jones was trying to provoke him, he could not help succumbing to resentment, anger. He had to restrain himself from resorting to sarcasm. "What do Greg's peccadilloes have to do with the police?"

"Pace's peccadilloes, as you put it, may have something to do with what happened to him. They often do."

"My friend wasn't an alley cat, *as you put it.*"

Jones studied Dennis for a moment before saying, "You should know we ordered an autopsy on Anton Hulse."

If this policeman was trying to rattle him, that was the wrong approach. Dennis forced a smile and said, "Tony had diabetes since he was a boy."

Jones said, "Have you traveled in the last two days, to Atlanta, by any chance?"

"I have not", Dennis said. "That should be easy enough for the police to verify."

"Do you know that your friend Benedict Carlson is dead?"

"His daughter informed me. You probably know that too." It stung Dennis' conscience to hear himself speak about Ben with a kind of Scroogish economy, the way Dickens' "man of business" had spoken about his ostensible friend and partner, Jacob Marley.

"You don't think these three deaths are coincidence, do you?"

Dennis said, "Greg disappeared; I have to take your word that he's dead. Tony was sick. According to his daughter, Ben committed suicide."

"That's one interpretation. Weren't they your best friends? You are doing an admirable job of keeping your composure. I have to ask you a question: How safe do you feel?"

Dennis shrugged and smiled. Inside, he was panicked.

Jones said, "The four of you grew up in Terrapin Township."

Dennis said, "So we did."

"You've met regularly since you went your separate ways."

Their long friendship had been reduced to that bloodless summary, but he had to play along. Dennis said, "We have."

"Have you ever been in business together?" Jones asked, blinking and wiping his eyes with a dirty handkerchief.

Dennis shook his head. Why hadn't Eva alerted him to Jones' visit?

"Did anyone owe anyone else money?"

Dennis said, "I didn't owe them any money, nor did they owe me any. I can't speak for the others."

"Were the four of you ever involved in something that might account for these deaths; anything at all?"

"Never", Dennis said, more forcefully than he had intended, and more forcefully than necessary. He was sure that Jones noticed.

"You're a scientist."

Dennis corrected him: "Engineer."

"You've heard of forensic evidence."

Dennis nodded.

"If there's evidence that Gregory Pace came to a bad end in that Hilton suite, we will discover it. The maid service isn't that efficient. One drop of blood is enough. It would be better to hear it from you before we learn it for ourselves."

Dennis said, "I don't expect you to find anything." But he didn't believe it; he was treading water. He hadn't seen any blood, but he knew that this policeman wasn't bluffing.

"Things are being analyzed as we speak. Do you want to amend your story, Dr. Cole?"

How could he? He was determined to tough it out for as long as he could. "No", he said.

"You're a successful man: a professor, a famous writer. It wouldn't do to get wrapped up in a murder if you don't need to. I'll give you one more chance. Do you understand me?"

"Perfectly", Dennis said.

The man shifted in the wobbly chair. Dennis could hear the legs tap against the tile. The policeman, with his deft questioning and subtle threats, was giving him an opportunity to reveal more, but not everything. Dennis told himself that walking this tightrope was his best chance to survive this ordeal with his reputation intact.

"Here's what happened", Dennis said, trying to stay as composed as possible. He told the policeman about finding Greg, and then returning to the room and discovering that he was missing.

"Why didn't you call the police?" Jones said, but not accusingly.

Dennis, fully aware that the tightrope had no net beneath it, said, "We thought it might have been a stunt. You didn't know Greg."

"But you were sure he was dead when you saw him on the bed."

Dennis said, "I thought so at the time, but later I wasn't sure. Neither were Tony and Ben."

"It's convenient that they're not able to corroborate that story", the man said, matter-of-factly.

"If you wish", Dennis said peevishly.

"Did you touch anything?"

"I removed the plastic bag."

"Were there any signs of violence on the body? Was the head battered? Were his hands bloody?"

Dennis said, "No. I'm not an expert . . . but no."

"Was the room disturbed?"

"No."

"Were Pace's things disturbed?"

"We didn't notice anything before we left the room. When we returned, all his things were gone. That made us suspect that Greg was behind it."

"Was the door locked when you got up in the morning?"

"I'm sure it was. The door wasn't open, and it locks automatically."

"Was the dead bolt engaged?"

"We couldn't remember. Tony said he would make sure the door was bolted the next night."

"Why, if Pace was pulling a prank?"

The more Dennis talked, the more this man learned.

When Dennis didn't reply, Jones said, "Did the others remark on anything else that happened that night?"

"No."

"No one admitted to hearing anything during the night?"

"That's correct."

"Is it possible that Anton Hulse or Benedict Carlson killed Gregory Pace?"

"It's not possible", Dennis insisted.

The lieutenant ran his hand through his gray hair and said, "If Carlson killed him, perhaps he was so remorseful that he killed himself."

"Like I told you, it's not possible."

Jones stood and leaned forward. His flabby face was close to Dennis'. Jones said, "How could someone enter a locked room and suffocate your friend without one of you hearing something?"

Dennis said, "I don't know. That's why we were doubtful that Greg was really dead when we returned to the room."

"Hmmm. You told me you haven't heard from Gregory Pace since then."

He could feel the vice tighten. "That's right."

"And you chose not to contact the police."

Dennis said, "I told you, we thought that Greg might be working for the CIA, or one of those alphabet-soup agencies. I grew up with Greg. He was a daredevil. He took risks. We thought he worked for the Smithsonian.

We learned he'd left that job years ago. We also learned that he was affiliated with the War College."

"So you conducted your own investigation. Why involve the police?" If Dennis hadn't known better, he might have taken this as a conciliatory remark, rather than another warning.

Dennis said, "That's not the way it was." It annoyed him that he was trying to wheedle something like respect from this policeman. In spite of all his success and accolades, he was that self-conscious Terrapin Township boy again.

"Who decided the police shouldn't be called?"

It would have been easy to accuse Ben or Tony, but he couldn't make himself do it. "All three of us. We didn't think it was necessary."

Jones said, "Why would Carlson commit suicide?"

"His wife recently died. Maybe he was despondent."

"Did he seem despondent to you?"

"I'm not a psychologist", Dennis said.

"You interviewed a waiter and a bartender at the hotel. What did you learn?" Jones asked him.

"Nothing. I'm sure you already know that. Wait ... we learned that Greg possessed some high-tech gadgets."

"That's better", Jones said.

Dennis said, "Do you believe me?"

Jones said, "I haven't made up my mind. You might be a murderer, and then again, you might be someone who needs to lock his door. I think you're a good liar."

The lieutenant took a step toward the door.

"Gregory Pace was married once; wasn't he? What was the woman's name?"

Had Jones talked to Susan? The policeman's face was impassive. "Susan", Dennis said.

"Have you talked to her since he died, or disappeared?"

"Yes."

"This isn't a courtroom, Dr. Cole. What did you and Susan Pace, I should say Decker, talk about?"

"We were trying to learn what Greg was up to."

"It was unwise to keep all this from the police."

"I suppose so."

"Hmmm. I wish you hadn't killed Leander Kelly off. I liked him, and he was a good detective", Jones said, turning and leaving the office.

You might be someone who needs to lock his door. Dennis didn't think he had an enemy in the world, certainly not someone who wanted him dead. If Greg had an enemy, and if his business was espionage, another spy might have killed him. Tony's enemy was the disease in his veins. Ben's enemy must have been a well-concealed despair. He didn't need to lock his doors; he needed this craziness to stop. At least now he could tell Marta what he had told this policeman without worrying that she would be at risk too.

The police had questioned Christine and Jorge; probably the maid too. He had done the right thing in admitting to what he had seen. The samples might produce something, even if he hadn't observed any blood. Jones seemed to be convinced that Greg was dead; what else did he know?

Instead of going home, he traversed Ann Arbor and parked in back of the Hilton. He had succumbed to an urge, an emotional compulsion. He knew it was risky, but he owed Greg, Tony, and Ben his best. As soon as he entered the dining room, he saw the waiter. The man saw him too, and walked away. Dennis wasn't having any of it. He caught up to the waiter and grabbed his arm before the man could escape into the kitchen.

"Remember me?" he said.

Jorge looked weary, but resigned. "Yes", he said.

"You've spoken to the police."

The waiter said, "Of course."

"I'm not here to cause trouble", Dennis said. "You know how to reach the police, and they know how to reach me. I want to ask some questions."

"Sí", the man said, warily. It was not lost on Dennis that he had reverted to his first language.

"We asked you if our friend had met anyone, if you noticed anything after the three of us left the bar."

"I told you everything I remembered."

"Was there anything that happened before we left the bar? Did you see anyone speaking to our friend? Was there anything you can think of that seemed odd?"

"No ... I'm sorry." Dennis released his grip on the man, and Jorge walked through the kitchen door.

Dennis was almost out of the dining area when he heard the waiter's voice from behind him.

"Wait."

Jorge had regained the self-confidence that Dennis was used to seeing in the man. "There is one thing I can tell you. It was probably nothing at all, but it seemed strange at the time. A man approached your table while the four of you were outside. You were gone for ... what, ten minutes? I thought this man was a member of your party. He sat in one of your chairs. After a few minutes, he got up and left."

"Was he writing something, a note?" Dennis asked eagerly.

"I could not tell. I was not paying such close attention. I thought he was known to you. He behaved perfectly natural."

Dennis said, "What did he look like?"

"He had a short beard... He was not so tall ... and he wore a jacket."

"What color jacket?"

"Dark blue, I think. I am not sure. It might have been black."

Dennis said, "Was he young or old?"

"He was not an old man, but as to his age I cannot tell. I had no reason to suspect him."

Dennis wondered if this man had left a message for Greg. But if that's what the stranger did, how could the man be sure Greg would find it, and no one else? Or was this just a convenient table for the man to bide time for a few minutes, something that had nothing to do with Greg?

"Do you remember where this man came from and where he went?" Dennis said.

Jorge said, "There is only one public entrance to that room. I didn't see him enter, but I presume he came that way. I saw him get up and leave. He went out the door as if he was in a hurry."

This wasn't much, Dennis told himself, but it was the first thing he had learned that might be connected to Greg's disappearance, or death.

"Did you serve the man in the wheelchair that evening?" Dennis said.

"Yes", Jorge said, with a smile. "He told me he was from Baltimore. It is not common to meet a man who comes to Ann Arbor for frogs."

"Was he still seated when the bearded man came to our table? Did he ask about us, or Greg, our friend?"

"I don't remember if the frog man was at table then. He did not ask me about your friend, or any of your party."

"Was the man with the chair staying at the hotel?" Dennis said.

"He charged his meal to his room."

Dennis said, "When did he leave?"

"The following day, I think."

"You noticed nothing that might connect him to our friend?"

"No . . . when your friend was working in the alcove, this man was reading in the common room across the way."

Dennis said, "So the man would have seen Greg leave the alcove."

"It is possible."

As Dennis drove home, he wondered how much of this information was just background noise and how much of it, if any, had meaning?

Some of the properties in the Barton Hills area of Ann Arbor boasted stunning vistas of the Huron River, and Dennis' home was one of these. The house wasn't overlarge, but it had been well built and occupied by its architect for thirty years before Dennis acquired it. The designer had an eye for the synthesis of earth, stone, and wood. Dennis and his wife weren't so close to the river that they had an unobstructed view in summer, but in winter, early spring, and late fall they could see the water clearly from a promontory on their property. They wouldn't have been able to afford the house on Dennis' university salary alone. Cole Porter Palmer had provided the added income to make the acquisition possible.

The car in front of the house was unfamiliar; then Dennis noticed that it was a rental.

Marta greeted him at the door, but before he could ask about the car she handed him a Fedex overnight package. The label identified the sender as Benedict Carlson.

Marta's features told the turmoil she was experiencing; not so much anguish as apprehension. Dennis sat in the nearest chair and tore into the package. It contained a short letter:

Dennis:

I'm sorry for everything. For killing Greg and for having the body moved. For Tony's death. For intending to kill you too. You could say that our HISTORY caught up with me. I couldn't find the strength to finish the job.

Ben

The world had officially gone berserk. Ben a murderer? But here was a letter from Ben, sent from Atlanta on the day he died. And what's more, a knowing letter: "our HISTORY". Could such demons have resided in Ben all these years without Dennis, Tony, or Greg knowing it? Was this person he'd known all his life capable of killing his best friends?

Dennis looked at Marta, who was looking at him with pity. She had an interesting, if not beautiful, face, an ideal tableau for a range of emotions and expressions. Her mouth was wide. Her face was wide too, her nose small. She had long, thin brows arched atop oval green eyes.

"Everything's wrong", he said to her.

"We're still here."

He said, "Are we? I can't be sure about anything."

"What is it?" Marta said.

"Ben confessed that he murdered Greg and Tony, and that he had planned to kill all of us."

Marta shook her head vigorously and said, "That's crazy."

"Crazy, and apparently true. Read it yourself."

Marta took the sheet of paper as if it were unexploded ordnance. She sat staring at it for a long period before saying, "Do you believe this?"

"I would never have believed it", he said, "if not for the last five days. Now what can't be true is, and what is true cannot be." He was exhausted, weary beyond measure.

At that moment, a man stepped into the room from the kitchen. Dennis had forgotten about the car in front of the house. He recognized the man immediately, even though the visitor was much changed from the last time they had met, at TA's funeral. Dennis looked at Marta, who met his eyes with something like defiance. So this had been the *idea* she had suggested on the phone.

When the man spoke, his voice was still strong. "I'm sorry to hear about your friends, Dennis. I remember them well, all of them."

Peter Kristov's wizened face startled Dennis. He couldn't be well, Dennis told himself. As he walked toward Dennis, Peter's steps were tentative. He said, "Marta called me. Of course I told her I'd come."

Dennis bristled; what business did Marta have calling Peter? He didn't need another father; he needed explanations. How was a man who couldn't keep up with his shoes supposed to make sense of what was going on?

In spite of Peter's fragility, his eyes were still bright and lively. His hair was completely grey, almost white, but still thick. The closer he approached, the more Dennis remembered, and the happier he was to see his godfather. Dennis saw the silver chain that was attached to the dog tags beneath his shirt. As he reached out for an embrace, Dennis saw bruises up and down the old man's arms.

Peter's eyes followed Dennis'. "I'm still a rough, tough, hard-to-bluff Marine. Don't let these bruises fool you. I can still whip you if I need to."

Dennis smiled and said, "I guess you can. Can I get you a beer, or a glass of wine?"

"I'll have a beer. I don't drink that sissy stuff. You remind me of TA. That's what happens when you get old. Give me a hug."

Peter Kristov enfolded Dennis in his arms, as he had when Dennis was a boy. Marta had been right to call him, Dennis realized. "Now, what the hell is going on?" Peter said, clutching both of Dennis' shoulders at arm's length.

"It seems that Greg, and maybe Tony, were murdered by Ben. Did you hear me talking to Marta?"

"Every word", Peter said. "What does your gut tell you?"

Dennis said, "I'm an engineer. I'm not much for guts."

"Neither was TA, but he could dig deep when he needed to. What does your gut tell you now? Did Ben kill Greg and Tony?"

"No", Dennis whispered. "I don't know how to explain this, but Ben said some things last weekend that would be absurd if he were guilty."

Peter said, "Ben was an unlikely candidate to go off his rocker. I know that much. How do you know that Ben wrote the letter?"

"I don't know; but if he didn't, then who did? I have a reason for believing that Ben wrote it."

"Someone else could have written it", Marta said.

"Someone else couldn't have written it", Dennis contradicted her. That statement proved that he was losing control, that he'd been buffeted beyond his limits. The expedient path would have been to accept Marta's explanation; doing so would prevent the inevitable demand for an explanation. Something had prevented him from taking the expedient path.

"Would you explain that?" She looked and sounded frustrated, and that wasn't like Marta.

"I can't."

"I'm your wife. This is Peter."

"I can't", Dennis said again.

"Dennis", she said pleadingly.

Peter interrupted her and said, "I fought in a war. I know something about things that can't be said. One thing I've learned over the years is, it can do some good to get it out, but I also know that getting it out has to come in a person's own time. Dennis, Marta invited me here to help, and I don't intend to leave without doing some good."

Dennis said, "What good can you do? There's no bringing any of them back."

Peter looked not at Dennis, but at Marta. "Sometimes, you have to hunker down in the foxhole and hope the hell passes by. And you're not dead yet, Dennis", he said to his godson.

"What do you mean by that?" Dennis said.

"No more, or less, than what I said."

Dennis had forgotten to get Peter the beer he had offered him. He walked to the refrigerator, using that time to try to compose himself.

While only Ben could have written the letter, it was impossible for Dennis to believe that he did. Nothing in Ben's past—and Dennis knew as much about it as anyone— suggested an inclination toward violence, or madness. Ben had not gone after the man who ran him off the road. Diane's death had produced profound sadness, but not depression or despair, much less his coming unhinged. On the contrary, Ben had always been the most rational of their group. Dennis brought back three bottled Harps.

"This isn't a sissy beer, is it?" Peter said skeptically.

"Not atall, atall", Dennis said, affecting a brogue. Leave it to Peter to provoke some needed humor.

Peter took a long pull on the beer and said, "Were any of your friends in distress when they arrived in Ann Arbor?"

"Everyone seemed fine. The first night we were all in great spirits. I could read Tony, Greg, and Ben like open books; at least, I thought I could."

"And yet", Peter said, as a district attorney might have done, "Ben was supposedly planning to murder all of you; and none of you, lifelong friends, suspected anything. But you still think Ben composed the note. It doesn't add up."

Peter had circled back to the thing that couldn't be explained. Dennis walked toward the kitchen and said, "Let's eat." Then he asked Peter, "How long can you stay?"

"As long as it takes", the man said. "I brought my toothbrush and an extra pair of shoes. I'm not about to let you get yourself killed—for Marta's sake."

Dennis said, "You're always welcome, but I don't need your help."

"*I* do", Marta said.

Dennis looked at his wife; then he let out a mournful sigh.

"Out with it", Peter said.

"You won't like it."

"I don't like a lot of what I've heard tonight. I didn't come to Ann Arbor for fun."

"Is my mother dead?"

"What kind of crazy question is that?" Peter asked.

Dennis had watched Peter carefully as he posed the question. The only thing he had detected on Peter's features was concern.

"Patricia Cole has been dead for forty . . . forty-five years. You know that as well as me."

"What is this all about, Dennis?" Marta said.

"I received an anonymous letter three years ago. The author claimed that Patricia Cole was still alive."

Marta said, "Why didn't you tell me?"

He couldn't meet her eyes, but he could feel them boring into him.

She said, "So instead of talking about it, you've kept it hidden, pent up. No doubt, that's what the author wanted. For a smart man, you're a fool."

He wasn't used to hearing that from Marta, but he could tell she'd been hurt by his not confiding in her.

Peter said, "I went to the funeral. I could have told you that three years ago if you'd asked."

"Did you see her?"

Peter frowned and said, "I'm giving you a pass because of Greg, Tony, and Ben. You're so shaken that you don't realize you're asking me if your father was a liar. He was the best man I ever knew, Dennis. Your father was on heaven's picket line; had been for a long time."

"What do you mean by that?"

"You figure it out. You're smart."

Dennis said, "Why would someone send me that letter?"

Peter said, "You have an enemy, or TA did, or there's a lunatic that needed an outlet for his madness. Did you receive any more letters?"

"No." Unspoken was Dennis' apprehension that the letter might be connected to what had transpired in the past week. If the same author wrote both letters, who else could it be but Ben? But if that were the case, Ben would have been certifiably crazy for the last three years. Nothing made any sense, but there was nothing more that Dennis could confide in Marta and Peter.

"Have I ever lied to you, Dennis?" Peter asked him.

"No."

"Your mother died in that accident. Your dad—what he did and said afterward—was living proof of that. All you had to do was open your eyes and ears."

Dennis saw that Marta was now regarding him with pity rather than frustration. She walked over to him and took his hand, and Dennis was relieved to have her support—and Peter's. Perhaps the time had come to lean on the only two people he could trust.

"You've delayed supper long enough", Peter said to Dennis. "I may not be as smart as TA, but I'm smart enough to eat when I'm hungry. Where's the chow, you punk kid?"

27

May 1999

The visitor turned into the neat grounds and followed the drive to the single-story building. He was shown to a clean, simple, and uncluttered room. It was as if TA had been preparing for this room all his life.

The man in the room was propped up in the bed. A book lay open on his lap, but his eyes were closed. The visitor dragged one of two chairs in the room to the man's bedside, and whispered, "Are you comfortable?"

"Most of the time", the man answered, opening his eyes. "How are you?"

"Good. Fine. Is Peter still coming?"

"He called. He's having his gall bladder removed in a few days. They won't let him travel for a week or so. I guess we're both coming unglued."

"Peter will bounce back. He always does."

"No one always does, but I think Peter will be okay. How are things going?"

"Fine. Good."

"Have you heard from Tony, Greg, or Ben?"

"I spoke to them last weekend."

"I hope I wasn't the reason."

"They'd like to see you. They all told me that."

"I'd like to see them too, but I don't like the idea of turning everyone's life upside down."

"You deserve it ..." He had come as close to saying *Dad* as he ever had.

"Thanks, but that's not the way I feel. Guess who stopped by last night."

"President Clinton?"

"Not yet." TA managed a smile. "Jonas."

"How is he?"

"Not great. We had a nice visit. I've always had hope for Jonas."

The visitor almost said that the man in the bed was the only one who did.

TA had not asked about the hippocampi, and Dennis would not bother to tell him that all but two had died. He hadn't asked Dennis to look after the animals. Jonas had been recruited for this task. Surely, TA knew that Jonas wasn't up to the challenge.

Dennis said, "Anyone else come yesterday?"

"It was like Grand Central Station, but I'm not complaining. Your Uncle Thomas and Cate Hulse visited earlier in the week. I was happy to see them, especially Thomas. Wanda and Alvin stopped by last night. Alvin wanted to break me out, said we needed to change a tire. I told him my tire-changing days are over. Marta came in the morning. She brought me soup and cake, even though I've told her not to bother, since I don't eat much. The priest came in the afternoon. He gave me the sacraments."

"Are they taking good care of you?"

The man in the bed closed his eyes. "Very good."

"Is there any pain?"

"None ... not much. It's been a great ride. Some bumps, but I've let all that go. I'm privileged to be your dad. It seems a good time to say what I hope you know."

"I do know."

"Make sure you tell Marta I ate every last drop of her soup, but don't tell her I skipped the cake."

"Okay."

"Be good to Marta. Don't take her for granted." The man opened his eyes, as if for emphasis.

"Sure."

"How's the book coming? I could use a good mystery story right about now."

"Slow. The quality has to be there. You taught me that."

"I did? I seem to be drifting off. I'd hate to fall asleep in mid-sentence."

"Don't mind me. It's not as if I've never seen you sleep."

"I guess not." The man closed his eyes again and extended a hand. The visitor took it, observing that now the strength resided in his hand.

"*Semper fi*", the man in the bed whispered.

The visitor looked down at the dying man, his father. "*Semper fi*", he said.

28

Day Six

Dennis went to the office that day for one reason and one reason only: to convince the police, if they were paying attention, that he was unperturbed by their suspicion. Otherwise, he had no motivation, no spark of interest in his work. Marta and Peter had tried to talk him out of it but hadn't been successful. He had left them at the kitchen table with their coffee. The sun was bright, and the air was warm. Cars and people traversed North Campus. He hardly noticed. He ascended the stairs to the third floor and entered his office.

There were his reference books, including those he had co-authored; there his degrees and honors. There was the big desk he had inherited from Professor Spooner. There were the photo of Marta and Lori's picture of TA. There was a collection of his Cole Porter Palmer stories, though few knew him to be the author. He had never been philosophical in the sense that TA had been, but he was struck that morning by the incongruity of this normal space and the abnormality that had taken hold of his life. Could it be, he wondered, that, like water, the consequences of an act, no matter how remote, continue to flow downhill, that only when the water is lifted by means of a pump—by a kind of restitution—could this flow be reversed?

There was also the old scrapbook that contained his mother's journalistic work. Dennis had never spoken to TA about it. The morning after he had found it on the kitchen table, it had been removed. Later, he had noticed that it was on TA's bookshelf in the front room, had probably been there all along. He sometimes wondered if he had gravitated to writing because he was unconsciously emulating his mother, or because he'd inherited the gift. Occasionally, when he had been alone in the house on Lincoln Street, he had reread an article, or looked at the photograph. Eventually this woman had merged with his former image of Patricia Cole so that the two became indistinguishable. For many years, that was how it had stood, until that anonymous letter from California arrived.

A knock on the door was followed by Eva Bright's entrance. Even she looked stretched. He knew her well enough to notice that she'd used more makeup that morning than was usual for her. "You have a visitor, Dr. Cole", she said.

"I'm busy", he said.

"It's Lieutenant Jones."

"Tell him I'll call him later."

"I don't think that will satisfy him", Eva said.

Dennis took a deep breath. Eva had barely left the room when the policeman entered the office. He sat in the wooden chair opposite Dennis. There were three loud taps as the chair legs rocked.

"You've been meddling again", Jones said to him.

Dennis said, "I expected Jorge to keep it quiet." He hadn't expected any such thing, but had said it anyway. He wasn't used to being on the defensive and didn't like it.

"He didn't. You knew he wouldn't. Maybe it was useful. We learned some things when he related your conversation."

"I'm happy to know it", Dennis said.

"I'm sure you are. For purposes of this conversation, let's call the two people you discussed with Jorge the bearded man and the legless man."

"Do you know who they are?" Dennis asked him.

Lieutenant Jones ignored the question. "Do *you* have any suspicions about who they are?"

Dennis said, "The bearded man could have been anyone. We were out of the room when he sat at our table."

Jones wagged a finger and said, "Not anyone. He didn't weigh three hundred pounds. He wasn't six foot six. Those things can't be disguised. We've identified the legless man", the policeman said. "Have you thought of anything else that might explain Benedict Carlson's death?"

"No", Dennis said.

"Hmmm. If something comes to mind, I'm sure you'll let me know. How about Gregory Pace?"

Dennis said, "I received a call from someone claiming to be a colleague of Greg's. He asks questions like you do, but I don't think he's a policeman."

Lieutenant Jones didn't pursue this, which supported Dennis' suspicion that his interlocutor knew something about the anonymous man who had called him and Ben. Dennis said, "Do you have the analytical results from the hotel room?"

"Nothing I can reveal. You do realize that you could be charged with obstruction of justice."

Dennis had been expecting that. He said, "You'd have to prove intent to deceive, not just negligence, or what you call meddling."

For the first time, the policeman's poker face showed signs of cracking. He shook his head, then smiled, but it was a cold smile. "Now that you've been advised—you may consider yourself advised—any further obstruction would clearly be intentional. Think about it. I'm sure you're keeping something important from me. I usually know, or strongly suspect, what that something is, and why it's being withheld. Not this time. You may attribute it to your guile, but it's very risky."

"That's a supposition", Dennis said.

"It's more than a supposition. Why would someone risk what you're risking unless something very important is at stake? I wonder what that something is."

"Keep supposing", Dennis said. This dogged man was proving to be relentless. He wondered if Jones knew about Ben's letter. If so, Dennis could never get away with the defense that he wasn't sure the letter was authentic, especially after the warning Jones had just given him.

"If you're hiding something, Dr. Cole, it's going to be a serious problem. We're investigating a murder, multiple murders. This dilatory approach might buy you a few days but we'll fill in the blanks. The DA doesn't take kindly to obstruction. I'd hate to have to arrest Henry Drake. Now, I'm going to instruct, not ask, you to stay away from the Hilton and Jorge Estrada."

The mask had come off. Jones was a shrewd, calculating investigator who was getting too close to the truth for comfort. Dennis wasn't looking for trouble, but he wouldn't be dissuaded from learning as much as he could about what had happened to his friends. If that meant another confrontation with the police, so be it, he told himself. Jones had admitted that he was investigating multiple murders. Dennis suspected that Jones wanted him to ask who had been murdered. Instead, he said, "Did you learn any more about Tony?'

Jones said, "We've completed the autopsy."

"Was Tony's death related to the diabetes?"

"That's privileged information", Jones said.

If Tony had died a natural death, Dennis reflected, why would the lieutenant keep it from him? He told himself that he would have to accept—at least accept the possibility—that Tony had been murdered. If that was what happened—now his mind was churning, and he was sure Jones knew it was churning—then Tony must have been poisoned.

"Think about it", Jones said.

When Dennis didn't answer, the lieutenant got up and walked out of the office without another word. Not a minute later, Eva came in without knocking. Those piercing dark eyes, not unsympathetic, met Dennis'. Despite the physical dissimilarities, she had never reminded him more of Lori than she did at that moment. "What's wrong?" she implored.

"Last weekend ... the police are interested. It's too complicated to go into, but if I've been testy, I'm sorry. It's liable to go on for a while; I may not be myself." As he said this, he realized that he didn't know what *myself* meant anymore.

She began doing what she did every day, sorting his in-box and out-box, filing, tidying up. "Did he try to intimidate you?" she asked. "Did he show you his badge?"

He hadn't, Dennis realized. For that matter, who had identified himself? What did he know about the man who claimed to be Greg's colleague? Was Jorge the waiter he represented himself to be? Was Christine just a doe-eyed bartender? Was the legless man a harmless naturalist?

Lieutenant Jones probably knew who this man was; did that exonerate the legless man or make the two of them collaborators? Was Susan still the person he had known years ago? He could go on, but these questions scared him. Mostly, he was frightened about becoming paranoid.

He said, "Eva, I'd like you to do me a favor."

"Name it."

"Find out if there was a conference on campus concerning reptiles and amphibians last weekend, especially frogs."

She looked puzzled.

"I'm serious", he said. "With your network, it shouldn't take long."

"I thought you were an engineer," she said wryly, "not a zoologist."

"Herpetologist", he said. "Let me know as soon as you can."

On the way out, Eva put her hand on his shoulder. She didn't speak; the gesture was enough. After she left the room, Dennis considered that Jones was beginning to look like a spider to his fly. He was not a man to be underestimated. Wouldn't it be ironic, Dennis thought, if he was charged and went to jail for something he *didn't* do?

He tried to work, but he couldn't concentrate. Several times, he looked up at the picture of TA. Not too much later, Eva walked into the room and said, "No frog-fest in Ann Arbor, Dr. Cole."

"Sure?"

Eva said, "I'm sure. I have a good network, remember?"

So the man in the wheelchair had lied, he told himself, and it had been an unnecessary lie at that, since there had been no apparent reason for prevarication.

329

He needed time to think, and he couldn't do it here. He said, "I'm going out, Eva."

"Will you be back?"

"I don't know", he admitted.

"Can I do anything at all?"

He shook his head and walked past her. He took the bus to the main campus and started walking, ending up at Zingerman's Deli, a bruised brick building at the junction of Kingsley and Detroit streets. As it was the busy lunch hour, the diners were elbow to elbow. He told himself it was as good a place as any to rest and try to eat, though his appetite was meager. He had thought about going home, but he felt the need to think without any of the emotional interruptions that would occur there. He had also thought of going to a quieter place, but he was afraid of being alone.

Waiting for his order, he called Jan Hulse. Tony's funeral was supposed to have been the day before, but with the police investigation, Dennis suspected it was delayed. Could Jan tell him something about Tony that Dennis didn't already know? He doubted it, as he had always been closer to Tony than Jan had been, but it was worth a try.

He got Jan's voicemail and left a message, but by the time he was finished picking at his favorite Zingerman's sandwich, Jan returned his call.

Tony's brother said, "They won't release the body, Dennis. What the hell is going on?"

Dennis said, "Greg is missing and Ben committed suicide. The police have come to see me, more than once."

"You can't be serious", Jan said.

"As serious as I've ever been."

"It doesn't add up, Dennis. Is there something else you want to tell me?" Jan said.

"The police are on a wild goose chase", Dennis said.

"Unfortunately, that wild goose chase affects our family", Jan said. "We can't have Tony's funeral. Cate is so distraught, she's useless. Wim has to get back to San Francisco."

"I'm so sorry", Dennis said.

Jan said, "Did Tony tell you about the girl he was going to marry, Maddie Harris? While they were engaged, Tony was a different man, lighthearted, if you can believe it. We lost touch with her when she and Tony split up, but I'm sure she'd like to know."

"He told us about her, but not very much."

"You know, I hate to say this, but I'm glad that Mom and Dad are dead. They wouldn't have been able to understand this."

"They were strong people", Dennis said.

"They were strong", Jan agreed. "They survived a world war. But this is different—Mom thought of you as another son. I resented it once; I don't anymore."

That was it. They hung up. "A wild goose chase", Dennis had said to Jan. He wondered if, instead, these events were actually like a line of dominos. Which was the domino that started the rest tumbling? he asked himself. For the first time since this madness began—with Greg on the bed with a bag over his head—Dennis tried to separate himself from the events themselves and view them as a disinterested observer, as Cole Porter Palmer did in the stories he wrote. He told himself a rational man would conclude that these rapid-fire deaths were a continuum rather than isolated events. If that was so,

Dennis could not help but wonder when *his* falcon would be uncapped.

He had the strong sense that he possessed a subterranean awareness of the truth and that he needed to dig deep to find it. As his mind stirred, he became less and less aware of the noisy, shoulder-to-shoulder Zingerman's crowd. He turned over the paper placemat, producing a clean white surface, and lifted his pen.

29

September 2007

Macklin, Eroica, nee Papandreou, born July 1, 1920, died September 6, 2007. Beloved mother of Jimmy Macklin and Billy Macklin (deceased). Wife of Peter Macklin (deceased). Mrs. Macklin was born in Athens, Greece, where her father, Bartholomew Papandreou, was the conductor of the Athens Symphony Orchestra. Mrs. Macklin was educated in Paris and Vienna and was a concert violinist in her youth. During the Nazi occupation, Mrs. Macklin and her father were active in the Greek Resistance. In 1943 they were captured by the Gestapo and imprisoned, escaping just days before their scheduled execution. Bartholomew and Eroica made their way to a secret airfield, where Bartholomew was killed defending his daughter. Mrs. Macklin moved to England, and from there she emigrated to America after the war. In 1946, she married Peter Macklin, a fourth-generation Terrapin Township farmer. She resided on the Macklin homestead until her death. A large portion of the Macklin property was subdivided and developed in the 1950s and 1960s. In later years, Mrs. Macklin and her sons kept a garden and raised chickens on the property. She was known to be a devoted

Red Wings fan, holding season tickets for over three decades.

Dennis folded the newspaper containing the obituary and set it on the table. Then he held his head in his hands. The voice he had heard when Gordie was threatening him, the "stay" he hadn't been able to purge from his mind all that night and even into the next day had belonged to the late Mrs. Macklin; he admitted that now. He also now understood that the violin music that emanated from the Macklin home wasn't a record but that woman's art.

As a youth, he had no inkling of the terror she must have experienced during the war, how it could make one pathologically suspicious of people, and he wondered how much that anxiety had been compounded when he and his friends invaded her property, when they invaded her home and injured her son.

The obituary was sitting on the Mercedes passenger seat as Dennis drove to the corner of Lincoln and Lee streets. He parked the car, opened the glove compartment, and removed a photograph. That moment in time, a joyful moment, had been memorialized on film by Alvin Pompay. In the foreground, from left to right, were the Flash, Green Lantern, Batman, and Wonder Woman. Even in costume, Tony and Lori were side by side. In the back were Superman and Aquaman, the two taller boys. Superman was dead, had been dead for over thirty years; Wonder Woman for almost as long. The photograph had faded to a degree that only someone who knew the subjects could recognize them. The subjects were fading too, or had become different people. Or were they, he asked himself, the same people, just further down the road that they had begun traveling so long ago?

He wasn't altogether sure why he'd made the drive from Ann Arbor to Terrapin Township. He supposed he had been prompted by the obituary; but to do what? He got out of the car and walked to the path that led to the frog pond; rather, what had once been the frog pond. Now, a fitness center and a parking lot occupied that space. Who was there to protest this desecration except for him and Tony, and both were too preoccupied to care. Tony, at least, had an excuse; he lived in Oregon.

Dennis felt nostalgic for those frog-hunting days with his friend, though he knew that it was foolish to pine for things that belonged to the past. He was a full professor at a prestigious university and a successful author. He had status, money—all the earmarks of success. He walked further down Lincoln Street, apprehensive about what he would see when he arrived at the next corner. In fact, there was nothing to see. The Big Tree was an ugly stump in a postage-stamp field, surrounded by newer houses, left alone because removing it would have been too much trouble.

Marta wouldn't have shaken the Terrapin Township dust from her feet no matter how successful she was, Dennis thought. Rather, she would have found a way to use that celebrity and prestige to benefit the community.

Thinking about his wife made him feel uncomfortable, guilty even. He could feel the two of them drifting apart. Actually, he was drifting away, in spite of Marta's efforts to bolster their marriage. His love for Marta had become a staccato to her continuo.

When they had first met, he had been less than overwhelmed. She had been a friend of a friend, a steady, dependable sort of girl, not glamorous by any means. But the more he got to know her, the more comfortable he became, the more he shared his love for writing with her. She encouraged him, and encouraged him again when he received innumerable rejections. It had seemed the most natural thing in the world to marry her since she had become his best friend and confidante. Lately, though—it made him uncomfortable to admit it to himself—he felt he had outgrown her.

Of course, the most serious cause of the distance in their marriage was their failure to have a child. Though both of them had tacitly come to terms with it, their mutual disappointment had fostered too much regret to ignore. Sometimes it made them try too hard; at other times, they didn't try hard enough. Either way, their marriage lacked the joyful spontaneity they had enjoyed in the early days.

He wished TA were still alive, though he would not have been able to talk to him about his marriage. Dennis had seriously considered an extramarital relationship; there had been such an opportunity. In retrospect, he suspected that TA's intangible, lingering influence prevented him. There would be other opportunities, he suspected, and he wondered if he would succumb the next time.

Now he had walked to the nexus of everything: the Cole, Hulse, Carlson, Pace, and Linus houses. He couldn't conceive of these structures in any other way, even though many of the original families were now gone. The house that first drew his attention was the one next to Tony's, where Jenny Holm lived. He had heard she had been committed to a psychiatric hospital and then released. He wondered if she still lived here on Lincoln Street.

He glanced between the Pace and Linus houses and could just see past the vines to the corner of the Macklin house. How tired it all looked, he reflected. He wondered if Jimmy was still there. The obituary mentioned that his brother had died, implying that Jimmy was still alive.

It wasn't his fault that Jimmy got hurt, Dennis insisted to himself. Breaking in hadn't been his idea. They hadn't meant to hurt anyone. Jimmy wasn't supposed to be there.

He kept walking and found himself in front of the house he and TA had shared. He recalled the day after TA's burial, when he cleaned out the place. It didn't take long. Dennis gave away or threw out everything except for a few books. After he had returned from donating the last surviving hippocampi to the zoo, there was still the matter of the empty aquarium. He stood in the basement, reflecting on all the hours he and TA had spent together caring for those delicate and beautiful creatures, and he realized for the first time how precious and formative that time had been.

In that dark basement, in that empty house, his grief gave way to bitter disappointment. He took a hammer and shattered the empty aquarium. Actually, he pulverized it. Beneath that shattered aquarium, he discovered the plans TA had drawn in order to build it, meticulously detailed and dimensioned. They had been there, like a cornerstone beneath a building, all those years.

Though Eroica Macklin's obituary had prompted this visit to the neighborhood, there was another reason he had returned to Terrapin Township—a single page of paper in his jacket pocket. He had received it in the mail three days earlier and had read it many times since. The ordinary white envelope had no return address and had been postmarked from San Diego, California. It had been typed and was undated and unsigned. With tremulous hands, he removed it from his jacket, unfolded it, and read:

> Patricia Cole did not die in Iowa. After a brief hospitalization, she ran away from you and your father. She and your brother are alive and well. They are living in a suburb of San Diego. She has taken a new name. Your brother is unaware of his past. She is writing for several local newspapers, a risk, but one she cannot resist.

The letter completely dumbfounded him the first time he read it. A part of him angrily rejected these revelations as vicious lies, but he could not help asking questions. Where could the author have learned so much about a woman who had, presumably, been dead for over forty years? Why would someone compose and send this letter if it wasn't true? Had TA's resistance to Dennis' search for his mother's killer been caused by the fear that he would learn the truth that Patricia Cole hadn't died?

Dennis had been five years old at the time of the accident; he had no memory of a funeral service. Couldn't TA—and that small family circle—have decided that it was better for Dennis, and their Lincoln Street neighbors, not to know that Patricia had abandoned them?

He had entertained the notion that his mother's killer had sent the letter. In researching his own literary projects, he had learned that some killers have a pathological need to punish their victim's loved ones. But if this was the explanation, why had the killer waited so long? If the assertions in the letter were true, another explanation was that Patricia Cole had made an enemy, someone she had confided in, someone so vindictive that he had resorted to this vile act.

But hadn't he seen his mother's crumpled body, like a rag doll that had been tossed in the backseat of the Buick? Hadn't he seen Andrew's lifeless body on the pavement? Images like that couldn't be manufactured, he told himself. Still, he counterargued, people survive terrible accidents every day.

And why hadn't he shown the letter to Marta? If the claim was so ludicrous, why not reveal it to her? He knew that it was shame that prevented him from revealing it to anyone. He couldn't abide anyone's suspicion that his mother had abandoned him. With the care one gives to a precious artifact, he refolded the page and put it back in his pocket, knowing that he would do nothing to corroborate or refute it. How ironic, he told himself, that when TA was alive, that man's resistance to Dennis' desire to learn the truth had made Dennis even more determined to know. Now that TA was gone, it was as if Dennis had assumed the curatorship of Patricia Cole's memory and reputation.

The Mercedes purred when he turned the key. Two kids on the corner were watching him with admiration. After all, he told himself, he was a success.

30

Day Six, Evening

So engrossed was Dennis in the ideas that tumbled from his mind onto that paper placemat that he spent most of the afternoon and early evening in his office, lining up the dominos. Now Dennis realized that he had missed dinner and had not even called Marta. He sent a text message informing her that he was working late and received a one-word acknowledgement. Peter was with her, Dennis reminded himself, and Peter would be better company than he would be.

The building was mostly empty, and the office cleaners didn't arrive until well after midnight. The traffic noise outside was much reduced because most of the students and staff had departed the academic buildings. The small work lamp on his desk shed its modest spotlight on his work: scribbles, lines, and balloons—unintelligible to anyone but Dennis.

He was trying to examine the events of the past six days as emotionlessly as possible, as Cole Porter Palmer or Sherlock Holmes might examine them. Every time he encountered a preconceived notion, he rejected it. Every time he experienced an emotional reaction to a question, he willed himself to go on.

His eyes came to rest on the bookshelf, the bookshelf that had belonged to his predecessor, and maybe his predecessor's predecessor. It was solid oak; in those days they built furniture to last. On one shelf were a handful of TA's books, the few he had kept when he emptied the house on Lincoln Street: Augustine's *City of God* and *Confessions*, Pascal's *Pensées*, and Aristotle's *Nicomachean Ethics*. There was also TA's battered notebook of derivative and original ideas that Dennis had almost thrown out; only TA's faded signature on the cover had prevented him.

What was inside the notebook turned out to be a window on TA's surprisingly fecund mind. In the immediate aftermath of TA's death, Dennis had recourse to it often, but just as often he found the contents more troubling than consoling. TA had been a searcher for truth and meaning, and anything that got in the way of that quest—pride, convention, affection—had been anathema to him.

Now—why, he couldn't have said—Dennis retrieved the notebook from the shelf and opened it. His eyes rested on this passage:

> Listen to what I shall call him; the Bottomless Abyss, the Insatiable, the Merciless, the Unsatisfied—he who never once said to poor, unfortunate mankind, "Enough."
> "Not enough." That is what he screamed at me.
> "I can't go further", whines miserable man.
> "You can!" the Lord replies.
> "I shall break in two", man whines again.
> "Break!" (Kazantzakis' *Saint Francis*)

In the margin, in TA's hand, was this: "Impenetrability, and not an evil act, is the demonic origin of despair, because not even an evil act can prevent the one who comes close to our 'I', whatever we have done!"

Dennis closed the notebook and groaned. He ought to have known better than to look for solace in TA's notebook. But was there something Dennis needed, before he could be comforted?

"Break!"

Why would anyone allow himself to be broken? Wasn't man programmed to resist this with all his might? Didn't one's prestige and position in the world depend on never being broken?

Dennis was hungry. He opened the desk drawer, and there was the Scotch, like a memory in a bottle. He rifled deeper, and his hand emerged with a package of crackers. So dinner would be Scotch and crackers. Going through all the drawers, he found a square of chocolate Marta had given him, and he made a dessert of it.

His attempted objective inquiry had produced a daunting list of questions. He had begun the project by making the bold assumption, which he had previously resisted, that all of the events of the past six days were connected. Since it was only an academic exercise, he told himself, why not see where these questions led him:

Who had knowledge that the four of them would be together that weekend?
Who had access to the room at the Hilton?
How was Greg murdered in the room, or conveyed into the room, without disturbing the other three?
How could Greg's killer count on them not to involve the police?
Who had knowledge of Tony's diabetes and medical paraphernalia?

Who knew enough about their history to ghost-write Ben's suicide note?

Who had been in Atlanta on Monday?

How did the bearded man (or the legless man) figure into Greg's death?

Who could have written the letter claiming that Patricia Cole was still alive?

How could the author have known so much, and why had it been written?

Who could have harbored such animosity for the four of them?

Ben might have said that these questions, and the speculation they provoked, belonged to the world of fiction, not real life. Still, the more Dennis considered them, the more they compelled him to conclude that if—and it was a big if—some*one* was behind these three deaths, then the acts had been planned meticulously and executed with clockwork precision. This conclusion led Dennis to another conclusion: that person wasn't finished as long as Dennis lived.

He remembered the night when he had confronted TA with the police file from the Iowa accident, that unsolved killing, as Dennis called it. Even then, Dennis had been building momentum in a dark direction, a direction that TA had been unable to discourage. Still, wasn't this exercise in logic, this Socratic questioning, exactly the gift that TA had bestowed on him that night? Then, TA had guided him to a credible conclusion using a series of questions. Here, Dennis was using the same process.

The sun had set, and a deep quiet had settled on the building. This was the point of decision: Take the next step or let it go? Then, he asked himself, what did letting it go mean if someone was behind the deaths of his friends and intended to kill him too? He needed to call Greg's mysterious colleague, whose number was still in his cell phone. If Greg had been working in intelligence, maybe his colleague could help Dennis confirm what he was beginning to suspect. He dialed the number on his desk phone.

"Yes, Dr. Cole", said the now-familiar voice. "I didn't expect to hear from you."

Dennis said, "I'm full of surprises. Are you ready to tell me your name?"

"As I've said, my name is unimportant. It wouldn't mean anything to you."

"Whom do you work for?"

"Also irrelevant. You must have called me for more than this. I hope so."

"I need your help", Dennis said, adding, "I'm desperate."

"With a matter of mutual interest?" the man asked.

"If you help me, I might be able to answer the riddle of Greg's disappearance."

"So tell me what I can do for you."

Dennis said, "You strike me as a resourceful man, and I need a resourceful man to help me track down somebody. There was a woman Tony Hulse knew in Portland: Maddie Harris. She was divorced when he met her. I need to know her maiden name."

"Tell me how this is connected to Gregory Pace."

"Supply the name, and I may be able to do that. I won't know until I know the name."

"I don't suppose you have a social security number."

"No."

"Hold on—Her age?"

"Forty to forty-five."

"Place of birth?"

"Michigan, I believe."

"You must think highly of my skills."

"Consider it a test."

"You promise it has something to do with Greg?"

"Yes."

There was a long delay, so long that Dennis wondered whether the connection had been broken.

The voice said, "Madeline Harris nee Bridgeman. Age forty-two. Mean anything to you?"

Though Dennis had entertained this possibility earlier in the evening, he could never have prepared himself to hear this man confirm it. The first domino was about to fall.

"I'll call you back", Dennis said. He hung up and opened his web browser with trembling hands. He splashed some Scotch in the glass and gulped it down, feeling its calming influence. He was accessing the university's historical-news library, and he knew what to look for.

Detroit Free Press

October 8, 1981

Senator's Son Killed by Vehicle

Police Investigating, but No Suspects

The son of U.S. Senator Ulysses S. Bridgeman, Michael Bridgeman, was struck and killed by a vehicle last night on North Territorial Road west of Ann Arbor. His disabled car was found on the shoulder of the road less than two hundred yards from the body. Police are considering this a case of hit-and-run, but given the identity of the victim, they are not ruling out foul play. At present there are no suspects.

The victim was discovered by a motorist, Ken Scott of Dexter, at 3 A.M. The police have confirmed that Mr. Scott is not a suspect.

Senator Bridgeman is en route from Washington, D.C., to the University of Michigan Medical Center, where the body is being held pending the police investigation.

Mr. Bridgeman was nineteen years of age and a sophomore at the University of Michigan, majoring in pre-law. In addition to the Senator, he is survived by his mother, Hilda Bridgeman, and a sister, Madeline Bridgeman.

Detroit Free Press
October 12, 1981
Senator Bridgeman's Son Buried

Michael Bridgeman, nineteen, son of U.S. Senator Ulysses S. Bridgeman, was buried today in a private service attended by close family and friends. Representing President Reagan was the First Lady. Six senators and eight congressmen were also in attendance.

Bridgeman was killed in a hit-and-run outside Ann Arbor, where he was attending the University of Michigan. Police are still investigating the incident but are admitting to no suspects at this time.

So many years ago, yet Dennis felt the same horror and fear and guilt.

As if it were yesterday, he saw the red Monte Carlo hurtling down North Territorial Road. Greg was driving; Ben and Tony were in the back. It was the anniversary of Davey's death, and they had been out drinking at their usual hole in the wall. It was Dennis who had suggested a ride in the car, though none of them was fit to drive. A young man was in the road trying to wave them down. When they drove past without stopping, the man saluted them with one finger.

Tony said, "Did you see that?"

Greg expelled a loud curse. The Monte Carlo spun around and accelerated in the opposite direction. Greg braked and veered at the last second, but the figure leapt in the same direction. The collision was all sounds and sensations, reminding Dennis of the Iowa wreck; the grinding of the brakes, the utter stillness when the car came to a stop.

Drunk, disoriented, and horrified, the driver and his friends did not even bother to check on the victim. Not a word was spoken as they sped back to campus. They inspected the car when they arrived at the apartment; just the smallest of dents on the bumper. They barely hit the man, or so they told each other; maybe he would be okay.

But the next day's newspaper told a different story. Though ever fearful that they would be found out, the four were never questioned by the police. Of course, they would never be suspected; there were no witnesses to the accident. But that fact didn't end their anguish. It never ended.

On the night of the ball game, hadn't that injured pedestrian on the side of the road dissolve the camaraderie the four of them so desperately sought to recover? Hadn't they resorted to their usual attempts at disassociation from that long-ago act? Dennis' hands were still trembling as he called the man back. "You said you were a friend of Greg's. Is that true?" he asked.

"Yes. Now you are the one asking all the questions. That hardly seems fair."

Dennis said, "It's necessary." Then he added, "Believe me."

"I will trust you, even if you don't trust me."

"I have another question: Did my assistant, Eva Bright, that's B-r-i-g-h-t, travel from Detroit to Atlanta on Monday the nineteenth and return to Michigan the same day, or early on Tuesday?"

"So that's who you think is responsible."

"Yes. That's the next domino."

"Hold on."

It was a shorter wait this time. "You called the right person. It helps to have . . . access to things that other people do not. Eva Bright was on a Delta flight to Atlanta the morning of Monday the nineteenth, and she returned the same day on the nine o'clock flight to Detroit."

Dennis dropped the phone on the desk. Michael Bridgeman's little sister, Madeline, became Maddie Harris. Tony must have confided everything to his former fiancée. Once she learned Tony's history, she canceled the wedding: How could she marry a man who had killed her brother? The fact that they hadn't intended to kill Michael Bridgeman—Tony must have told her that too—was irrelevant to her. Now Maddie Harris was Eva Bright. And why would Eva Bright be here, working for Dennis, unless it had been part of a grand scheme to—

Dennis clumsily picked up the phone and asked, "Are you still there?"

"Yeah, but if this Eva Bright killed Greg, there are things I need to do—I'd keep your door locked if I were you." That was what Lieutenant Jones had told him.

Dennis hung up the phone, and it rang within seconds. "Yes." Dennis could barely speak. More than his hands were shaking.

"You should know that I don't think our call was secure."

Dennis said, "What do you mean?"

"Someone was listening. Where are you?"

Dennis hesitated before answering. "At my university office."

"Like I said, keep your door locked—and call the police."

The man had hung up, and Dennis moved as quickly as he could, banging his knee so hard against the desk that he cried out. As soon as he closed the door and turned the dead bolt, he heard the handle rattle. Then came a knock, firm and steady.

"Who's there?" he said, as calmly as he could.

"It's Eva. I was working late. I didn't know you were still here. Can I talk to you?"

He said, "I'm busy, Eva. I'll talk to you tomorrow."

"I'll just be a minute."

He hesitated, searching frantically for something to say.

"Why is your door locked?" she asked.

He didn't answer her. He heard a siren in the street, getting louder, and then fainter.

Eva said, "Tomorrow is too late, Dennis." She had never called him Dennis.

He found himself fumbling with his keys: something, anything, to release nervous energy. When he removed his hand from his pocket, he found that it held the half-dollar from the hotel. It was a perverse memento, something he had retained to keep him connected to Greg and Tony, and now Ben. The ordinary half-dollar had been minted in 1981: another domino, one he had missed. Eva hadn't been able to resist this calling card containing a message they were unlikely to decipher. It confirmed what he suspected, as unbelievable as it seemed: Eva, his extraordinary assistant for the last three years, had been playing a role and plotting revenge all that time.

"You've been under a lot of pressure", Eva said. "I just want to help."

Was there another way into the office? He didn't think so; he hoped not. The door was solid wood, old but substantial. Nonetheless, he was frightened. For all intents and purposes, the baleful ghost of Michael Bridgeman was on the other side of the door, returned from a twenty-nine-year-old grave to take vengeance on him.

Dennis now admitted that the dominos had started falling on that road in 1981 and had been tumbling inexorably ever since. But then he stopped himself. No, in reality, the chain reaction had begun long before then. Their invasion of the Macklin home had twisted something inside them. The act itself was not the culprit, but the individual and corporate lack of remorse. Each of those boys had the freedom to admit guilt and make amends, but none of them had chosen to do so. TA had tried to help Dennis own up to his responsibility, but TA had encountered a heart of stone and a psychological dismissal of the gravity of his son's actions.

By harboring hatred for the driver who robbed him of his mother and brother, Dennis had been hardening his heart for years, despite TA's warnings. Injuring Jimmy, Davey's death that same night, and the bitterness that came in its wake, sealed his cynicism and that of his friends. Lori's death and Ben's accident only magnified their resentment.

"I do need to speak to you, Dennis." Eva continued.

Dennis said, "Is Joseph with you?"

"Why would Joseph be here?"

"Weren't you together Friday night, at the hotel?"

"What makes you think I was at the hotel?" Eva asked.

"We left drinks on the table when Joseph arrived", Dennis explained, only too happy to keep Eva listening and talking. "We were away from the table less than ten minutes to see the new car. According to our waiter, a bearded man sat at the table while we were away. We slept too soundly that night, and Tony, Ben, and I felt exhausted the next day. You drugged our drinks, didn't you, Eva?"

"Yes, and it was poetic justice. Tony told me that Carlson used pentobarbital to knock the dog out the night you four invaded the Macklin house. You see, Dennis, the argument that my brother's murder was an accident doesn't hold water. You four had been making misery long before the night you killed Michael.

"If it was ironic that Tony fell in love with me, I compounded the irony by using pentobarbital to drug all of you the night I eliminated Pace. I needed a dose that would induce sound sleep, but not too soon, and not too conspicuously. I practiced on Joseph, and the doses worked beautifully. Clumsy bottles and syringes wouldn't do. We made a special device to dispense the drug. It was strapped to my arm and hidden beneath my shirt sleeve. All I had to do was push a button on my wrist, and an aliquot went into the drink. It was an excellent performance, if I may say so."

"Tony complained about the beer when we returned."

"He would. He was a connoisseur when it came to beer. But he drank it; that's all that mattered. Poor Tony."

Dennis thought he detected genuine concern in Eva's voice.

"Eva, Tony loved you. He didn't intend for your brother to die. None of us did. In spite of what happened at the

Macklins, we weren't thugs; we were . . . reckless kids. Greg hitting your brother . . . it wasn't murder." Hadn't TA said the same thing to him years ago when they discussed the accident in Iowa?

"Twenty-one-year-old men, kids? What do you think a judge or a jury would say to that defense? What do you think they would call it, Dennis?"

"Manslaughter", Dennis said hesitantly.

"*Man slaughter*", she said, enunciating each word separately. "That's why I'm here, isn't it?"

"Tony must have told you that Greg was only . . . being Greg . . . trying to scare him, or something."

"By driving a car at him? I don't have to believe your convenient memory; I don't believe it."

Dennis said, "I'm sorry, Eva. I have been for twenty-nine years."

He could hear the handle rattle again. Eva had always been persistent. That quality was one of the things that made her so valuable.

"Let me tell you a story", she said. "There was a girl whose father was a senator. He was a warm and generous man. When she was little, he would sit her on one knee and read to her. He had the most beautiful voice in the world. Her big brother treated her like a princess.

"Then, her father was away more and more, and one day her brother didn't come home. Her mother began drinking, then drinking more; then she died. Her father retreated from everything that had once so animated him, including the daughter who was becoming a woman. The storybook life turned dark."

"Killing Greg, Tony, and Ben won't change that", Dennis said.

"It satisfies blood with blood. I wonder if that's Shake-speare or the Bible. Tony was the hardest. Still, it had to be done. I knew all about his diabetes and the needles. There was nothing to it . . . just an exchange of syringes in his bag. I couldn't be sure when Tony would use it, but I knew he would sooner or later.

"Suffocating Pace was easy; no noise, no fuss. He was out cold. All I had to do was attach the bag.

"The morning after I killed Pace, you encountered me in the corridor—remember? Uniforms come in handy; people don't bother looking at faces. The ham-per was just the right size for Pace and a convenient way to remove him and his belongings from the build-ing. I was tempted to keep that tiny computer, but Joseph said no—he was in the Presidential Guard in Jordan. He even understood that we had to dispose of it sepa-rate from the body."

Dennis was considering his options: hole up until the cleaning crew or someone else arrived, call 911, or take his chances jumping out the window.

"The greatest peril wasn't getting in or out of your suite", Eva went on, "or the risk of encountering Tony, or even the trip to Atlanta. It was the presence of an invalid at the table next to yours in the hotel lounge when I drugged your drinks. I could tell he was watch-ing me, and he unnerved me, even though I have per-formed in male roles, and I took care in creating my disguise. Tony's card house also gave me a bad start, but I had worked hard at putting down my feelings for him. Well, fate almost did me in, but then it saved me. Another man came to the invalid's table and distracted him for a minute, enough time to drug the drinks and exit before you returned."

Dennis couldn't help but wonder if the legless man would have revealed Eva's visit to their table if they hadn't been so belligerent toward him.

"Can you imagine how difficult it is to kill four people in less than a week, and with virtuosity? Pace wasn't easy, but I knew you wouldn't call the police; not immediately anyway. And I knew you'd have to leave the room sooner or later. The hard part was waiting for you to leave without being observed by someone from the hotel. Tony's death was the easiest to plan but the hardest to execute. I suppose I fell in love with Tony. He certainly fell in love with me. Before I learned what he—all of you—had done, I pitied Tony because I didn't have the capacity to love him the way he loved me.

"Tony told me everything, told me about your pathological fear of the police, told me that every day you expected the police to apprehend you for the murder of my brother. He even told me about the assault on your neighbor.... Yes, he told me everything. He needed to get it out, you see, and I have made good use of that knowledge.

"I spent a lot of time in Atlanta following Carlson and learning his habits. He wasn't a careful man when it came to locking doors, and it helped that he lived alone. Still, staging a credible suicide isn't easy. I'll never forget the expression on his face when he saw me in the house."

"What if we had turned the dead bolt that first night?" Dennis said, stalling for time.

"Do you think I'd have relied on whether you bolted the door or not? I got a key to the suite when I reserved it, and while you were at the game, I decommissioned the dead bolt. Community theater honed more than my acting skills; it made a respectable handyman out of me too. I recommissioned the lock after I tidied up the room and substituted the syringe in Tony's bag."

Eva finally paused.

"So now it's my turn", Dennis said.

"Yes, but your suicide note will be more revealing than Carlson's. It's high time everyone learned the whole truth, and nothing but the truth."

"You did a good job of hiding your hatred", he said.

"It wasn't so hard. I'm an actress. I approached my job as if I were playing a role. And you were a good boss, for what it's worth."

The door to his office had become a fragile barrier between different times and places. Dennis wasn't in the present, and his assistant, Eva, wasn't on the other side. He was in the past, and a person he had never met, an avenging angel, was on the other side of the door, ready to deal out justice for Jimmy and Michael. He himself had been living on both sides of the door for decades, justifying himself on one hand, and accusing himself on the other. Now the reality that existed in his mind had assumed tangible form.

"You could have killed all of us when you killed Greg", Dennis said.

"That would have lacked artistry. Think of all the years that girl suffered. Would it have been fair for you to have avoided your share of suffering? What I am doing would be incomplete unless one of you knew. I've worked too hard to let all of you slip away into the darkness without feeling the desperation and terror I have felt. Haven't the last six days been painful?"

"Yes . . . painful", he said. If they had confessed, asked forgiveness, would the Bridgeman family have spiraled to such depths? Who could say, but the decision to keep the secret for all these years had affected every one of the actors in this drama.

"I've been planning my revenge for a long time. Learning where each of you lived. Finding this job three years ago. Until you turned the dead bolt on this door, everything had gone famously."

Dennis said, "It was you who sent me the letter about my mother. Tony told you how she died, and he told you how much I wanted to find her killer."

"I suffer; you suffer. That's a universe that makes sense to me."

He heard an explosion and a thud. The door splintered near the handle and something ricocheted off a metal cabinet in his office.

"Are you okay, Dennis?" she asked in a monotone.

"Someone will hear", he said.

"Eventually. You'll be dead by then."

Another thud. This time the bullet didn't penetrate the door.

"I'm calling the police, Eva."

"You wouldn't dare. A successful professor, a pillar of the community. What would they think when they found out you're a murderer?"

Dennis said, "You made the mistake of believing we were incapable of remorse. You've given me six days of pain, but I've had twenty-nine years of pain and regret. I'm calling the police, and when they arrive, I'm telling them everything."

"I don't believe you. You're bluffing."

"I'm not the man I was a week ago. You're responsible for that, Eva."

"Let me in, Dennis. I'll put away the gun."

Like a man in a trance obeying his hypnotist, Dennis made a move for door. But another bullet and then another shattered the door in two places. He should have felt terrified—by Eva's assault, by the prospect of talking to the police—but a sort of serenity took hold of him instead. He could see Ben's turtle on the beach extending one leg, then another, one arm, then another.

He heard her voice, more frantic now: "Do you think I enjoyed killing a man who loved me?"

"You still have a choice, Eva", Dennis said. "You don't have to kill me."

"I made that choice a long time ago when I let that demon in . . . and there's no getting rid of him now."

"You have a choice too, Joseph."

A man's voice said, "I'm sorry, Dr. Cole. I'm committed."

Dennis told himself that they couldn't keep blasting away at the door without alarming someone. He doubted that the building was completely empty, even at this hour. There may be someone on the way already; surely Eva and Joseph knew that.

He heard a rustling sound above him. He had forgotten about the ceiling panels and the communicating space above them. He felt a surge of panic. He was trapped with nowhere to go.

He thought about throwing open the door and making a dash for it, but they'd be expecting that. Death would be quick at least, he told himself, and after all he had been through, there was a certain appeal to that outcome.

Then Dennis recalled something Peter had said: "Sometimes, you have to hunker down in the foxhole and hope the hell passes by."

The noise above him was getting louder. He ran to the window and threw open the sash, banging it as loudly as he could, hoping Eva would hear. He leaned out the window and looked down on Beal Avenue, almost thirty-five feet below. He took his jacket off and dropped it on the floor beneath the window. He grabbed the dark blanket that he sometimes used to help seal the leakiest window on frigid days and ran back to his desk. Lastly, he squeezed himself into the leg space beneath the top of his desk and pulled the blanket over him, trying to make himself disappear into the dark shadow.

He waited. It sounded as if an army of rats were scuttling above him. One or more of the ceiling panels came crashing down on top of the desk. Then something large struck the desktop, an object that moved—first to the window and then to the door. He heard the door open and Joseph's voice: "Where is he?"

"Gone", Eva replied. "He's gone."

"It is too high to jump", Joseph protested.

"He might have gotten to the roof."

"He isn't an acrobat", Joseph said.

"He has gone out the window, I tell you", Eva said. "Look, it's open. There's his jacket. He's a coward. Even if he broke both legs, he'd prefer it to facing me."

Joseph said, "A coward doesn't jump out of a third-story window."

"Then where is he?"

Hearing Joseph ransacking the room, Dennis quaked, but there was nothing he could do except stay as still as possible. Then he heard a loud siren.

"The police are here", Joseph said, his voice breaking with panic.

"I came so close, Joseph", Eva lamented. "This last misery I can give him at least." There was a rending sound, as if fabric was being torn.

After a moment of silence, Joseph pleaded, "Don't do it, Eva. Please . . . we can go somewhere."

"There's nowhere I can go. The performance is over. The curtain is coming down."

There were two shots, separated by about ten seconds. Then, all was silent, and stayed silent.

Dennis didn't emerge until the police arrived. They found the bodies of Eva and Joseph on the office floor— a lovers' quarrel turned violent, a murder-suicide. Dennis refused to look at the dead Eva as he stepped through the debris on the floor, but he picked up what remained of Lori's portrait of TA. His father's searching eyes looked up at him, but a huge gash tore through the face. The painting was beyond repair.

Dennis told the police that he had heard Eva and Joseph heatedly arguing. When Joseph ran into his office and shut the door, and Eva began shooting, Dennis hid under his desk until it was over.

Now, no one else in the world knew the whole story, and he was finally free.

Day Seven

"Your phone is ringing", Marta said.

"Let it ring", Dennis mumbled.

A few minutes later, it started ringing again.

"What time is it?" he asked her.

"Six."

"Good God. I'm tired to death." After hours of police questioning, not to mention Marta's interrogation when he arrived home, he'd finally gotten to bed at 3 A.M.

"Yes?" he heard Marta say. "Who is this? . . . I'm sorry, he's not available. . . . I said he's not available." Marta didn't often lose her composure, but he sensed that she was close to doing so now. She shook Dennis and said, "He insists on talking to you. He said he talked to you last night about airplanes and Atlanta. What does that mean?"

Dennis lifted a hand, and she gave him the phone. "Yes", he said.

The voice said, "I need to talk to you, in person."

Dennis tried to think, but it was useless. Exhaustion, sadness, and anger at the man's impertinence had crowded out everything else. He said, "There's nothing to talk about."

"There's a lot to talk about. I'll be at the south door of the mall at eight. Meet me there."

Dennis dropped the phone on the carpet.

"Who was that?" Marta said.

"Someone who knew Greg."

"Is Greg in trouble?"

Dennis said, "He's dead."

"Dead? How long have you known that?"

"I don't *know* anything. This man knew Greg. He wants to meet me."

Marta shook him so hard he had to sit up. She stared at him and said, "Let's see if I understand. Tony's dead, Ben's dead, Eva's dead, and Greg's dead, and you're going to meet a stranger who claims to know Greg. Have you lost your mind?"

"Maybe I have, but I have to meet him."

"Why, Dennis? Just tell me why. Please."

He saw Marta as he never had before; strong and vulnerable, determined and frightened, "all in" as he had never been "all in". He told her everything, starting with the Macklin home invasion, then the night on North Territorial Road, and ending with what had really happened last night.

She didn't interrupt. There were tears in her eyes when he finished. She said, "So that's it. Thank you for telling me. What hell you must have been living in; all of you. Go ahead and meet this man. I'll be waiting for you. And I'll make coffee so you can have a cup before you leave." She didn't try to hug or kiss him. She didn't even touch him. She just pulled on her robe and left the room.

Dennis got dressed and accepted the cup of black coffee from his wife in the kitchen. He and Marta sipped in silence, but as he rose from his chair, he said, "The police will probably call. They're not finished with me. Tell them I've done a bunk to Acapulco."

She managed a wan smile and said, "Shhh. Peter's still asleep on the recliner in the den. Try not to wake him. He was bound and determined to stay awake until you got home, but he's old, and he's not well. See how much he loves you."

On his way out of the house, Dennis went into his office for his car keys, turned on the light, and saw *The Deadly Dart Mystery*, a story he was writing for a new anthology, on his desk. When would he be able to write again, if ever? he wondered.

He passed the door of the den, where he saw the old man asleep in the chair. Marta was right. How brittle he looked. Even at rest, Peter Kristov was all straight lines and acute angles. But, like a sentinel at the gate, his shoes were still on, and still tied.

Dennis drove to the south side of Ann Arbor. When he entered the mall, there was a man standing at the end of the corridor. There was no mistaking that thin projecting nose. Face and frame were spare, but one would be more apt to call him wiry than gaunt. As he stood there, he reminded Dennis of a marathoner, a colossal irony considering the disguise the man had adopted in the hotel bar, at the table across from him and his friends.

Two older women were speed-walking and talking enthusiastically. Dennis let them pass before he approached the man.

"We meet again", the man said. He spoke with a British accent.

"You seem to have sprouted legs", Dennis said.

"I understand you had a trying night."

Neither had bothered with the formality of shaking hands. Dennis said, "Will you be supplying a name?"

The man smiled and said, "I won't insult your intelligence with an alias, and I can't reveal my name; so no."

Dennis said, "You seem to know more than I do, so why did you bring me here?"

The man's eyes moved up and down from Dennis' face to his shoes. He said, "Greg and I found out, quite by accident, that we would both be in Ann Arbor. I'm on assignment in Dearborn. We had agreed to a covert meeting at the hotel; sort of a private amusement."

Dennis said, "There was no frog seminar. I did my homework too."

"Bravo. Greg told me that would be an appropriate ruse." Then the man said, "Information is power in my line of work. Eva killed Greg, didn't she?"

"Yes", Dennis said.

"Why?"

"Who can say? She did it masterfully. It was a neurosis connected to me, I suppose."

The man said, "Would you care to walk the circuit?"

Dennis said, "If your legs are up to it."

"They have to be nimble to carry off the illusion. I was a gymnast and an acrobat. Combine those skills with my organization's genius and, presto."

"My compliments", Dennis said wryly.

"Now that you know, I may have to kill you", the man said. Then he added, "You don't smile much, do you?"

"I lost three friends in the past week. I don't feel like smiling."

The man looked Dennis in the eye and said, "If one can't smile, what is to keep him from despair?"

It was too early for music, just a silent procession of walkers. As if reading Dennis' thoughts, the man said, "It was the most private place I could think of. I can tell you this. My chair was especially designed; also the slacks and harness I use when I'm out of the chair, which isn't often when I'm working. By the way, I mustn't appear in one of your stories. You must resist that temptation."

Dennis glanced at the man to see if he was serious, but there was no telling.

"I've found it's remarkable what can be accomplished with clothing and posture, a few expert accessories, and an accent—I Americanized my speech on the phone."

It was hard for Dennis to reconcile this virile man with the legless eccentric in the hotel. He said, "The police interrogated you. At least they told me they did."

"We had a conversation."

"Meaning?"

"It wasn't exactly an interrogation. I would call it a give-and-take."

Dennis said, "Here's something you may not know. The bearded man who sat at our table the night we arrived at the hotel was Eva Bright."

"You don't say", the man exclaimed, stopping in his tracks. His dark eyes, wide and unblinking, dazzled Dennis like headlights. "I'm in the business of creating illusions, and I fell for one myself. I had an eye on her, but I was interrupted by the hotel manager. It was a case of two actors deceiving each other."

They bought a coffee and an espresso from the kiosk in the center court. Dennis desperately needed another cup to clear his head.

"Much better", the man said, after sipping from his tiny cup with his pinky extended. "You weren't the only one to lose sleep last night. Now listen, for many reasons it is vitally important for me to know why Greg was murdered, not least of which is the fact that he was my

364

friend. You understand, of course, that even if you don't tell me, I will find out eventually."

Dennis shrugged. "I told you what I suspect. An unbalanced mind, a secret hatred that grew into an obsession to destroy my friends."

"That's more than you told the police. They're inclined to believe it was a lovers' quarrel that turned ugly. I happen to know too much to accept that explanation.

"Listen Dennis, I'm not a policeman. In fact, I've been trained to ignore inconvenient laws. I can't afford it in my line of work. But I need to know about Greg as much as you needed to know what happened in Iowa."

Dennis mind leaped the tracks again, as it had so often in recent days. How much did this stranger know about that, and how had he learned it? Why had he learned it?

Even though Dennis knew that he was out of his league, he was determined not to tell this man what he had no right to know, what Dennis intended to bury, once and for all, with the dead.

"There are too many gaps in your explanation", the man continued, seeing that Dennis chose to remain silent. He set down his cup and led Dennis back into the stream of walkers. "Why were you so interested in knowing if Eva Bright lived in Portland? I happen to know that Tony lived in Portland. That's an odd coincidence if the reason for the killings—and they were all acts of murder—were prompted by a neurotic hatred she developed for you later."

Dennis said, "Portland is a big town. It's not such a coincidence that Eva and Tony lived there at the same time."

"Perhaps. Your interest in whether they lived there at the same time interests me. Can you explain it?"

"No", Dennis said.

"You can't, or you won't?"

"There are things neither of us is willing to explain", Dennis said.

"So that's how it is", the man said. "I'm not easily put off when I set my mind to getting to the bottom of something. If I reveal everything I know to the police—I haven't as yet—it will be troublesome for you."

"There are things I can reveal too. You wouldn't want me to do that."

The man laughed softly and said, "That was the answer I expected. Very well. I must tell you it is the wrong answer if I had the least suspicion that you were complicit in Greg's death."

Even though Dennis knew that this man operated extra-legally, this was the first time that he felt threatened by him. Why was this man so intent on discovering the truth? Surely in his line of work he had experienced the death of collaborators, as he called them. Dennis said, "There was a lot about Greg we didn't know. We didn't even know he was divorced until Susan told us."

The man said, "The honest truth is that he was ashamed to tell you. In his mind, divorcing Susan was a kind of betrayal, not just on her account, but on all your accounts. I heard Greg's life story when we were both on assignment in Prague. I came to feel like I knew all of you. I had never experienced that sense of camaraderie. My mother was a Pashtu princess, and my father . . . well, he was an English adventurer; we will leave it at that. There was little room for a child in their complicated relationship. Greg vicariously provided me the childhood I never had. My determination to know the truth isn't only about Greg. It's about all of you. But Greg didn't tell me all of your stories."

"What do you mean?" Dennis said.

"He forgot to tell me the story of how all of you incurred the wrath of Eva Bright, aka Madeline Bridgeman, of how all of you were connected. I have my suspicions. It helps to have an army of myrmidons at one's beck and call. I thought I might be able to convince you to tell me, but I see I've overreached. Just because Greg made me feel like one of you doesn't make it so."

The man knew how to push every button, Dennis thought. The sooner he could extricate himself the better. "Not everything we did together is worth remembering", he said.

"Most of us can say the same. I see we've come full circle. Here is your entrance. Thank you for coming. It says something about who you are, or how you've been trained, that you were able to rouse yourself today." The man hesitated, then grasped Dennis' sleeve and said, "I have some influence with the police. I'll see what I can do."

"I appreciate it", Dennis said, but did he, or would the man's help make the decision he faced even harder?

They shook hands, and the man said, "Pleased to have met you, Dennis Cole—Oh, and one more thing." Then he handed Dennis a folded sheet of paper and added, "You're not the only one who likes a good puzzle."

Dennis waited for the man to leave the building before unfolding the paper:

Edgar Perkins, Stanhope, Iowa, 1963 Ford F100 (blue), died June 6, 1993

What, at one time, wouldn't Dennis have given to acquire this information?

He had made the killer of his mother and brother into a diabolical fiend who deserved to be hunted down and destroyed. Now, seeing the name, knowing that the man was dead, and having experienced the devastating events of recent days, he could summon no hatred, not even rancor. It was even possible, he admitted to himself, that he and Edgar Perkins had more in common than the boy, Dennis Cole, could ever have imagined.

As battered as he felt, he wasn't finished for the day. There was another destination that he had been contemplating, at first indistinctly, and now more explicitly, ever since he had learned of Ben's death. It was a destination that evoked fear, but also a kind of liberating hope.

He got into the car and drove to the other side of town. All the while, he was thinking of something Lori had said on the day they had all gone to Bob-Lo Island: *"If Dennis doesn't have enough money to get into the park, we'll have to smuggle him in."*

Now, looking at the tall stone building in his path, that was exactly what Dennis was thinking: someone would have to smuggle him in.

He finally understood the nature of his struggle. His conflict wasn't with the police, or fate, or TA, or Marta, or even Eva Bright. It was with himself, a battle to become what TA had called authentically human.

Dennis Cole hesitated outside the heavy door, then pushed it open. Inside, the building was cool and dark. A small light glowed above a door along one wall of the building, and there Dennis entered a box big enough for one person, like a vertical casket. He emerged knowing there was a choice to be made; he had known that even before he came, but now the choice was less daunting, less debilitating.

Dennis placed a call. "Marta, meet me at the Gandy Dancer. Bring Peter. I need to talk to both of you."

Appendix

The Deadly Dart Mystery

By Henry Drake

The big SUV wound its way out of the City of Livonia heading west. At the wheel was a funny-looking beauty named Portia Kendall, a woman with one of the best business minds in Michigan and a mother of two girls. The truck was filled with women on their way to inspect an undeveloped site for the new Center for Development of Women in Leadership. This truck full of women made up the steering committee for the project, and they had decided to visit the site firsthand in preparation for the groundbreaking that weekend.

"I'm an east-sider", a striking blond in jeans and a pullover said. "Where are we going?" She was Missy Amsler, an executive with an auto-parts supplier.

"It's not far", an older woman, equally striking, said. She was Frances Grund, the chair of the committee, and she was sitting up front with Portia. "The site's in Plymouth Township, not far from M-14 and Gottfredson Road. It's a good location. I think you'll be satisfied." Frances Grund was an executive with Ford.

"I like Plymouth", a high-pitched voice from the back with a pronounced accent said. "Good shopping and good food." This was Shiva Raj, the owner of a fast-growing tech consulting firm. Having grown up in an Indian mountain community, she was rapidly becoming Americanized. She was wearing a lemon golf suit and a black cap.

"It's not far from Ann Arbor. That's a big plus too", Missy Amsler added.

"I had a friend in Ann Arbor", Portia remarked, and her voice broke a little.

"An old love?" the woman directly behind Portia asked. She was a tall, big-boned woman with a voice like a trumpet. Her name was Theresa Klink, and she was a partner in a prominent Detroit law firm. The last member of the party was a young black woman. She was seated behind Frances Grund. Her hair was close cropped, and she was dressed all in black.

"You're too quiet, Medora", Frances turned and said to the black woman. "Aren't we serious enough for you?"

"I'm thinking and enjoying the drive", Medora Withers replied. She was a professor at Eastern Michigan University.

"Portia didn't answer my question", Frances observed. "Does your husband know about this mysterious stranger, Portia?"

"We're here", Portia said.

"Not very impressive, is it?" Theresa Klink boomed, and she laughed.

It was a big open field, muddy from the recent rains. In fact, the last half-mile had been driven on a gravel road, an adventure Portia and her big SUV took in stride. There was some allowance made for the adverse conditions in that a gravel pedestrian path had been constructed from the shoulder of the road to a platform in the field about twenty yards away. It would have been more accurate to call it a wooden floor than a platform, as it was no more than two feet high and eight feet square, more a place to be out of the dirt and mud than anything else. Even so, it was a well-built "floor", with four sides down to the ground and two-by-four planking. There were a few gaps on the ends, but none in the center area to interfere with heels.

"Is this the best we could do?" Theresa Klink asked.

"It's just for the groundbreaking, fifty people, the media, then we're gone", Frances replied. "Next time we visit, there'll be roads and foundations."

"Remind me to wear old shoes", Missy remarked. "I hope it doesn't rain."

"Don't even think about that", Portia said. "This will be a mud bowl if it gets any wetter."

That afternoon was sunny and humid. The women were wearing tennis shoes or hiking boots, and Frances led the way along the narrow gravel path to the platform. "This is the script", she said. "I'll be on the platform with the township supervisor. The county exec might be here too. It'll be a tight squeeze on this bandbox." She stepped gingerly up to the wooden floor. "Guests will be on the tarmac, where you are now." The women had moved forward to be as close as possible to the stage without wandering into the mud. Theresa Klink lit a cigarette. Missy Amsler removed a mobile phone from her bag and made a call. Medora Withers was taking notes with a pen and notepad. Shiva Raj and Portia looked at each other with bemused expressions. All of these female champions of industry standing in a muddy field made a humorous image.

"This will be the sequence", Frances Grund continued. "The township supervisor will introduce the project, how wonderful, et cetera. Then, the exec will say a few words—I hope it's a few words—if he's here. I think he'll be here. There'll be media, and he has gender credibility problems. Then, I'll come up to the platform, introduce all of you—don't try to come up; you'll only crowd the platform—and give my address."

"Pray God it's short", Shiva Raj whispered to Portia. Portia tried her best not to laugh.

"Any questions?" Frances Grund asked.

"What happens when you're finished?" Missy Amsler queried.

"When I'm finished, we go home", Frances said seriously.

"I think there's some business with a spade first", Shiva Raj suggested.

"That won't take long", Frances remarked. "Just a few photos and we'll be back in Portia's truck. You don't mind driving, do you, dear?" Frances asked with a frown. "I'd hate to bring my Lincoln into this mess."

"Happy to", Portia replied. "What's a little mud on a truck?"

"My sentiments exactly", Frances observed. "It's amazing how we think so alike."

Frances Grund had a confused expression on her face. Then she stood ramrod straight. Her lips moved, but no sound emerged, and her body was as still as a mannequin.

"Practicing her stage presence", Shiva Raj sniggered from behind a cupped hand. Medora Withers had stopped taking notes, perhaps expecting Frances to continue her description of the ceremony. Theresa Klink tossed her cigarette into the mud, reached over with her foot, and pushed it into the ooze. Missy Amsler put her mobile phone back into her Coach bag.

"Impressive", Missy said loudly to Frances.

Frances Grund fell forward, like a sack of potatoes, hit the little platform hard, and rolled off into the mud, face-down.

Medora Withers screamed like a banshee, loud and sustained.

"My God", Shiva Raj said.

Portia and Theresa raced into the mud and rolled Frances over on her back. Despite the mud in her hair and on her features, they could see that the blood had already drained from her face.

"Pulse?" Theresa asked. Portia was holding Frances' wrist. She shook her head.

"Look!" Theresa reached down and extracted a small object from the mud, where it was half-buried. It was small and colorful, sharp on one end and feathered on the other. The feathers contributed the vibrant colors.

"It looks like a dart", Portia said.

"What did you find? Is she OK?" Shiva Raj asked hopefully.

"I don't think so", Theresa replied nervously. "Someone call 911. We need help fast."

Missy Amsler retrieved the mobile phone from her purse and made the call. Theresa and Portia returned to Frances, opening her blouse, rechecking for even a faint pulse.

"Don't lose that dart", Portia instructed. "Here. Drop it in my purse, in this pocket." Theresa hesitated, then obeyed. She looked suspiciously at Portia.

"Missy, Shiva, look in every direction. Do you see anyone? In that grove over there." Portia pointed to a mature stand of trees about one hundred yards to the west. "Have you seen any cars pass in the last few minutes?"

"No cars", Shiva answered. "I don't see anything in the trees, but they're dense. I can't be sure."

"Go look", Portia said firmly. "No, wait. If someone's in there, it might be dangerous. We'll let the police do it."

"They might be gone by then", Missy Amsler replied. "Was she shot? I didn't hear anything."

"She's dead. I'm sure of it", Theresa Klink whispered to Portia.

Portia bit her lip. She closed Frances' eyes with her fingers. It took all her resolve. She could hear sirens in the distance. Missy Amsler and Shiva Raj had backed away toward the road. Theresa Klink didn't appear to be intimidated by the corpse of her friend. She kept checking for a pulse and scanning the landscape.

An EMS vehicle, followed by a police car, came racing down the road. Both stopped on the shoulder; a man and a woman exited the EMS vehicle. A single officer from the patrol car led the way to the platform.

"What happened?" asked the officer, a man with a bulging waist. The EMS team was already with the body.

"She fell off the platform", Portia answered. "We tried to help but I think she was already dead."

The officer made eye contact with one of the EMS technicians. It was thumbs down.

"Was she sick? Do you think she had a heart attack?" the officer asked.

Theresa Klink shrugged. "Maybe. She seemed to be in distress before she collapsed, but we didn't know it was anything serious at the time. I thought she was hamming it up. We found a dart in the mud."

"A what?" the officer asked.

Portia carefully removed the dart from her purse. If that brightly colored little projectile had anything to do with Frances' sudden death, she couldn't be too careful.

The officer was also careful to avoid the business end. "I've never seen anything like this", he ruminated. "There's a carved wooden barrel, and the feathers look real. You say it was in the mud near the body."

"Yes", Theresa replied succinctly.

"Can something like this be fired with a gun?" Medora Withers asked.

The officer shook his head but didn't answer. He was still examining the dart. The EMS team had returned from their vehicle with a cart and were lifting the body. The mud-splattered corpse made a hideous contrast to the white linen on the cart. They put another sheet over the body, secured it with straps and returned to their vehicle. So quickly, Portia thought. Less than an hour earlier, they had been laughing and talking together, mistresses of all they surveyed, and now Frances had been reduced to this.

The officer held the dart up in the air. "I'll ask this for the record: Does this little missile belong to any of you?"

There was a chorus of no's.

"Someone could have fired it from an air gun", Missy asserted. "From that stand of trees over there. That must be what happened. Or maybe Frances had a heart attack. The dart may have had nothing to do with it. It might have been here for days or weeks."

"What were you doing when she was on the platform?" the officer asked.

"I was taking notes", Medora replied immediately. "When I looked up, Frances was rolling off the platform. It was horrible."

"I was watching", Theresa said. "I told you she seemed to be in distress before she collapsed. I didn't see anything suspicious. When she fell into the mud, Portia and

I went to help, but it was too late. If it was a heart attack, it was a bad one. If it was the dart, it was a bad poison."

"Who said anything about poison?"

"I did. If she was killed with that little dart, what else could it have been?" Theresa exclaimed. Medora gasped, and Shiva bowed her head and hugged herself tightly with both arms.

"I had just finished making a call", Missy Amsler offered. "I saw her fall, but I couldn't believe my eyes. It didn't make any sense. Healthy people don't fall down and die."

"Sometimes they do", the officer said. "Sometimes, they're helped along. And how about you?" he looked hard at Portia.

"When Frances fell, I tried to help. Theresa and I found the dart. We did everything we could, but it was too late."

"Names, addresses, and phones", the officer handed a notebook and pencil to the women. "That's the thing about sudden death, suspicious death; everyone on the scene's a suspect. It's nothing personal." And he was holding the dart by one red feather and scratching his head.

It was later that same day but the clouds had rolled in and the humidity had produced thunder. It wasn't raining yet, but the skies were threatening. Still, there were a few hours of daylight left and the pair on the platform hoped to learn something that would help explain that terrible event.

"That's what happened", Portia concluded. The man next to her was big and balding, probably close to fifty, unimpressive except for his size. His name was Thomas Jefferson Penn; he was a private investigator, and a good one.

"And all you found was the dart", Thomas said.

"There was nothing else", Portia said firmly. "The police scoured the area after they finished with us. The others wanted to go, but I watched the police. I couldn't hear what they said to one another, but I could see what they were doing. If they discovered anything else, they did a good job of concealing it."

A few drops of rain splattered on Thomas' bald head. He looked up at the sky and scowled. At that moment, a car came to a stop on the shoulder behind Portia's truck, and a man exited. He was dark-haired and of average size; he might have been anywhere from his late thirties to late forties. As he walked toward the platform, his eyes darted across the landscape but never higher than eye level, as if he had no interest in anything up above. When he reached them, he shook hands with Thomas and then surveyed Portia with almost clinical interest.

"Portia Kendall, this is Cole Porter Palmer." Cole shook Portia's hand.

Thomas had been looking for an excuse to contact Cole. He needed a partner. He had too much work, and Christine and the children had been doing without him of late. Also, he had been impressed with Cole's work. Thomas had delayed calling Cole because he was afraid the former police detective would question his motives, but he needed expert help, and Portia's call for assistance had been the last straw.

"Hi", Portia said to Cole. From certain angles, she was spectacularly beautiful. From others, her features looked sharp and angular, making her something of an ugly duckling. Portia was as tall as Cole, though both of them had to look up to Thomas.

"Cole is helping me", Thomas said.

Portia repeated her story. During the telling, Cole sometimes looked at her with a surprising intensity. At other moments, he was prowling the area as if he was ignoring her. When she finished, he didn't say a word. He was down on his knees in the mud, scooping and turning. Then, without getting up or turning around, he said, "You'll find that I'm a lot different from Leander Kelly. He was a brain man, and I'm a bloodhound. If I have to put my nose in the mud to get evidence, it's just a matter of how deep." He got up and rejoined them. His hands and pants were filthy.

"Not made to order, I hope", Portia said.

Cole grinned. "Kmart blue-light special. One dart. No other evidence. No one within arm's reach of the victim. If the dart is the agent of death, then there has to be a projector." He saw the confusion on their features. "Something like an air gun or a blowpipe. I haven't seen the dart, so I can't make a judgment. Is Theresa Klink a frequent smoker?"

"Yes", Portia answered.

"And Medora Withers was using a pen to take notes, and Missy Amsler was using her mobile phone. How about Shiva Raj? Did she have anything in her hands?"

A light went on in Portia's eyes, and Thomas too was more engaged. Portia took a little time trying to remember. "You're right about Medora and Missy. I don't remember Shiva holding anything, but it's possible she was. Theresa had finished her cigarette by the time Frances collapsed, but she had been smoking a few minutes earlier. Do you believe that someone from our group fired or launched that dart?"

"Based on what I know, I believe that a dart with a strong poison on its tip killed Frances Grund, and someone

378

launched that dart at her using a device of some kind. It wouldn't need to be large at such close quarters."

"What about an air gun?" Portia asked.

Cole shook his head. "I don't think so. Those trees are too far away and air guns aren't very accurate. It's possible. I like the theory that one of your group used a disguised dart launcher."

"I don't share your enthusiasm, Mr. Palmer", Portia said with emotion.

"Call me Cole. Thomas, you've been silent too long."

Penn relaxed his owlish features. "We'll wait for the police report. We may be making a mountain out of a molehill, or a murder out of a malady. If she was poisoned, I'm not sure I buy the dart-launcher theory. Maybe the dart's nothing but a red herring. Let's say poison was introduced earlier in her food, and then someone tossed the dart on the ground to make it look like it caused her death. When they find poison in her system, we would be apt to think that the dart was the agent."

"Excellent", Cole exclaimed, but he was back on his knees. When he stood up, he lost his balance and ended up sitting on the platform with his shoes in the mud. He said to Portia, "You were counting on this wooden stage to keep you clean and dry?" It was raining harder. Portia removed a small black umbrella from her bag and opened it.

"Gather round", she said.

"I'm a mess already, but thanks", Cole replied. "There are four possible explanations." He was still seated on the platform. When he moved, it could be seen that he had ripped his pants.

"Nice boxers", Portia observed.

Cole turned red, but continued. "Explanation one: she died from natural causes. Explanation two: she was poisoned earlier and the dart was used to confuse us. Explanation three: someone fired an air gun from a shielded location, like the woods. Explanation four: a device was used by one of the women to launch the dart. The first explanation will be proved or disproved in short order. The second is intriguing and has possibilities, but I think we can prove or disprove this one quickly too. Thomas, call the police and find out if they found a puncture wound. If they did, and if she was poisoned, was that poison detected at the site of the puncture wound? The third explanation requires an expert marksman and good fortune, but it's not impossible. The fourth explanation requires a suitable device and some training."

Cole and Thomas were getting drenched.

"Let's go", Portia said. "Is there a place nearby that'll accept wet, muddy guys with exposed underpants?"

"There's a bar in Plymouth that's dark", Thomas answered. "It's just east of Main Street across from the Kellogg Park. Can you find it?"

Portia frowned. "I'll meet you there. I don't mind if the outside of my truck gets dirty, but the inside is another matter."

By the time they reconvened in Plymouth, it was raining hard. Portia arrived first and had a table by the window. There were few patrons, but all eyes were on Thomas and Cole as they entered. Both were still wet, and Cole was still dirty.

"Soccer", he shouted defensively.

"I couldn't find any flaws in your explanations", Portia remarked, once the two were seated. The waitress brought a basket of popcorn and three beers.

"I ordered for you", Portia explained.

Cole pushed the beer aside. "Black coffee", he said to the retreating waitress. "Which explanation do you favor?"

"I don't think any of the women are murderers. They're successful businesswomen. They're not close friends, but I've known all of them for years. They are—were—all conventional with a capital *C*. I don't believe the dart was a coincidence. I want to believe that a marksman in the woods did it. I'm not a firearms expert, but I can imagine the difficulty in accurately firing a dart at a distance of a hundred yards."

"How about you, Thomas?" Cole said.

"One of the women. Sorry, Portia. I made a few calls on the way over. There was a fast-acting nerve toxin in her bloodstream. It was powerful enough to shut down her nervous system in just a few minutes, so the poison-in-the-food theory is out. There was plenty of toxin residue at the site of the puncture wound in the neck. It's clear that the dart was the agent and that it was directed at her while she was on the platform."

"If it was one of the women, how was the dart launched?" Cole asked. "Some kind of dart gun? Some kind of blowgun? By hand? We know that Theresa Klink was smoking, that Missy Amsler was using a mobile phone, that Medora Withers was using a pen. Shiva Raj was close enough to have used a device of some kind, as yet unknown."

"Why?" Portia asked.

"That's just a detail for Cole", Thomas interjected.

"Tell us about them", Cole said.

Portia seemed to be collecting her thoughts. She took a sip of beer and grabbed a handful of popcorn. Cole couldn't make up his mind if she was a beauty or a clown.

"Start with Frances", Thomas directed.

Portia pursed her lips and took another sip. "Frances wasn't bashful. I guess you could say that she thought a lot of herself. When she wanted something, she went after it, and she generally got it. She wasn't the most intelligent person I've ever known, but she was the most tenacious. Her motives were usually obvious; there was no secret about what she was after. Frances had been divorced twice; no children from either marriage.

"Shiva Raj is fun. She and I are a lot alike. We both like to test limits. Shiva is married, but she doesn't have any children yet. Maybe I've made her cautious—just kidding! She's been in America for about five years. She's a fast learner, and she's made a great success of her business. I think it caused friction between Shiva and her husband. I've seen it before; one spouse absorbed in their business, the other gets lonely and, well, you know. She wants to save the marriage; I know that much.

"Missy Amsler is in her early thirties, and she's single. I don't think she's involved with anyone, but I'm not sure. She's candid enough that she'd broadcast it, unless the man was married. She received an MBA from the University of Chicago. I think her family is active in the Chicago financial market, but she's been here, in Troy, since she graduated.

"I don't know much about Theresa. She's the sort of person who lets you see what she wants you to see. She's a respected attorney, and she's friendly and outgoing. I can't say exactly why I'm not as comfortable with her as I am with the others. I don't think she's married; see, I don't even know for sure.

"Medora is thoughtful and friendly. She teaches literature at Eastern Michigan University. She's divorced, and her son and daughter live with her in Ann Arbor. I've seen her work; it's good. She has a periodic column in the Free Press. I like Medora but she plays her cards close to the vest too. I suppose we're all alike in that regard."

"And what about Portia Kendall?" Cole asked.

Portia didn't miss a beat. "She's a scientist by training and an entrepreneur by choice. She has two daughters. She has a lot of acquaintances and casual friends, but few close friends. If she got mad enough, it's hard to say what she'd do."

Cole sipped his coffee. "You said you didn't think any of the women were capable of murder."

"I said that I hoped they weren't capable of murder", Portia corrected him.

"If one of them did it, who would you suspect?"

"That's not a fair question. I'd have to be indiscreet to answer."

"Try", Cole said curtly.

"I'll try," Portia answered, "but I don't have to like it. If anyone, I'd have picked Frances as the most likely candidate. But she's the victim. I've already said that Theresa is an enigma. Shiva comes from a part of the world where violence is common. I suppose it's ethnocentric to suggest it, but maybe that's how they settle things over there."

"How about the others?" Cole prodded.

"Missy and Medora don't have the temperament for murder. They'd do it by beating your brains out in business or by skewering you in an article. But who knows what evil lurks in the mind of man, as some poet said."

"That was the Shadow", Thomas offered.

"Who cares", Portia replied. "I hope you have the good sense to keep this information to yourselves."

"I'm discretion itself", Cole said, smiling.

"I've heard that before, from a boyfriend at college. I'll deny this too, if I have to."

"Did any of the women have a business relationship with Frances, or each other, for that matter?" Cole asked.

"Shiva worked for Frances several years ago when she came to the States, and I think they continued seeing each other socially after Shiva started her own company. Missy and Frances bought property together. Theresa represented Frances and Missy in private legal matters. That's the extent of it, as far as I know. Oh yes, Frances and I were both involved in a limited partnership. She introduced me to it last year as a tax shelter."

"The web expands", Cole observed.

"You make it sound insidious. You're not as nice as you look", Portia said.

"I'm not nice period when it comes to murder."

"Can you two suspend your sparring so we can get down to business?" Thomas asked.

"Let's see", Cole said. "If one of the women committed the crime, as Thomas believes, then they had to get the dart into Frances Grund's neck. I don't believe they could have done it before she ascended the platform. It was a deep penetration, and she would have reacted quickly. That would also contradict Thomas' statement that the toxin was so fast-acting it must have been introduced after she stepped on the platform."

"Then someone near the platform must have fired or propelled the dart into Frances' neck, a neat little trick considering they couldn't set up a tripod and take aim", Thomas said, and finished his beer with a big swallow. "That means it was planned in advance, because someone had to construct a device that was invisible to the others."

"What would such a dart launcher look like?" Cole reflected.

"Small, probably innocent-looking", Thomas suggested.

There was a peal of thunder. Cole and Thomas had stopped dripping. The beer mugs and coffee cup were empty.

"I have to get back to my girls", Portia said, rising.

"You're lucky", Cole said softly.

"I am lucky", Portia admitted. "Do you have any children?"

"One, but she's gone away."

No one dared to ask any more questions.

They were lucky. The dedication was held on a nice day, and they had a good turnout. The county executive showed up, and he didn't try to capture too much of the spotlight. Portia stood in for Frances; it was somber in that the publicity about the murder had darkened the spirits of some and attracted a throng of ambulance chasers and media. When these tried to pry information from Portia, she referred them to the authorities, though she would have liked to have kicked them in the pants.

An hour later, the spade removed the dirt and the crowd dispersed, all except the five women and two men. It was Portia's job to gather them on the platform. Theresa Klink eyed the two men suspiciously. Missy Amsler gave Cole a curious and not unfriendly smile.

"That's that", Shiva Raj said. "Poor Frances. You did a good job, Portia."

"Who are you?" Theresa asked Cole.

Portia said, "His name is Cole Porter Palmer. He used to be a police detective, and he's now working with Thomas Jefferson Penn." She indicated the other man, who was slouching and frowning on the edge of the platform.

"What the hell do they want?" Theresa roared.

"We want to remove the onus of guilt from four of you", Cole said succinctly. "That's a noble goal, isn't it?"

"That depends on whether you're one of the four", Medora said wryly. "I happen to like it. Can you deliver?"

"Be careful", Theresa advised. "These people have no legal standing. Portia, you should have said something. I resent being confronted like this."

"You'll get over it", Thomas said, and the two glared at each other.

"Is everyone willing to participate?" Portia asked.

"Within limits", Theresa replied. The others nodded.

The scene was comical. First, there were seven people standing on a rustic platform, which was beginning to dry and even crack. There was no one else in sight.

"Does anyone have anything to say?" Cole said.

"I don't, or I would have told the police", Medora Withers replied. "I've discovered that withholding evidence from the police is dangerous."

"I'm still too upset to think about it", Missy Amsler said. "I just want to get out of here and forget it."

"But you can't," Shiva said, "not as long as all of us are suspects. I agree with Mr. Palmer. We are better off getting to the bottom of this, even if it is painful. Then we can really put it behind us."

"Just be careful", Theresa cautioned. "How long will this take?"

"If everyone cooperates, not long", Cole answered. "Just a list of facts and questions. And if you're ready, I'll start with a fact."

No one objected. Theresa retrieved a cigarette from her purse, but everyone else seemed to be frozen in place. Medora looked resigned to the ordeal. Shiva was smiling, though wanly. Missy Amsler removed her heels and replaced them with sandals from her bag.

"Fact", Cole began. "Frances Grund was killed by a fast-acting toxin. Based on this fact, it's reasonable to conclude that she was infected with the toxin while she was on the platform. I admit there's a slight possibility that the deed was done before she reached the platform. This wasn't a pinprick. The dart penetrated her neck a full one-eighth inch. The potency of the toxin also precludes any other form of introduction, such as food or drink. Someone propelled the dart into Frances Grund's neck while she stood on the platform."

"What if she did it herself?" Theresa Klink speculated. "Maybe her life was crumbling, and this was her exit."

"There's no evidence, or any behavior to suspect it", Portia replied. "Anyway," she continued, "if she'd wanted to make an *exit*"—and she expressed the word scornfully— "she would have waited until the ceremony, when there was a large audience and media."

"Maybe", Theresa admitted. "Maybe not."

Cole continued. "If Frances Grund was attacked on the platform, the attacker must have been in close proximity to her. I've spoken to an expert on darts. Do you know how hard it is for expert darters to hit a bull's-eye at twenty feet? Even that requires careful preparation. A blowgun or air gun would require the same meticulous setup. You'd have only one chance too. To take the risk of missing the target, hitting a collar, would be very dangerous.

"That rules out marksmen in the forest and passing cars. The person I consulted said that those scenarios are all but impossible. Even if such an attack were to succeed, it would be monumentally lucky, and this crime was too carefully planned for luck."

"That means one of us did it", Missy Amsler remarked. "That's preposterous. It's frightening. We were friends. Why would any one of us want to kill her? I'm anxious enough as it is, and this isn't helping."

"We're not here to make anyone anxious. We're after the truth", Thomas interjected.

"Let's dispense with philosophy", Medora said, with uncharacteristic acerbity.

Cole walked to the center of the platform. "Complicating this business is the fact that Frances didn't stand still. She was a moving target. Granted the platform is small, but motion would be a severe complication if one is trying to propel a small, feathered projectile into a small patch of flesh. I asked my darter how difficult it would be to hit a bull's-eye if it swung like a pendulum. The man just shook his head and groaned.

"This means two things: it required an expert, and it required a careful and steady aim. But how could this have been achieved, even by the women who were next to the platform?"

"Theresa propped her faux cigarette against her forearm and blew hard. Presto", Missy suggested.

"Probably slanderous", Theresa observed, but she had seen Missy's devilish grin and responded in kind.

"No matter how steady, we're still faced with a moving target. There's nothing in your backgrounds to suggest that any of you have this skill."

"We can be devious", Shiva offered, smiling.

Cole continued. "We've established that this attack required careful aim while the victim was on the platform—"

"Speculation", Theresa interrupted. "Establishing it is another matter."

"Quit bedeviling the man", Portia quipped. Theresa Klink got redder.

Cole didn't seem to be annoyed. He plodded on. "From where, then, was the attack launched? Is there an invisible location close to the platform?"

"You said the woods are too far away", Missy Amsler remarked.

"Yes", Cole admitted. "We're standing on an eight-foot by eight-foot platform, twenty-four inches high. It looks like nothing more than a series of two-by-fours against the ground. But I asked myself a question: Would a person lying on his back have enough room beneath this platform? Yes, he would. Twenty-four inches is plenty of room for a trained assassin to lie hidden from a group of people outside, and above."

Anguished words, ranging from incredulity to horror, were expressed by all of them.

Theresa Klink was the first to say something intelligible. "You're suggesting that someone lying on their back beneath this platform launched a dart—there would have to be an opening in the deck—into Frances' neck? That's absurd; it's comical."

"What other explanation is there? There are several one-inch holes at the western edge of this platform, where someone looking up could have viewed the proceedings, could have supported a blowpipe, could have taken careful aim from a distance of six to seven feet, and launched the dart! Not only are there four openings, which have been made to look like imperfections in a temporary platform, but we discovered residue of materials in the soil common to perfumes and colognes."

"I'm sure of one thing", Theresa asserted. "We were all upright. Unless one of us has been cloned, we couldn't have been under this platform. And don't give me any disguise mumbo jumbo. It was broad daylight, and no one was wearing a veil or mask."

"No disguise," Cole agreed, "but the part about cloning isn't far from the truth."

Theresa guffawed. "Portia, have you introduced us to a lunatic?"

"Oh, shut up", Portia said. This time, Theresa Klink's eyes were daggers.

"Then we're all off the hook", Theresa said, composing herself. "When Palmer began, he said that four of us would be able to resume our lives. If none of us was beneath the platform—and I still have a hard time believing that explanation—then we're all innocent and, I presume, free to go."

Cole waited for Theresa to finish. He didn't seem to be in a hurry. Instead, he was watching the women. "I believe the killer planned in advance to be in that confined space before you arrived. He must have been an assassin or had training in the craft. He had to lie still and remain silent for a long period of time. He had to bore holes at just the right locations and in just the right manner, so that they would appear natural and not raise suspicion. He had to have the talent to hit the target on the first try. And he had to possess the patience and courage to remain beneath the platform while the police swarmed all over the area. He was a special person."

"*Special* is not the word I'd use", Missy Amsler exclaimed.

"In the sense of talent, not character", Cole admitted. "His skill is extraordinary. I'd hate to meet him in a dark alley."

"Can we go?" Shiva asked.

"Do you have a brother?" Cole said, ignoring her question.

"Who are you asking?" Medora queried.

Cole turned to Shiva Raj. "Do you?"

"Yes."

"Is he in the States?"

She hesitated.

"I've already said we've been investigating. Be careful not to tell obvious lies."

"That inference is resented, Mr. Palmer", Shiva answered.

"Don't answer if you don't want to", Theresa advised.

"He's in the States", Shiva Raj said defiantly.

"In Michigan?"

"I think so."

"He is", Cole said bluntly and forcefully. "You and your brother both hail from Jammu. It has a clannish mountain culture. I've consulted a colleague of Leander Kelly at the University of Michigan. The people of Jammu are impulsive, prone to desperate action when provoked."

"Who isn't?" Medora volunteered.

"I'll finish with a story, more speculative than proven. We've built a foundation, but the structure requires work. I'll leave that to the police. They have the resources for that sort of thing.

"Here it is: Shiva's marriage has been in trouble, in jeopardy of dissolving. She and her husband knew Frances Grund professionally and socially; that's been established. Frances had a reputation for getting what she wanted,

391

and she wanted Shiva's husband. She got him. Shiva Raj is a proud woman determined to save her marriage, but is she a match for the forceful and clever Frances? Shiva's brother arrived in the States less than a month ago. Why? To neutralize the threat to his sister's marriage? The ceremony for the new center and the invisibility of the space beneath the platform would have presented a perfect opportunity to murder Frances while protecting Shiva from suspicion. It was executed flawlessly. There is motive. The means and opportunity, though brilliantly concealed, have also been demonstrated."

They all looked at Shiva, who was inscrutable. No more frivolity on her features, instead, the hard determination of a person who once had to fight the elements and struggle for the basic necessities of life. It was as if everyone in the group—except one person—were invisible, or inconsequential.

Shiva took Theresa's hand. "I must speak with you."

The attorney was no longer a friend, but an officer of the court.